CLEA

by *Lawrence Durrell*

CLEA

a novel

by

LAWRENCE
DURRELL

NEW YORK

E. P. Dutton & Co., Inc.

1960

First Printing, March 1960

Second Printing, March 1960

Third Printing, April 1960

Fourth Printing, April 1960

Fifth Printing, June 1960

Sixth Printing, November 1960

Seventh Printing, January 1961

Library of Congress Catalog Card Number: 60-5969

To
MY FATHER

AUTHOR'S NOTE

This is the fourth volume of a group of novels intended to be judged as a single work. It is a sequel to JUSTINE, BALTHAZAR, *and* MOUNT-OLIVE. *Together the four novels constitute "The Alexandria Quartet"; a suitable descriptive subtitle would be "a word continuum". The prefatory note to* BALTHAZAR *has already described my intentions as far as the form of the books is concerned.*

Among the workpoints at the end of this volume I have sketched a number of possible ways of continuing to deploy these characters and situations in further instalments—but this is only to suggest that even if the series were extended indefinitely the result would never become a roman fleuve *(an expansion of the matter in serial form) but would remain strictly part of the present word-continuum. If the axis has been well and truly laid down in the quartet it should be possible to radiate in any direction without losing the strictness and congruity of the continuum. But to all intents and purposes the present set of four volumes may be judged as a completed whole.*

L.D.

The Primary and most beautiful of Nature's qualities is motion, which agitates her at all times, but this motion is simply the perpetual consequence of crimes, it is conserved by means of crimes alone.

(D. A. F. de Sade)

BOOK I

I

The oranges were more plentiful than usual that year. They glowed in their arbours of burnished green leaf like lanterns, flickering up there among the sunny woods. It was as if they were eager to celebrate our departure from the little island—for at last the long-awaited message from Nessim had come, like a summons back to the Underworld. A message which was to draw me back inexorably to the one city which for me always hovered between illusion and reality, between the substance and the poetic images which its very name aroused in me. A memory, I told myself, which had been falsified by the desires and intuitions only as yet half-realised on paper. Alexandria, the capital of memory! All the writing which I had borrowed from the living and the dead, until I myself had become a sort of postscript to a letter which was never ended, never posted. . . .

How long had I been away? I could hardly compute, though calendar-time gives little enough indication of the aeons which separate one self from another, one day from another; and all this time I had been living there, truly, in the Alexandria of my heart's mind. And page by page, heartbeat by heartbeat, I had been surrendering myself to the grotesque organism of which we had all once been part, victors and vanquished alike. An ancient city changing under the brush-strokes of thoughts which besieged meaning, clamouring for identity; somewhere there, on the black thorny promontories of Africa the aromatic truth of the place lived on, the bitter unchewable herb of the past, the pith of memory. I had set out once to store, to codify, to annotate the past before it was utterly lost—that at least was a task I had set myself. I had failed in it (perhaps it was hopeless?)—for no sooner had I embalmed one aspect of it in words than the intrusion of new knowledge disrupted the frame of reference, everything flew asunder, only to reassemble again in unforeseen, unpredictable patterns. . . .

"To re-work reality" I had written somewhere; temeritous, presumptuous words indeed—for it is reality which works and reworks us on its slow wheel. Yet if I had been enriched by the experience of this island interlude, it was perhaps because of this total failure to record the inner truth of the city. I had now come face to face with the nature of time, that ailment of the human psyche. I had been forced to admit defeat on paper. Yet curiously enough the act of writing had in itself brought me another sort of increase; by the very *failure* of words, which sink one by one into the measureless caverns of the imagination and gutter out. An expensive way to begin living, yes; but then we artists are driven towards personal lives nourished in these strange techniques of self-pursuit.

But then . . . if I had changed, what of my friends—Balthazar, Nessim, Justine, Clea? What new aspects of them would I discern after this time-lapse, when once more I had been caught up in the ambience of a new city, a city now swallowed by a war? Here was the rub. I could not say. Apprehension trembled within me like a lodestar. It was hard to renounce the hard-won territory of my dreams in favour of new images, new cities, new dispositions, new loves. I had come to hug my own dreams of the place like a monomaniac. . . . Would it not, I wondered, be wiser to stay where I was? Perhaps. Yet I knew I must go. Indeed *this very night* I should be gone! The thought itself was so hard to grasp that I was forced to whisper it aloud to myself.

We had passed the last ten days since the messenger called in a golden hush of anticipation; and the weather had matched it, turning up a succession of perfectly blue days, windless seas. We stood between the two landscapes, unwilling to relinquish the one yet aching to encounter the other. Poised, like gulls upon the side of a cliff. And already the dissimilar images mixed and baulked in my dreams. This island house, for example, its smoke-silvered olives and almonds where the red-footed partridge wandered . . . silent glades where only the goat-face of a Pan might emerge. Its simple and lucent perfection of form and colour could not mix with the other premonitions crowding in upon us. (A sky full of falling-stars, emerald wash of tides on lonely beaches, crying of gulls on the white roads of the south.) This Grecian world was already being invaded by the odours of the forgotten city—promontories where the sweating sea-captains had boozed and eaten until their intestines cracked, had drained their bodies, like kegs, of every lust, foundering in the embrace of black slaves with spaniels' eyes. (The mirrors, the heart-rending sweetness of the voices of blinded canaries, the bubble of *narguilehs* in their rose-water bowls, the smell of patchouli and joss.) They were eating into one another, these irreconcilable dreams. And I saw my friends once again (not as names now), irradiated anew by the knowledge of this departure. They were no longer shadows of my own writing but refreshed anew—even the dead. At night I walked again those curling streets with Melissa (situated now somewhere beyond regrets, for even in my dreams I knew she was dead), walking comfortably arm in arm; her narrow legs like scissors gave her a swaying walk. The habit of pressing her thigh to mine at every step. I could see everything with affection now—even the old cotton frock and cheap shoes which she wore on holidays. She had not been able to powder out the faint blue lovebite on her throat. . . . Then she vanished and I awoke with a cry of regret. Dawn was breaking among the olives, silvering their still leaves.

Somewhere along the road I had recovered my peace of mind. This handful of blue days before saying farewell—I treasured them, luxuriating in their simplicity: fires of olive-wood blazing in the old hearth whose painting of Justine would be the last item to be packed, jumping and gleaming on the battered table and chair, on the blue enamel bowl of early cyclamen. What

13

had the city to do with all this—an Aegean spring hanging upon a thread between winter and the first white puffs of almond blossom? It was a word merely, and meant little, being scribbled on the margins of a dream, or being repeated in the mind to the colloquial music of time, which is only desire expressed in heartbeats. Indeed, though I loved it so much, I was powerless to stay; the city which I now knew I hated held out something different for me—a new evaluation of the experience which had marked me. I must return to it once more in order to be able to leave it forever, to shed it. If I have spoken of time it is because the writer I was becoming was learning at last to inhabit those deserted spaces which time misses— beginning to live between the ticks of the clock, so to speak. The continuous present, which is the real history of that collective anecdote, the human mind; when the past is dead and the future represented only by desire and fear, what of that adventive moment which can't be measured, can't be dismissed? For most of us the so-called Present is snatched away like some sumptuous repast, conjured up by fairies—before one can touch a mouthful. Like the dead Pursewarden I hoped I might soon be truthfully able to say: "I do not write for those who have never asked themselves this question: 'at what point does real life begin?' "

Idle thoughts passing through the mind as I lay on a flat rock above the sea, eating an orange, perfectly circumscribed by a solitude which would soon be engulfed by the city, the ponderous azure dream of Alexandria basking like some old reptile in the bronze Pharaonic light of the great lake. The mastersensualists of history abandoning their bodies to mirrors, to poems, to the grazing flocks of boys and women, to the needle in the vein, to the opium-pipe, to the death-in-life of kisses without appetite. Walking those streets again in my imagination I knew once more that they spanned, not merely human history, but the whole biological scale of the heart's affections —from the painted ecstasies of Cleopatra (strange that the vine

14

should be discovered here, near Taposiris) to the bigotry of Hypatia (withered vine-leaves, martyr's kisses). And stranger visitors: Rimbaud, student of the Abrupt Path, walked here with a belt full of gold coins. And all those other swarthy dream-interpreters and politicians and eunuchs were like a flock of birds of brilliant plumage. Between pity, desire and dread, I saw the city once more spread out before me, inhabited by the faces of my friends and subjects. I knew that I must re-experience it once more and this time forever.

Yet it was to be a strange departure, full of small unforeseen elements—I mean the messenger being a hunchback in a silver suit, a flower in his lapel, a perfumed handkerchief in his sleeve! And the sudden springing to life of the little village which had for so long tactfully ignored our very existence, save for an occasional gift of fish or wine or coloured eggs which Athena brought us, folded in her red shawl. She, too, could hardly bear to see us go; her stern old wrinkled mask crumpled into tears over each item of our slender baggage. But "They will not let you leave without a hospitality" she repeated stubbornly. "The village will not let you go like that." We were to be offered a farewell banquet!

As for the child I had conducted the whole rehearsal of this journey (of her whole life, in truth) in images from a fairy story. Many repetitions had not staled it. She would sit staring up at the painting and listening attentively. She was more than prepared for it all, indeed almost ravenous to take up her own place in the gallery of images I had painted for her. She had soaked up all the confused colours of this fanciful world to which she had once belonged by right and which she would now recover—a world peopled by those presences—the father, a dark pirate-prince, the stepmother a swarthy imperious queen. . . .

"She is like the playing-card?"

"Yes. The Queen of Spades."

"And her name is Justine."

"Her name is Justine."

15

"In the picture she is smoking. Will she love me more than my father or less?"

"She will love you both."

There had been no other way to explain it to her, except in terms of myth or allegory—the poetry of infant uncertainty. I had made her word-perfect in this parable of an Egypt which was to throw up for her (enlarged to the size of gods or magi) the portraits of her family, of her ancestors. But then is not life itself a fairy-tale which we lose the power of apprehending as we grow? No matter. She was already drunk upon the image of her father.

"Yes, I understand everything." With a nod and a sigh she would store up these painted images in the treasure-box of her mind. Of Melissa, her dead mother, she spoke less often, and when she did I answered her in the same fashion from the story-book; but she had already sunk, pale star, below the horizon into the stillness of death, leaving the foreground to those others—the playing-card characters of the living.

The child had thrown a tangerine into the water and now leaned to watch it roll softly down to the sandy floor of the grotto. It lay there, flickering like a small flame, nudged by the swell and fall of the currents.

"Now watch me fetch it up."

"Not in this icy sea, you'll die of cold."

"It isn't cold to-day. Watch."

By now she could swim like a young otter. It was easy, sitting here on the flat rock above the water, to recognise in her the dauntless eyes of Melissa, slanted a little at the edges; and sometimes, intermittently, like a forgotten grain of sleep in the corners, the dark supposing look (pleading, uncertain) of her father Nessim. I remembered Clea's voice saying once, in another world, long ago: "Mark, if a girl does not like dancing and swimming she will never be able to make love." I smiled and wondered if the words were true as I watched the little creature turn over smoothly in the water and flow gracefully

16

downwards to the target with the craft of a seal, toes pressed back against the sky. The glimmer of the little white purse between her legs. She retrieved the tangerine beautifully and spiralled to the surface with it gripped in her teeth.

"Now run and dry quickly."

"It isn't cold."

"Do as you are told. Be off. Hurry."

"And the man with the hump?"

"He has gone."

Mnemjian's unexpected appearance on the island had both started and thrilled her—for it was he who brought us Nessim's message. It was strange to see him walking along the shingle beach with an air of grotesque perturbation, as if balancing on corkscrews. I think he wished to show us that for years he had not walked on anything but the finest pavements. He was literally unused to terra firma. He radiated a precarious and overbred finesse. He was clad in a dazzling silver suit, spats, a pearl tie-pin, and his fingers were heavily ringed. Only the smile, the infant smile was unchanged, and the oiled spitcurl was still aimed at the frontal sinus.

"I have married Halil's widow. I am the richest barber in all Egypt to-day, my dear friend."

He blurted this out all in one breath, leaning on a silver-knobbed walking-stick to which he was clearly as unaccustomed. His violet eye roved somewhat disdainfully round our somewhat primitive cottage, and he refused a chair, doubtless because he did not wish to crease those formidable trousers. "You have a hard style of life here, eh? Not much *luxe*, Darley." Then he sighed and added, "But now you will be coming to us again." He made a vague gesture with the stick intended to symbolise the hospitality we should once more enjoy from the city. "Myself I cannot stay. I am on my way back. I did this purely as a favour to Hosnani." He spoke of Nessim with a sort of pearly grandeur, as if he were now his equal socially; then he caught sight of my smile and had the grace to giggle once before

17

becoming serious again. "There is no time, anyway" he said, dusting his sleeves.

This had the merit of being true, for the Smyrna boats stays only long enough to unload mail and occasional merchandise—a few cases of macaroni, some copper sulphate, a pump. The wants of the islanders are few. Together we walked back towards the village, across the olive-groves, talking as we went. Mnemjian still trudged with that slow turtle-walk. But I was glad, for it enabled me to ask him a few questions about the city, and from his answers to gain some inkling of what I was to find there in the matter of changed dispositions, unknown factors.

"There are many changes since this war. Dr. Balthazar has been very ill. You know about the Hosnani intrigue in Palestine? The collapse? The Egyptians are trying to sequestrate. They have taken much away. Yes, they are poor now, and still in trouble. She is still under house-detention at Karm Abu Girg. Nobody has seen her for an age. He works by special permission as an ambulance driver in the docks, twice a week. Very dangerous. And there was a bad air-raid; he lost one eye and a finger."

"Nessim?" I was startled. The little man nodded self-importantly. This new, this unforeseen image of my friend struck me like a bullet. "Good God" I said, and the barber nodded as if to approve the appropriateness of the oath. "It was bad" he said. "It is the war, Darley." Then suddenly a happier thought came into his mind and he smiled the infant smile once more which reflected only the iron material values of the Levant. Taking my arm he continued: "But the war is also good business. My shops are cutting the armies' hair day and night. Three saloons, twelve assistants! You will see, it is superb. And Pombal says, as a joke, 'Now you are shaving the dead while they are still alive.' " He doubled up with soundless refined laughter.

"Is Pombal back there?"

"Of course. He is a high man of the Free French now. He has conferences with Sir Mountolive. He is also still there.

18

Many have remained from your time, Darley, you will see."

Mnemjian seemed delighted to have been able to astonish me so easily. Then he said something which made my mind do a double somersault. I stood still and asked him to repeat it, thinking that I had misheard him. "I have just visited Capodistria." I stared at him with utter incredulity. Capodistria! "But he *died!*" I exclaimed in surprise.

The barber leaned far back, as if on a rocking-horse, and tittered profusely. It was a very good joke this time and lasted him a full minute. Then at last, still sighing luxuriously at the memory of it, he slowly took from his breast-pocket a postcard such as one buys upon any Mediterranean seafront and held it out to me, saying: "Then who is this?"

It was a murky enough photograph with the heavy developing-marks which are a feature of hasty street-photography. It depicted two figures walking along a seafront. One was Mnemjian. The other . . . I stared at it in growing recognition. . . .

Capodistria was clad in tubular trousers of an Edwardian style and very pointed black shoes. With this he wore a long academician's topcoat with a fur collar and cuffs. Finally, and quite fantastically, he was sporting a *chapeau melon* which made him look rather like a tall rat in some animal cartoon. He had grown a thin Rilkean moustache which drooped a little at the corner of his mouth. A long cigarette-holder was between his teeth. It was unmistakably Capodistria. "What on earth . . ." I began, but the smiling Mnemjian shut one eye and laid a finger across his lips. "Always" he said "there are mysteries"; and in the act of guarding them he swelled up toad-like, staring into my eyes with a mischievous content. He would perhaps have deigned to explain but at that minute a ship's siren rang out from the direction of the village. He was flustered. "Quickly"; he began his trudging walk. "I mustn't forget to give you the letter from Hosnani." It was carried doubled in his breast pocket and he fished it out at last. "And now goodbye" he said. "All is arranged. We will meet again."

19

I shook his hand and stood looking after him for a moment, surprised and undecided. Then I turned back to the edge of the olive grove and sat down on a rock to read the letter from Nessim. It was brief and contained the details of the travel arrangements he had made for us. A little craft would be coming to take us off the island. He gave approximate times and instructions as to where we should wait for it. All this was clearly set out. Then, as a postscript Nessim added in his tall hand: "It will be good to meet again, without reserves. I gather that Balthazar has recounted all our misadventures. You won't exact an unduly heavy repentance from people who care for you so much? I hope not. Let the past remain a closed book for us all."

That was how it fell out.

For those last few days the island regaled us nobly with the best of its weather and those austere Cycladean simplicities which were like a fond embrace—for which I knew I should be longing when once more the miasma of Egypt had closed over my head.

On the evening of departure the whole village turned out to give us the promised farewell dinner of lamb on the spit and gold *rezina* wine. They spread the tables and chairs down the whole length of the small main street and each family brought its own offerings to the feast. Even those two proud dignitaries were there—mayor and priest—each seated at one end of the long table. It was cold to sit in the lamplight thus, pretending that it was really a summer evening, but even the moon collaborated, rising blindly out of the sea to shine upon the white tablecloths, polish the glasses of wine. The old burnished faces, warmed by drink, glowed like copperware. Ancient smiles, archaic forms of address, traditional pleasantries, courtesies of the old world which was already fading, receding from us. The old sea-captains of the sponge-fleets sucking their bounty of wine from blue enamel cans, their warm embraces smelt like wrinkled crab-apples, their great moustaches tanned by tobacco curled towards their ears.

At first I had been touched, thinking all this ceremony was for me; I was not the less so to find that it was for my country. To be English when Greece had fallen was to be a target for the affection and gratitude of every Greek, and the humble peasants of this hamlet felt it no less keenly than Greeks everywhere. The shower of toasts and pledges echoed on the night, and all the speeches flew like kites, in the high style of Greek, orotund and sonorous. They seemed to have the cadences of immortal poetry—the poetry of a desperate hour; but of course they were only words, the wretched windy words which war so easily breeds and which the rhetoricians of peace would soon wear out of use.

But tonight the war lit them up like tapers, the old men, giving them a burning grandeur. Only the young men were not there to silence and shame them with their hangdog looks—for they had gone to Albania to die among the snows. The women spoke shrilly, in voices made coarsely thrilling with unshed tears, and among the bursts of laughter and song fell their sudden silences—like so many open graves.

It had come so softly towards us over the waters, this war; gradually, as clouds which quietly fill in a horizon from end to end. But as yet it had not broken. Only the rumour of it gripped the heart with conflicting hopes and fears. At first it had seemed to portend the end of the so-called civilised world, but this hope soon proved vain. No, it was to be as always simply the end of kindness and safety and moderate ways; the end of the artist's hopes, of nonchalance, of joy. Apart from this everything else about the human condition would be confirmed and emphasised; perhaps even a certain truthfulness had already begun to emerge from behind appearances, for death heightens every tension and permits us fewer of the half-truths by which we normally live.

This was all we had known of it, to date, this unknown dragon whose claws had already struck elsewhere. All? Yes, to be sure, once or twice the upper sky had swollen with the slur of invisible bombers, but their sounds could not drown the buzzing, nearer at hand, of the island bees: for each household owned a few whitewashed hives. What else? Once (this seemed more real) a submarine poked up a periscope in the bay and surveyed the coastline for minutes on end. Did it see us bathing on the point? We waved. But a periscope has no arms with which to wave back. Perhaps on the beaches to the north it had discovered something else more rare—an old bull seal dozing in the sun like a Moslem on his prayer-mat. But this again could have had little to do with war.

Yet the whole business became a little more real when the little *caique* which Nessim had sent fussed into the dusk-filled harbour that night, manned by three sullen-looking sailors armed with automatics. They were not Greek, though they spoke the tongue with waspish authority. They had tales to tell of shattered armies and death by frostbite, but in a sense it was already too late, for the wine had fuddled the wits of the old men. Their stories palled rapidly. Yet they impressed me, these three leather-faced specimens from an unknown civilisation called "war". They sat uneasily in such good fellowship. The flesh was stretched tight over their unshaven cheek-bones as if from fatigue. They smoked gluttonously, gushing the blue smoke from mouth and nostrils like voluptuaries. When they yawned they seemed to fetch their yawns up from the very scrotum. We confided ourselves to their care with misgiving for they were the first unfriendly faces we had seen for a long time.

At midnight we slipped out slantwise from the bay upon a high moonlight—the further darkness made more soft, more confiding, by the warm incoherent goodbyes which poured out across the white beaches towards us. How beautiful are the Greek words of greeting and farewell!

We shuttled for a while along the ink-shadowed line of cliffs where the engine's heartbeats were puckered up and thrown back at us in volleys. And so at last outwards upon the main deep, feeling the soft swelling unction of the water's rhythms

22

begin to breast us up, cradle and release us, as if in play. The night was superlatively warm and fine. A dolphin broke once, twice at the bow. A course was set.

Exultation mixed with a profound sadness now possessed us; fatigue and happiness in one. I could taste the good salt upon my lips. We drank some warm sage-tea without talking. The child was struck speechless by the beauties of this journey—the quivering phosphorescence of our wake, combed out behind us like a comet's hair, flowing and reviving. Above us, too, flowed the plumed branches of heaven, stars scattered as thick as almond-blossom on the enigmatic sky. So at last, happy with these auguries and lulled by pulses of the water and the even vibrations of the engine, she fell asleep with a smile upon parted lips, with the olive-wood doll pressed against her cheek.

How could I help but think of the past towards which we were returning across the dense thickets of time, across the familiar pathways of the Greek sea? The night slid past me, an unrolling ribbon of darkness. The warm sea-wind brushed my cheek—soft as the brush of a fox. Between sleep and waking I lay, feeling the tug of memory's heavy plumb-line: tug of the leaf-veined city which my memory had peopled with masks, malign and beautiful at once. I should see Alexandria again, I knew, in the elusive temporal fashion of a ghost—for once you become aware of the operation of a time which is not calendar-time you become in some sort a ghost. In this other domain I could hear the echoes of words uttered long since in the past by other voices. Balthazar saying: "This world represents the promise of a unique happiness which we are not well-enough equipped to grasp." The grim mandate which the city exercised over its familiars, crippling sentiment, steeping everything in the vats of its own exhausted passions. Kisses made more passionate by remorse. Gestures made in the amber light of shuttered rooms. The flocks of white doves flying upwards among the minarets. These pictures seemed to me to represent the city as I would see it again. But I was wrong—for each new approach is different. Each time we deceive ourselves that it will be the same. The Alexandria I now saw, the first vision of it from the sea, was something I could not have imagined.

It was still dark when we lay up outside the invisible harbour with its remembered outworks of forts and anti-submarine nets. I tried to paint the outlines on the darkness with my mind. The boom was raised only at dawn each day. An all-obliterating darkness reigned. Somewhere ahead of us lay the invisible coast of Africa, with its "kiss of thorns" as the Arabs say. It was intolerable to be so aware of them, the towers and minarets of the city, and yet to be unable to will them to appear. I could not see my own fingers before my face. The sea had become a vast empty ante-room, a hollow bubble of blackness.

Then suddenly there passed a sudden breath, a whiff like a wind passing across a bed of embers, and the nearer distance glowed pink as a sea-shell, deepening gradually into the rose-richness of a flower. A faint and terrible moaning came out across the water towards us, pulsing like the wing-beats of some fearful prehistoric bird—sirens which howled as the damned must howl in limbo. One's nerves were shaken like the branches of a tree. And as if in response to this sound lights began to prick out everywhere, sporadically at first, then in ribbons, bands, squares of crystal. The harbour suddenly out-lined itself with complete clarity upon the dark panels of heaven, while long white fingers of powder-white light began to stalk about the sky in ungainly fashion, as if they were the legs of some awkward insect struggling to gain a purchase on the slippery black. A dense stream of coloured rockets now began to mount from the haze among the battleships, emptying on the sky their brilliant clusters of stars and diamonds and smashed pearl snuff-boxes with a marvellous prodigality. The air shook in strokes. Clouds of pink and yellow dust arose with the maroons to shine upon the greasy buttocks of the barrage bal-loons which were flying everywhere. The very sea seemed to tremble. I had had no idea that we were so near, or that the city

could be so beautiful in the mere saturnalia of a war. It had
begun to swell up, to expand like some mystical rose of the
darkness, and the bombardment kept it company, overflowing
the mind. To our surprise we found ourselves shouting at each
other. We were staring at the burning embers of Augustine's
Carthage, I thought to myself, we were observing the fall of
city man.

It was as beautiful as it was stupefying. In the top left-hand
corner of the tableau the searchlights had begun to congregate,
quivering and sliding in their ungainly fashion, like daddy-
long-legs. They intersected and collided feverishly, and it was
clear that some signal had reached them which told of the
struggles of some trapped insect on the outer cobweb of darkness. Again and again they crossed, probed, merged, divided.
Then at last we saw what they were bracketing: six tiny silver
moths moving down the skylanes with what seemed unbearable slowness. The sky had gone mad around them yet they still
moved with this fatal languor; and languidly too curled the
curving strings of hot diamonds which spouted up from the
ships, or the rank lacklustre sniffs of cloudy shrapnel which
marked their progress.

And deafening as was the roaring which now filled our ears it
was possible to isolate many of the separate sounds which
orchestrated the bombardment. The crackle of shards which
fell back like a hailstorm upon the corrugated roofs of the
waterside cafés: the scratchy mechanical voices of ships' sig-
nallers repeating, in the voices of ventriloquists' dummies,
semi-intelligible phrases which sounded like "Three o'clock
red, Three o'clock red". Strangely too, there was music somewhere at the heart of all the hubbub, jagged quartertones which
stabbed; then, too, the foundering roar of buildings falling.
Patches of light which disappeared and left an aperture of
darkness at which a dirty yellow flame might come and lap like
a thirsty animal. Nearer at hand (the water smacked the echo
out) we could hear the rich harvest of spent cannon-shells pour-

25

ing upon the decks from the Chicago Pianos: an almost continuous splashing of golden metal tumbling from the breeches of the skypointed guns.

So it went on, feasting the eye yet making the vertebrae quail before the whirlwind of meaningless power it disclosed. I had not realised the impersonality of war before. There was no room for human beings or thought of them under this vast umbrella of coloured death. Each drawn breath had become only a temporary refuge.

Then, almost as suddenly as it had started, the spectacle died away. The harbour vanished with theatrical suddenness, the string of precious stones was turned off, the sky emptied, the silence drenched us, only to be broken once more by that famished crying of the sirens which drilled at the nerves. And then, nothing—a nothingness weighing tons of darkness out of which grew the smaller and more familiar sounds of water licking at the gunwales. A faint shore-wind crept out to invest us with the alluvial smells of an invisible estuary. Was it only in my imagination that I heard from far away the sounds of wildfowl on the lake?

We waited thus for a long time in great indecision; but meanwhile from the east the dawn had begun to overtake the sky, the city and desert. Human voices, weighted like lead, came softly out, stirring curiosity and compassion. Children's voices—and in the west a sputum-coloured meniscus on the horizon. We yawned, it was cold. Shivering, we turned to one another, feeling suddenly orphaned in this benighted world between light and darkness.

But gradually it grew up from the eastern marches, this familiar dawn, the first overflow of citron and rose which would set the dead waters of Mareotis a-glitter; and fine as a hair, yet so indistinct that one had to stop breathing to verify it, I heard (or thought I heard) the first call to prayer from some as yet invisible minaret.

Were there, then, still gods left to invoke? And even as the

26

question entered my mind I saw, shooting from the harbour-mouth, the three small fishing-boats—sails of rust, liver and blue plum. They heeled upon a freshet and stooped across our bows like hawks. We could hear the rataplan of water lapping their prows. The small figures, balanced like riders, hailed us in Arabic to tell us that the boom was up, that we might enter harbour.

This we now did with circumspection, covered by the apparently deserted batteries. Our little craft trotted down the main channel between the long lines of ships like a *vaporetto* on the Grand Canal. I gazed around me. It was all the same, yet at the same time unbelievably different. Yes, the main theatre (of the heart's affections, of memory, of love?) was the same; yet the differences of detail, of décor stuck out obstinately. The liners now grotesquely dazzle-painted in cubist smears of white, khaki and North-Sea greys. Self-conscious guns, nesting awkwardly as cranes in incongruous nests of tarpaulin and webbing. The greasy balloons hanging in the sky as if from gibbets. I compared them to the ancient clouds of silver pigeon which had already begun to climb in wisps and puffs among the palms, diving upwards into the white light to meet the sun. A troubling counterpoint of the known and the unknown. The boats, for example, drawn up along the slip at the Yacht Club, with the remembered dew thick as sweat upon their masts and cordage. Flags and coloured awnings alike hanging stiffly, as if starched. (How many times had we not put out from there, at this same hour, in Clea's small boat, loaded with bread and oranges and wicker-clothed wine?) How many old sailing-days spent upon this crumbling coast, landmarks of affection now forgotten? I was amazed to see with what affectionate emotion one's eye could travel along a line of inanimate objects tied to a mossy wharf, regaling itself with memories which it was not conscious of having stored. Even the French warships (though now disgraced, their breech-blocks confiscated, their crews in nominal internment aboard) were exactly where I had last seen

27

them in that vanished life, lying belly-down upon the dawn murk like malevolent tomb-stones: and still, as always, backed by the paper-thin mirages of the city, whose fig-shaped minarets changed colour with every lift of the sun.

Slowly we passed down the long green aisle among the tall ships, as if taking part in some ceremonial review. The surprises among so much that was familiar, were few but choice: an ironclad lying dumbly on its side, a corvette whose upper works had been smeared and flattened by a direct hit—gun-barrels split like carrots, mountings twisted upon themselves in a contortion of scorched agony. Such a large package of grey steel to be squashed at a single blow, like a paper bag. Human remains were being hosed along the scuppers by small figures with a tremendous patience and quite impassively. This was surprising as it might be for someone walking in a beautiful cemetery to come upon a newly dug grave. ("It is beautiful" said the child.) And indeed it was so—the great forests of masts and spires which rocked and inclined to the slight swell set up by water-traffic, the klaxons mewing softly, the reflections dissolving and reforming. There was even some dog-eared jazz flowing out upon the water as if from a waste-pipe somewhere. To her it must have seemed appropriate music for a triumphal entry into the city of childhood. *"Jamais de la vie"* I caught myself humming softly in my own mind, amazed how ancient the tune sounded, how dated, how preposterously without concern for myself! She was looking into the sky for her father, the image which would form like a benevolent cloud above us and envelop her.

Only at the far end of the great dock were there evidences of the new world to which we were coming: long lines of trucks and ambulances, barriers, and bayonets, manned by the blue and khaki races of men like gnomes. And here a slow, but purposeful and continuous activity reigned. Small troglodytic figures emerged from iron cages and caverns along the wharves, busy upon errands of differing sorts. Here too there were ships

28

split apart in geometrical sections which exposed their steaming intestines, ships laid open in Caesarian section: and into these wounds crawled an endless ant-like string of soldiers and blue-jackets humping canisters, bales, sides of oxen on blood-stained shoulders. Oven doors opened to expose to the firelight white-capped men feverishly dragging at oven-trays of bread. It was somehow unbelievably slow, all this activity, yet immense in compass. It belonged to the instinct of a race rather than to its appetites. And while silence here was only of comparative value small sounds became concrete and imperative—sentries stamping iron-shod boots upon the cobbles, the yowl of a tug, or the buzz of a liner's siren like the sound of some giant blue-bottle caught in a web. All this was part of the newly acquired city to which I was henceforth to belong.

We drew nearer and nearer, scouting for a berth among the small craft in the basin; the houses began to go up tall. It was a moment of exquisite delicacy, too, and my heart was in my mouth (as the saying goes) for I had already caught sight of the figure which I knew would be there to meet us—away across the wharves there. It was leaning against an ambulance, smoking. Something in its attitude struck a chord and I knew it was Nessim, though I dared not as yet be sure. It was only when the ropes went out and we berthed that I saw, with beating heart (recognising him dimly through his disguise as I had with Capodistria), that it was indeed my friend. Nessim!

He wore an unfamiliar black patch over one eye. He was dressed in a blue service greatcoat with clumsy padded shoulders and very long in the knee. A peaked cap pulled well down over his eyes. He seemed much taller and slimmer than I remembered—perhaps it was this uniform which was half chauffeur's livery, half airman's rig. I think he must have felt the force of my recognition pressing upon him for he suddenly stood upright, and after peering briefly about him, spotted us. He threw the cigarette away and walked along the quay with his swift and graceful walk, smiling nervously. I waved but he did not

29

respond, though he half nodded as he moved towards us. "Look" I said, not without apprehension. "Here he comes at last, your father." She watched with wide and frozen eyes following the tall figure until it stood smiling at us, not six feet away. Sailors were busy with ropes. A gang plank went down with a bang. I could not decide whether that ominous black patch over his eye added to or subtracted from, the old distinction. He took off his cap and still smiling, shyly and somewhat ruefully, stroked his hair into place before putting it on again. "Nessim" I called, and he nodded, though he did not respond. A silence seemed to fall upon my mind as the child stepped out upon the plank. She walked with an air of bemused rapture, spellbound by the image rather than the reality. (Is poetry, then, more real than observed truth?) And putting out her arms like a sleepwalker she walked chuckling into his embrace. I came hard on her heels, and as he still laughed and hugged her Nessim handed me the hand with the missing finger. It had become a claw, digging into mine. He uttered a short dry sob disguised as a cough. That was all. And now the child crawled up like a sloth into a tree-trunk and wound her legs about his hips. I did not quite know what to say, gazing into that one all-comprehending dark eye. His hair was quite white at the temples. You cannot squeeze a hand with a missing finger as hard as you would like.

"And so we meet again."

He backed away briskly and sat down upon a bollard, groping for his cigarette case to offer me the unfamiliar delicacy of a French cigarette. We were both dumb. The matches were damp and only struck with difficulty. "Clea was to have come" he said at last, "but she turned tail at the last moment. She has gone to Cairo. Justine is out at Karm!" Then ducking his head he said under his breath "You know about it eh?" I nodded and he looked relieved. "So much the less to explain. I came off duty half an hour ago and waited for you to take you out. But perhaps. . . ."

But at this moment a flock of soldiers closed on us, verifying our identities and checking on our destinations. Nessim was busy with the child. I unpacked my papers for the soldiers. They studied them gravely, with a certain detached sympathy even, and hunted for my name upon a long sheet of paper before informing me that I should have to report to the Consulate, for I was a "refugee national". I returned to Nessim with the clearance slips and told him of this. "As a matter of fact it does not fall badly. I had to go there anyway to fetch a suitcase I left with all my respectable suits in it . . . how long ago, I wonder?"

"A lifetime" he smiled.

"How shall we arrange it?"

We sat side by side smoking and reflecting. It was strange and moving to hear around us all the accents of the English shires. A kindly corporal came over with a tray full of tin mugs, steaming with that singular brew, Army tea, and decorated with slabs of white bread smeared with margarine. In the middle distance a stretcher-party walked apathetically offstage with a sagging load from a bombed building. We ate hungrily and became suddenly aware of our swimming knees. At last I said: "Why don't you go on and take her with you? I can get a tram at the dock-gate and visit the Consul. Have a shave. Some lunch. Come out this evening to Karm if you will send a horse to the ford."

"Very well" he said, with a certain relief, and hugging the child suggested this plan to her, whispering in her ear. She offered no objection, indeed seemed eager to accompany him—for which I felt thankful. And so we walked, with a feeling of unreality, across the slimy cobbles to where the little ambulance was parked, and Nessim climbed into the driver's seat with the child. She smiled and clapped her hands, and I waved them away, delighted that the transition was working so smoothly. Nevertheless it was strange to find myself thus, alone with the city, like a castaway on a familiar reef. 'Familiar'—yes! For once one had left the semi-circle of the harbour nothing had

31

changed whatsoever. The little tin tram groaned and wriggled along its rusty rails, curving down those familiar streets which spread on either side of me images which were absolute in their fidelity to my memories. The barbers' shops with their fly-nets drawn across the door, tingling with coloured beads: the cafés with their idlers squatting at the tin tables (by El Bab, still the crumbling wall and the very table where we had sat motionless, weighed down by the blue dusk). Just as he let in the clutch Nessim had peered at me sharply and said: "Darley, you have changed very much", though whether in reproof or commendation I could not tell. Yes, I had: seeing the old crumbled arch of El Bab I smiled, remembering a now prehistoric kiss upon my fingers. I remembered the slight flinch of the dark eyes as she uttered the sad brave truth: "One learns nothing from those who return our love." Words which burnt like surgical spirit on an open wound, but which cleansed, as all truth does. And busy with these memories as I was, I saw with another part of my mind the whole of Alexandria unrolling once more on either side of me—its captivating detail, its insolence of colouring, its crushing poverty and beauty. The little shops, protected from the sun by bits of ragged awning in whose darkness was piled up every kind of merchandise from live quail to honeycombs and lucky mirrors. The fruit-stalls with their brilliant stock made doubly brilliant by being displayed upon brighter papers; the warm gold of oranges lying on brilliant slips of magenta and crimson-lake. The smoky glitter of the coppersmiths' caves. Gaily tasselled camel-saddlery. Pottery and blue jade beads against the Evil Eye. All this given a sharp prismatic brilliance by the crowds milling back and forth, the blare of the café radios, the hawkers' long sobbing cries, the imprecations of street-arabs, and the demented ululations of distant mourners setting forth at a jog-trot behind the corpse of some notable sheik. And here, strolling in the foreground of the painting with the insolence of full possession, came plum-blue Ethiopians in snowy turbans, bronze Sudanese with puffy charcoal

lips, pewter-skinned Lebanese and Bedouin with the profiles of
kestrels, woven like brilliant threads upon the monotonous
blackness of the veiled women, the dark Moslem dream of the
hidden Paradise which may only be glimpsed through the key-
hole of the human eye. And lurching down these narrow streets
with their packs scraping the mud walls plunged the sumpter
camels with cargoes of green clover, putting down their huge
soft pads with infinite delicacy. I suddenly remembered Scobie
giving me a lesson on the priority of salutation: "You must
realise that it's a question of form. They're regular Britishers
for politeness, my boy. No good throwing your *Salaam Aleikum*
around just anyhow. It must be given first by a camel-rider to a
man on a horse, by a horseman to a man on a donkey, by a
donkey-rider to a man on foot, by a man walking to a man
seated, by a small party to a large one, by the younger to the
older. . . . It's only in the great schools at home they teach such
things. But here every nipper has it at his fingers' ends. Now
repeat the order of battle after me!" It was easier to repeat the
phrase than to remember the order at this remove in time.
Smiling at the thought, I strove to re-establish those forgotten
priorities from memory, while I gazed about me. The whole
toybox of Egyptian life was still there, every figure in place—
street-sprinkler, scribe, mourner, harlot, clerk, priest—untouched, it seemed, by time or by war. A sudden melancholy
invaded me as I watched them, for they had now become a part
of the past. My sympathy had discovered a new element inside
itself—detachment. (Scobie used to say, in an expansive moment: "Cheer up, me boyo, it takes a lifetime to grow. People
haven't the patience any more. *My* mother waited nine months
for me!" A singular thought.)

Jolting past the Goharri Mosque I remembered finding one-
eyed Hamid there one afternoon rubbing a slice of lemon on a
pilaster before sucking it. This, he had said, was an infallible
specific against the stone. He used to live somewhere in this
quarter with its humble cafés full of native splendours like rose-

scented drinking water and whole sheep turning on spits, stuffed with pigeons, rice, nuts. All the paunch-beguiling meals which delighted the ventripotent pachas of the city!

Somewhere up here, skirting the edge of the Arab quarter the tram gives a leap and grinds round abruptly. You can for one moment look down through the frieze of shattered buildings into the corner of the harbour reserved for craft of shallow draught. The hazards of the war at sea had swollen their numbers to overflowing. Framed by the coloured domes there lay feluccas and lateen-rig giassas, wine-caiques, schooners, and brigantines of every shape and size, from all over the Levant. An anthology of masts and spars and haunting Aegean eyes; of names and rigs and destinations. They lay there coupled to their reflections with the sunlight on them in a deep water-trance. Then abruptly they were snatched away and the Grande Corniche began to unroll, the magnificent long sea-parade which frames the modern city, the Hellenistic capital of the bankers and cotton-visionaries—all those European bagmen whose enterprise had re-ignited and ratified Alexander's dream of conquest after the centuries of dust and silence which Amr had imposed upon it.

Here, too, it was all relatively unchanged save for the dull khaki clouds of soldiers moving everywhere and the rash of new bars which had sprung up everywhere to feed them. Outside the Cecil long lines of transport-trucks had overflowed the taxi-ranks. Outside the Consulate an unfamiliar naval sentry with rifle and bayonet. I could not say it was all irremediably changed, for these visitors had a shiftless and temporary look, like countrymen visiting a capital for a fair. Soon a sluice gate would open and they would be drawn off into the great reservoir of the desert battles. But there were surprises. At the Consulate, for example, a very fat man who sat like a king prawn at his desk, pressing white hands together whose long filbert nails had been carefully polished that morning, and who addressed me with familiarity. "My task may seem invidious" he fluted, "yet it is necessary. We are trying to grab everyone who has a special aptitude before the Army gets them. I have been sent your name by the Ambassador who had designated you for the censorship department which we have just opened, and which is grotesquely understaffed."

"The Ambassador?" It was bewildering.

"He's a friend of yours is he not?"

"I hardly know him."

"Nevertheless I am bound to accept his direction, even though I am in charge of this operation."

There were forms to be filled in. The fat man, who was not unamiable, and whose name was Kenilworth, obliged by helping me. "It is a bit of mystery" I said. He shrugged his shoulders and spread his white hands. "I suggest you discuss it with him when you meet."

"But I had no intention . . ." I said. But it seemed pointless to discuss the matter further until I discovered what lay behind it. How could Mountolive. . . ? But Kenilworth was talking again. "I suppose you might need a week to find yourself lodgings here before you settle in. Shall I tell the department so?"

"If you wish" I said in bewilderment. I was dismissed and spent some time in the cellars unearthing my battered cabin-trunk and selecting from it a few respectable city-clothes. With these in a brown paper parcel I walked slowly along the Corniche towards the Cecil, where I purposed to take a room, have a bath and shave, and prepare myself for the visit to the country-house. This had begun to loom up rather in my mind, not exactly with anxiety but with the disquiet which suspense always brings. I stood for a while staring down at the still sea, and it was while I was standing thus that the silver Rolls with the daffodil hub-caps drew up and a large bearded personage jumped out and came galloping towards me with hands out-stretched. It was only when I felt his arms hugging my shoulders and the beard brushing my cheek in a Gallic greeting that I was able to gasp "Pombal!"

35

"Darley". Still holding my hands as tenderly, and with tears in his eyes, he drew me to one side and sat down heavily on one of the stone benches bordering the marine parade. Pombal was in the most elegant *tenue*. His starched cuffs rattled crisply. The dark beard and moustache gave him an imposing yet somehow forlorn air. Inside all these trappings he seemed quite unchanged. He peered through them, like a Tiberius in fancy-dress. We gazed at each other for a long moment of silence, with emotion. Both knew that the silence we observed was one of pain for the fall of France, an event which symbolised all too clearly the psychic collapse of Europe itself. We were like mourners at an invisible cenotaph during the two minutes' silence which commemorates an irremediable failure of the human will. I felt in his handclasp all the shame and despair of this graceless tragedy and I sought desperately for the phrase which might console him, might reassure him that France itself could never truly die so long as artists were being born into the world. But this world of armies and battles was too intense and too concrete to make the thought seem more than of secondary importance—for art really means freedom, and it was this which was at stake. At last the words came. "Never mind. To-day I've seen the little blue cross of Lorraine flowering everywhere."

"You understand" he murmured and squeezed my hand again. "I knew you would understand. Even when you most criticised her you knew that she meant as much to you as to us." He blew his nose suddenly, with startling loudness, in a clean handkerchief and leaned back on the stone bench. With amazing suddenness he had become his old self again, the timid, fat, irrepressible Pombal of the past. "There is so much to tell you. You will come with me now. At once. Not a word. Yes, it is Nessim's car. I bought it to save it from the Egyptians. Mountolive has fixed you an excellent post. I am still in the old flat, but now we have taken the building. You can have the whole top floor. It will be like old times again." I was carried

36

off my feet by his volubility and by the bewildering variety of prospects he described so rapidly and confidently, without apparently expecting comment. His English had become practically perfect.

"Old times" I stammered.

But here an expression of pain crossed his fat countenance and he groaned, pressing his hands between his knees as he uttered the word: "Fosca!" He screwed up his face comically and stared at me. "You do not know." He looked almost terrified. "I am in love with her."

I laughed. He shook his head rapidly. "No. Don't laugh."

"I must, Pombal."

"I beseech you." And leaning forward with a look of despair on his countenance he lowered his voice and prepared to confide something to me. His lips moved. It was clearly something of tragic importance. At last he brought it out, and the tears came into his eyes as he spoke the words: "You don't understand. *Je suis fidèle malgré moi.*" He gasped like a fish and repeated *"Malgré moi.* It has never happened before, *never.*" And then abruptly he broke into a despairing whinny with the same look of awed bewilderment on his face. How could I forbear to laugh? At a blow he had restored Alexandria to me, complete and intact—for no memory of it could be complete without the thought of Pombal in love. My laughter infected him. He was shaking like a jelly. "Stop" he pleaded at last with comic pathos, interjecting into the forest of bearded chuckles the words. "And I have never slept with her, not once. That is the insane thing." This made us laugh more than ever.

But the chauffeur softly sounded the horn, recalling him to himself abruptly, reminding him that he had duties to perform. "Come" he cried. "I have to take a letter to Pordre before nine. Then I'll have you dropped at the flat. We can lunch together. Hamid is with me, by the way; he'll be delighted. Hurry up." Once more my doubts were not given time to formulate themselves. Clutching my parcel I accompanied him to the familiar

37

car, noticing with a pang that its upholstery now smelt of expensive cigars and metal-polish. My friend talked rapidly all the way to the French Consulate, and I was surprised to find that his whole attitude to the Chief had changed. All the old bitterness and resentment had vanished. They had both, it seemed, abandoned their posts in different capitals (Pombal in Rome) in order to join the Free French in Egypt. He spoke of Pordre now with tender affection. "He is like a father to me. He has been marvellous" said my friend rolling his expressive dark eye. This somewhat puzzled me until I saw them both together and understood in a flash that the fall of their country had created this new bond. Pordre had become quite white-haired; his frail and absent-minded gentleness had given place to the calm resolution of someone grappling with responsibilities which left no room for affectation. The two men treated each other with a courtesy and affection which in truth made them seem like father and son rather than colleagues. The hand that Pordre placed so lovingly on Pombal's shoulder, the face he turned to him, expressed a wistful and lonely pride.

But the situation of their new Chancery was a somewhat unhappy one. The broad windows looked out over the harbour, over the French Fleet which lay there at anchor like a symbol of all that was malefic in the stars which governed the destiny of France. I could see that the very sight of it lying there idle was a perpetual reproach to them. And there was no escaping it. At every turn taken between the high old-fashioned desks and the white wall their eyes fell upon this repellent array of ships. It was like a splinter lodged in the optic nerve. Pordre's eye kindled with self-reproach and the zealot's hot desire to reform these cowardly followers of the personage whom Pombal (in his less diplomatic moments) was henceforward to refer to as "*ce vieux Putain*". It was a relief to vent feelings so intense by the simple substitution of a letter. The three of us stood there, looking down into the harbour at this provoking sight, and suddenly the old man burst out: "Why don't you British intern them? Send them to India with the Italians. I shall never understand it. Forgive me. But do you realise that they are allowed to keep their small arms, mount sentries, take shore leave, just as if they were a neutral fleet? The admirals wine and dine in the town, all intriguing for Vichy. There are endless *bagarres* in the cafés between our boys and their sailors." I could see that it was a subject which was capable of making them quite beside themselves with fury. I tried to change it, since there was little consolation I could offer.

I turned instead to Pombal's desk on which stood a large framed photograph of a French soldier. I asked who it was and both men replied simultaneously: "He saved us." Later of course I would come to recognise this proud, sad Labrador's head as that of de Gaulle himself.

Pombal's car dropped me at the flat. Forgotten whispers stirred in me as I rang the bell. One-eyed Hamid opened to me, and after a moment of surprise he performed a curious little jump in the air. The original impulse of this jump must have been an embrace which he repressed just in time. But he put two fingers on my wrist and jumped like a solitary penguin on an ice-floe before retreating to give himself room for the more elaborate and formal greeting. "Ya Hamid" I cried, as delighted as he was. We crossed ourselves ceremonially at each other.

The whole place had been transformed once more, repainted and papered and furnished in massive official fashion. Hamid led me gloatingly from room to room while I mentally tried to reconstruct its original appearance from memories which had by now become faded and transposed. It was hard to see Melissa shrieking, for example. On the exact spot now stood a handsome sideboard crowded with bottles. (Pursewarden had once gesticulated from the far corner.) Bits of old furniture came back to mind. "Those old things must be knocking about somewhere" I thought in quotation from the poet of the city.* The only recognisable item was Pombal's old gout-chair which had mysteriously reappeared in its old place under the window. Had he perhaps flown back with it from Rome? That would be like him. The little box-room where Melissa and I. . . . It was now Hamid's own room. He slept on the same uncomfortable bed which I looked at with a kind of shrinking feeling, trying to recapture the flavour and ambience of those long enchanted afternoons when. . . . But the little man was talking. He must prepare lunch. And then he rummaged in a corner and thrust into my hand a crumpled snapshot which he must at some time have stolen from Melissa. It was a street-photograph and very faded. Melissa and I walked arm in arm talking down Rue Fuad. Her face was half turned away from me, smiling—dividing her attention between what I was saying so earnestly and the lighted shop-windows we passed. It must have been taken, this snapshot, on a winter afternoon around the hour of four. What on earth could I have been telling her with such earnestness? For the life of me I could not recall the time and place; yet there it was, in black and white, as they say. Perhaps the words I was uttering were momentous, significant—or perhaps they were meaningless! I had a pile of books under my arm and was wearing the dirty old mackintosh which I finally gave to Zoltan. It was in need of a dry-clean. My hair, too, seemed to need cutting at the back. Impossible to restore this vanished afternoon to mind! I gazed carefully at the circumstantial detail of the picture like someone bent upon restoring an irremediably faded fresco. Yes, it was winter, at four o'clock. She was wearing her tatty seal-skin and carried a handbag which I had not ever seen in her possession. "Sometime in August—*was* it August?" I mentally quoted to myself again.*

Turning back to the wretched rack-like bed again I whispered her name softly. With surprise and chagrin I discovered that she had *utterly vanished*. The waters had simply closed over her head. It was as if she had never existed, never inspired in me the pain and pity which (I had always told myself) would live

40

on, transmuted into other forms perhaps—but live triumph-antly on forever. I had worn her out *like an old pair of socks,* and the utterness of this disappearance surprised and shocked me. Could "love" simply wear out like this? "Melissa" I said again, hearing the lovely word echo in the silence. Name of a sad herb, name of a pilgrim to Eleusis. Was she less now than a scent or a flavour? Was she simply a nexus of literary cross-references scribbled in the margins of a minor poem? And had my love dissolved her in this strange fashion, or was it simply the literature I had tried to make out of her? Words, the acid-bath of words! I felt guilty. I even tried (with that lying self-deception so natural to sentimentalists) to *force* her to reappear by an act of will, to re-evoke a single one of those afternoon kisses which had once been for me the sum of the city's many meanings. I even tried deliberately to squeeze the tears into my eyes, to hypnotise memory by repeating her name like a charm. The experiment yielded nothing. Her name had been utterly worn out of use! It was truly shameful not to be able to evoke the faintest tribute to so all-engulfing an unhappiness. Then like the chime of a distant bell I heard the tart voice of the dead Pursewarden saying "But our unhappiness was sent to regale us. We were intended to revel in it, enjoy it to the full." Melissa had been simply one of the many costumes of love!

I was bathed and changed by the time Pombal hurried in to an early lunch, full of the incoherent rapture of his new and remarkable state of mind. Fosca, the cause of it, was, he told me, a refugee married to a British officer. "How could it have come about, this sudden passionate understanding?" He did not know. He got up to look at his own face in the hanging mirror. "I who believed so many things about love" he went on moodily, half addressing his own reflection and combing his beard with his fingers, "but never something like this. Even a year ago had you said what I am just saying I would have answered: '*Pouagh!* It is simply a Petrarchian obscenity. Med-iaeval rubbish!'. I even used to think that continence was medically unhealthy, that the damned thing would atrophy or fall off if it were not frequently used. Now look at your unhappy—no *happy* friend! I feel bound and gagged by Fosca's very existence. Listen, the last time Keats came in from the desert we went out and got drunk. He took me to Golfo's tavern. I had a sneaking desire—sort of experimental—to *ramoner une poule*. Don't laugh. Just to see what had gone wrong with my feelings. I drank five Armagnacs to liven them up. I began to feel quite like it theoretically. Good, I said to myself, I will crack this virginity. I will *dépuceler* this romantic image once and for all lest people begin to talk and say that the great Pombal is unmanned. But what happened? I became panic-stricken! My feelings were quite quite *blindés* like a bloody tank. The sight of all those girls made me memorise Fosca in detail. Everything, even her hands in her lap with her knitting! I was cooled as if by an ice cream down my collar. I emptied my pockets on the table and fled in a hail of slippers and a torrent of cat-calls from my old friends. I was swearing, of course. Not that Fosca expects it, no. She tells me to go ahead and have a girl if I must. Perhaps this very freedom keeps me in prison? Who knows? It is a complete mystery to me. It is strange that this girl should drag me by the hair down the paths of honour like this—an unfamiliar place."

Here he struck himself softly on the chest with a gesture of reproof mixed with a certain doubtful self-commendation. He came and sat down once more saying moodily: "You see, she is pregnant by her husband and her sense of honour would not permit her to trick a man on active service, who may be killed at any time. Specially when she is bearing his child. *Ça se conçoit.*"

We ate in silence for a few moments, and then he burst out: "But what have I to do with such ideas? Tell me please. We only talk, yet it is enough." He spoke with a touch of self-contempt.

"And he?"

Pombal sighed: "He is an extremely good and *kind* man, with that national kindliness which Pursewarden used to say was a kind of compulsion neurosis brought on by the almost suicidal boredom of English life! He is handsome, gay, speaks three languages. And yet . . . it is not that he is *froid*, exactly, but he is *tiède*—I mean somewhere in his inner nature. I am not sure if he is typical or not. At any rate he seems to embody notions of honour which would do credit to a troubadour. It isn't that we Europeans lack honour, of course, but we don't stress things unnaturally. I mean self-discipline should be more than a concession to a behaviour-pattern. I sound confused. Yes, I am a little confused in thinking of their relationship. I mean something like this: in the depths of his national conceit he really believes foreigners incapable of fidelity in love. Yet in being so truthful and so faithful she is only doing what comes naturally to her, without a false straining after a form. *She acts as she feels*. I think if he really loved her in the sense I mean he would not appear always to have merely condescended to rescue her from an intolerable situation. I think somewhere inside herself, though she is not aware of it, the sense of injustice rankles a little bit; she is faithful to him . . . how to say? Slightly contemptuously? I don't know. But she does love him in this peculiar fashion, the only one he permits. She is a girl of delicate feelings. But what is strange is that our own love—which neither doubts, and which we have confessed and accepted—has been coloured in a curious way by these circumstances. If it has made me happy it has also made me a little uncertain of myself; at times I get rebellious. I feel that our love is beginning to wear a penitential air—this glorious adventure. It gets coloured by his own grim attitude which is like one of atonement. I wonder if love for a *femme galante* should be quite like this. As for him he also is a *chevalier* of the middle class, as incapable of inflicting pain as of giving physical pleasure I should say. Yet withal gentle and quite overwhelming in his kindness and uprightness. But *merde*, one cannot love

43

judicially, out of a sense of justice, can one? Somewhere along the line he fails her without being conscious of the fact. Nor do I think she *knows* this, at any rate in her conscious mind. But when they are together you feel in the presence of something incomplete, something which is not cemented but just soldered together by good manners and convention. I am aware that I sound unkind, but I am only trying to describe exactly what I see. For the rest we are good friends and indeed I really admire him; when he comes on leave we all go out to dinner and talk politics! Ouf!"

He lay back in his chair, exhausted by this exposition, and yawned heavily before consulting his watch. "I suppose" he went on with resignation "that you will find it all very strange, these new aspects of people; but then everything sounds strange here, eh? Pursewarden's sister, Liza, for example—you don't know her? She is stone blind. It seems to us all that Mountolive is madly in love with her. She came out originally to collect his papers and also to find materials for a book about him. Allegedly. Anyway she has stayed on at the Embassy ever since. When he is in Cairo on duty he visits her every weekend! He looks somehow unhappy now—perhaps I do too?" He once more consulted the mirror and shook his head decisively. Apparently he did not. "Well anyway" he conceded "I am probably wrong."

The clock on the mantelpiece struck and he started up. "I must get back to the office for a conference" he said. "What about you?" I told him of my projected trip to Karm Abu Girg. He whistled and looked at me keenly. "You will see Justine again, eh?" He thought for a moment and then shrugged his shoulders doubtfully. "A recluse now, isn't she? Put under house-arrest by Memlik. Nobody has seen her for ages. I don't know what's going on with Nessim either. They've quite broken with Mountolive and as an official I have to take his line, so we would never even try to meet: even if it were allowed, I mean. Clea sees him sometimes. I'm sorry for

44

Nessim. When he was in hospital she could not get permission to visit him. It is all a merry-go-round, isn't it? Like a Paul Jones. New partners until the music stops! But you'll come back, won't you, and share this place? Good. Then I'll tell Hamid. I must be off. Good luck."

I had only intended to lie down for a brief siesta before the car came, but such was my fatigue that I plunged into a heavy sleep the moment my head touched the pillow; perhaps I should have slept the clock round had not the chauffeur awakened me. Half-dazed as yet I sat in the familiar car and watched the unreal lakelands grow up around with their palms and water-wheels—the Egypt which lives outside the cities, ancient, pastoral and veiled by mists and mirages. Old memories stirred now, some bland and pleasing, others rough as old cicatrices. Scar-tissue of old emotions which I should soon be shedding. The first momentous step would be to encounter Justine again. Would she help or hinder me in the task of controlling and evaluating these precious "reliques of sensation" as Coleridge calls them? It was hard to know. With every succeeding mile I felt anxiety and expectation running neck and neck. The Past!

o   o   o   o   o

II

Ancient lands, in all their prehistoric intactness: lake-solitudes hardly brushed by the hurrying feet of the centuries where the uninterrupted pedigrees of pelican and ibis and heron evolve their slow destinies in complete seclusion. Clover-patches of green baize swarming with snakes and clouds of mosquitoes. A landscape devoid of songbirds yet full of owls, hoopoes and kingfishers hunting by day, pluming themselves on the banks of the tawny waterways. The packs of half-wild dogs foraging, the blindfolded water-buffaloes circling the water-wheels in an eternity of darkness. The little wayside chancels built of dry mud and floored with fresh straw where the pious traveller might say a prayer as he journeyed. Egypt! The goose-winged sails scurrying among the freshets with perhaps a human voice singing a trailing snatch of song. The click-click of the wind in the Indian corn, plucking at the coarse leaves, shumbling them. Liquid mud exploded by rainstorms in the dust-laden air throwing up mirages everywhere, despoiling perspectives. A lump of mud swells to the size of a man, a man to the size of a church. Whole segments of the sky and land displace, open like a lid, or heel over on their side to turn upside down. Flocks of sheep walk in and out of these twisted mirrors, appearing and disappearing, goaded by the quivering nasal cries of invisible shepherds. A great confluence of pastoral images from the forgotten history of the old world which still lives on side by side with the one we have inherited. The clouds of silver winged ants floating up to meet and incandesce in the sunlight. The clap of a horse's hoofs on the mud floors of this lost world echo like a pulse and the brain swims among these veils and melting rainbows.

And so at last, following the curves of the green embank-

46

ments you come upon an old house built sideways upon an intersection of violet canals, its cracked and faded shutters tightly fastened, its rooms hung with dervish trophies, hide shields, bloodstained spears and magnificent carpets. The gardens desolate and untended. Only the little figures on the wall move their celluloid wings—scarecrows which guard against the Evil Eye. The silence of complete desuetude. But then the whole countryside of Egypt shares this melancholy feeling of having been abandoned, allowed to run to seed, to bake and crack and moulder under the brazen sun.

Turn under an arch and clatter over the cobbles of a dark courtyard. Will this be a new point of departure or a return to the starting-point?

It is hard to know.

o o o o o

S he stood at the very top of the long outer staircase looking down into the dark courtyard like a sentinel and holding in her right hand a branch of candles which threw a frail circle of light around her. Very still, as if taking part in a *tableau vivant*. It seemed to me that the tone in which she first uttered my name had been deliberately made flat and unemphatic, copied perhaps from some queer state of mind which she had imposed upon herself. Or perhaps, uncertain that it was I, she was merely interrogating the darkness, trying to unearth me from it like some obstinate and troublesome memory which had slipped out of place. But the familiar voice was to me like the breaking of a seal. I felt like someone at last awakened from a sleep which had lasted centuries and as I walked slowly and circumspectly up the creaking wooden stairway I felt, hovering over me, the breath of a new self-possession. I was halfway up when she spoke again, sharply this time, with something almost comminatory in her tone. "I heard the horses and went all-overish suddenly. I've spilt scent all over my dress. I stink, Darley. You will have to forgive me."

She seemed to have become very much thinner. Holding the candle high she advanced a step to the stairhead, and after gazing anxiously into my eyes placed a small cold kiss upon my right cheek. It was as cold as an obituary, dry as leather. As she did so I smelt the spilt perfume. She did indeed give off overpowering waves of it. Something in the enforced stillness of her attitude suggested an inner unsteadiness and the idea crossed my mind that perhaps she had been drinking. I was a trifle shocked too to see that she had placed a bright patch of rouge on each cheek-bone which showed up sharply against a dead white, overpowdered face. If she was beautiful still it was the passive beauty of some Propertian mummy which had been clumsily painted to give the illusion of life, or a photograph carelessly colour-tinted. "You must not look at my eye" she next said, sharply, imperatively: and I saw that her left eyelid drooped slightly, threatening to transform her expression into something like a leer—and most particularly the welcoming smile which she was trying to adopt at this moment. "Do you understand?" I nodded. Was the rouge, I wondered, designed to distract attention from that drooping eyelid? "I had a small stroke" she added under her breath, as if explaining to herself. And as she still stood before me with the raised branch of candles she seemed to be listening to some other sound. I took her hand and we stood together for a long moment thus, staring at one another.

"Have I changed very much?"

"Not at all."

"Of course I have. We all have." She spoke now with a contemptuous shrillness. She raised my hand briefly and put it to her cheek. Then nodding with a puzzled air she turned and drew me towards the balcony, walking with a stiff proud step. She was clad in a dress of dark taffeta which whispered loudly at every movement. The candlelight jumped and danced upon the walls. We stopped before a dark doorway and she called out "Nessim" in a sharp tone which shocked me, for it was the tone in which one would call a servant. After a moment Nessim appeared from the shadowy bedroom, obedient as a djinn.

"Darley's here" she said, with the air of someone handing over a parcel, and placing the candles on a low table reclined swiftly in a long wicker chair and placed her hand over her eyes.

Nessim had changed into a suit of a more familiar cut, and he came nodding and smiling towards me with the accustomed expression of affection and solicitude. Yet it was somehow different again; he wore a faintly cowed air, shooting little

49

glances sideways and downwards towards the figure of Justine, and speaking softly as one might in the presence of someone asleep. A constraint had suddenly fallen upon us as we seated ourselves on that shadowy balcony and lit cigarettes. The silence locked like a gear which would not disengage.

"The child is in bed, delighted with the palace as she calls it, and the promise of a pony of her own. I think she will be happy."

Justine suddenly sighed deeply and without uncovering her eyes said slowly: "He says we have not changed."

Nessim swallowed and continued as if he had not heard the interruption in the same low voice: "She wanted to stay awake till you came but she was too tired."

Once again the reclining figure in the shadowy corner interrupted to say: "She found Narouz' little circumcision cap in the cupboard. I found her trying it on." She gave a short sharp laugh, like a bark, and I saw Nessim wince suddenly and turn away his face.

"We are short of servants" he said in a low voice, hastily as if to cement up the holes made in the silence by her last remark.

His air of relief was quite patent when Ali appeared and bade us to dinner. He picked up the candles and led us into the house. It had a somewhat funereal flavour—the white-robed servant with his scarlet belt leading, holding aloft the candles in order to light Justine's way. She walked with an air of pre-occupation, of remoteness. I followed next with Nessim close behind me. So we went in Indian file down the unlighted corridors, across high-ceilinged rooms with their walls covered in dusty carpets, their floors of rude planks creaking under our feet. And so we came at last to a supper-room, long and narrow, and suggesting a forgotten sophistication which was Ottoman perhaps; say, a room in a forgotten winter palace of Abdul Hamid, its highly carved window-screens of filigree looking out upon a neglected rose-garden. Here the candlelight with its luminous shadows was ideal as an adjunct to furnishings which were, in themselves, strident. The golds and the reds and the violets would in full light have seemed unbearable. By candlelight they had a subdued magnificence.

We seated ourselves at the supper-table and once more I became conscious of the almost cowed expression of Nessim as he gazed around him. It is perhaps not the word. It was as if he expected some sudden explosion, expected some unforeseen reproach to break from her lips. He was mentally prepared to parry it, to fend it off with a tender politeness. But Justine ignored us. Her first act was to pour out a glass of red wine. This she raised to the light as if to verify its colour. Then she dipped it ironically to each of us in turn like a flag and drank it off all in one motion before replacing the glass on the table. The touches of rouge gave her an enflamed look which hardly matched the half-drowsy stupefaction of her glance. She was wearing no jewelry. Her nails were painted with gold polish. Putting her elbows on the table she propped her chin for a long moment as she studied us keenly, first one and then the other. Then she sighed, as if replete, and said: "Yes, we have all changed", and turning swiftly like an accuser she stabbed her finger at her husband and said: "*He* has lost an eye."

Nessim pointedly ignored this, passing some item of table fare towards her as if to distract her from so distressing a topic. She sighed again and said: "Darley, you look much better, but your hands are cracked and calloused. I felt it on my cheek."

"Wood-cutting I expect."

"Ah. So! But you look well, very well."

(A week later she would telephone Clea and say: "Dear God, how coarse he has become. What little trace of sensibility he had has been swamped by the peasant.")

In the silence Nessim coughed nervously and fingered the black patch over his eye. Clearly he misliked the tone of her voice, distrusted the weight of the atmosphere under which one could feel, building up slowly like a wave, the pressure of a hate which was the newest element among so many novelties of speech and manner. Had she really turned into a shrew? Was she ill? It was difficult to disinter the memory of that magical dark mistress of the past whose every gesture, however ill-advised and ill-considered, rang with the newly minted splendour of complete generosity. ("So you come back" she was saying harshly "and find us all locked up in Karm. Like old figures in a forgotten account book. Bad debts, Darley. Fugitives from justice, eh Nessim?")

There was nothing to be said in answer to such bitter sallies. We ate in silence under the quiet ministration of the Arab servant. Nessim addressed an occasional hurried remark to me on some neutral topic, brief, monosyllabic. Unhappily we felt the silence draining out around us, emptying like some great reservoir. Soon we should be left there, planted in our chairs like effigies. Presently the servant came in with two charged thermos flasks and a package of food which he placed at the end of the table. Justine's voice kindled with a kind of insolence as she said: "So you are going back tonight?"

Nessim nodded shyly and said: "Yes, I'm on duty again." Clearing his throat he added to me: "It is only four times a week. It gives me something to do."

"Something to do" she said clearly, derisively. "To lose his eye and his finger gives him something to do. Tell the truth, my dear, you would do anything to get away from this house." Then leaning forward towards me she said: "To get away from me, Darley. I drive him nearly mad with my scenes. That is what he says." It was horribly embarrassing in its vulgarity.

The servant came in with his duty clothes carefully pressed and ironed, and Nessim rose, excusing himself with a word and a wry smile. We were left alone. Justine poured out a glass of wine. Then, in the act of raising it to her lips she surprised me with a wink and the words: "Truth will out."

"How long have you been locked up here?" I asked.

"Don't speak of it."

"But is there no way. . . ."

"He has managed to partly escape. Not me. Drink, Darley, drink your wine."

I drank in silence, and in a few minutes Nessim appeared once more, in uniform and evidently ready for his night journey. As if by common consent we all rose, the servant took up the candles and once more conducted us back to the balcony in lugubrious procession. During our absence one corner had been spread with carpets and divans while extra candlesticks and smoking materials stood upon inlaid side-tables. The night was still, and almost tepid. The candle-flames hardly moved. Sounds of the great lake came ebbing in upon us from the outer darkness. Nessim said a hurried good-bye and we heard the diminishing clip of his horse's hoofs gradually fade as he took the road to the ford. I turned my head to look at Justine. She was holding up her wrists at me, her face carved into a grimace. She held them joined together as if by invisible manacles. She exhibited these imaginary handcuffs for a long moment before dropping her hands back into her lap, and then, abruptly, swift as a snake, she crossed to the divan where I lay and sat down at my feet, uttering as she did so, in a voice vibrating with remorseful resentment, the words: "Why, Darley? O *why*?" It was as if she were interrogating not merely destiny or fate but the very workings of the universe itself in these thrilling poignant tones. Some of the old beauty almost flashed out in this ardour to trouble me like an echo. But the perfume! At such close quarters the spilled perfume was over-powering, almost nauseating.

Yet suddenly now all our constraint vanished and we were at last able to talk. It was as if this outburst had exploded the bubble of listlessness in which we had been enveloped all evening. "You see a different me" she cried in a voice almost of triumph. "But once again the difference lies in you, in what you imagine you see!" Her words rattled down like a hail of sods on an empty coffin. "How is it that you can feel no

53

resentment against me? To forgive such treachery so easily—why, it is unmanly. Not to hate such a vampire? It is unnatural. Nor could you ever understand my sense of humiliation at not being able to regale, yes *regale* you, my dear, with the treasures of my inner nature as a mistress. And yet, in truth, I enjoyed deceiving you, I must not deny it. But also there was regret in only offering you the pitiful simulacrum of a love (Ha! that word again!) which was sapped by deceit. I suppose this betrays the bottomless female vanity again: to desire the worst of two worlds, of both words—love and deceit. Yet it is strange that now, when you know the truth, and I am free to offer you affection, I feel only increased self-contempt. Am I enough of a woman to feel that the real sin against the Holy Ghost is dishonesty in love? But what pretentious rubbish—for love admits of no honesty by its very nature."

So she went on, hardly heeding me, arguing my life away, moving obsessively up and down the cobweb of her own devising, creating images and beheading them instantly before my eyes. What could she hope to prove? Then she placed her head briefly against my knee and said: "Now that I am free to hate or love it is comical to feel only fury at this new self-possession of yours! You have escaped me somewhere. But what else was I to expect?"

In a curious sort of way this was true. To my surprise I now felt the power to wound her for the first time, even to subjugate her purely by my indifference! "Yet the truth" I said "is that I feel no resentment for the past. On the contrary I am full of gratitude because an experience which was perhaps banal in itself (even perhaps disgusting for you) was for me immeasurably enriching!" She turned away saying harshly: "Then we should both be laughing now."

Together we sat staring out into the darkness for a long while. Then she shivered, lighted a cigarette and resumed the thread of her interior monologue. "The post-mortems of the undone! What could you have seen in it all I wonder? We are after all totally ignorant of one another, presenting selected fictions to each other! I suppose we all observe each other with the same immense ignorance. I used, in my moments of guilt long afterwards, to try and imagine that we might one day become lovers again, on a new basis. What a farce! I pictured myself making it up to you, expiating my deceit, repaying my debt. But . . . I knew that you would always prefer your own mythical picture, framed by the five senses, to anything more truthful. But now, then, tell me—which of us was the greater liar? I cheated you, you cheated yourself."

These observations, which at another time, in another context, might have had the power to reduce me to ashes, were now vitally important to me in a new way. "However hard the road, one is forced to come to terms with truth at last" wrote Pursewarden somewhere. Yes, but unexpectedly I was discovering that truth was nourishing—the cold spray of a wave which carried one always a little further towards self-realisation. I saw now that my own Justine had indeed been an illusionist's creation, raised upon the faulty armature of misinterpreted words, actions, gestures. Truly there was no blame here; the real culprit was my love which had invented an image on which to feed. Nor was there any question of dishonesty, for the picture was coloured after the necessities of the love which invented it. Lovers, like doctors, colouring an unpalatable medicine to make it easier for the unwary to swallow! No, this could not have been otherwise, I fully realised.

Something more, fully as engrossing: I also saw that lover and loved, observer and observed, throw down a field about each other ("Perception is shaped like an embrace—the poison enters with the embrace" as Pursewarden writes). They then infer the properties of their love, judging it from this narrow field with its huge margins of unknown ("the refraction"), and proceed to refer it to a generalised conception of something constant in its qualities and universal in its operation. How valuable a lesson this was, both to art and to life! I had only

55

been attesting, in all I had written, to the power of an image which I had created involuntarily by the *mere act of seeing* Justine. There was no question of true or false. Nymph? Goddess? Vampire? Yes, she was all of these, and none of them. She was, like every woman, everything that the mind of a man (let us define "man" as a poet perpetually conspiring against himself) —that the mind of man wished to imagine. She was there for-ever, and she had never existed! Under all these masks there was only another woman, every woman, like a lay figure in a dress-maker's shop, waiting for the poet to clothe her, breathe life into her. In understanding all this for the first time I began to realise with awe the enormous reflexive power of woman—the fecund passivity with which, like the moon, she borrows her second-hand light from the male sun. How could I help but be anything but grateful for such vital information? What did they matter, the lies, deceptions, follies, in comparison to this truth?

Yet while this new knowledge compelled my admiration for her more than ever—as symbol of woman, so to speak—I was puzzled to explain the new element which had crept in here: a flavour of disgust for her personality and its attributes. The scent! Its cloying richness half sickened me. The touch of the dark head against my knee stirred dim feelings of revulsion in me. I was almost tempted to embrace her once more in order to explore this engrossing and inexplicable novelty of feeling further! Could it be that a few items of information merely, *facts* like sand trickling into the hour-glass of the mind, had irrevocably altered the image's qualities—turning it from something once desirable to something which now stirred dis-gust? Yes, the same process, the very same love-process, I told myself. This was the grim metamorphosis brought about by the acid-bath of truth—as Pursewarden might say.

Still we sat together on that shadowy balcony, prisoners of memory, still we talked on: and still it remained unchanged, this new disposition of selves, the opposition of new facts of mind.

56

At last she took a lantern and a velvet cloak and we walked about for a while in that tideless night, coming at last to a great *nubk* tree whose branches were loaded with votive offerings. Here Nessim's brother had been found dead. She held the lantern high to light the tree, reminding me that the "nubk" forms the great circular palisade of trees which encircles the Moslem Paradise. "As for Narouz, his death hangs heavy on Nessim because people say that he ordered it himself —the Copts say so. It has become like a family curse to him. His mother is ill, but she will never return to this house, she says. Nor does he wish her to. He gets quite cold with rage when I speak of her. He says he wishes shè would die! So here we are cooped up together. I sit all night reading—guess what? —a big bundle of love-letters to her which she left behind! Mountolive's love-letters! More confusion, more unexplored corners!" She raised the lantern and looked closely into my eyes: "Ah, but this unhappiness is not just ennui, spleen. There is also a desire to swallow the world. I have been experimenting with drugs of late, the sleep-givers!"

And so back in silence to the great rustling house with its dusty smells.

"He says we will escape one day and go to Switzerland where at least he still has money. But when, but when? And now this war! Pursewarden said that my sense of guilt was atrophied. It is simply that I have no power to decide things now, any more. I feel as if my will had snapped. But it will pass." Then suddenly, greedily she grasped my hand and said: "But thank God, you are here. Just to talk is such a *soulagement*. We spend whole weeks together without exchanging a word."

We were seated once more on the clumsy divans by the light of candles. She lit a silver-tipped cigarette and smoked with short decisive inspirations as the monologue went on, unrolling on the night, winding away in the darkness like a river.

"When everything collapsed in Palestine, all our dumps discovered and captured, the Jews at once turned on Nessim

57

accusing him of treachery, because he was friendly with Mount-olive. We were between Memlik and the hostile Jews, in disgrace with both. The Jews expelled me. This was when I saw Clea again; I so badly needed news and yet I couldn't confide in her. Then Nessim came over the border to get me. He found me like a mad woman. I was in despair! And he thought it was because of the failure of our plans. It was, of course, it was; but there was another and deeper reason. While we were conspirators, joined by our work and its dangers, I could feel truly passionate about him. But to be under house-arrest, compelled to idle away my time alone with him, in his company. . . . I knew I should die of boredom. My tears, my lamentations were those of a woman forced against her will to take the veil. Ah but you will not understand, being a northerner. How could you? To be able to love a man fully, but only in a single posture, so to speak. You see, when he does not act, Nessim is nothing; he is completely flavourless, not in touch with himself at any point. Then he has no real self to interest a woman, to grip her. In a word he is really a pure idealist. When a sense of destiny consumes him he becomes truly splendid. It was as an actor that he magnetised me, illuminated me for myself. But as a fellow prisoner, in defeat—he predisposes to ennui, migraine, thoughts of utter banality like suicide! That is why from time to time I drive my claws into his flesh. In despair!"

"And Pursewarden?"

"Ah! Pursewarden. That is something different again. I cannot think of him without smiling. There my failure was of a totally different order. My feeling for him was—how shall I say?—almost incestuous, if you like; like one's love for a beloved, an incorrigible elder brother. I tried so hard to penetrate into his confidences. He was too clever, or perhaps too egotistical. He defended himself against loving me by *making me laugh*. Yet I achieved with him, even so very briefly, a tantalising inkling that there might be other ways of living open to me if only I could find them. But he was a tricky one. He used to say: 'An artist saddled with a woman is like a spaniel with a tick in its ear; it itches, it draws blood, one cannot reach it. Will some kindly grown-up please. . . ?' Perhaps he was utterly lovable because quite out of reach? It is hard to say these things. One word 'love' has to do service for so many different kinds of the same animal. It was he, too, who reconciled me to that whole business of the rape, remember? All that nonsense of Arnauti's in *Moeurs*, all those psychologists! His single observation stuck like a thorn. He said: 'Clearly you enjoyed it, as any child would, and probably even invited it. You have wasted all this time trying to come to terms with an imaginary conception of damage done to you. Try dropping this invented guilt and telling yourself that the thing was both pleasurable and meaningless. Every neurosis is made to measure!' It was curious that a few words like this, and an ironic chuckle, could do what all the others could not do for me. Suddenly everything seemed to lift, get lighter, move about. Like cargo shifting in a vessel. I felt faint and rather sick, which puzzled me. Then later on a space slowly cleared. It was like feeling creeping back into a paralysed hand again.''

She was silent for a moment before going on. ''I still do not quite know how he saw us. Perhaps with contempt as the fabricators of our own misfortunes. One can hardly blame him for clinging to his own secrets like a limpet. Yet he hardly kept them, for he had a so-called Check hardly less formidable than mine, something which had plucked and gutted all sensation for him; so really in a way perhaps his strength was really a great weakness! You are silent, have I wounded you? I hope not, I hope your self-esteem is strong enough to face these truths of our old relationship. I should like to get it *all* off my chest, to come to terms with you—can you understand? To confess everything and wipe the slate clean. Look, even that first, that very first afternoon when I came to you —remember? You told me once how momentous it was. When you were ill in bed with sunburn, remember? Well, I had just been kicked out of his hotel-room against my will and was quite beside myself with fury. Strange to think that every word I then addressed to you was spoken mentally to him, to Pursewarden! In your bed it was he I embraced and subjugated in my mind. And yet again, in another dimension, *everything* I felt and did then was really for Nessim. At the bottom of my rubbish heap of a heart there was really Nessim, and the plan. My innermost life was rooted in this crazy adventure. Laugh now, Darley! Let me see you laugh for a change. You look rueful, but why should you? We are all in the grip of the emotional field which we throw down about one another—you yourself have said it. Perhaps our only sickness is to desire a truth which we cannot bear rather than to rest content with the fictions we manufacture out of each other."

She suddenly uttered a short ironic laugh and walked to the balcony's edge to drop the smouldering stub of her cigarette out into the darkness. Then she turned, and standing in front of me with a serious face, as if playing a game with a child, she softly patted her palms together, intoning the names, "Pursewarden and Liza, Darley and Melissa, Mountolive and Leila, Nessim and Justine, Narouz and Clea. . . . Here comes a candle to light them to bed, and here comes a chopper to chop off their heads. The sort of pattern we make should be of interest to someone; or is it just a meaningless display of coloured fireworks, the actions of *human* beings or of a set of dusty puppets which could be hung up in the corner of a writer's mind? I suppose you ask yourself the question."

"Why did you mention Narouz?"

"After he died I discovered some letters to Clea; in his cupboard along with the old circumcision-cap there was a huge nosegay of wax flowers and a candle the height of a man. As you know a Copt proposes with these. But he never had the courage to send them! How I laughed!"

"You laughed?"

60

"Yes, laughed until the tears ran down my cheeks. But I was really laughing at myself, at you, at all of us. One stumbles over it at every turn of the road, doesn't one; under every sofa the same corpse, in every cupboard the same skeleton? What can one do but laugh?"

It was late by now, and she lighted my way to the gaunt guest-bedroom where I found a bed made up for me, and placed the candles on the old-fashioned chest of drawers. I slept almost at once.

It must have been at some time not far off dawn when I awoke to find her standing beside the bed naked, with her hands joined in supplication like an Arab mendicant, like some beggar-woman of the streets. I started up. "I ask nothing of you" she said, "nothing at all but only to lie in your arms for the comfort of it. My head is bursting tonight and the medicines won't bring sleep. I do not want to be left to the mercies of my own imagination. Only for the comfort, Darley. A few strokes and endearments, that is all I beg you."

I made room for her listlessly, still half asleep. She wept and trembled and muttered for a long time before I was able to quieten her. But at last she fell asleep with her dark head on the pillow beside me.

I lay awake for a long time to taste, with perplexity and wonder, the disgust that had now surged up in me, blotting out every other feeling. From where had it come? The perfume! The unbearable perfume and the smell of her body. Some lines from a poem of Pursewarden's drifted through my mind.

"Delivered by her to what drunken caresses,
Of mouths half eaten like soft rank fruit,
From which one takes a single bite,
A mouthful of the darkness where we bleed."

The once magnificent image of my love lay now in the hollow of my arm, defenceless as a patient on an operating table, hardly breathing. It was useless even to repeat her name which

61

once held so much fearful magic that it had the power to slow the blood in my veins. She had become a woman at last, lying there, soiled and tattered, like a dead bird in a gutter, her hands crumpled into claws. It was as if some huge iron door had closed forever in my heart.

I could hardly wait for that slow dawn to bring me release. I could hardly wait to be gone.

o   o   o   o   o

IV

Walking about the streets of the summer capital once more, walking by spring sunlight, and a cloudless skirmishing blue sea—half-asleep and half-awake—I felt like the Adam of the mediaeval legends: the world-compounded body of a man whose flesh was soil, whose bones were stones, whose blood water, whose hair was grass, whose eyesight sunlight, whose breath was wind, and whose thoughts were clouds. And weightless now, as if after some long wasting illness, I found myself turned adrift again to float upon the shallows of Mareotis with its old tide-marks of appetites and desires refunded into the history of the place: an ancient city with all its cruelties intact, pitched upon a desert and a lake. Walking down with remembered grooves of streets which extended on every side, radiating out like the arms of a starfish from the axis of its founder's tomb. Footfalls echoing in the memory, forgotten scenes and conversations springing up at me from the walls, the café tables, the shuttered rooms with cracked and peeling ceilings. Alexandria, princess and whore. The royal city and the *anus mundi*. She would never change so long as the races continued to seethe here like must in a vat; so long as the streets and squares still gushed and spouted with the fermentation of these diverse passions and spites, rages and sudden calms. A fecund desert of human loves littered with the whitening bones of its exiles. Tall palms and minarets marrying in the sky. A hive of white mansions flanking those narrow and abandoned streets of mud which were racked all night by Arab music and the cries of girls who so easily disposed of their body's wearisome baggage (which galled them) and offered to the night the passionate kisses which money could not disflavour. The sadness and beatitude of this human conjunction which perpetuated itself to eternity, an endless cycle of rebirth and annihilation which alone could teach and reform by its destructive power. ("One makes love only to confirm one's loneliness" said Pursewarden, and at another time Justine added like a coda "A woman's best love letters are always written to the man she is betraying" as she turned an immemorial head on a high balcony, hanging above a lighted city where the leaves of the trees seemed painted by the electric signs, where the pigeons tumbled as if from shelves. . . .) A great honeycomb of faces and gestures.

"We become what we dream" said Balthazar, still hunting among these grey paving stones for the key to a watch which is Time. "We achieve in reality, in substance, only the pictures of the imagination." The city makes no answer to such propositions. Unheeding it coils about the sleeping lives like some great anaconda digesting a meal. Among those shining coils the pitiable human world went its way, unaware and unbelieving, repeating to infinity its gestures of despair, repentance, and love. Demonax the philosopher said: "Nobody wishes to be evil" and was called a cynic for his pains. And Pursewarden in another age, in another tongue replied: "Even to be half-awake among sleep-walkers is frightening at first. Later one learns to dissimulate!"

I could feel the ambience of the city on me once more, its etiolated beauties spreading their tentacles out to grasp at my sleeve. I felt more summers coming, summers with fresh despairs, fresh onslaughts of the "bayonets of time". My life would rot away afresh in stifling offices to the tepid whirl of electric fans, by the light of dusty unshaded bulbs hanging from the cracked ceilings of renovated tenements. At the Café Al Aktar, seated before a green *menthe*, listening to the sulky bubbles in the *narguilehs* I would have time to catechise the silences which followed the cries of the hawkers and the clatter of backgammon-boards. Still the same phantoms would pass and repass in the Nebi Daniel, the gleaming limousines of the bankers would bear their choice freight of painted ladies to distant bridge-tables, to the synagogue, the fortune-teller, the smart café. Once all this had power to wound. And now? Snatches of a quartet squirted from a café with scarlet awnings reminded me of Clea once saying: "Music was invented to confirm human loneliness." But if I walked here with attention and even a certain tenderness it was because for me the city was something which I myself had deflowered, at whose hands I had learned to ascribe some particular meaning to fortune. These patched and faded walls, the lime wash cracking into a million oyster-coloured patches, only imitated the skins of the lepers who whined here on the edge of the Arab quarter; it was simply the hide of the place itself, peeling and caking away under the sun.

Even the war had come to terms with the city, had indeed stimulated its trade with its bands of aimless soldiers walking about with that grim air of unflinching desperation with which Anglo-Saxons embark upon their pleasures; their own demagnetised women were all in uniform now which gave them a ravenous air—as if they could drink the blood of the innocents while it was still warm. The brothels had over-flowed and gloriously engulfed a whole quarter of the town around the old square. If anything the war had brought an air of tipsy carnival rather than anything else; even the nightly bombardments of the harbour were brushed aside by day, shrugged away like nightmares, hardly remembered as more than an inconvenience. For the rest, nothing had fundamentally changed. The brokers still sat on the steps of the Mohammed Ali club sipping their newspapers. The old horse-drawn gharries still clopped about upon their listless errands. The crowds still thronged the white Corniche to take the frail spring sunlight. Balconies crowded with wet linen and tittering girls. The Alexandrians still moved inside the murex-tinted cyclorama of the life they imagined. ("Life is more complicated

65

than we think, yet far simpler than anyone dares to imagine.")
Voices of girls, stabbing of Arab quarter-tones, and from the
synagogue a metallic drone punctuated by the jingle of a sis-
trum. On the floor of the Bourse they were screaming like one
huge animal in pain. The money-changers were arranging their
currencies like sweets upon the big squared boards. Pashas in
scarlet flower-pots reclining in immense cars like gleaming
sarcophagi. A dwarf playing a mandolin. An immense eunuch
with a carbuncle the size of a brooch eating pastry. A legless
man propped on a trolley, dribbling. In all this furious
acceleration of the mind I thought suddenly of Clea—her thick
eyelashes fragmenting every glance of the magnificent eyes—
and wondered vaguely when she would appear. But in the
meantime my straying footsteps had led me back to the narrow
opening of the Rue Lepsius, to the worm-eaten room with the
cane chair which creaked all night, and where once the old
poet of the city had recited 'The Barbarians'. I felt the stairs
creak again under my tread. On the door was a notice in
Arabic which said 'Silence'. The latch was hooked back.

Balthazar's voice sounded strangely thin and far away as he
bade me to enter. The shutters were drawn and the room was
shrouded in half-darkness. He was lying in bed. I saw with a
considerable shock that his hair was quite white which made
him look like an ancient version of himself. It took me a
moment or two to realise that it was not dyed. But how he had
changed! One cannot exclaim to a friend: "My God, how
much you have aged!" Yet this is what I almost did, quite
involuntarily.

"Darley!" he said feebly, and held up in welcome hands
swollen to the size of boxing-gloves by the bandages which
swathed them.

"What on earth have you been doing to yourself?"

He drew a long sad sigh of vexation and nodded towards a
chair. The room was in great disorder. A mountain of books
and papers on the floor by the window. An unemptied chamber-

pot. A chessboard with the pieces all lying in confusion. A newspaper. A cheese-roll on a plate with an apple. The wash-basin full of dirty plates. Beside him in a glass of some cloudy fluid stood a glittering pair of false teeth on which his feverish eye dwelt from time to time with confused perplexity. "You have heard nothing? That surprises me. Bad news, news of a scandal, travels so fast and so far I should have thought that by now you had heard. It is a long story. Shall I tell you and provoke the look of tactful commiseration with which Mount-olive sits down to play chess with me every afternoon?"

"But your hands. . . ."

"I shall come to those in due course. It was a little idea I got from your manuscript. But the real culprits are these, I think, these false teeth in the glass. Don't they glitter bewitchingly? I am sure it was the teeth which set me off. When I found that I was about to lose my teeth I suddenly began to behave like a woman at the change of life. How else can I explain falling in love like a youth?" He cauterised the question with a dazed laugh.

"First the Cabal—which is now disbanded; it went the way of all words. Mystagogues arose, theologians, all the resource-ful bigotry that heaps up around a sect and spells dogma! But the thing had to me a special meaning, a mistaken and un-conscious meaning, but nevertheless a clear one. I thought that slowly, by degrees, I should be released from the bondage of my appetites, of the flesh. I should at last, I felt, find a philo-sophic calm and balance which would expunge the passional nature, sterilise my actions. I thought of course that I had no such *préjugés* at the time; that my quest for truth was quite pure. But unconsciously I was using the Cabal to this precise end—instead of letting it use me. First miscalculation! Pass me some water from the pitcher over there." He drank thirstily through his new pink gums. "Now comes the absurdity. I found I must lose my teeth. This caused the most frightful up-heaval. It seemed to me like a death-sentence, like a confirma-

67

tion of growing old, of getting beyond the reach of life itself.
I have always been fastidious about mouths, always hated rank
breath and coated tongues; but most of all false teeth! Unconsciously, then, I must have somehow pushed myself to this
ridiculous thing—as if it were a last desperate fling before old
age settled over me. Don't laugh. *I fell in love* in a way that I
have never done before, at least not since I was eighteen.
'Kisses sharp as quills' says the proverb; or as Pursewarden
might say 'Once more the cunning gonads on the prowl, the
dragnet of the seed, the old biological terror'. But my dear
Darley, this was no joke. I still had my own teeth! But the
object of my choice, a Greek actor, was the most disastrous that
anyone could hit upon. To look like a god, to have a charm
like a shower of silver arrows—and yet to be simply a small-
spirited, dirty, venal and empty personage: that was Pana-
giotis! I knew it. It seemed to make no difference whatsoever.
I cursed myself in the mirror. But I was powerless to behave
otherwise. And, in truth, all this might have passed off as so
much else had he not pushed me to outrageous jealousies,
terrific scenes of recrimination. I remember that old Pursewarden used to say: 'Ah! you Jews, you have the knack of
suffering' and I used to reply with a quotation from Mommsen
about the bloody Celts: 'They have shaken all states and
founded none. They nowhere created a great state or developed
a distinctive culture of their own.' No, this was not simply an
expression of minority-fever: this was the sort of murderous
passion of which one has read, and for which our city is
famous! Within a matter of months I became a hopeless
drunkard. I was always found hanging about the brothels. I
obtained drugs under prescription for him to sell. Anything,
lest he should leave me. I became as weak as a woman. A
terrific scandal, rather a series of them, made my practice
dwindle until it is now non-existent. Amaril is keeping the
clinic going out of kindness until I can pick myself off the
floor. I was dragged across the floor of the club, holding on to

his coat and imploring him not to leave me! I was knocked down in Rue Fuad, thrashed with a cane outside the French Consulate. I found myself surrounded by long-faced and concerned friends who did everything they could to avert disaster. Useless. I had become quite impossible! All this went on, this ferocious life—and really I enjoyed being debased in a queer way, being whipped and scorned, reduced to a wreck! It was as if I wanted to swallow the world, to drain the sore of love until it healed. I was pushed to the very extremity of myself, yet I myself was doing the pushing: or was it the teeth?" He cast a sulky furious look in their direction and sighed, moving his head about as if with inner anguish at the memory of these misdeeds.

"Then of course it came to an end, as everything does, even presumably life! There is no merit in suffering as I did, dumbly like a pack animal, galled by intolerable sores it cannot reach with its tongue. It was then that I remembered a remark in your manuscript about the ugliness of my hands. Why did I not cut them off and throw them in the sea as you had so thoughtfully recommended? This was the question that arose in my mind. At the time I was so numb with drugs and drink that I did not imagine I would feel anything. However I made an attempt, but it is harder than you imagine, all that gristle! I was like those fools who cut their throats and come bang up against the oesophagus. They always live. But when I desisted with pain I thought of another writer, Petronius. (The part that literature plays in our lives!) I lay down in a hot bath. But the blood wouldn't run, or perhaps I had no more. The colour of bitumen it seemed, the few coarse drops I persuaded to trickle. I was about to try other ways of alleviating the pain when Amaril appeared at his most abusive and brought me to my senses by giving me a deep sedation of some twenty hours during which he tidied up my corpse as well as my room. Then I was very ill, with shame I believe. Yes, it was chiefly shame, though of course I was much weakened by the absurd excesses

69

to which I had been pushed. I submitted to Pierre Balbz who removed the teeth and provided me with this set of glittering snappers—*art nouveau!* Amaril tried in his clumsy way to analyse me—but what is one to say of this very approximate science which has carelessly overflowed into anthropology on one side, theology on the other? There is much they do not know as yet: for instance that one kneels in church because one kneels to enter a woman, or that circumcision is derived from the clipping of the vine, without which it will run to leaf and produce no fruit! I had no philosophic system on which to lean as even Da Capo did. Do you remember Capodistria's exposition of the nature of the universe? 'The world is a biological phenomenon which will only come to an end when every single man has had all the women, every woman all the men. Clearly this will take some time. Meanwhile there is nothing to do but to help forward the forces of nature by treading the grapes as hard as we can. As for an afterlife—what will it consist of but satiety? The play of shadows in Paradise—pretty *hanoums* flitting across the screens of memory, no longer desired, no longer desiring to be desired. Both at rest at last. But clearly it cannot be done all at once. Patience! *Avanti!*' Yes, I did a lot of slow and careful thinking as I lay here, listening to the creak of the cane chair and the noises from the street. My friends were very good and often visited me with gifts and conversations that left me headaches. So I gradually began to swim up to the surface again, with infinite slowness. I said to myself 'Life is the master. We have been living against the grain of our intellects. The real teacher is endurance.' I had learned something, but at what a cost!

"If only I had had the courage to tackle my love wholeheartedly I would have served the ideas of the Cabal better. A paradox, you think? Perhaps. Instead of letting my love poison my intellect and my intellectual reservations my love. Yet though I am rehabilitated, and ready once more to enter the world, everything in nature seems to have disappeared! I still

70

awake crying out: 'He has gone away forever. True lovers exist for the sake of love.' "

⁻He gave a croaky sob and crawled out from between the sheets, looking ridiculous in his long woollen combinations, to hunt for a handkerchief in the chest of drawers. To the mirror he said: "The most tender, the most tragic of illusions is perhaps to believe that our actions can add or subtract from the total quantity of good and evil in the world." Then he shook his head gloomily and returned to his bed, settling the pillows at his back and adding: "And that fat brute Father Paul talks of acceptance! Acceptance of the world can only come from a full recognition of its measureless extents of good and evil; and to really inhabit it, explore it to the full uninhibited extent of this finite human understanding—that is all that is necessary in order to accept it. But what a task! One lies here with time passing and wonders about it. Every sort of time trickling through the hour-glass, 'time immemorial' and 'for the time being' and 'time out of mind'; the time of the poet, the philosopher, the pregnant woman, the calendar. . . . Even 'time is money' comes into the picture; and then, if you think that money is excrement for the Freudian, you understand that time must be also! Darley you have come at the right moment, for I am to be rehabilitated tomorrow by my friends. It was a touching thought which Clea first had. The shame of having to put in a public appearance again after all my misdeeds has been weighing on me very heavily. How to face the city again—that is the problem. It is only in moments like this that you realise who your friends are. Tomorrow a little group is coming here to find me dressed, my hands less conspicuously bandaged, my new teeth in place. I shall of course wear dark glasses. Mountolive, Amaril, Pombal and Clea, two on each arm. We will walk the whole length of Rue Fuad thus and take a lengthy public coffee on the pavement outside Pastroudi. Mountolive has booked the largest lunch table at the Mohammed Ali and proposes to offer me a lunch of twenty people to celebrate my

71

resurrection from the dead. It is a wonderful gesture of solidarity, and will certainly quell spiteful tongues and sneers. In the evening the Cervonis have asked me to dinner. With such lucky help I feel I may be able in the long run to repair my damaged confidence and that of my old patients. Is it not fine of them—and in the traditions of the city? I may live to smile again, if not to love—a fixed and glittering smile which only Pierre will gaze at with affection—the affection of the artificer for his handiwork." He raised his white boxing-gloves like a champion entering the ring and grimly saluted an imaginary crowd. Then he flopped back on his pillows once more and gazed at me with an air of benign sorrow.

"Where has Clea gone?" I asked.

"Nowhere. She was here yesterday afternoon asking for you."

"Nessim said she had gone somewhere."

"Perhaps to Cairo for the afternoon; where have you been?"

"Out to Karm for the night."

There was a long silence during which we eyed each other. There were clearly questions in his mind which he tactfully did not wish to inflict on me; and for my part there was little that I felt I could explain. I picked up an apple and took a bite from it.

"And the writing?" he said after a long silence.

"It has stopped. I don't seem to be able to carry it any further for the moment. I somehow can't match the truth to the illusions which are necessary to art without the gap show-ing—you know, like an unbasted seam. I was thinking of it at Karm, confronted again by Justine. Thinking how despite the factual falsities of the manuscript which I sent you the portrait was somehow poetically true—psychographically if you like. But an artist who can't solder the elements together falls short somewhere. I'm on the wrong track."

"I don't see why. In fact this very discovery should encourage rather than hamper you. I mean about the mutability of all truth. Each fact can have a thousand motivations, all equally

72

valid, and each fact a thousand faces. So many truths which have little to do with fact! Your duty is to hunt them down. At each moment of time all multiplicity waits at your elbow. Why, Darley, this should thrill you and give your writing the curves of a pregnant woman."

"On the contrary, it has faulted me. For the moment anyway. And now that I am back here in the real Alexandria from which I drew so many of my illustrations I don't feel the need for more writing—or at any rate writing which doesn't fulfil the difficult criteria I see lurking behind art. You remember Pursewarden writing: 'A novel should be an act of divination by entrails, not a careful record of a game of pat-ball on some vicarage lawn!'"

"Yes."

"And so indeed it should. But now I am confronted once more with my models I am ashamed to have botched them up. If I start again it will be from another angle. But there is still so much I don't know, and presumably never will, about all of you. Capodistria, for example, where does he fit in?"

"You sound as if you knew he was alive!"

"Mnemjian told me so."

"Yes. The mystery isn't a very complicated one. He was working for Nessim and compromised himself by a serious slip. It was necessary to clear out. Conveniently it happened at a time when he was all but bankrupt financially. The insurance money was most necessary! Nessim provided the setting and I provided the corpse. You know we get quite a lot of corpses of one sort or another. Paupers. People who donate their bodies, or actually sell them in advance for a fixed sum. The medical schools need them. It wasn't hard to obtain a private one, relatively fresh. I tried to hint at the truth to you once but you did not take my meaning. Anyway the thing's worked smoothly. Da Capo now lives in a handsomely converted Martello tower, dividing his time between studying black magic and working on certain schemes of Nessim's about which I

73

know nothing. Indeed I see Nessim only rarely, and Justine not at all. Though guests are permitted by special police order they never invite anyone out to Karm. Justine telephones people from time to time for a chat, that is all. You have been privileged, Darley. They must have got you a permit. But I am relieved to see you cheerful and undesponding. You have made a step forward somewhere, haven't you?"

"I don't know. I worry less."

"But you will be happy this time, I feel it; much has changed but much has remained the same. Mountolive tells me he has recommended you for a censorship post, and that you will probably live with Pombal, until you have had a chance to look round a bit."

"Another mystery! I hardly know Mountolive. Why has he suddenly constituted himself my benefactor?"

"I don't know, possibly because of Liza."

"Pursewarden's sister?"

"They are up at the summer legation for a few weeks. I gather you will be hearing from him, from them both."

There was a tap at the door and a servant entered to tidy the flat; Balthazar propped himself up and issued his orders. I stood up to take my leave.

"There is only one problem" he said "which occupies me. Shall I leave my hair as it is? I look about two hundred and seventy when it isn't dyed. But I think on the whole it would be better to leave it to symbolise my return from the dead with a vanity chastened by experience, eh? Yes, I shall leave it. I think I shall definitely leave it."

"Toss a coin."

"Perhaps I will. This evening I must get up for a couple of hours and practise walking about; extraordinary how weak one feels simply from lack of practice. After a fortnight in bed one loses the power of one's legs. And I mustn't fall down tomorrow or people will think I am drunk again and that would never do. As for you, you must find Clea."

74

"I'll go round to the studio and see if she is working."

"I'm glad you are back."

"In a strange way so am I."

And in the desultory brilliant life of the open street it was hard not to feel like an ancient inhabitant of the city, returning from the other side of the grave to visit it. Where would I find Clea?

o o o o o

V

She was not at the flat, though her letter-box was empty, which suggested that she had already collected her mail and gone out to read it over a *café crème*, as had been her wont in the past. There was nobody at the studio either. It fitted in with my mood to try and track her down in one of the familiar cafés and so I dutifully walked down Rue Fuad at a leisurely pace towards Baudrot, the Café Zoltan and the Coquin. But there was no sign of her. There was one elderly waiter at the Coquin who remembered me however, and he had seen her walking down Rue Fuad earlier in the morning with a portfolio. I continued my circuit, peering into the shop-windows, examining the stalls of second-hand books, until I reached the Select on the seafront. But she was not there. I turned back to the flat and found a note from her saying that she would not be able to make contact before the later after-noon, but that she would call there for me; it was annoying, for it meant that I should have to pass the greater part of the day alone, yet it was also useful, for it enabled me to visit Mnem-jian's redecorated emporium and indulge in a post-Pharaonic haircut and shave. ("The natron-bath" Pursewarden used to call it.) It also gave me time to unpack my belongings.

But we met by chance, not design. I had gone out to buy some stationery, and had taken a short cut through the little square called Bab El Fedan. My heart heeled half-seas over for a moment, for she was sitting where once (that first day) Melissa had been sitting, gazing at a coffee cup with a wry reflective air of amusement, with her hands supporting her chin. The exact station in place and time where I had once found Melissa, and with such difficulty mustered enough courage at last to enter the place and speak to her. It gave me a strange sense of unreality to repeat this forgotten action at such a great remove of time, like unlocking a door which had remained closed and bolted for a generation. Yet it was in truth Clea and not Melissa, and her blonde head was bent with an air of childish concentration over her coffee cup. She was in the act of shaking the dregs three times and emptying them into the saucer to study them as they dried into the contours from which fortune-tellers "skry"—a familiar gesture.

"So you haven't changed. Still telling fortunes."

"Darley." She sprang up with a cry of pleasure and we embraced warmly. It was with a queer interior shock, almost like a new recognition, that I felt her warm laughing mouth on mine, her hands upon my shoulders. As though somewhere a window had been smashed, and the fresh air allowed to pour into a long-sealed room. We stood thus embracing and smiling for a long moment. "You startled me! I was just coming on to the flat to find you."

"You've had me chasing my tail all day."

"I had work to do. But Darley, how you've changed! You don't stoop any more. And your spectacles. . . ."

"I broke them by accident ages ago, and then found I didn't really need them."

"I'm delighted for you. Bravo! Tell me, do you notice my wrinkles? I'm getting some I fear. Have I changed very much would you say?"

She was more beautiful than I could remember her to have been, slimmer, and with a subtle range of new gestures and expressions suggesting a new and troubling maturity.

"You've grown a new laugh."

"Have I?"

"Yes. It's deeper and more melodious. But I must not flatter you! A nightingale's laugh—if they do laugh."

"Don't make me self-conscious because I so much want to laugh with you. You'll turn it into a croak."

"Clea, why didn't you come and meet me?"

She wrinkled up her nose for a moment, and putting her hand on my arm, bent her head once more to the coffee grounds which were drying fast into little whorls and curves like sand-dunes. "Light me a cigarette" she said pleadingly.

"Nessim said you turned tail at the last moment."

"Yes, I did, my dear."

"Why?"

"I suddenly felt it might be inopportune. It might have been a complication somehow. You had old accounts to render, old scores to settle, new relationships to explore. I really felt powerless to do anything about you until . . . well, until you had seen Justine. I don't know why. Yes, I do though. I wasn't sure that the cycle would really change, I didn't know how much you had or hadn't changed yourself. You are such a bloody correspondent I hadn't any way of judging about your inside state of mind. Such a long time since you wrote, isn't it? And then the child and all that. After all, people sometimes get stuck like an old disc and can't move out of a groove. That might have been your fate with Justine. So it wasn't for me to intrude, since my side of you. . . . Do you see? I had to give you air."

"And supposing I have stuck like some old disc?"

"No it hasn't turned out like that."

"How can you tell?"

"From your face, Darley. I could tell in a flash!"

"I don't know quite how to explain. . . ."

"You don't *need* to" her voice curved upwards with elation and her bright eyes smiled. "We have such totally different claims upon each other. We are free to *forget!* You men are the strangest creatures. Listen, I have arranged this first day together like a tableau, like a charade. Come first and see the queer immortality one of us has gained. Will you put yourself in my hands? I have been so looking forward to acting as dragoman on . . . but no, I won't tell you. Just let me pay for this coffee."

78

"What does your fortune say in the grounds?"

"Chance meetings!"

"I think you invent."

The afternoon had been overcast and dusk fell early. Already the sunset violets had begun to tamper with the perspectives of the streets along the seafront. We took an old horse-drawn gharry which was standing forlornly in a taxi rank by Ramleh Station. The ancient jarvey with his badly cicatriced face asked hopefully if we wished for a "carriage of love" or an "ordinary carriage", and Clea, giggling, selected the latter variety of the same carriage as being cheaper. "O son of truth!" she said. "What woman would take a lusty husband in such a thing when she has a good bed at home which costs nothing."

"Merciful is God" said the old man with sublime resignation.

So we set off down the white curving Esplanade with its fluttering awnings, the quiet sea spreading away to the right of us to a blank horizon. In the past we had so often come this way to visit the old pirate in his shabby rooms in Tatwig Street.

"Clea, where the devil are we going?"

"Wait and see."

I could see him so clearly, the old man. I wondered for a moment if his shabby ghost still wandered about those dismal rooms, whistling to the green parrot and reciting: "*Taisez-vous, petit babouin.*" I felt Clea's arm squeeze mine as we sheered off left and entered the smoking ant-heap of the Arab town, the streets choked with smoke from the burning refuse-heaps, or richly spiced with cooking meat and whiffs of baking bread from the bakeries.

"Why on earth are you taking me to Scobie's rooms?" I said again as we started to clip-clop down the length of the familiar street. Her eyes shone with a mischievous delight as putting her lips to my ear she whispered: "Patience. You shall see."

It was the same house all right. We entered the tall gloomy archway as we had so often in the past. In the deepening dusk

79

it looked like some old faded daguerrotype, the little court-yard, and I could see that it had been much enlarged. Several supporting walls of neighbouring tenements had been razed or had fallen down and increased its mean size by about two hundred square feet. It was just a shattered and pock-marked no-man's-land of red earth littered with refuse. In one corner stood a small shrine which I did not remember having re-marked before. It was surrounded by a huge ugly modern grille of steel. It boasted a small white dome and a withered tree, both very much the worse for wear. I recognised in it one of the many *Maquams* with which Egypt is studded, spots made sacred by the death of a hermit or holy man and where the faithful repair to pray or solicit his help by leaving ex-votos. This little shrine looked as so many do, utterly shabby and forlorn, as if its existence had been overlooked and forgotten for centuries. I stood looking around me, and heard Clea's clear voice call: "Ya Abdul!" There was a note in it which suggested suppressed amusement but I could not for the life of me tell why. A man advanced towards us through the shadows peering. "He is almost blind. I doubt if he'll recognise you."

"But who is it?" I said, almost with exasperation at all this mystery. "Scobie's Abdul" she whispered briefly and turned away to say: "Abdul, have you the key of the *Maquam* of El Scob?"

He greeted her in recognition making elaborate passes over his breast, and produced a clutch of tall keys saying in a deep voice: "At once O lady" rattling the keys together as all guar-dians of shrines must do to scare the djinns which hang about the entrances to holy places.

"Abdul!" I exclaimed with amazement in a whisper. "But he was a youth." It was quite impossible to identify him with this crooked and hunched anatomy with its stooping centenar-ian's gait and cracked voice. "Come" said Clea hurriedly, "explanations later. Just come and look at the shrine." Still bemused I followed in the guardian's footsteps. After a very thorough rattling and banging to scare the djinns he unlocked the rusty portals and led the way inside. It was suffocatingly hot in that little airless tomb. A single wick somewhere in a recess had been lighted and gave a wan and trembling yellow light. In the centre lay what I presumed must be the tomb of the saint. It was covered with a green cloth with an elaborate design in gold. This Abdul reverently removed for my inspection, revealing an object under it which was so surprising that I uttered an involuntary exclamation. It was a galvanised iron bath-tub on one leg of which was engraved in high relief the words: " 'The Dinky Tub' Crabbe's. Luton." It had been filled with clean sand and its four hideous crocodile-feet heavily painted with the customary anti-djinn blue colour. It was an astonishing object of reverence to stumble upon in such surroundings, and it was with a mixture of amusement and dismay that I heard the now completely unrecognisable Abdul, who was the object's janitor, muttering the conventional prayers in the name of El Scob, touching as he did so the ex-votos which hung down from every corner of the wall like little white tassels. These were, of course, the slips of cloth which women tear from their underclothes and hang up as offerings to a saint who, they believe, will cure sterility and enable them to conceive. The devil! Here was old Scobie's bath-tub apparently being invoked to confer fertility upon the childless—and with success, too, if one could judge by the great number of the offerings.

"El Scob was a holy one?" I said in my halting Arabic.

The tired, crooked bundle of humanity with its head encircled in a tattered shawl nodded and bowed as he croaked: "From far away in Syria he came. Here he found his rest. His name enlightens the just. He was a student of harmlessness!"

I felt as if I were dreaming. I could almost hear Scobie's voice say: "Yes, it's a flourishing little shrine as shrines go. Mind you, I don't make a fortune, but I do give service!" The laughter began to pile up inside me as I felt the trigger of

81

Clea's fingers on my elbow. We exchanged delighted squeezes as we retired from that fuggy little hole into the dusky court-yard, while Abdul reverently replaced the cloth over the bath-tub, attended to the oil wick, and then joined us. Carefully he locked the iron grille, and accepting a tip from Clea with many hoarse gratitudes, shuffled away into the shadows, leaving us to sit down upon a heap of tumbled masonry.

"I didn't come right in" she said. "I was afraid we'd start laughing and didn't want to risk upsetting Abdul."

"Clea! Scobie's *bath-tub*!"

"I know."

"How the devil did this happen?"

Clea's soft laughter!

"You must tell me."

"It is a wonderful story. Balthazar unearthed it. Scobie is now officially El Yacoub. At least that is how the shrine is registered on the Coptic Church's books. But as you have just heard he is really El Scob! You know how these saints' *Maquams* get forgotten, overlooked. They die, and in time people completely forget who the original saint was; sometimes a sand-dune buries the shrine. But they also spring alive again. Suddenly one day an epileptic is cured there, or a prophecy is given by the shrine to some mad woman—and presto! the saint wakes up, revives. Well, all the time our old pirate was living in this house El Yacoub was there, at the end of the garden, though nobody knew it. He had been bricked in, surrounded by haphazard walls—you know how crazily they build here. He was utterly forgotten. Meanwhile Scobie, after his death, had become a figure of affectionate memory in the neighbourhood. Tales began to circulate about his great gifts. He was clever at magic potions (like Mock Whisky?). A cult began to blossom around him. They said he was a necromancer. Gamblers swore by his name. 'El Scob spit on this card' became quite a proverb in the quarter. They also said that he had been able to change himself into a woman at will (!) and by sleeping with impotent men regenerate their forces. He could also make the barren conceive. Some women even called their children after him. Well, in a little while he had already joined the legendary of Alexandrian saints, but of course he had no actual shrine—because everyone knew with one half of his mind that Father Paul had stolen his body, wrapped it in a flag, and buried it in the Catholic cemetery. They knew because many of them had been there for the service and much enjoyed the dreadful music of the police band of which I believe Scobie had once been a member. I often wonder whether he played any instrument and if so what. A slide trombone? Anyway, it was during this time, while his sainthood was only, so to speak, awaiting a Sign, a Portent, a Confirmation, that that wall obligingly fell down and revealed the (perhaps indignant?) Yacoub. Yes, but there was no tomb in the shrine. Even the Coptic Church which has at last reluctantly taken Yacoub on their books knows nothing of him except that he came from Syria. They are not even sure whether he was a Moslem or not! He sounds distinctly Jewish to me. However they diligently questioned the oldest inhabitants of the quarter and at least established his name. But nothing more. And so one fine day the neighbourhood found that it had an empty shrine free for Scobie. He must have a local habitation to match the power of his name. A spontaneous festival broke out at which his bath-tub which had been responsible for so many deaths (great is Allah!) was solemnly enshrined and consecrated after being carefully filled with holy sand from the Jordan. Officially the Copts could not concede Scob and insisted on sticking to Yacoub for official purposes; but Scob he remained to the faithful. It might have been something of a dilemma, but being magnificent diplomatists, the clergy turned a blind eye to El Scob's reincarnation; they behave *as if* they thought it was really El Yacoub in a local pronunciation. So everyone's face is saved. They have, in fact, even—and here is that marvellous tolerance which exists nowhere else on earth—formally registered Scobie's birthday,

83

suppose because they do not know Yacoub's. Do you know that he is even to have a yearly *mulid* in his honour on St. George's Day? Abdul must have remembered his birthday because Scobie always hung up from each corner of his bed a string of coloured flags-of-all-nations which he borrowed from the newsagent. And he used to get rather drunk, you told me once, and sing sea-chanties and recite 'The Old Red Duster' until the tears flowed!"

"What a marvellous immortality to enjoy."

"How happy the old pirate must be."

"How happy! To be the patron saint of his own *quartier*! O Darley I knew you'd enjoy it. I often come here at this time in the dusk and sit on a stone and laugh inwardly, rejoicing for the old man."

So we sat together for a long time as the shadows grew up around the shrine, quietly laughing and talking as people should at the shrine of a saint! Reviving the memory of the old pirate with the glass eye whose shade still walked about those mouldering rooms on the second floor. Vaguely glimmered the lights of Tatwig Street. They shone, not with their old accustomed brilliance, but darkly—for the whole harbour quarter had been placed under blackout and one sector of it included the famous street. My thoughts were wandering.

"And Abdul" I said suddenly. "What of him?"

"Yes, I promised to tell you; Scobie set him up in a barber's shop, you remember. Well, he was warned for not keeping his razors clean, and for spreading syphilis. He didn't heed the warnings perhaps because he believed that Scobie would never report him officially. But the old man did, with terrible results. Abdul was nearly beaten to death by the police, lost an eye. Amaril spent nearly a year trying to tidy him up. Then he got some wasting disease on top of it and had to abandon his shop. Poor man. But I'm not sure that he isn't the appropriate guardian for the shrine of his master."

"El Scob! Poor Abdul!"

84

"But now he has taken consolation in religion and does some mild preaching and reciting of the Suras as well as this job. Do you know I believe that he has forgotten the real Scobie. I asked him one evening if he remembered the old gentleman on the upper floor and he looked at me vaguely and muttered something; as if he were reaching far back in his memory for something too remote to grasp. The real Scobie had disappeared just like Yacoub, and El Scob had taken his place."

"I feel rather as one of the Apostles must have—I mean to be in on the birth of a saint, a legend; think, we actually knew the real El Scob! We heard his voice. . . ."

To my delight Clea now began to mimic the old man quite admirably, copying the desultory scattered manner of his conversation to the life; perhaps she was only repeating the words from memory?

"Yes, mind you, on St. George's Day I always get a bit carried away for England's sake as well as my own. Always have a sip or two of the blushful, as Toby would say, even bubbly if it comes my way. But, bless you, I'm no horse-drawn conveyance—always stay on my two pins. It's the cup that cheers and not in . . . in . . . inebriates for me. Another of Toby's expressions. He was full of literary illustrations. As well he might be—for why? *Ber*corse he was never without a book under his arm. In the Navy he was considered quite queer, and several times had rows. 'What yer got there?' they used to shout, and Toby who could be pert at times used to huff up and answer quite spontaneous. 'What d'yer think, Puffy? Why me marriages lines of course.' But it was always some heavy book which made *my* head swim though I love reading. One year it was Stringbag's Plays, a Swedish author as I understand it. Another year it was Goitre's 'Frowst'. Toby said it was a liberal education. My education just wasn't up to his. The school of life, as you might say. But then my mum and dad were killed off early on and we were left, three perishing little orphans. They had destined us for high things, my father had;

85

one for the church, one for the army, one for the navy. Quite shortly after this my two brothers were run over by the Prince Regent's private train near Sidcup. That was the end of *them*. But it was in all the papers and the Prince sent a wreath. But there I was left quite alone. I had to make my own way without influence—otherwise I should have been an Admiral I expect by now. . . ."

The fidelity of her rendering was absolutely impeccable. The little old man stepped straight out of his tomb and began to stalk about in front of us with his lopsided walk, now toying with his telescope on the cake-stand, now opening and shutting his battered Bible, or getting down on one creaking knee to blow up his fire with the tiny pair of bellows. His birthday! I recalled finding him one birthday evening rather the worse for brandy, but dancing around completely naked to music of his own manufacture on a comb and paper.

Recalling this celebration of his Name Day I began, as it were, to mimic him back to Clea, in order to hear once more this thrilling new laugh she had acquired. "O! it's you, Darley! You gave me quite a turn with your knock. Come in, I'm just having a bit of a dance round in my *tou tou* to recall old times. It's my birthday, yes. I always dwell a bit on the past. In my youth I was a proper spark, I don't mind admitting. I was a real dab at the Velouta. Want to watch me? Don't laugh, just *ber*corse I'm *in puris*. Sit on the chair over there and watch. Now, advance, take your partners, shimmy, bow, reverse! It looks easy but it isn't. The smoothness is deceptive. I could do them all once, my boy, Lancers, Caledonians, Circassian Circle. Never seen a *demi-chaine Anglais*, I suppose? Before your time I think. Mind you, I loved dancing, and for years I kept up to date. I got up as far as the Hootchi-Kootchi—have you ever seen that? Yes, the haitch is haspirated as in 'otel. It's got some fetching little movements they call oriental allurements. Undulations, like. You take off one veil after another until all is revealed. The suspense is terrific, but you have to waggle as you
86

glide, see?" Here he took up a posture of quite preposterous oriental allurement and began to revolve slowly, wagging his behind and humming a suitable air which quite faithfully copied the lag and fall of Arab quartertones. Round and round the room he went until he began to feel dizzy and flopped back triumphantly on his bed, chuckling and nodding with self-approval and self-congratulation, and reaching out for a swig of *arak*, the manufacture of which was also among his secrets. He must have found the recipe in the pages of Postlethwaite's Vade Mecum For Travellers in Foreign Lands, a book which he kept under lock and key in his trunk and by which he absolutely swore. It contained, he said, everything that a man in Robinson Crusoe's position ought to know—even how to make fire by rubbing sticks together; it was a mine of marvellous information. ("To achieve Bombay arrack dissolve two scruples of flowers of benjamin in a quart of good rum and it will impart to the spirit the fragrance of arrack.") That was the sort of thing. "Yes" he would add gravely, "old Postlethwaite can't be bettered. There's something in him for every sort of mind and every sort of situation. He's a genius I might say."

Only once had Postlethwaite failed to live up to his reputation, and that was when Toby said that there was a fortune to be made in Spanish Fly if only Scobie could secure a large quantity of it for export. "But the perisher didn't explain what it was or how, and it was the only time Postlethwaite had me beat. D'you know what he says about it, under Cantharides? I found it so mysterious I memorised the passage to repeat to Toby when next he came through. Old Postle says this: 'Cantharides when used internally are diuretic and stimulant; when applied externally they are epispastic and rubefacient.' Now what the devil can he mean, eh? And how does this fit in with Toby's idea of a flourishing trade in the things? Sort of worms, they must be. I asked Abdul but I don't know the Arabic word."

Refreshed by the interlude he once more advanced to the mirror to admire his wrinkled old tortoise-frame. A sudden thought cast a gloom over his countenance. He pointed at a portion of his own wrinkled anatomy and said: "And to think that *that* is what old Postlethwaite describes as '*merely* erectile tissue'. Why the *merely*, I always ask myself. Sometimes these medical men are a puzzle in their language. Just a sprig of erectile tissue indeed! And think of all the trouble it causes. Ah me; if you'd seen what I've seen you wouldn't have half the nervous energy I've got today."

And so the saint prolonged his birthday celebrations by putting on pyjamas and indulging in a short song-cycle which included many old favourites and one curious little ditty which he only sang on birthdays. It was called "The Cruel Cruel Skipper" and had a chorus which ended:

> *So he was an old sky plant, tum tum,*
> *So he was an old meat loaf, tum tum,*
> *So he was an old cantankeroo.*

And now, having virtually exhausted his legs by dancing and his singing-voice with song, there remained a few brief conundrums which he enunciated to the ceiling, his arms behind his head.

"Where did King Charles' executioner dine, and what did he order?"

"I don't know."

"Give in?"

"Yes."

"Well he took a chop at the King's Head."

Delighted clucks and chuckles!

"When may a gentleman's property be described as feathers?"

"I don't know."

"Give in?"

"Yes."

"When his estates are all entails (hen-tails, see?)"

The voice gradually fading, the clock running down, the eyes closing, the chuckles trailing away languorously into sleep. And it was thus that the saint slept at last, with his mouth open, upon St. George's Day.

So we walked back, arm in arm, through the shadowy archway, laughing the compassionate laughter which the old man's image deserved—laughter which in a way regilded the ikon, refuelled the lamps about the shrine. Our footfalls hardly echoed on the streets' floor of tamped soil. The partial blackout of the area had cut off the electric light which so brilliantly illuminated it under normal conditions, and had been replaced by the oil lamps which flickered wanly everywhere, so that we walked in a dark forest by glow-worm light which made more than ever mysterious the voices and the activities in the buildings around us. And at the end of the street, where the rickety gharry stood awaiting us, came the stirring cool breath of the night-sea which would gradually infiltrate the town and disperse the heavy breathless damps from the lake. We climbed aboard, the evening settling itself about us cool as the veined leaves of a fig.

"And now I must dine you, Clea, to celebrate the new laughter!"

"No. I haven't finished yet. There is another tableau I want you to see, of a different kind. You see, Darley, I wanted to sort of recompose the city for you so that you could walk back into the painting from another angle and feel quite at home—though that is hardly the word for a city of exiles, is it? Anyhow . . ." And leaning forward (I felt her breath on my cheek) she said to the jarvey, "Take us to the Auberge Bleue!"

"More mysteries."

"No. Tonight the Virtuous Semira makes her first appearance on the public stage. It is rather like a *vernissage* for me— you know, don't you, that Amaril and I are the authors of her lovely nose? It has been a tremendous adventure, these long months; and she has been very patient and brave under the

89

bandages and grafts. Now it's complete. Yesterday they were married. Tonight all Alexandria will be there to see her. We shouldn't absent ourselves, should we? It characterises something which is all too rare in the city and which you, as an earnest student of the matter, will appreciate. *Il s'agit de* Romantic Love with capital letters. My share in it has been a large one so let me be a bit boastful; I have been part duenna, part nurse, part artist, all for the good Amaril's sake. You see, she isn't very clever, Semira, and I have had to spend hours with her sort of preparing her for the world. Also brushing up her reading and writing. In short, trying to educate her a bit. It is curious in a way that Amaril does not regard this huge gap in their different educations as an obstacle. He loves her the more for it. He says: 'I know she is rather simple-minded. That is what makes her so exquisite.'

"This is the purest flower of romantic logic, no? And he has gone about her rehabilitation with immense inventiveness. I should have thought it somewhat dangerous to play at Pygmalion, but only now I begin to understand the power of the image. Do you know, for example, what he has devised for her in the way of a profession, a skill of her own? It shows brilliance. She would be too simple-minded to undertake anything very specialised so he has trained her, with my help, to be a doll's surgeon. His wedding-present to her is a smart little surgery for children's dolls which has already become tremendously fashionable though it won't officially open until they come back from the honeymoon. But this new job Semira has really grasped with both hands. For months we have been cutting up and repairing dolls together in preparation for this! No medical student could have studied harder. 'It is the only way' says Amaril 'to hold a really stupid woman you adore. Give her something of her own to do.' "

So we swayed down the long curving Corniche and back into the lighted area of the city where the blue street-lamps came up one by one to peer into the gharry at us as we talked; and

90

all at once it seemed that past and present had joined again without any divisions in it, and that all my memories and impressions had ordered themselves into one complete pattern whose metaphor was always the shining city of the disinherited —a city now trying softly to spread the sticky prismatic wings of a new-born dragon-fly on the night. Romantic Love! Pursewarden used to call it "The Comic Demon".

The Auberge had not changed at all. It remained a lasting part of the furniture of my dreams, and here (like faces in a dream) were the Alexandrians themselves seated at flower-decked tables while a band softly punctuated their idleness with the Blues. The cries of welcome recalled vanished generosities of the old city. Athena Trasha with the silver crickets in her ears, droning Pierre Balbz who drank opium because it made the "bones blossom", the stately Cervonis and the rash dexterous Martinengo girls, they were all there. All save Nessim and Justine. Even the good Pombal was there in full evening-dress so firmly ironed and starched as to give him the air of a monumental relief executed for the tomb of François Premier. With him was Fosca, warm and dark of colouring, whom I had not met before. They sat with their knuckles touching in a curious stiff rapture. Pombal was perched quite upright, attentive as a rabbit, as he gazed into her eyes—the eyes of this handsome young matron. He looked absurd. ("She calls him 'Georges-Gaston' which for some reason quite delights him" said Clea.)

So we made our slow way from table to table, greeting old friends as we had often done in the past until we came to the little alcove table with its scarlet celluloid reservation card marked in Clea's name, where to my surprise Zoltan the waiter materialised out of nothing to shake my hand with warmth. He was now the resplendent *maître d'hôtel* and was in full fig, his hair cut *en brosse*. It seemed also that he was fully in the secret for he remarked under his breath to Clea that everything had been prepared in complete secrecy, and even went so far as to wink. "I have Anselm outside watching. As soon as he sees Dr. Amaril's car he will signal. Then the music will play —Madame Trasha has asked for the old 'Blue Danube'." He clasped his hands together in ecstasy and swallowed like a toad. "O what a good idea of Athena's. Bravo!" cried Clea. It was indeed a gesture of affection for Amaril was the best Viennese waltzer in Alexandria, and though not a vain man was always absurdly delighted by his own prowess as a dancer. It could not fail to please him.

Neither had we long to wait; anticipation and suspense had hardly had time to become wearying when the band, which had been softly playing with one ear cocked for the sound of a car, so to speak, fell silent. Anselm appeared at the corner of the vestibule waving his napkin. They were coming! The musicians struck out one long quivering arpeggio such as normally brings a tzigane melody to a close, and then, as the beautiful figure of Semira appeared among the palms, they swung softly and gravely into the waltz measure of 'The Blue Danube'. I was suddenly quite touched to see the shy way that Semira hesitated on the threshold of that crowded ballroom; despite the magnificence of her dress and grooming those watching eyes intimidated her, made her lose her self-possession. She hovered with a soft indecision which reminded me of the way a sailing boat hangs pouting when the painter is loosed, the jib shaken out—as if slowly meditating for a long moment before she turns, with an almost audible sigh, to take the wind upon her cheek. But in this moment of charming irresolution Amaril came up behind her and took her arm. He himself looked, I thought, rather white and nervous despite the customary foppishness of his attire. Caught like this, in a moment of almost panic, he looked indeed absurdly young. Then he registered the waltz and stammered something to her with trembling lips, at the same time leading her down gravely among the tables to the edge of the floor where with a slow and perfectly turned movement they began to dance.

92

With the first full figure of the waltz the confidence poured into them both—one could almost see it happening. They calmed, became still as leaves, and Semira closed her eyes while Amaril recovered his usual gay, self-confident smile. And everywhere the soft clapping welled up around them from every corner of the ballroom. Even the waiters seemed moved and the good Zoltan groped for a handkerchief, for Ameril was much-beloved.

Clea too looked quite shaken with emotion. "O quick, let's have a drink" she said "for I've a huge lump in my throat and if I cry my make-up will run."

The batteries of champagne-bottles opened up from every corner of the ballroom now, and the floor filled with waltzers, the lights changed colour. Now blue now red now green I saw the smiling face of Clea over the edge of her champagne glass turned towards me with an expression of happy mockery. "Do you mind if I get a little tipsy tonight to celebrate her successful nose? I think we can drink to their future without reserve for they will never leave each other; they are drunk with the knightly love one reads about in the Arthurian legends— knight and rescued lady. And pretty soon there will be children all bearing my lovely nose."

"Of that you can't be sure."

"Well, let me believe it."

"Let's dance a while."

And so we joined the thronging dancers in the great circle which blazed with spinning prismatic light hearing the soft drum-beats punctuate our blood, moving to the slow grave rhythms like the great wreaths of coloured seaweed swinging in some under-water lagoon, one with the dancers and with each other.

We did not stay late. As we came out into the cold damp air she shivered and half-fell against me, catching my arm.

"What is it?"

"I felt faint all of a sudden. It's passed."

So back into the city along the windless seafront, drugged by the clop of the horse's hooves on the macadam, the jingle of harness, the smell of straw, and the dying strains of music which flowed out of the ballroom and dwindled away among the stars. We paid off the cab at the Cecil and walked up the winding deserted street towards her flat arm-in-arm, hearing our own slow steps magnified by the silence. In a bookshop window there were a few novels, one by Pursewarden. We stopped for a moment to peer into the darkened shop and then resumed our leisurely way to the flat. "You'll come in for a moment?" she said.

Here, too, the air of celebration was apparent, in the flowers and the small supper-table on which stood a champagne-bucket. "I did not know we'd stay to dine at the Auberge, and prepared to feed you here if necessary" said Clea, dipping her fingers in the ice-water; she sighed with relief. "At least we can have a night-cap together."

Here at least there was nothing to disorient or disfigure memory, for everything was exactly as I remembered it; I had stepped back into this beloved room as one might step into some favourite painting. Here it all was, the crowded book-shelves, heavy drawing-boards, small cottage piano, and the corner with the tennis racquet and fencing foils; on the writing desk, with its disorderly jumble of letters, drawings and bills, stood the candlesticks which she was now in the act of lighting. A bundle of paintings stood against the wall. I turned one or two round and stared at them curiously.

"My God! You've gone abstract, Clea."

"I know! Balthazar hates them. It's just a phase I expect, so don't regard it as irrevocable or final. It's a different way of mobilising one's feelings about paint. Do you loathe them?"

"No, they are stronger I think."

"Hum. Candle-light flatters them with false chiaroscuro."

"Perhaps."

"Come, sit down; I've poured us a drink."

As if by common consent we sat facing each other on the carpet as we had so often done in the past, cross-legged like "Armenian tailors", as she had once remarked. We toasted each other in the rosy light of the scarlet candles which stood unwinking in the still air defining with their ghostly radiance the smiling mouth and candid features of Clea. Here, too, at last, on this memorable spot on the faded carpet, we embraced each other with—how to say it?—a momentous smiling calm, as if the cup of language had silently overflowed into these eloquent kisses which replaced words like the rewards of silence itself, perfecting thought and gesture. They were like soft cloud-formations which had distilled themselves out of a novel innocence, the veritable ache of desirelessness. My steps had led me back again, I realised, remembering the night so long ago when we had slept dreamlessly in each other's arms, to the locked door which had once refused me admission to her. Led me back once more to that point in time, that threshold, behind which the shade of Clea moved, smiling and irresponsible as a flower, after a huge arid detour in a desert of my own imaginings. I had not known then how to find the key to that door. Now of its own accord it was slowly opening. Whereas the other door which had once given me access to Justine had now locked irrevocably. Did not Pursewarden say something once about "sliding-panels"? But he was talking of books, not of the human heart. In her face now there was neither guile nor premeditation mirrored, but only a sort of magnificent mischief which had captured the fine eyes, expressed itself in the firm and thoughtful way she drew my hands up inside her sleeves to offer herself to their embrace with the uxorious gesture of a woman offering her body to some priceless cloak. Or else to catch my hand, place it upon her heart and whisper "Feel! It has stopped beating!" So we lingered, so we might have stayed, like rapt figures in some forgotten painting, unhurriedly savouring the happiness given to those who set out to enjoy each other without reservations or self-contempts, without the premeditated costumes of selfishness—the invented limitations of human love: but that suddenly the dark air of the night outside grew darker, swelled up with the ghastly tumescence of a sound which, like the frantic wing-beats of some prehistoric bird, swallowed the whole room, the candles, the figures. She shivered at the first terrible howl of the sirens but did not move; and all around us the city stirred to life like an ants' nest. Those streets which had been so dark and silent now began to echo with the sound of feet as people made their way to the air-raid shelters, rustling like a gust of dry autumn leaves whirled by the wind. Snatches of sleepy conversation, screams, laughter, rose to the silent window of the little room. The street had filled as suddenly as a dry river-bed when the spring rains fall.

"Clea, you should shelter."

But she only pressed closer, shaking her head like someone drugged with sleep, or perhaps by the soft explosion of kisses which burst like bubbles of oxygen in the patient blood. I shook her softly, and she whispered: "I am too fastidious to die with a lot of people in a shelter like an old rats' nest. Let us go to bed together and ignore the loutish reality of the world."

So it was that love-making itself became a kind of challenge to the whirlwind outside which beat and pounded like a thunder-storm of guns and sirens, igniting the pale skies of the city with the magnificence of its lightning-flashes. And kisses themselves became charged with the deliberate affirmation which can come only from the foreknowledge and presence of death. It would have been good to die at any moment then, for love and death had somewhere joined hands. It was an expression of her pride, too, to sleep there in the crook of my arm like a wild bird exhausted by its struggles with a limed twig, for all the world as if it were an ordinary summer night of peace. And lying awake at her side, listening to the infernal racket of gun-fire and watching the stabbing and jumping of light behind the blinds I remembered how once in the remote past she had reminded me of the limitations which love illuminated in us: saying something about its capacity being limited to an iron ration for each soul and adding gravely: "The love you feel for Melissa, the same love, is trying to work itself out through Justine." Would I, by extension, find this to be true also of Clea? I did not like to think so—for these fresh and spontaneous embraces were as pristine as invention, and not like ill-drawn copies of past actions. They were the very improvisations of the heart itself—or so I told myself as I lay there trying so hard to recapture the elements of the feelings I had once woven around those other faces. Yes, improvisations upon reality itself, and for once devoid of the bitter impulses of the will. We had sailed into this calm water completely without premeditation, all canvas crowded on; and for the first time it felt natural to be where I was, drifting into sleep with her calm body lying beside me. Even the long rolling cannonades which shook the houses so, even the hail of shards which swept the streets, could not disturb the dreaming silence we harvested together. And when we awoke to find everything silent once more she lit a single candle and we lay by its flickering light, looking at each other, and talking in whispers.

"I am always so bad the first time, why is it?"

"So am I."

"Are you afraid of me?"

"No. Nor of myself."

"Did you ever imagine this?"

"We must both have done. Otherwise it would not have happened."

"Hush! Listen."

Rain was now falling in sheets as it so often did before dawn in Alexandria, chilling the air, washing down the stiffly clicking leaves of the palms in the Municipal Gardens, washing the iron grilles of the banks and the pavements. In the Arab town the earthen streets would be smelling like a freshly dug graveyard.

The flower-sellers would be putting out their stocks to catch the freshness. I remembered their cry of "Carnations, sweet as the breath of a girl!" From the harbour the smells of tar, fish and briny nets flowing up along the deserted streets to meet the scentless pools of desert air which would later, with the first sunlight, enter the town from the east and dry its damp façades. Somewhere, briefly, the hushing of the rain was pricked by the sleepy pang of a mandoline, inscribing on it a thoughtful and melancholy little air. I feared the intrusion of a single thought or idea which, inserting itself between these moments of smiling peace, might inhibit them, turn them to instruments of sadness. I thought too of the long journey we made from this very bed, since last we lay here together, through so many climates and countries, only to return once more to our starting-point again, captured once more by the gravitational field of the city. A new cycle which was opening upon the promise of such kisses and dazed endearments as we could now exchange—where would it carry us? I thought of some words of Arnauti, written about another woman, in another context: "You tell yourself that it is a woman you hold in your arms, but watching the sleeper you see all her growth in time, the unerring unfolding of cells which group and dispose themselves into the beloved face which remains always and for ever mysterious—repeating to infinity the soft boss of the human nose, an ear borrowed from a sea-shell's helix, an eyebrow thought-patterned from ferns, or lips invented by bivalves in their dreaming union. All this process is human, bears a name which pierces your heart, and offers the mad dream of an eternity which time disproves in every drawn breath. And if human personality is an illusion? And if, as biology tells us, every single cell in our bodies is replaced every seven years by another? At the most I hold in my arms something like a fountain of flesh, continuously playing, and in my mind a rainbow of dust." And like an echo from another point of the compass I heard the sharp voice of Pursewarden saying: "There is no

Other; there is only oneself facing forever the problem of one's self discovery!"

I had drifted into sleep again; and when I woke with a start the bed was empty and the candle had guttered away and gone out. She was standing at the drawn curtains to watch the dawn break over the tumbled roofs of the Arab town, naked and slender as an Easter lily. In that spring sunrise, with its dense dew, sketched upon the silence which engulfs a whole city before the birds awaken it, I caught the sweet voice of the blind *muezzin* from the mosque reciting the *Ebed*—a voice hanging like a hair in the palm-cooled upper airs of Alexandria. "I praise the perfection of God, the Forever existing; the perfection of God, the desired, the Existing, the Single, the Supreme; the Perfection of God, the One, the Sole". . . . The great prayer wound itself in shining coils across the city as I watched the grave and passionate intensity of her turned head where she stood to observe the climbing sun touch the minarets and palms with light: rapt and awake. And listening I smelt the warm odour of her hair upon the pillow beside me. The buoyancy of a new freedom possessed me like a draught from what the Cabal once called "The Fountain of All Existing Things". I called "Clea" softly, but she did not heed me; and so once more I slept. I knew that Clea would share everything with me, withholding nothing—not even the look of complicity which women reserve only for their mirrors.

o   o   o   o   o

BOOK II

I

So the city claimed me once more—the same city made now somehow less poignant and less terrifying than it had been in the past by new displacements in time. If some parts of the old fabric had worn away, others had been restored. In the first few weeks of my new employment I had time to experience both a sense of familiarity and one of alienation, measuring stability against change, past against present tense. And if the society of my friends remained relatively the same, new influences had entered, new winds had sprung up; we had all begun, like those figures on revolving turntables in jewellers' shops, to turn new facets of ourselves towards each other. Circumstances also helped to provide a new counterpoint, for the old, apparently unchanged city had now entered the penumbra of a war. For my part I had come to see it as it must always have been—a shabby little seaport built upon a sand-reef, a moribund and spiritless backwater. True this unknown factor "war" had given it a specious sort of modern value, but this belonged to the invisible world of strategies and armies, not to ourselves, the inhabitants; it had swollen its population by many thousands of refugees in uniform and attracted those long nights of dull torment which were only relatively dangerous, for as yet the enemy was confining his operations strictly to the harbour area. Only a small area of the Arab quarter came under direct fire; the upper town remained relatively untouched, except perhaps for an occasional error of judgement. No, it was only the harbour at which the enemy scratched and scratched, like a dog at an inflamed scab. A mile away from it the bankers conducted their affairs by day as if from the immunity of New York. Intrusions into their world were rare and accidental. It came as a painful surprise to confront a shop-front which had been blasted in, or a lodging-house blown inside out with all its inhabitants' clothes hanging in festoons from the neighbouring trees. This was not part of the normal expectation of things; it had the shocking rarity value merely of some terrible street accident.

How had things changed? It was not danger, then, but a less easily analysable quality which made the notion of war distinctive; a sensation of some change in the specific gravity of things. It was as if the oxygen content of the air we breathed were being steadily, invisibly reduced day by day; and side by side with this sense of inexplicable blood-poisoning came other pressures of a purely material kind brought about by the huge shifting population of soldiers in whom the blossoming of death released the passions and profligacies which lie buried in every herd. Their furious gaiety tried hard to match the gravity of the crisis in which they were involved; at times the town was racked by the frenetic outbursts of their disguised spleen and boredom until the air became charged with the mad spirit of carnival; a saddening and heroic pleasure-seeking which disturbed and fractured the old harmonies on which personal relationships had rested, straining the links which bound us. I am thinking of Clea, and her loathing for the war and all it stood for. She feared, I think, that the vulgar blood-soaked reality of this war world which spread around her might one day poison and infect our own kisses. "Is it fastidious to want to keep your head, to avoid this curious sexual rush of blood to the head which comes with war, exciting the women beyond endurance? I would not have thought the smell of death could be so exciting to them! Darley, I don't want to be a part of this mental saturnalia, these overflowing brothels. And all these poor men crowded up here. Alexandria has become a huge orphanage, everyone grabbing at the last chance of life. You haven't been long enough yet to feel the strain. The disorientation. The city was always perverse, but it took its pleasures with style at an old-fashioned tempo, even in rented beds: never up against a wall or a tree or a truck! And now at times the town seems to be like some great public urinal. You step over the bodies of drunkards as you walk home at night. I suppose the sunless have been robbed even of sensuality and drink compensates them for the loss! But there is no place in all this for me. I cannot see these soldiers as Pombal does. He gloats on them like a child—as if they were bright lead soldiers—because he sees in them the only hope that France will be freed. I only feel ashamed for them, as one might to see friends in convict garb; out of shame and sympathy I feel like turning my face away. O Darley, it isn't very sensible, and I know I am doing them a grotesque injustice. Possibly it is just selfishness. So I force myself to serve them teas at their various canteens, roll bandages, arrange concerts. But inside myself I shrink smaller every day. Yet I always believed that a love of human beings would flower more strongly out of a common misfortune. It isn't true. And now I am afraid that you too will begin to like me the less for these absurdities of thought, these revulsions of feeling. To be here, just the two of us, sitting by candle-light is almost a miracle in such a world. You can't blame me for trying to hoard and protect it against the intrusive world outside can you? Curiously, what I hate most about it all is the sentimentality which spells violence in the end!''

I understood what she meant, and what she feared; and yet from the depths of my own inner selfishness I was glad of these external pressures, for they circumscribed our world perfectly, penned us up more closely together, isolated us! In the old world I would have had to share Clea with a host of other friends and admirers. Not now.

Curiously, too, some of these external factors around us, involving us in its death-struggles—gave our newest passion a fulfilment not based on desperation yet nevertheless built just as certainly upon the sense of impermanence. It was of the same order, though different in kind to the dull orgiastic rut of the various armies; it was quite impossible to repudiate the truth, namely, that death (not even at hand, but in the air) sharpens kisses, adds unbearable poignance to every smile and handclasp. Even though I was no soldier the dark question mark hovered over our thoughts, for the real issues of the heart were influenced by something of which we were all, however reluctantly, part: a whole world. If the war did not mean a way of dying, it meant a way of ageing, of tasting the true staleness in human things, and of learning to confront change bravely. No-one could tell what lay beyond the closed chapter of every kiss. In those long quiet evenings before the bombardment began we would sit upon that small square of carpet by the light of candles, debating these matters, punctuating our silences with embraces which were the only inadequate answer we could offer to the human situation. Nor, lying in each other's arms during those long nights of fitful sleep broken by the sirens, did we ever (as if by a silent convention) speak of love. To have uttered the word might acknowledge a more rare yet less perfect variety of the state which now bewitched us, perfected this quite un-premeditated relationship. Somewhere in *Moeurs* there is a passionate denunciation of the word. I cannot remember into whose mouth the speech has been put—perhaps Justine's. "It may be defined as a cancerous growth of unknown origin which may take up its site anywhere without the subject knowing or wishing it. How often have you tried to love the 'right' person in vain, even when your heart knows it has found him after so much seeking? No, an eyelash, a perfume, a haunting walk, a strawberry on the neck, the smell of almonds on the breath—these are the accomplices the spirit seeks out to plan your overthrow."

Thinking of such passages of savage insight—and they are many in that strange book—I would turn to the sleeping Clea and study her quiet profile in order to . . . to ingest her, drink the whole of her up without spilling a drop, mingle my very heart-beats with hers. "However near we would wish to be, so far exactly do we remain from each other" wrote Arnauti. It seemed to be no longer true of our condition. Or was I simply deluding myself once more, refracting truth by the disorders inherent in my own vision? Strangely enough I neither knew nor cared now; I had stopped rummaging through my own mind, had learned to take her like a clear draught of spring water.

"Have you been watching me asleep?"

"Yes."

"Unfair! But what thinking?"

"Many things."

"Unfair to watch a sleeping woman, off her guard."

"Your eyes have changed colour again. Smoke."

(A mouth whose paint blurred slightly under kisses. The two small commas, which were almost cusps, almost ready to turn into dimples when the lazy smiles broke surface. She stretches and places her arms behind her head, pushing back the helmet of fair hair which captures the sheen of the candle-light. In the past she had not possessed this authority over her own beauty. New gestures, new tendrils had grown, languorous yet adept to express this new maturity. A limpid sensuality which was now undivided by hesitations, self-questionings. A transformation of the old "silly goose" into this fine, indeed impressive, personage, quite at one with her own body and mind. How had this come about?)

I: "That commonplace book of Pursewarden's. How the devil did you come by it? I took it to the office today."

She: "Liza. I asked her for something to remember him by. Absurd. As if one could forget the brute! He's everywhere. Did the notes startle you?"

I: "Yes. It was as if he had appeared at my elbow. The first thing I fell upon was a description of my new chief, Maskelyne by name. It seems Pursewarden worked with him once. Shall I read it to you?"

She: "I know it."

("Like most of my compatriots he had a large hand-illuminated sign hanging up on the front of his mind reading ON NO ACCOUNT DISTURB. At some time in the distant past he had been wound up and set like a quartz clock. He will run his course unfaltering as a metronome. Do not let the pipe alarm you. It is intended to give a judicial air. White man smoke puff puff, white man ponder puff puff. In fact white man is deeply deeply asleep under the badges of office, the pipe, the nose, the freshly starched handkerchief sticking out of his sleeve.")

She: "Did you read it to Maskelyne?"

I: "Naturally not."

She: "There are wounding things about all of us in it; perhaps that is why I took a fancy to it! I could hear the brute's voice as he uttered them. You know, my dear, I think I am the only person to have loved old Pursewarden for himself while he was alive. I got his wavelength. I loved him for himself, I say, because strictly he *had* no self. Of course he could be tiresome, difficult, cruel—like everyone else. But he exemplified something—a grasp on something. That is why his work will live and go on giving off light, so to speak. Light me a cigarette. He had cut a foothold in the cliff a bit higher than I could dare to go—the point where one looks at the top because one is afraid to look down! You tell me that Justine also says something like this. I suppose she got the same thing in a way—but I suspect her of being merely grateful to him, like an animal whose master pulls a thorn from its paw. His intuition was very feminine and much sharper than hers—and you know that women instinctively like a man with plenty of female in him; *there*, they suspect, is the only sort of lover who can sufficiently identify himself with them to . . . deliver them of being just women, catalysts, strops, oil-stones. Most of us have to be content to play the role of *machine à plaisir!*"

I: "Why do you laugh, suddenly like that?"

"I was remembering making a fool of myself with Pursewarden. I suppose I should feel ashamed of it! You will see what he says about me in the notebook. He calls me 'a juicy Hanoverian goose, the only truly kallipygous girl in the city'! I cannot think what possessed me, except that I was so worried about my painting. It had dried up on me. I couldn't get any further somehow, canvas gave me a headache. I finally decided that the question of my own blasted virginity was the root cause of the business. You know it is a terrible business to be a virgin—it is like not having one's Matric or Bac. You long to be delivered from it yet . . . at the same time this valuable experience should be with someone whom you care for, otherwise it will be without value to your inside self. Well, there I was, stuck. So with one of those characteristic strokes of fancy which in the past confirmed for everyone my stupidity I decided —guess what? To offer myself grimly to the only artist I knew I could trust, to put me out of my misery. Pursewarden, I thought, might have an understanding of my state and some consideration for my feelings. I'm amused to remember that I dressed myself up in a very heavy tweed costume and flat shoes, and wore dark glasses. I was timid, you see, as well as desperate. I walked up and down the corridor of the hotel outside his room for ages in despair and apprehension, my dark glasses firmly on my nose. He was inside. I could hear him whistling as he always did when he was painting a water colour; a maddening tuneless whistle! At last I burst in on him like a fireman into a burning building, startling him, and said with trembling lips: 'I have come to ask you to *dépuceler* me, please, because I cannot get any further with my work unless you do.' I said it in French. It would have sounded dirty in English. He was startled. All sorts of conflicting emotions flitted across his face for a second. And then, as I burst into tears and sat down suddenly on a chair he threw his head back and roared with laughter. He laughed until the tears ran down his cheeks while I sat there in my dark glasses sniffing. Finally he collapsed exhausted on his bed and lay staring at the ceiling. Then he got up, put his arms on my shoulders, removed my glasses, kissed me, and put them back.

Then he put his hands on his hips and laughed again. 'My dear Clea' he said, 'it would be anyone's dream to take you to bed, and I must confess that in a corner of my mind I have often allowed the thought to wander but . . . dearest angel, you have spoilt everything. *This* is no way to enjoy you, and no way for you to enjoy yourself. Forgive my laughing! You have effectively spoiled my dream. Offering yourself *this* way, without *wanting* me, is such an insult to my male vanity that I simply would not be able to comply with your demand. It is, I suppose, a compliment that you chose me rather than someone else—but my vanity is larger than that! In fact your request is like a pailful of slops emptied over my head! I shall always treasure the compliment and regret the refusal but . . . if only you had chosen some other way to do it, how glad I would have been to oblige! Why did you have to let me see that you really did not care for *me?*'

"He blew his nose gravely in a corner of the sheet, took my glasses and placed them on his own nose to examine himself in the mirror. Then he came and stared at me until the comedy overflowed again and we both started laughing. I felt an awful sense of relief. And when I had repaired my damaged make-up in the mirror he allowed me to take him to dinner to discuss the problem of paint with magnificent, generous honesty. The poor man listened with such patience to my rigmarole! He said: 'I can only tell you what I know, and it isn't much. First you have to know and understand intellectually what you want to do—then you have to sleep-walk a little to reach it. The real obstacle is oneself. I believe that artists are composed of vanity, indolence and self-regard. Work-blocks are caused by the swelling-up of the ego on one or all of these fronts. You get a bit scared about the imaginary importance of what you are doing! Mirror-worship. My solution would be to slap a poultice on the inflamed parts—tell your ego to go to hell and not make a misery of what should be essentially *fun, joy.*' He said many other things that evening, but I have forgotten the rest; but the funny thing was that just talking to him, just being talked to, seemed to clear the way ahead again. I started work again, clear as a bell, the next morning. Perhaps in a funny sort of way he did *dépuceler* me? I regretted not being able to reward him as he deserved, but I realised that he was right. I would have to wait for a tide to turn. And this did not happen until later, in Syria. There was something bitter and definitive about it when it came, and I made the usual mistakes one makes from inexperience and paid for them. Shall I tell you?"

I: "Only if you wish."

She: "I found myself suddenly and hopelessly entangled with someone I had admired some years before but never quite imagined in the context of a lover. Chance brought us together for a few short months. I think that neither of us had foreseen this sudden *coup de foudre*. We both caught fire, as if somewhere an invisible burning glass had been playing on us without our being aware. It is curious that an experience so wounding can also be recognised as good, as positively nourishing. I suppose I was even a bit eager to be wounded—or I would not have made the mistakes I did. He was somebody already committed to someone else, so there was never, from the beginning, any pretence of permanence in our liaison. Yet (and here comes my famous stupidity again) I very much wanted to have a child by him. A moment's thought would have shown me that it would have been impossible; but the moment's thought only supervened when I was already pregnant. I did not, I thought, care that he must go away, marry someone else. I would at least have his child! But when I confessed it—at the very moment the words left my lips—I suddenly woke up and realised that this would be to perpetuate a link with him to which I had no right. To put it plainly I should be taking advantage of him, creating a responsibility which would shackle him throughout his marriage. It came to me in a flash, and I swallowed my tongue. By the greatest luck he had not heard my words. He was lying like you are now, half asleep, and had not caught my whisper.

'What did you say?' he said. I substituted another remark, made up on the spur of the moment. A month later he left Syria. It was a sunny day full of the sound of bees. I knew I should have to destroy the child. I bitterly regretted it, but there seemed no other honourable course to take in the matter. You will probably think I was wrong, but even now I am glad I took the course I did, for it would have perpetuated something which had no right to exist outside the span of these few golden months. Apart from that I had nothing to regret. I had been immeasurably grown-up by the experience. I was full of gratitude, and still am. If I am generous now in my love-making it is perhaps because I am paying back the debt, refunding an old love in a new. I entered a clinic and went through with it. Afterwards the kindly old anaesthetist called me to the dirty sink to show me the little pale homunculus with its tiny nails and members. I wept bitterly. It looked like a smashed yolk of an egg. The old man turned it over curiously with a sort of spatula—as one might turn over a rasher of bacon in a frying-pan. I could not match his cold scientific curiosity and felt rather sick. He smiled and said: 'It is all over. How relieved you must feel!' It was true, with my sadness there was a very real relief at having done what I recognised as the right thing. Also a sense of loss; my heart felt like a burgled swallow's nest. And so back to the mountains, to the same easel and white canvas. It is funny but I realised that precisely what wounded me most as a woman nourished me most as an artist. But of course I missed him for a long time: just a physical being whose presence attaches itself without one's knowing, like a piece of cigarette paper to the lip. It hurts to pull it away. Bits of the skin come off! But hurt or not, I learned to bear it and even to cherish it, for it allowed me to come to terms with another illusion. Or rather to see the link between body and spirit in a new way—for the physique is only the outer periphery, the contours of the spirit, its solid part. Through smell, taste, touch we apprehend each other, ignite each other's minds;

information conveyed by the body's odours after orgasm, breath, tongue-taste—through these one 'knows' in quite primeval fashion. Here was a perfectly ordinary man with no exceptional gifts but in his elements, so to speak, how good for me; he gave off the odours of good natural objects: like newly baked bread, roasting coffee, cordite, sandalwood. In this field of *rapport* I missed him like a skipped meal—I know it sounds vulgar! Paracelsus says that thoughts are acts. Of them all, I suppose, the sex act is the most important, the one in which our spirits most divulge themselves. Yet one feels it is a sort of clumsy paraphrase of the poetic, the noetic, *thought* which shapes itself into a kiss or an embrace. Sexual love *is* knowledge, both in etymology and in cold fact; 'he knew her' as the Bible says! Sex is the joint or coupling which unites the male and female ends of knowledge merely—a cloud of unknowing! When a culture goes bad in its sex all knowledge is impeded. We women know that. That was when I wrote to you asking if I should come to visit you in your island. How grateful I am that you did not answer me! It would have been a wrong move at the time. Your silence saved me! Ah! my dear, forgive me if I bore you with my wanderings, for I see that you are looking somewhat sleepy! But with you it is such a pleasure to talk away the time between love-making! It is a novelty for me. Apart from you there is only dear Balthazar—whose rehabilitation, by the way, is going on apace. But he has told you? He has been inundated with invitations since the Mountolive banquet, and it seems will have little difficulty in rebuilding the clinic practice again."

I: "But he is far from reconciled to his teeth."

She: "I know. And he is still rather shaken and hysterical—as who would not be. But everything goes forward steadily, and I think he will not lapse."

I: "But what of this sister of Pursewarden's?"

She: "Liza! I think you will admire her, though I can't tell if you will like her. She is rather impressive, indeed perhaps just a little bit frightening. The blindness does not seem like an in-capacity, rather it gives an expression of double awareness. She listens to one as if one were music, an extra intentness which makes one immediately aware of the banality of most of one's utterances. She's unlike him, yet very beautiful though deathly pale, and her movements are swift and absolutely certain, un-like most blind people. I have never seen her miss a door-handle or trip on a mat, or pause to get her bearings in a strange place. All the little errors of judgement the blind make, like talking to a chair which has just been vacated by its owner . . . they are absent. One wonders sometimes if she really is blind. She came out here to collect his effects and to gather material about him for a biography."

I: "Balthazar hinted at some sort of mystery."

She: "There is little doubt that David Mountolive is hopelessly in love with her; and from what he told Balthazar it began in London. It is certainly an unusual liaison for someone so cor-rect, and it obviously gives them both a great deal of pain. I often imagine them, the snow falling in London, suddenly finding themselves face to face with the Comic Demon! Poor David! And yet why should I utter such a patronising phrase? Lucky David! Yes, I can tell you a little, based on a scrap of Balthazar's conversation. Suddenly, in a moribund taxi speeding away to the suburbs she turned her face to him and told him that she had been told to expect him many years ago; that the moment she heard his voice she knew that he was the dark princely stranger of the prophecy. He would never leave her. And she only asked leave to verify it, pressing her cold fingers to his face to feel it all over, before sinking back on the cold cushions with a sigh! Yes, it was he. It must have been strange to feel the fingers of the blind girl pressing one's features with a sculptor's touch. David said that a shudder ran through him, all the blood left his face, and his teeth began to chatter! He groaned aloud and clenched them together. So they sat there, hand in hand, trembling while the snowlit suburbs shuttled by the windows. Later she placed his finger upon the exact configuration in her hand which portended an altered life, and the emergence of this unexpected figure which would dominate it! Balthazar is sceptical of such prophecies, as you are, and he cannot avoid a note of amused irony in recounting the story. But so far the enchantment seems to have lasted, so perhaps you will concede something to the power of prophecy, sceptic that you are! And well: with her brother's death she arrived here, has been sorting out papers and manuscripts, as well as interviewing people who knew him. She came here once or twice to talk to me; it wasn't altogether easy for me, though I told her all that I could remember of him. But I think the question which really filled her mind was one which she did not actually utter, namely, had I ever been Pursewarden's mistress? She circled round and round it warily. I think, no, I am sure that she thought me a liar because what I had to tell her was so inconsequent. Indeed perhaps its vagueness suggested that I had something to conceal. In the studio I still have the plaster negative of the death-mask which I showed Balthazar how to make. She held it to her breast for a moment as if to suckle it, with an expression of intense pain, her blind eyes seeming to grow larger and larger until they overflowed the whole face, and turned it into a cave of interrogation. I was horribly embarrassed and sad to suddenly notice, sticking in the plaster, a few little shreds of his moustache. And when she tried to place the negative together and apply it to her own features I almost caught her hand lest she feel them. An absurdity! But her manner startled and upset me. Her questions put me on edge. There was something shamefully inconclusive about these interviews, and I was mentally apologising to Pursewarden all the time in my mind for not making a better showing; one should, after all, be able to find something sensible to say of a great man whom one fully recognised in his lifetime. Not like poor Amaril who was so furious to see Pursewarden's death-mask lying near that of Keats and Blake in the National Portrait

115

Gallery. It was all he could do, he says, to prevent himself from giving the insolent thing a smack with his hand. Instead he abused the object, saying: '*Salaud!*' Why did you not tell me you were a great man passing through my life? I feel defrauded in not noticing your existence, like a child whom someone forgot to tell, and who missed the Lord Mayor riding by in his coach!' I had no such excuse myself, and yet what could I find to say? You see, I think a cardinal factor in all this is that Liza lacks a sense of humour; when I said that in thinking of Pursewarden I found myself instinctively smiling she put on a puzzled frown of interrogation merely. It is possible that they never laughed together, I told myself; yet their only real similarity in the physical sense is in the alignment of teeth and the cut of the mouth. When she is tired she wears the rather insolent expression which, on his face, heralded a witticism! But I expect you too will have to see her, and tell her what you know, what you can remember. It is not easy, facing those blind eyes, to know where to begin! As for Justine, she has luckily been able to escape Liza so far; I suppose the break between Mountolive and Nessim has presented an effective enough excuse. Or perhaps David has convinced her that any contact might be compromising to him officially. I do not know. But I am certain that she has not seen Justine. Perhaps you will have to supply her with a picture, for the only references in Pursewarden's notes are cruel and perfunctory. Have you reached the passages yet in the commonplace book? No. You will. I'm afraid none of us gets off very lightly there! As for any really profound mystery I think Balthazar is wrong. Essentially I think that the problem which engulfs them is simply the effect upon him of her blindness. In fact I am sure from the evidence of my own eyes. Through the old telescope of Nessim . . . yes, the same one! It used to be in the Summer Palace, do you recall? When the Egyptians began to expropriate Nessim all Alexandria got busy to defend its darling. We all bought things from him, intending to hold them for him until everything had blown over. The Cervonis bought the Arab stock, Ganzo the car, which he resold to Pombal, and Pierre Balbz the telescope. As he had nowhere to house it Mountolive let him put it on the verandah of the summer legation, an ideal site. One can sweep the harbour, and most of the town, and in the summer dinner guests can do a little mild star-gazing. Well, I went up there one afternoon and was told that they were both out for a walk, which by the way was a daily custom all winter with them. They would take the car down to the Corniche and walk along the Stanley Bay front arm in arm for half an hour. As I had time to kill I started to fool with the telescope, and idly trained it on the far corner of the bay. It was a blowy day, with high seas running, and the black flags out which signalled dangerous bathing. There were only a few cars about in that end of the town, and hardly anyone on foot. Quite soon I saw the Embassy car come round the corner and stop on the sea-front. Liza and David got down and began to walk away from it towards the beach end. It was amazing how clearly I could see them; I had the impression that I could touch them by just putting out a hand. They were arguing furiously, and she had an expression of grief and pain on her face. I increased the magnification until I discovered with a shock that I could literally lip-read their remarks! It was startling, indeed a little frightening. I could not 'hear' him because his face was half turned aside, but Liza was looking into my telescope like a giant image on a cinema screen. The wind was blowing her dark hair back in a shock from her temples, and with her sightless eyes she looked like some strange Greek statue come to life. She shouted through her tears, 'No, you *could* not have a blind Ambassadress', turning her head from side to side as if trying to find a way of escaping this fearful truth—which I must admit had not occurred to me until the words registered. David had her by the shoulders and was saying something very earnestly, but she wasn't heeding. Then with a sudden twist she broke free and with a single jump cleared the parapet like a stag, to

117

land upon the sand. She began to run towards the sea. David shouted something, and stood for a second gesticulating at the top of the stone steps to the beach. I had such a distinct picture of him then, in that beautifully cut suit of pepper and salt, the flower in his button-hole and the old brown waistcoat he loves with its gun-metal buttons. He looked a strangely ineffectual and petulant figure, his moustache flying in the wind as he stood there. After a second of indecision he too jumped down on to the sand and started after her. She ran very fast right into the water which splashed up, darkening her skirt about her thighs and braking her. Then she halted in sudden indecision and turned back, while he, rushing in after her, caught her by the shoulders and embraced her. They stood for a moment—it was so strange—with the waves thumping their legs; and then he drew her back to the shore with a strange look of gratitude and exultation on his face—as if he were simply delighted by this strange gesture. I watched them hurry back to the car. The anxious chauffeur was standing in the road with his cap in his hand, obviously relieved not to have been called upon to do any life-saving. I thought to myself then: 'A blind Ambassadress? Why not? If David were a meaner-spirited man he might think to himself: "The originality alone would help rather than hinder my career in creating for me artificial sympathies to replace the respectful admiration which I dare only to claim by virtue of my position!" But he would be too single-minded for any such thoughts to enter his mind.'

"Yet when they arrived back for tea, soaked, he was strangely elated. 'We had a little accident' he called gaily as he retired with her for a change of clothes. And of course there was no further reference to the escapade that evening. Later he asked me if I would undertake a portrait of Liza and I agreed. I do not know quite why I felt a sense of misgiving about it. I could not refuse, yet I have found several ways of delaying the business and would like to put it off indefinitely if I could. It is curious to feel as I do, for she would be a splendid subject and perhaps if she had several sittings we might get to know each other a little and ease the constraint I feel when I am with her. Besides, I would really like to do it for his sake, for he has always been a good friend. But there it is. . . . I shall be curious to know what she has to ask you about her brother. And curious to see what you will find to say about him."

I: "He seems to change shape so quickly at every turn of the road that one is forced to revise each idea about him almost as soon as it is formulated. I'm beginning to wonder about one's right to pronounce in this fashion on unknown people."

She: "I think, my dear, you have a mania for exactitude and an impatience with partial knowledge which is . . . well, unfair to knowledge itself. How can it be anything but imperfect? I don't suppose reality ever bears a close resemblance to human truth as, say, El Scob to Yacoub. Myself I would like to be content with the poetic symbolism it presents, the shape of nature itself as it were. Perhaps this was what Pursewarden was trying to convey in those outrageous attacks upon you—have you come to the passages called 'My silent conversations with Brother Ass'?"

I: "Not yet."

She: "Don't be too wounded by them. You must exonerate the brute with a good-natured laugh, for after all he was one of us, one of the tribe. Relative size of accomplishment doesn't matter. As he himself says: 'There is not enough faith, charity or tenderness to furnish this world with a single ray of hope— yet so long as that strange sad cry rings out over the world, the birth-pangs of an artist—all cannot be lost! This sad little squeak of rebirth tells us that all still hangs in the balance. Heed me, reader, for the artist is you, all of us—the statue which must disengage itself from the dull block of marble which houses it and start to live. But when? But when? And then in another place he says: 'Religion is simply art bastardised out of all recognition'—a characteristic remark. It was the central point of his difference with Balthazar and the Cabal.

Pursewarden had turned the whole central proposition upside down."

I: "To suit his private ends."

She: "No. To suit his own immortal needs. There was nothing dishonest about it all. If you are born of the artist tribe it is a waste of time to try and function as a priest. You have to be faithful to your angle of vision, and at the same time fully recognise its partiality. There is a kind of perfection to be achieved in matching oneself to one's capacities—at every level. This must, I imagine, do away with striving, and with illusions too. I myself always admired old Scobie as a thoroughly success-ful example of this achievement in his own way. He was quite successfully himself, I thought."

I: "Yes, I suppose so. I was thinking of him today. His name cropped up at the office in some connection. Clea, imitate him again. You do it so perfectly that I am quite dumb with admiration."

She: "But you know all his stories."

I: "Nonsense. They were inexhaustible."

She: "And I wish I could imitate his expression! That look of portentous owlishness, the movement of the glass eye! Very well; but close your eyes and hear the story of Toby's downfall, one of his many downfalls. Are you ready?"

I: "Yes."

She: "He told it to me in the course of a dinner-party just before I went to Syria. He said he had come into some money and insisted on taking me to the Lutetia in ceremonial fashion where we dined on *scampi* and Chianti. It began like this in a low confidential tone. 'Now the thing about Toby that charac-terised him was a superb effrontery, the fruit of perfect breed-ing! I told you his father was an M.P.? No? Funny, I thought I mentioned it in passing. Yes, he was very highly placed, you might say. But Toby never boasted of it. In fact, and *this* shows you, he actually asked me to treat the matter with discretion and not mention it to his shipmates. He didn't want any

120

favours, he said. He didn't want people sucking up to him neither, just because his father was an M.P. He wanted to go through life incognito, he said, and make his own career by hard work. Mind you, he was almost continuously in trouble with the upper deck. It was his religious convictions more than anything, I think. He had a remorseless taste for the cloth did old Toby. He was vivid. The only career he wanted was to be a sky-pilot. But somehow he couldn't get himself ordained. *They* said he drank too much. But *he* said it was because his vocation was so strong that it pushed him to excesses. If only they'd ordain him, he said, everything would be all right. He'd come right off the drink. He told me this many a time when he was on the Yokohama run. When he was drunk he was always trying to hold services in Number One hold. Naturally people complained and at Goa the captain made a bishop come aboard to reason with him. It was no go. "Scurvy" he used to say to me, "Scurvy, I shall die a martyr to my vocation, that's what." But there's nothing in life like determination. Toby had plenty of it. And I wasn't at all surprised one day, after many years, to see him come ashore ordained. Just how he'd squeezed into the Church he never would tell. But one of his mates said that he got a slightly tainted Chinese Catholic bishop to ordain him on the sly in Hong Kong. Once the articles were all signed sealed and wrapped up there was nothing anyone could do, so the Church had to put a good face on it, taint and all. After that he became a holy terror, holding services everywhere and distributing cigarette cards of the saints. The ship he was serving on got fed up and paid him off. They framed him up; said he had been seen going ashore carrying a lady's handbag! Toby denied it and said it was something religious, a chasuble or something that they mistook for a handbag. Anyway he turned up on a passenger-ship next carrying pilgrims. He said that at last he had fulfilled himself. Services all day long in "A" Lounge, and no one to hinder the word of the Lord. But I noticed with alarm that he was drinking more heavily than before and he had a funny cracked sort of laugh. It wasn't the old Toby. I wasn't surprised to hear he had been in trouble again. Apparently he had been suspected of being drunk on duty and of having made an unflattering reference to a bishop's posterior. Now this shows his superb cleverness, for when he came up for court martial he had the perfect answer ready. I don't quite know how they do court martials in the Church, but I suppose this pilgrim boat was full of bishops or something and they did it drum-head fashion in "A" Lounge. But Toby was too fast for them with his effrontery. There's nothing like breeding to make you quick at answering. His defence was that if anyone *had* heard him breathing heavily at Mass it was his asthma; and secondly he hadn't never mentioned anyone's posterior. He had talked about a bishop's *fox terrier*! Isn't it dazzling? It was the smartest thing he ever did, old Toby, though I've never known him at a loss for a clever answer. Well, the bishops were so staggered that they let him off with a caution and a thousand Ave Marias as a penance. This was pretty easy for Toby; in fact it was no trouble at all because he'd bought a little Chinese prayer-wheel which Budgie had fixed up to say Ave Marias for him. It was a simple little device, brilliantly adapted to the times as you might say. One revolution was an Ave Maria or fifty beads. It simplified prayer, he said; in fact one could go on praying without thinking. Later someone told on him and it was confiscated by the head bloke. Another caution for poor Toby. But nowadays he treated everything with a toss of the head and a scornful laugh. He was riding for a fall, you see. He had got a bit above himself. I couldn't help noticing how much he'd changed because he touched here nearly every week with these blinking pilgrims. I think they were Italians visiting the Holy Places. Back and forth they went, and with them Toby. But he had changed. He was always in trouble now, and seemed to have thrown off all restraint. He had gone completely fanciful. Once he called on me dressed as a cardinal with a red beret and a sort of lampshade in his hand. "Cor!" I gasped.

"You aren't half orchidaceous, Toby!" Later he got very sharply told off for dressing above his rank, and I could see that it was only a matter of time before he fell out of the balloon, so to speak. I did what I could as an old friend to reason with him but somehow I couldn't bring him to see the point. I even tried to get him back on to beer but it wasn't any go at all. Nothing but fire water for Toby. Once I had to have him carried back aboard by the police. He was all figged up in a prelate's costume. I think they call it a shibboleth. And he tried to pronounce an anathema on the city from "A" Boat Deck. He was waving an apse or something. The last thing I saw of him was a lot of real bishops restraining him. They were nearly as purple as his own borrowed robes. My, how those Italians carried on! Then came the crash. They nabbed him in fragrant delicto swigging the sacramental wine. You know it has the Pope's Seal on it, don't you? You buy it from Cornford's, the Ecclesiastical Retailers in Bond Street, ready sealed and blessed. Toby had *broken the seal*. He was finished. I don't know whether they ex-communicate or what, but anyway he was struck off the register properly. The next time I saw him he was a shadow of his old self and dressed as an ordinary seaman. He was still drinking heavily but in a different way now, he said. "Scurvy" he said. "Now I simply drink to expiate my sins. I'm drinking as a punishment now, not a pleasure." The whole tragedy had made him very moody and restless. He talked of going off to Japan and becoming a religious body there. The only thing that prevented him was that there you have to shave your head and he couldn't bear to part with his hair which was long, and was justly admired by his friends. "No" he said, after discussing the idea, "no, Scurvy old man, I couldn't bring myself to go about as bald as an egg, after what I've been through. It would give me a strangely roofless appearance at my age. Besides once when I was a nipper I got ringworm and lost my crowning glory. It took ages to grow again. It was so slow that I feared it never would come into bloom again. Now I couldn't bear to be parted from it. Not for anything." I saw his dilemma perfectly, but I didn't see any way out for him. He would always be a square peg would old Toby, swimming against the stream. Mind you, it was a mark of his originality. For a little while he managed to live by blackmailing all the bishops who'd been to confession while he was O.C. Early Mass, and twice he got a free holiday in Italy. But then other troubles came his way and he shipped to the Far East, working in Seamen's Hostels when he was ashore, and telling everyone that he was going to make a fortune out of smuggled diamonds. I see him very rarely now, perhaps once every three years, and he never writes; but I'll never forget old Toby. He was always such a gentleman in spite of his little mishaps, and when his father dies he expects to have a few hundred a year of his own. Then we're going to join forces in Horsham with Budgie and put the earth-closet trade on a real economic basis. Old Budgie can't keep books and files. That's a job for me with my police training. At least so old Toby always said. I wonder where he is now?' "

The recital ended, the laughter suddenly expired and a new expression appeared on Clea's face which I did not remember ever having seen before. Something between a doubt and an apprehension which played about the mouth like a shadow. She added with a studied naturalness which was somehow strained: "Afterwards he told my fortune. I know you will laugh. He said he could only do it with certain people and at certain times. Will you believe me if I tell you that he described with perfect fidelity and in complete detail the whole Syrian episode?" She turned her face to the wall with an abrupt movement and to my surprise I saw her lips were trembling. I put my hand up her warm shoulder and said "Clea" very softly. "What is it?" Suddenly she cried out: "O leave me alone. Can't you see I want to sleep?"

o   o   o   o   o

124

MY CONVERSATIONS WITH BROTHER ASS
(being extracts from Pursewarden's Notebook)

With what a fearful compulsion we return to it again and again—like a tongue to a hollow tooth—this question of writing! Can writers talk nothing but shop then? No. But with old Darley I am seized with a sort of convulsive vertigo for, while we have everything in common, I find I cannot talk to him at all. But wait. I mean that I do talk: endlessly, passionately, hysterically without uttering a word aloud! There is no way to drive a wedge between his ideas which, *ma foi*, are thoughtful, orderly, the very essence of "soundness". Two men propped on bar-stools thoughtfully gnawing at the universe as if at a stick of sugar-cane! The one speaks in a low, modulated voice, using language with tact and intuition; the other shifts from buttock to listless buttock shamefacedly shouting in his own mind, but only answering with an occasional affirmative or negative to these well-rounded propositions which are, for the most part, incontestably valuable and true! This would perhaps make the germ of a short story? ("But Brother Ass, there is a whole dimension lacking to what you say. How is it possible for one to convey this in Oxford English?") Still with sad penitential frowns the man on the high bar-stool proceeds with his exposition about the problem of the creative act—I ask you! From time to time he shoots a shyish sideways glance at his tormentor—for in a funny sort of way I do seem to torment him; otherwise he would not always be at me, aiming the button of his foil at the chinks in my self-esteem, or at the place where he believes I must keep my heart. No, we would be content with simpler conversational staples like the weather. In me he scents an enigma, something crying out for the probe. ("But Brother Ass, I am as clear as a bell—a sancing bell! The problem is there, here, nowhere!") At times while he is talking like this I have the sudden urge to jump on his back and ride him frantically up and down Rue Fuad, thrashing him with a Thesaurus and crying: "Awake, moon-calf! Let me take you by your long silken jackass's ears and drive you at a gallop through the waxworks of our literature, among the clicking of Box Brownies each taking its monochrome snapshots of so-called reality! Together we will circumvent the furies and become celebrated for our depiction of the English scene, of English life which moves to the stately rhythm of an autopsy! Do you hear me, Brother Ass?"

He does not hear, he will not hear. His voice comes to me from a great way off, as if over a faulty land-line. "Hullo! Can you hear me?" I cry, shaking the receiver. I hear his voice faintly against the roaring of Niagara Falls. "What is that? Did you say that you wished to contribute to English literature? What, to arrange a few sprigs of parsley over this dead turbot? To blow diligently into the nostrils of this corpse? Have you mobilised your means, Brother Ass? Have you managed to annul your early pot-training? Can you climb like a cat-burglar with loosened sphincters? But then what will you say to people whose affective life is that of hearty Swiss hoteliers? I will tell you. I will say it and save all you artists the trouble. A simple word. *Edelweiss.* Say it in a low well-modulated voice with a refined accent, and lubricate it with a sigh! The whole secret is there, in a word which grows above snowline! And then, having solved the problem of ends and means you will have to face another just as troublesome—for if by any chance a work of art should cross the Channel it would be sure to be turned back at Dover on the grounds of being improperly dressed! It is not easy, Brother Ass. (Perhaps it would be wisest to ask the French for intellectual asylum?) But I see you will not

126

heed me. You continue in the same unfaltering tone to describe for me the literary scene which was summed up once and for all by the poet Gray in the line 'The lowing herd winds slowly o'er the lea'! Here I cannot deny the truth of what you say. It is cogent, it is prescient, it is carefully studied. But I have taken my own precautions against a nation of mental grannies. Each of my books bears a scarlet wrapper with the legend: *NOT TO BE OPENED BY OLD WOMEN OF EITHER SEX*. (Dear D.H.L. so wrong, so right, so great, may his ghost breathe on us all!)"

He puts down his glass with a little click and sighing runs his fingers through his hair. Kindness is no excuse, I tell myself. Disinterested goodness is no exoneration from the basic demands of the artist's life. You see, Brother Ass, there is my life and then the life of my life. They must belong as fruit and rind. I am not being cruel. It is simply that I am not indulgent!

"How lucky not to be interested in writing" says Darley with a touch of plaintive despair in his tone. "I envy you." But he does not, really, not at all. Brother Ass, I will tell you a short story. A team of Chinese anthropologists arrived in Europe to study our habits and beliefs. Within three weeks they were all dead. They died of uncontrollable laughter and were buried with full military honours! What do you make of that? We have turned ideas into a paying form of tourism.

Darley talks on with slanting eye buried in his gin-sling. I reply wordlessly. In truth I am deafened by the pomposity of my own utterances. They echo in my skull like the reverberating eructations of Zarathustra, like the wind whistling through Montaigne's beard. At times I mentally seize him by the shoulders and shout: "Should literature be a path-finder or a bromide? Decide! Decide!"

He does not heed, does not hear me. He has just come from the library, from the pot-house, or from a Bach concert (the gravy still running down his chin). We have aligned our shoes upon the polished brass rail below the bar. The evening has begun to yawn around us with the wearisome promise of girls to be ploughed. And here is Brother Ass discoursing upon the book he is writing and from which he has been thrown, as from a horse, time and time again. It is not really art which is at issue, it is ourselves. Shall we always be content with the ancient tinned salad of the subsidised novel? Or the tired ice-cream of poems which cry themselves to sleep in the refrigerators of the mind? If it were possible to adopt a bolder scansion, a racier rhythm we might all breathe more freely! Poor Darley's books—will they always be such painstaking descriptions of the soul-states of . . . the human omelette? (Art occurs at the point where a form is sincerely honoured by an awakened spirit.)

"This one's on me."

"No, old man, on me"

"No. No; I insist."

"No. It's my turn."

This amiable quibble allows me just the split second I need to jot down the salient points for my self-portrait on a rather ragged cuff. I think it covers the whole scope of the thing with admirable succinctness. Item one. "Like all fat men I tend to be my own hero." Item two. "Like all young men I set out to be a genius, but mercifully laughter intervened." Item three. "I always hoped to achieve the Elephant's Eye view." Item four. "I realised that to become an artist one must shed the whole complex of egotisms which led to the choice of self-expression as the only means of growth! This because it is impossible I call The Whole Joke!"

Darley is talking of disappointments! But Brother Ass, disenchantment is the essence of the game. With what high hopes we invaded London from the provinces in those old dead days, our manuscripts bagging out suitcases. Do you recall? With what emotion we gazed over Westminster Bridge, reciting Wordsworth's indifferent sonnet and wondering if his daughter grew up less beautiful for being French. The whole metropolis seemed to quiver with the portent of our talent, our skill, our discernment. Walking along the Mall we wondered who all those men were—tall hawk-featured men perched on balconies and high places, scanning the city with heavy binoculars. What were they seeking so earnestly? Who were they—so composed and steely-eyed? Timidly we stopped a policeman to ask him. "They are publishers" he said mildly. Publishers! Our hearts stopped beating. "They are on the look out for new talent." Great God! It was for *us* they were waiting and watching! Then the kindly policeman lowered his voice confidentially and said in hollow and reverent tones: "*They are waiting for the new Trollope to be born!*" Do you remember, at these words, how heavy our suitcases suddenly felt? How our blood slowed, our footsteps lagged? Brother Ass, we had been bashfully thinking of a kind of illumination such as Rimbaud dreamed of—a nagging poem which was not didactic or expository but which *infected*—was not simply a rationalised intuition, I mean, clothed in isinglass! We had come to the wrong shop, with the wrong change! A chill struck us as we saw the mist falling in Trafalgar Square, coiling around us its tendrils of ectoplasm! A million muffin-eating moralists were waiting, not for us, Brother Ass, but for the plucky and tedious Trollope! (If you are dissatisfied with your form, reach for the *curette*.) Now do you wonder if I laugh a little off-key? Do you ask yourself what has turned me into nature's bashful little aphorist?

> *Disguised as an eiron, why who should it be*
> *But tuft-hunting, dram-drinking, toad-eating Me!*

We who are, after all, simply poor co-workers in the psyche of our nation, what can we expect but the natural automatic rejection from a public which resents interference? And quite right too. There is no injustice in the matter, for I also resent interference, Brother Ass, just as you do. No, it is not a question of being aggrieved, it is a question of being unlucky. Of the ten thousand reasons for my books' unpopularity I shall only bother to give you the first, for it includes all the others.

A puritan culture's conception of art is of something which will endorse its morality and flatter its patriotism. Nothing else. I see you raise your eyebrows. Even you, Brother Ass, realise the basic unreality of this proposition. Nevertheless it explains everything. A puritan culture, *argal*, does not know what art is—how can it be expected to care? (I leave religion to the bishops—there it can do most harm!)

> No croked legge, no blered eye,
> no part deformed out of kinde
> Nor yet so onolye half can be
> As is the inward suspicious minde.

> The wheel is patience on to which I'm bound.
> Time is this nothingness within the round.

Gradually we compile our own anthologies of misfortune, our dictionaries of verbs and nouns, our copulas and gerundives. That symptomatic policeman of the London dusk first breathed the message to us! That kindly father-figure put the truth in a nutshell. And here we are both in a foreign city built of smegma-tinted crystal and tinsel whose *moeurs*, if we described them, would be regarded as the fantasies of our disordered brains. Brother Ass, we have the hardest lesson of all to learn as yet—that truth cannot be forced but must be allowed to plead for itself! Can you hear me? The line is faulty again, your voice has gone far away. I hear the water rushing!

> Be bleak, young man, and let who will be sprightly,
> And honour Venus if you can twice nightly.
> All things being equal you should not refuse
> To ring the slow sad cowbell of the English muse!

> Art's Truth's Nonentity made quite explicit.
> If it ain't this then what the devil is it?

Writing in my room last night I saw an ant upon the table.

It crossed near the inkwell, and I saw it hesitate at the whiteness of a sheet of paper on which I had written the word "Love"; my pen faltered, the ant turned back, and suddenly my candle guttered and went out. Clear octaves of yellow light flickered behind my eyeballs. I had wanted to start a sentence with the words "Proponents of love"—but the thought had guttered out with the candle! Later on, just before dropping off to sleep an idea struck me. On the wall above my bed I wrote in pencil the words: "What is to be done when one cannot share one's own opinions about love?" I heard my own exasperated sigh as I was dropping off to sleep. In the morning I awoke, clear as a perforated appendix, and wrote my own epitaph on the mirror with my shaving-stick:

"I never knew which side my art was buttered"
Were the Last Words that poor Pursewarden uttered!

As for the proponents of love, I was glad they had vanished for they would have led me irresistibly in the direction of sex—that bad debt which hangs upon my compatriots' consciences. The quiddity! The veritable nub and quiddity of this disordered world, and the only proper field for the deployment of our talents, Brother Ass. But one true, honest unemphatic word in this department will immediately produce one of those neighing and whinnying acts peculiar to our native intellectuals! For them sex is either a Gold Rush or a Retreat from Moscow. And for us? No, but if we are to be a moment serious I will explain what I mean. (Cuckow, Cuckow, a merry note, unpleasing to the pigskin ear.) I mean more than they think. (The strange sad hermaphrodite figure of the London dusk—the Guardsman waiting in Ebury Street for the titled gent.) No, quite another region of enquiry which cannot be reached without traversing this *terrain vague* of the partial spirits. Our topic, Brother Ass, is the same, always and irremediably the same—I spell the word for you: l-o-v-e. Four letters, each letter a volume! The *point faible* of the human psyche, the very site of the carcinoma maxima! How, since the Greeks, has it got mixed up with the cloaca maxima? It is a complete mystery to which the Jews hold the key unless my history is faulty. For this gifted and troublesome race which has never known art, but exhausted its creative processes purely in the construction of ethical systems, has fathered on us all, literally impregnated the Western European psyche with, the whole range of ideas based on "race" and sexual containment in the furtherance of the race! I hear Balthazar growling and lashing his tail! But where the devil do these fantasies of purified bloodstreams come from? Am I wrong to turn to the fearful prohibitions listed in Leviticus for an explanation of the manic depressive fury of Plymouth Brethren and a host of other dismal sectarians? We have had our testicles pinched for centuries by the Mosaic Law; hence the wan and pollarded look of our young girls and boys. Hence the mincing effrontery of adults willed to perpetual adolescence! Speak, Brother Ass! Do you need me? If I am wrong you have only to say so! But in my conception of the four-letter word—which I am surprised has not been black-listed with the other three by the English printer—I am some-what bold and sweeping. I mean the *whole bloody range*—from the little greenstick fractures of the human heart right up to its higher spiritual connivance with the . . . well, the absolute ways of nature, if you like. Surely, Brother Ass, this is the improper study of man? The main drainage of the soul? We could make an atlas of our sighs!

> *Zeus gets Hera on her back*
> *But finds that she has lost the knack.*
> *Extenuated by excesses*
> *She is unable, she confesses.*
>
> *Nothing daunted Zeus, who wise is,*
> *Tries a dozen good disguises.*
> *Eagle, ram, and bull and bear*
> *Quickly answer Hera's prayer.*

One knows a God should be prolix,
*But . . . think of all those different ******!*

But I break off here in some confusion, for I see that I am in danger of not taking myself as seriously as I should! And this is an unpardonable offence. Moreover I missed your last remark which was something about the choice of a style. Yes, Brother Ass, the choice of a style is most important; in the market garden of our domestic culture you will find strange and terrible blooms with every stamen standing erect. O to write like Ruskin! When poor Effie Grey tried to get to his bed, he shoo'd the girl away! O to write like Carlyle! Haggis of the mind. When a Scotsman comes to toun Can Spring be far behind? No. Everything you say is truthful and full of point; relative truth, and somewhat pointless point, but nevertheless I will try and think about this invention of the scholiasts, for clearly style is as important to you as matter to me.

How shall we go about it? Keats, the word-drunk, searched for resonance among vowel-sounds which might give him an echo of his inner self. He sounded the empty coffin of his early death with patient knuckles, listening to the dull resonances given off by his certain immortality. Byron was off-hand with English, treating it as master to servant; but the language, being no lackey, grew up like tropic lianas between the cracks of his verses, almost strangling the man. He really lived, his life was truly imaginary; under the figment of the passional self there is a mage, though he himself was not aware of the fact. Donne stopped upon the exposed nerve, jangling the whole cranium. Truth should make one wince, he thought. He hurts us, fearing his own facility; despite the pain of the stopping his verse must be chewed to rags. Shakespeare makes all Nature hang its head. Pope, in an anguish of method, like a constipated child, sandpapers his surfaces to make them slippery for our feet. Great stylists are those who are least certain of their effects. The secret lack in their matter haunts them without knowing it!

133

Eliot puts a cool chloroform pad upon a spirit too tightly braced by the information it has gathered. His honesty of measure and his resolute bravery to return to the headsman's axe is a challenge to us all; but where is the smile? He induces awkward sprains at a moment when we are trying to dance! He has chosen greyness rather than light, and he shares his portion with Rembrandt. Blake and Whitman are awkward brown paper parcels full of vessels borrowed from the temple which tumble all over the place when the string breaks. Longfellow heralds the age of invention for he first thought out the mechanical piano. You pedal, it recites. Lawrence was a limb of the genuine oak-tree, with the needed girth and span. Why did he show them that it mattered, and so make himself vulnerable to their arrows? Auden also always talks. He has manumitted the colloquial. . . .

But here, Brother Ass, I break off; for clearly this is not higher or even lower criticism! I do not see this sort of fustian going down at our older universities where they are still pain-fully trying to extract from art some shadow of justification for their way of life. Surely there must be a grain of hope, they ask anxiously? After all, there must be a grain of hope for decent honest Christian folk in all this rigmarole which is poured out by our tribe from generation to generation. Or is art simply the little white stick which is given to the blind man and by the help of which he tap tap taps along a road he cannot see but which he is certain is there? Brother Ass, it is for you to decide!

When I was chided by Balthazar for being equivocal I replied, without a moment's conscious thought: "Words being what they are, people being what they are, perhaps it would be better always to say the opposite of what one means?" Afterwards, when I reflected on this view (which I did not know that I held) it seemed to me really eminently sage! So much for conscious thought: you see, we Anglo-Saxons are incapable of thinking *for* ourselves; *about*, yes. In thinking *about* ourselves we put up every kind of pretty performance in every sort of voice, from cracked Yorkshire to the hot-potato-in-the-mouth voice of the BBC. There we excel, for we see ourselves at one remove from reality, as a subject under a microscope. This idea of objectivity is really a flattering extension of our sense of humbug. When you start to think *for* yourself it is impossible to *cant*—and we live by cant! Ah! I hear you say with a sigh, another of those English writers, eminent jailors of the soul! How they weary and disturb us! Very true and very sad.

> *Hail! Albion drear, fond home of cant!*
> *Pursewarden sends thee greetings scant.*
> *Thy notions he's turned back to front*
> *Abhorring cant, adoring* ****

But if you wish to enlarge the image turn to Europe, the Europe which spans, say, Rabelais to de Sade. A progress from the belly-consciousness to the head-consciousness, from flesh and food to sweet (sweet!) reason. Accompanied by all the interchanging ills which mock us. A progress from religious ecstasy to duodenal ulcer! (It is probably healthier to be entirely brainless.) But, Brother Ass, this is something which you did not take into account when you chose to compete for the Heavyweight Belt for Artists of the Millennium. It is too late to complain. You thought you would somehow sneak by the penalties without being called upon to do more than demonstrate your skill with words. But words . . . they are only an Aeolian harp, or a cheap xylophone. Even a sea-lion can learn to balance a football on its nose or to play the slide trombone in a circus. What lies beyond. . . ?

No, but seriously, if you wished to be—I do not say original but merely contemporary—you might try a four-card trick in the form of a novel; passing a common axis through four stories, say, and dedicating each to one of the four winds of heaven. A continuum, forsooth, embodying not a *temps retrouvé* but a *temps délivré*. The curvature of space itself would give you stereoscopic narrative, while human personality seen across a continuum would perhaps become prismatic? Who can say? I throw the idea out. I can imagine a form which, if satisfied, might raise in human terms the problems of causality or indeterminacy. . . . And nothing very *recherché* either. Just an ordinary Girl Meets Boy story. But tackled in this way you would not, like most of your contemporaries, be drowsily cutting along a dotted line!

That is the sort of question which you will one day be forced to ask yourself ("We will never get to Mecca!" as the Tchekhov sisters remarked in a play, the title of which I have forgotten.)

> *Nature he loved, and next to nature nudes,*
> *He strove with every woman worth the strife,*
> *Warming both cheeks before the fire of life,*
> *And fell, doing battle with a million prudes.*

Who dares to dream of capturing the fleeting image of truth in all its gruesome multiplicity? (No, no, let us dine cheerfully off scraps of ancient discarded poultice and allow ourselves to be classified by science as wet and dry bobs.)

Whose are the figures I see before me, fishing the brackish reaches of the C. of E.?

One writes, Brother Ass, for the spiritually starving, the castaways of the soul! They will always be a majority even when everyone is a state-owned millionaire. Have courage, for here you will always be master of your audience! Genius which cannot be helped should be politely ignored.

Nor do I mean that it is useless to master and continuously practise your craft. No. A good writer should be able to write anything. But a great writer is the servant of compulsions which are ordained by the very structure of the psyche and cannot be disregarded. Where is he? Where is he?

Come, let us collaborate on a four- or five-decker job, shall we? "Why the Curate Slipped" would be a good title. Quick, they are waiting, those hypnagogic figures among the London minarets, the *muezzin* of the trade. "Does Curate get girl *as well as* stipend, or *only* stipend? Read the next thousand pages and find out!" English life in the raw—like some pious melodrama acted by criminal churchwardens sentenced to a lifetime of sexual misgivings! In this way we can put a tea-cosy over reality to our mutual advantage, writing it all in the plain prose which is only just distinguishable from galvanised iron. In this way we will put a lid on a box with no sides! Brother Ass, let us conciliate a world of listless curmudgeons who read to verify, not their intuitions, but their prejudices!

I remember old Da Capo saying one afternoon: "Today I had five girls. I know it will seem excessive to you. I was not trying to prove anything to myself. But if I said that I had merely blended five teas to suit my palate or five tobaccos to suit my pipe, you would not give the matter a second thought. You would, on the contrary, admire my eclecticism, would you not?"

The belly-furbished Kenilworth at the F.O. once told me plaintively that he had "just dropped in" on James Joyce out of curiosity, and was surprised and pained to find him rude, arrogant and short-tempered. "But" I said "he was paying for his privacy by giving lessons to niggers at one and six an hour! He might have been entitled to feel safe from ineffables like yourself who imagine that art is something to which a good education automatically entitles you; that it is a part of a social equipment, class aptitude, like painting water-colours was for a Victorian gentlewoman! I can imagine his poor heart sinking as he studied your face, with its expression of wayward condescension—the fathomless self-esteem which one sees occasionally flit across the face of a goldfish with a hereditary title!" After this we never spoke, which was what I wanted. The art of making necessary enemies! Yet one thing I liked in him: he pronounced the word 'Civilisation' as if it had an S-bend in it.

(Brother Ass is on symbolism now, and really talking good sense, I must admit.) Symbolism! The abbreviation of language into poem. The heraldic aspect of reality! Symbolism is the great repair-outfit of the psyche, Brother Ass, the *fond de pouvoir* of the soul. The sphincter-loosening music which copies the ripples of the soul's progress through human flesh, playing in us like electricity! (Old Parr, when he was drunk, said once: "Yes, but it *hurts* to realise!")

Of course it does. But we know that the history of literature is the history of laughter and pain. The imperatives from which there is no escape are: *Laugh till it hurts, and hurt till you laugh!*

The greatest thoughts are accessible to the least of men. Why do we have to struggle so? Because understanding is a function not of ratiocination but of the psyche's stage of growth. There, Brother Ass, is the point at which we are at variance. No amount of explanation can close the gap. Only realisation! One day you are going to wake from your sleep shouting with laughter. *Ecco!*

About Art I always tell myself: while they are watching the firework display, yclept Beauty, you must smuggle the truth into their veins like a filter-passing virus! This is easier said than done. How slowly one learns to embrace the paradox! Even I am not there as yet; nevertheless, like that little party of explorers, "Though we were still two days' march from the falls we suddenly heard their thunder growing up in the distance"! Ah! those who merit it may one day be granted a rebirth-certificate by a kindly Government Department. This will entitle them to receive everything free of charge—a prize reserved for those who want nothing. Celestial economics, about which Lenin is strangely silent! Ah! the gaunt faces of the English muses! Pale distressed gentlewomen in smocks and beads, dispensing tea and drop-scones to the unwary!

> *The foxy faces*
> *Of Edwardian Graces*
> *Horse-faces full of charm*
> *With strings of beads*
> *And a packet of seeds*
> *And an ape-tuft under each arm!*

Society! Let us complicate existence to the point of drudgery so that it acts as a drug against reality. Unfair! Unfair! But, my dear Brother Ass, the sort of book I have in mind will be characterised by the desired quality which will make us rich and famous: it will be characterised by a *total lack of codpiece*!

When I want to infuriate Balthazar I say: "Now if the Jews would only *assimilate* they would give us a valuable lead in the matter of breaking down puritanism everywhere. For they are the licence-holders and patentees of the closed system, the ethical response! Even our absurd food prohibitions and inhibitions are copied from their melancholy priest-ridden rigmarole about flesh and fowl. Aye! We artists are not interested in policies but in values—this is our field of battle! If once we could loosen up, relax the terrible grip of the so-called Kingdom of Heaven which has made the earth such a blood-soaked place, we might rediscover in sex the key to a metaphysical search which is our *raison d'être* here below! If the closed system and the moral exclusiveness on divine right were relaxed a little what could we not do?" What indeed? But the good Balthazar smokes his Lakadif gloomily and shakes his shaggy head. I think of the black velvet sighs of Juliet and fall silent. I think of the soft white knosps—unopened flower-shapes—which decorate the tombs of Moslem women! The slack, soft insipid mansuetude of these females of the mind! No, clearly my history is pretty weak. Islam also libs as the Pope does.

Brother Ass, let us trace the progress of the European artist from problem-child to case-history, from case-history to cry-baby! He has kept the psyche of Europe alive by his ability to be wrong, by his continual cowardice—this is his function! Cry-baby of the Western World! Cry-babies of the world unite! But let me hasten to add, lest this sounds cynical or despairing, that I am full of hope. For always, at every moment of time, there is a chance that the artist will stumble upon what I can only call The Great Inkling! Whenever this happens he is at once free to enjoy his fecundating rôle; but it can never really happen as fully and completely as it deserves until the miracle comes about—the miracle of Pursewarden's Ideal Commonwealth! Yes, I believe in this miracle. Our very existence as artists affirms it! It is the act of yea-saying about which the old poet of the city speaks in a poem you once showed me in translation.* The *fact* of an artist being born affirms and reaffirms this in every generation. The miracle is there, on ice so to speak. One fine day it will blossom: then the artist suddenly grows up and accepts the full responsibility for his origins in the people, and when *simultaneously* the people recognise his peculiar significance and value, and greet him as the unborn child in themselves, the infant Joy! I am certain it will come. At the moment they are like wrestlers nervously circling one another, looking for a hold. But when it comes, this great blinding second of illumination—only then shall we be able to dispense with hierarchy as a social form. The new society—so different from anything we can imagine now—will be born around the small strict white temple of the infant Joy! Men and women will group themselves around it, the proto-plasmic growth of the village, the town, the capital! Nothing stands in the way of this Ideal Commonwealth, save that in every generation the vanity and laziness of the artist has always matched the self-indulgent blindness of the people. But prepare, prepare! It is on the way. It is here, there, nowhere!

The great schools of love will arise, and sensual and intel-lectual knowledge will draw their impetus from each other. The human animal will be uncaged, all his dirty cultural straw and coprolitic refuse of belief cleaned out. And the human spirit, radiating light and laughter, will softly tread the green grass like a dancer; will emerge to cohabit with the time-forms and give children to the world of the elementaries—undines and salamanders, sylphs and sylvestres, Gnomi and Vulcani, angels and gnomes.

Yes, to extend the range of physical sensuality to embrace mathematics and theology: to nourish not to stunt the intuitions. For culture means sex, the root-knowledge, and where the faculty is derailed or crippled, its derivatives like religion come up dwarfed or contorted—instead of the emblematic mystic rose you get Judaic cauliflowers like Mormons or Vegetarians, instead of artists you get cry-babies, instead of philosophy semantics.

The sexual and the creative energy go hand in hand. They convert into one another—the solar sexual and the lunar spiritual holding an eternal dialogue. They ride the spiral of time together. They embrace the whole of the human motive. The truth is only to be found in our own entrails—the truth of Time.

"Copulation is the lyric of the mob!" Aye, and also the university of the soul: but a university at present without endowments, without books or even students. No, there are a few.

How wonderful the death-struggle of Lawrence: to realise his sexual nature fully, to break free from the manacles of the Old Testament; flashing down through the firmament like a great white struggling man-fish, the last Christian martyr. His struggle is ours—to rescue Jesus from Moses. For a brief moment it looked possible, but St. Paul restored the balance and the iron handcuffs of the Judaic prison closed about the growing soul forever. Yet in *The Man Who Died* he tells us plainly what must be, what the reawakening of Jesus should have meant—the true birth of free man. Where is he? What has happened to him? Will he ever come?

My spirit trembles with joy as I contemplate this city of light which a divine accident might create before our very eyes at any moment! Here art will find its true form and place, and the artist can play like a fountain without contention, without even trying. For I see art more and more clearly as a sort of manuring of the psyche. It has no intention, that is to say no *theology*. By nourishing the psyche, by dunging it up, it helps it to find its own level, like water. That level is an original inno-

141

cence—who invented the perversion of Original Sin, that filthy obscenity of the West? Art, like a skilled masseur on a playing-field, is always standing by to help deal with casualties; and just as a masseur does, its ministrations ease up the tensions of the psyche's musculature. That is why it always goes for the sore places, its fingers pressing upon the knotted muscles, the tendon afflicted with cramp—the sins, perversions, displeasing points which we are reluctant to accept. Revealing them with its harsh kindness it unravels the tensions, relaxes the psyche. The other part of the work, if there is any other work, must belong to religion. Art is the purifying factor merely. It predicates nothing. It is the handmaid of silent content, essential only to joy and to love! These strange beliefs, Brother Ass, you will find lurking under my mordant humours, which may be described simply as a technique of therapy. As Balthazar says: "A good doctor, and in a special sense the psychologist, makes it quite deliberately, slightly harder for the patient to recover too easily. You do this to see if his psyche has any real bounce in it, for the secret of healing is in the patient and not the doctor. The only measure is the reaction!"

I was born under Jupiter, Hero of the Comic Mode! My poems, like soft music invading the encumbered senses of young lovers left alone at night. . . . What was I saying? Yes, the best thing to do with a great truth, as Rabelais discovered, is to bury it in a mountain of follies where it can comfortably wait for the picks and shovels of the elect.

Between infinity and eternity stretches the thin hard tightrope human beings must walk, joined at the waist! Do not let these unamiable propositions dismay you, Brother Ass. They are written down in pure joy, uncontaminated by a desire to preach! I am really writing for an audience of the blind—but aren't we all? Good art points, like a man too ill to speak, like a baby! But if instead of following the direction it indicates you take it for a thing in itself, having some sort of absolute value, or as a thesis upon something which can be paraphrased, surely you miss the point; you lose yourself at once among the barren abstractions of the critic? Try to tell yourself that its fundamental object was only to invoke the ultimate healing silence—and that the symbolism contained in form and pattern is only a frame of reference through which, as in a mirror, one may glimpse the idea of a universe at rest, a universe in love with itself. Then like a babe in arms you will "milk the universe at every breath"! We must learn to read between the lines, between the lives.

Liza used to say: "But its very perfection makes one sure that it will come to an end." She was right; but women will not accept time and the dictates of the death-divining second. They do not see that a civilisation is simply a great metaphor which describes the aspirations of the individual soul in collective form—as perhaps a novel or a poem might do. The struggle is always for greater consciousness. But alas! Civilisations die in the measure that they become conscious of themselves. They realise, they lose heart, the propulsion of the unconscious motive is no longer there. Desperately they begin to copy themselves in the mirror. It is no use. But surely there is a catch in all this? Yes, Time is the catch! Space is a concrete idea, but Time is abstract. In the scar tissue of Proust's great poem you see that so clearly; his work is the great academy of the time-consciousness. But being unwilling to mobilise the meaning of time he was driven to fall back on memory, the ancestor of hope!

Ah! but being a Jew he had hope—and with Hope comes the irresistible desire to meddle. Now we Celts mate with despair out of which alone grows laughter and the desperate romance of the eternally hopeless. We hunt the attainless, and for us there is only a search unending.

For him it would mean nothing, my phrase "the prolongation of childhood into art". Brother Ass, the diving-board, the trapeze, lie just to the eastward of this position! A leap through the firmament to a new status—only don't miss the ring!

Why for example don't they recognise in Jesus the great Ironist that he is, the comedian? I am sure that two-thirds of the Beatitudes are jokes or squibs in the manner of Chuang Tzu. Generations of mystagogues and pedants have lost the sense. I am sure of it however because he must have known that Truth disappears with the telling of it. It can only be conveyed, not stated; irony alone is the weapon for such a task.

Or let us turn to another aspect of the thing; it was you, just a moment ago, who mentioned our poverty of observation in all that concerns each other—the limitations of sight itself. Bravely spoken! But translated spiritually you get the picture of a man walking about the house, hunting for the spectacles which are on his forehead. To see is to imagine! And what, Brother Ass, could be a better illustration than your manner of seeing Justine, fitfully lit up in the electric signs of the imagination? It is not the same woman evidently who set about besieging me and who was finally driven off by my sardonic laughter. What you saw as soft and appealing in her seemed to me a specially calculated hardness, not which she invented, but which you evoked in her. All that throaty chatter, the compulsion to exteriorise hysteria, reminded me of a feverish patient plucking at a sheet! The violent necessity to incriminate life, to *explain* her soul-states, reminded me of a mendicant soliciting pity by a nice exhibition of sores. Mentally she always had me scratching myself! Yet there was much to admire in her and I indulged my curiosity in exploring the outlines of her character with some sympathy—the configurations of an unhappiness which was genuine, though it always smelt of grease paint! The child, for example!

"I found it, of course. Or rather Mnemjian did. In a brothel. It died from something, perhaps meningitis. Darley and Nessim came and dragged me away. All of a sudden I realised that I could not bear to find it; all the time I hunted I lived on the hope of finding it. But this thing, once dead, seemed suddenly to deprive me of all purpose. I recognised it, but my inner mind kept crying out that it was not true, refusing to let me recognise it, even though I already had consciously done so!"

The mixture of conflicting emotions was so interesting that I jotted them down in my notebook between a poem and a recipe for angel bread which I got from El Kalef. Tabulated thus:

1. Relief at end of search.
2. Despair at end of search; no further motive force in life.
3. Horror at death.
4. Relief at death. What future possible for it?
5. Intense shame (don't understand this).
6. Sudden desire to continue search uselessly rather than admit truth.
7. Preferred to continue to feed on false hopes!

A bewildering collection of fragments to leave among the analects of a moribund poet! But here was the point I was trying to make. She said: "Of course neither Nessim nor Darley noticed anything. Men are so stupid, they never do. I would have been able to forget it even perhaps, and dream that I had never really discovered it, but for Mnemjian, who wanted the reward, and was so convinced of the truth of his case that he made a great row. There was some talk of an autopsy by Balthazar. I was foolish enough to go to his clinic and offer to bribe him to say it was not my child. He was pretty astonished. I wanted him to deny a truth which I so perfectly knew to be true, *so that I should not have to change my outlook*. I would not be deprived of my sorrow, if you like; I wanted it to go on—to go on passionately searching for what I did not dare to find. I even frightened Nessim and incurred his suspicions with my antics over his private safe. So the matter passed off, and for a long time I still went on automatically searching until underneath I could stand the strain of the truth and come to terms with it. I see it so clearly, the divan, the tenement."

Here she put on her most beautiful expression, which was one of intense sadness, and put her hands upon her breasts.

Shall I tell you something? *I suspected her of lying*; it was an unworthy thought but then . . . I am an unworthy person.

I: "Have you ever been back to the place?"

She: "No. I have often wanted to, but did not dare." She shuddered a little. "In my memory I have become attached to that old divan. It must be knocking about somewhere. You see, I am still half convinced it was all a dream."

At once I took up my pipe, violin and deerstalker like a veritable Sherlock. I have always been a X-marks-the-spot man. "Let us go and revisit it," I said briskly. At the worst, I thought, such a visitation would be cathartic. It was in fact a supremely practical thing to suggest, and to my surprise she at once rose and put on her coat. We walked silently down through the western edges of the town, arm in arm.

There was some kind of festival going on in the Arab town which was blazing with electric light and flags. Motionless sea, small high clouds, and a moon like a disapproving archimandrite or another faith. Smell of fish, cardamon seed and frying entrails packed with cummin and garlic. The air was full of the noise of mandolines scratching their little souls out on the night, as if afflicted with fleas—scratching scratching until the blood came on the lice-intoxicated night! The air was heavy. Each breath invisibly perforated it. You felt it come in and out of the lungs as if in a leather bellows. Eheu! It was grisly all that light and noise, I thought. And they talk of the romance of the East! Give me the Metropole at Brighton any day! We traversed this sector of light with quick deliberate step. She walked unerringly, head bent, deep in thought. Then gradually the streets grew darker, faded into the violet of darkness, became narrower, twisted and turned. At last we came to a great empty space with starlight. A dim great barrack of a building. She moved slowly now, with less certainty, hunting for a door. In a whisper she said "This place is run by old Mettrawi. He is bedridden. The door is always open. But he hears everything from his bed. Take my hand." I was never a great fire-eater and

I must confess to a certain uneasiness as we walked into this bandage of total blackness. Her hand was firm and cool, her voice precise, unmarked by any range of emphasis, betraying neither excitement nor fear. I thought I heard the scurrying of immense rats in the rotten structure around me, the very rafters of night itself. (Once in a thunderstorm among the ruins I had seen their fat wet glittering bodies flash here and there as they feasted on garbage.) "Please God, remember that even though I am an English poet I do not deserve to be eaten by rats" I prayed silently. We had started to walk down a long corridor of blackness with the rotten wooden boards creaking under us; here and there was one missing, and I wondered if we were not walking over the bottomless pit itself! The air smelt of wet ashes and that unmistakable odour of black flesh when it is sweating. It is quite different from white flesh. It is dense, foetid, like the lion's cage at the Zoo. The Darkness itself was sweating—and why not? The Darkness must wear Othello's skin. Always a timorous fellow, I suddenly wanted to go to the lavatory but I crushed the thought like a blackbeetle. Let my bladder wait. On we went, and round two sides of a . . . piece of darkness floored with rotten boards. Then suddenly she whispered: "I think we are there!" and pushed open a door upon another piece of impenetrable darkness. But it was a room of some size for the air was cool. One felt the space though one could see nothing whatsoever. We both inhaled deeply.

"Yes" she whispered thoughtfully and, groping in her velvet handbag for a box of matches, hesitantly struck one. It was a tall room, so tall that it was roofed by darkness despite the yellow flapping of the match-flame; one huge shattered window faintly reflected starlight. The walls were of verdigris, the plaster peeling everywhere, and their only decoration was the imprint of little blue hands which ran round the four walls in a haphazard pattern. As if a lot of pygmies had gone mad with blue paint and then galloped all over the walls standing on their hands! To the left, a little off centre, reposed a large gloomy divan, floating upon the gloom like a Viking catafalque; it was a twice-chewed relic of some Ottoman calif, riddled with holes. The match went out. "There it is" she said and putting the box into my hand she left my side. When I lit up again she was sitting beside the divan with her cheek resting upon it, softly stroking it with the palm of her hand. She was completely composed. She stroked it with a calm voluptuous gesture and then crossed her paws on it, reminding me of a lioness sitting astride its lunch. The moment had a kind of weird tension, but this was not reflected on her face. (Human beings are like pipe-organs, I thought. You pull out a stop marked "Lover" or "Mother" and the requisite emotions are unleashed—tears or sighs or endearments. Sometimes I try and think of us all as habit-patterns rather than human beings. I mean, wasn't the idea of the individual soul grafted on us by the Greeks in the wild hope that, by its sheer beauty, it would "take"—as we say of vaccination? That we might grow up to the size of the concept and grow the heavenly flame in each of our hearts? *Has* it taken or hasn't it? Who can say? Some of us still have one, but how vestigial it seems. Perhaps. . . .)

"They have heard us."

Somewhere in the darkness there was a thin snarl of voice, and the silence became suddenly padded out with the scamper of feet upon rotted woodwork. In the expiring flicker of the match I saw, as if somewhere very far away, a bar of light—like a distant furnace door opening in heaven. And voices now, the voices of ants! The children came through a sort of hatch or trap-door made of darkness, in their cotton nightgowns, absurdly farded. With rings on their fingers and bells on their toes. She shall have music wherever she goes! One of them carried a waxlight floating in a saucer. They twanged nasally about us, interrogating our needs with blasting frankness—but they were surprised to see Justine sitting beside the Viking catafalque, her head (now smiling) half turned towards them.

148

"I think we should leave" I said in a low voice, for they smelt dreadfully these tiny apparitions, and they showed a disagreeable tendency to twine their skinny arms about my waist as they wheedled and intoned. But Justine turned to one and said: "Bring the light here, where we can all see." And when the light was brought she suddenly turned herself, crossed her legs under her, and in the high ringing tone of the street story-teller she intoned: "Now gather about me, all ye blessed of Allah, and hear the wonders of the story I shall tell you." The effect was electric; they settled about her like a pattern of dead leaves in a wind, crowding up close together. Some even climbed on to the old divan, chuckling and nudging with delight. And in the same rich triumphant voice, saturated with unshed tears, Justine began again in the voice of the professional story-teller: "Ah, listen to me, all ye true believers, and I will unfold to you the story of Yuna and Aziz, of their great many-petalled love, and of the mishaps which befell them from the doing of Abu Ali Saraq el-Maza. In those days of the great Califate, when many heads fell and armies marched. . . ."

It was a wild sort of poetry for the place and the time—the little circle of wizened faces, the divan, the flopping light; and the strangely captivating lilt of the Arabic with its heavy damascened imagery, the thick brocade of alliterative repetitions, the nasal twanging accents, gave it a laic splendour which brought tears to my eyes—gluttonous tears! It was such a rich diet for the soul! It made me aware how thin the fare is which we moderns supply to our hungry readers. The epic contours, that is what her story had! I was envious. How rich these beggar children were. And I was envious too of her audience. Talk of suspended judgement! They sank into the imagery of her story like plummets. One saw, creeping out like mice, their true souls—creeping out upon those painted masks in little expressions of wonder, suspense and joy. In that yellow gloaming they were expressions of a terrible truth. You saw how they would be in middle age—the witch, the good wife, the gossip, the shrew.

149

The poetry had stripped them to the bone and left only their natural selves to flower thus in expressions faithfully portraying their tiny stunted spirits!

How could I help but admire her for giving me one of the most significant and memorable moments of a writer's life? I put my arm about her shoulders and sat, as rapt as any of them, following the long sinuous curves of the immortal story as it unfolded before our eyes.

They could hardly bear to part with us when at last the story came to an end. They clung to her, pleading for more. Some picked the hem of her skirt and kissed it in an agony of pleading. "There is no time" she said, smiling calmly. "But I will come again, my little ones." They hardly heeded the money she distributed but thronged after us along the dark corridors to the blackness of the square. At the corner I looked back but could only see the flicker of shadows. They said farewell in voices of heartbreaking sweetness. We walked in deep contented silence across the shattered, time-corrupted town until we reached the cool seafront; and stood for a long time leaning upon the cold stone piers above the sea, smoking and saying nothing! At last she turned to me a face of tremendous weariness and whispered: "Take me home, now. I'm dead tired." And so we hailed a pottering gharry and swung along the Corniche as sedately as bankers after a congress. "I suppose we are all hunting for the secrets of growth!" was all she said as we parted.

It was a strange remark to make at parting. I watched her walk wearily up the steps to the great house groping for her key. I still felt drunk with the story of Yuna and Aziz!

Brother Ass, it is a pity that you will never have a chance to read all this tedious rigmarole; it would amuse me to study your puzzled expression as you did so. Why should the artist always be trying to saturate the world with his own anguish, you asked me once. Why indeed? I will give you another phrase: emotional gongorism! I have always been good at polite phrase-making.

Loneliness and desire,
Lord of the Flies,
Are thy unholy empire and
The self's inmost surprise!
Come to these arms, my dear old Dutch
And firmly bar the door
I could not love thee, dear, so much
Loved I not ******* more!

And later, aimlessly walking, who should I encounter but the slightly titubating Pombal just back from the Casino with a chamber-pot full of paper money and a raging thirst for a last beaker of champagne which we took together at the Étoile. It was strange that I had no taste for a girl that night; somehow Yuna and Aziz had barred the way. Instead I straggled back to Mount Vulture with a bottle in my mackintosh pocket, to confront once more the ill-starred pages of my book which, twenty years from now, will be the cause of many a thrashing among the lower forms of our schools. It seemed a disastrous sort of gift to be offering to the generations as yet unborn; I would rather have left them something like Yuna and Aziz, but it hasn't been possible since Chaucer; the sophistication of the laic audience is perhaps to blame? The thought of all those smarting little bottoms made me close my notebooks with a series of ill-tempered snaps. Champagne is a wonderfully soothing drink, however, and prevented me from being too cast-down. Then I stumbled upon the little note which you, Brother Ass, had pushed under the door earlier in the evening: a note which complimented me on the new series of poems which the Anvil was producing (a misprint per line); and writers being what they are I thought most kindly of you, I raised my glass to you. In my eyes you had become a critic of the purest discernment; and once more I asked myself in exasperated tones why the devil I had never wasted more time on you? It was really remiss of me. And falling asleep I made a

151

mental note to take you to dinner the next evening and talk your jackass's head off—about writing, of course, what else? Ah! but that is the point. Once a writer seldom a talker; I knew that, speechless as Goldsmith, I should sit hugging my hands in my armpits while *you* did the talking!

In my sleep I dug up a mummy with poppy-coloured lips, dressed in the long white wedding dress of the Arab sugar-dolls. She smiled but would not awake, though I kissed her and talked to her persuasively. Once her eyes half opened; but they closed again and she lapsed back into smiling sleep. I whispered her name which was Yuna, but which had unaccountably become Liza. And as it was no use I interred her once more among the shifting dunes where (the wind-shapes were changing fast) there would be no trace remaining of the spot. At dawn I woke early and took a gharry down to the Rushdi beach to cleanse myself in the dawn-sea. There was not a soul about at that time save Clea, who was on the far beach in a blue bathing-costume, her marvellous hair swinging about her like a blonde Botticelli. I waved and she waved back, but showed no inclination to come and talk which made me grateful. We lay, a thousand yards apart, smoking and wet as seals. I thought for an instant of the lovely burnt coffee of her summer flesh, with the little hairs on her temples bleached to ash. I inhaled her metaphorically, like a whiff of roasting coffee, dreaming of the white thighs with those small blue veins in them! Well, well . . . she would have been worth taking trouble over had she not been so beautiful. That brilliant glance exposed everything and forced me to take shelter from her.

One could hardly ask her to bandage them in order to be made love to! And yet . . . like the black silk stockings some men insist on! Two sentences ending with a preposition! What is poor Pursewarden coming to?

His prose created grievous lusts
Among the middle classes

152

His propositions were decried
As dangerous for the masses

His major works were classified
Among the noxious gases
                    England awake!

Brother Ass, the so-called act of living is really an act of the imagination. The world—which we always visualise as "the outside" World—yields only to self-exploration! Faced by this cruel, yet necessary paradox, the poet finds himself growing gills and a tail, the better to swim against the currents of unenlightenment. What appears to be perhaps an arbitrary act of violence is precisely the opposite, for by reversing process in this way, he unites the rushing, heedless stream of humanity to the still, tranquil, motionless, odourless, tasteless plenum from which its own motive essence is derived. (Yes, but it *hurts* to realise!) If he were to abandon his rôle all hope of gaining a purchase on the slippery surface of reality would be lost, and everything in nature would disappear! But this act, the poetic act, will cease to be necessary when everyone can perform it for himself. What hinders them, you ask? Well, we are all naturally afraid to surrender our own pitifully rationalised morality —and the poetic jump I'm predicating lies the other side of it. It is only terrifying because we refuse to recognise in ourselves the horrible gargoyles which decorate the totem poles of our churches—murderers, liars, adulterers and so on. (Once recognised, these papier-mâché masks fade.) Whoever makes this enigmatic leap into the heraldic reality of the poetic life discovers that truth has its own built-in morality! There is no need to wear a truss any longer. Inside the penumbra of this sort of truth morality can be disregarded because it is a *donnée*, a part of the thing, and not simply a brake, an inhibition. It is there to be lived out and not thought out! Ah, Brother Ass, this will seem a far cry to the "purely literary" preoccupations which

153

beset you; yet unless you tackle this corner of the field with your sickle you will never reap the harvest in yourself, and so fulfil your true function here below.

But how? you ask me plaintively. And truly here you have me by the short hairs, for the thing operates differently with each one of us. I am only suggesting that you have not become desperate enough, determined enough. Somewhere at the heart of things you are still lazy of spirit. But then, why struggle? If it is to happen to you it will happen of its own accord. You may be quite right to hang about like this, waiting. I was too proud. I felt I must take it by the horns, this vital question of my birthright. For me it was grounded in an act of will. So for people like me I would say: "Force the lock, batter down the door. Outface, defy, disprove the Oracle in order to become the poet, the darer!"

But I am aware the test may come under any guise, perhaps even in the physical world by a blow between the eyes or a few lines scribbled in pencil on the back of an envelope left in a café. The heraldic reality can strike from any point, above or below: it is not particular. But without it the enigma will remain. You may travel round the world and colonise the ends of the earth with your lines and yet never hear the singing yourself.

o   o   o   o   o

III

I found myself reading these passages from Pursewarden's
notebooks with all the attention and amusement they
deserved, and without any thought of "exoneration"—
to use the phrase of Clea. On the contrary, it seemed to
me that his observation was not lacking in accuracy and whatever whips and scorpions he had applied to my image were well
justified. It is, moreover, useful as well as salutary to see oneself portrayed with such blistering candour by someone one
admires! Yet I was a trifle surprised not to feel even a little
wounded in my self-esteem. Not only were no bones broken,
but at times, chuckling aloud at his sallies, I found myself
addressing him under my breath as if he were actually present
before me, uttering rather than writing down these unpalatable
home-truths. "You bastard" I said under my breath. "You just
wait a little bit." Almost as if one day I might right the
reckoning with him, pay off the score! It was troubling to raise
my head and realise suddenly that he had already stepped
behind the curtains, vanished from the scene; he was so much
of a presence, popping up everywhere, with the strange mixture
of strengths and weaknesses which made up his enigmatic
character.

"What are you chuckling at?" said Telford, always anxious
to share a jocose exchange of office wit provided it had the
requisite moribund point.

"A notebook."

Telford was a large man draped in ill-cut clothes and a
spotted blue bow tie. His complexion was blotchy and of the
kind which tears easily under a razor-blade; consequently there
was always a small tuft of cotton wool sticking to chin or ear,
stanching a wound. Always voluble and bursting with the

155

wrong sort of expansive *bonhomie* he gave the impression of being at war with his dentures, which were ill-fitting. He gobbled and gasped, biting on loose stoppings, or swallowing a soft palate, gasping like a fish as he uttered his pleasantries or laughed at his own jokes like a man riding a bone-shaker, his top set of teeth bumping up and down on his gums. "I say, old fruit, that was rich" he would exclaim. I did not find him too disagreeable an inmate of the office which we shared at the censorship, for the work was not exacting and he, as an old hand, was always ready to give me advice or help with it; I enjoyed too his obstinately recurring stories of the mythical "old days", when he, Little Tommy Telford, had been a personage of great importance, second only in rank and power to the great Maskelyne, our present Chief. He always referred to him as "The Brig", and made it very clear that the department, which had once been Arab Bureau, had seen better times, had in fact been downgraded to a mere censorship department dealing with the ebb and flow of civilian correspondence over the Middle East. A menial rôle compared to "Espionage" which he pronounced in four separate syllables.

Stories of this ancient glory, which had now faded beyond recall, formed part of the Homeric Cycle, so to speak, of office life: to be recited wistfully during intervals between snatches of work or on afternoons when some small mishap like a broken fan had made concentration in those airless buildings all but impossible. It was from Telford that I learned of the long internecine struggle between Pursewarden and Maskelyne—a struggle which was, in a sense, continuing on another plane between the silent Brigadier and Mountolive, for Maskelyne was desperately anxious to rejoin his regiment and shed his civilian suit. This desire had been baulked. Mountolive, explained Telford with many a gusty sigh (waving chapped and podgy hands which were stuffed with bluish clusters of veins like plums in a cake)—Mountolive had "got at" the War Office and persuaded them not to countenance Maskelyne's resignation. I must say the Brigadier, whom I saw perhaps twice a week, did convey an impression of sullen, saturnine fury at being penned up in a civilian department while so much was going on in the desert, but of course any regular soldier would. "You see" said Telford ingenuously, "when a war comes along there's bags of promotion, old thing, bags of it. The Brig has a right to think of his career like any other man. It is different for us. We were born civilians, so to speak." He himself had spent many years in the currant trade in the Eastern Levant residing in places like Zante and Patras. His reasons for coming to Egypt were obscure. Perhaps he found life more congenial in a large British colony. Mrs. Telford was a fattish little duck who used mauve lipstick and wore hats like pincushions. She only appeared to live for an invitation to the Embassy on the King's birthday. ("Mavis loves her little official 'do', she does.")

But if the administrative war with Mountolive was so far empty of victory there were consolations, said Telford, from which the Brig could derive a studied enjoyment: for Mountolive was very much in the same boat. This made him (Telford) "chortle"—a characteristic phrase which he often used. Mountolive, it seemed, was no less eager to abandon his post, and had indeed applied several times for a transfer from Egypt. Unluckily, however, the war had intervened with its policy of "freezing personnel" and Kenilworth, no friend of the Ambassador, had been sent out to execute this policy. If the Brigadier was pinned down by the intrigues of Mountolive, the latter had been pinned down just as certainly by the newly appointed Personnel Adviser—pinned down "for the duration"! Telford rubbed unctuous hands as he retailed all this to me! "It's a case of the biter bit all right" he said. "And if you ask me the Brig will manage to get away sooner than Sir David. Mark my words, old fruit." A single solemn nod was enough to satisfy him that his point had been taken.

Telford and Maskelyne were united by a curious sort of bond which intrigued me. The solitary monosyllabic soldier and the effusive bagman—what on earth could they have had in common? (Their very names on the printed duty rosters irresistibly suggested a music-hall team or a firm of respectable undertakers!) Yet I think the bond was one of admiration, for Telford behaved with a grotesque wonder and respect when in the presence of his Chief, fussing around him anxiously, eagerly, longing to anticipate his commands and so earn a word of commendation. His heavily salivated "Yes, sir" and "No, sir" popped out from between his dentures with the senseless regularity of cuckoos from a clock. Curiously enough there was nothing feigned in this sycophancy. It was in fact something like an administrative love-affair, for even when Maskelyne was not present Telford spoke of him with the greatest possible reverence, the profoundest hero-worship—compounded equally of social admiration for his rank and deep respect for his character and judgement. Out of curiosity I tried to see Maskelyne through my colleague's eyes but failed to discern more than a rather bleak and well-bred soldier of narrow capacities and a clipped world-weary public school accent. Yet . . . "The Brig is a real cast-iron gentleman" Telford would say with an emotion so great that it almost brought tears to his eyes. "He's as straight as string, is the old Brig. Never stoop to do anything beneath him." It was perhaps true, yet it did not make our Chief less unremarkable in my eyes.

Telford had several little menial duties which he himself had elected to perform for his hero—for example, to buy the week-old *Daily Telegraph* and place it on the great man's desk each morning. He adopted a curious finicky walk as he crossed the polished floor of Maskelyne's empty office (for we arrived early at work): almost as if he were afraid of leaving footprints behind him. He positively stole across to the desk. And the tenderness with which he folded the paper and ran his fingers down the creases before laying it reverently on the green blotter reminded me of a woman handling a husband's newly starched and ironed shirt.

Nor was the Brigadier himself unwilling to accept the burden of this guileless admiration. I imagine few men could resist it. At first I was puzzled by the fact that once or twice a week he would visit us, clearly with no special matter in mind, and would take a slow turn up and down between our desks, occasionally uttering an informal monochrome pleasantry—indicating the recipient of it by pointing the stem of his pipe at him lightly, almost shyly. Yet throughout these visitations his swarthy greyhound's face, with its small crowsfeet under the eyes, never altered its expression, his voice never lost its studied inflections. At first, as I say, these appearances somewhat puzzled me, for Maskelyne was anything but a convivial soul and could seldom talk of anything but the work in hand. Then one day I detected, in the slow elaborate figure he traced between our desks, the traces of an unconscious coquetry—I was reminded of the way a peacock spreads its great studded fan of eyes before the female, or of the way a mannequin wheels in an arabesque designed to show off the clothes she is wearing. Maskelyne had in fact simply come to be admired, to spread out the riches of his character and breeding before Telford. Was it possible that this easy conquest provided him with some inner assurance he lacked? It would be hard to say. Yet he was inwardly basking in his colleague's wide-eyed admiration. I am sure it was quite unconscious—this gesture of a lonely man towards the only whole-hearted admirer he had as yet won from the world. From his own side, however, he could only reciprocate with the condescension bred by his education. Secretly he held Telford in contempt for not being a gentleman. "Poor Telford" he would be heard to sigh when out of the other's hearing. "Poor Telford". The commiserating fall of the voice suggested pity for someone who was worthy but hopelessly uninspired.

These, then, were my office familiars during the whole of that first wearing summer, and their companionship offered me no problem. The work left me easy and untroubled in mind.

My ranking was a humble one and carried with it no social obligations whatsoever. For the rest we did not frequent each other outside the office. Telford lived somewhere near Rushdi in a small suburban villa, outside the centre of the town, while Maskelyne seldom appeared to stir from the gaunt bedroom on the top floor of the Cecil. Once free from the office, therefore, I felt able to throw it off completely and once more resume the life of the town, or what was left of it.

With Clea also the new relationship offered no problems, perhaps because deliberately we avoided defining it too sharply, and allowed it to follow the curves of its own nature, to fulfil its own design. I did not, for example, always stay at her flat—for sometimes when she was working on a picture she would plead for a few days of complete solitude and seclusion in order to come to grips with her subject, and these intermittent intervals, sometimes of a week or more, sharpened and refreshed affection without harming it. Sometimes, however, after such a compact we would stumble upon each other by accident and out of weakness resume the suspended relationship before the promised three days or a week was up! It wasn't easy.

Sometimes at evening I might come upon her sitting absently alone on the little painted wooden terrace of the Café Baudrot, gazing into space. Her sketching blocks lay before her, unopened. Sitting there as still as a coney, she had forgotten to remove from her lips the tiny moustache of cream from her *café viennois!* At such a moment it needed all my self-possession not to vault the wooden balustrade and put my arms round her, so vividly did this touching detail seem to light up the memory of her; so childish and serene did she look. The loyal and ardent image of Clea the lover rose up before my eyes and all at once separation seemed unendurable! Conversely I might suddenly (sitting on a bench in a public garden, reading) feel cool hands pressed over my eyes and turn suddenly to embrace her and inhale once more the fragrance of her body through her crisp summer frock. At other times, and very often at moments when

160

I was actually thinking of her, she would walk miraculously into the flat saying: "I felt you calling me to come" or else "It suddenly came over me to need you very much." So these encounters had a breathless sharp sweetness, unexpectedly reigniting our ardour. It was as if we had been separated for years instead of days.

This self-possession in the matter of planned absences from each other struck a spark of admiration from Pombal, who could no more achieve the same measure in his relations with Fosca than climb to the moon. He appeared to wake in the morning with her name on his lips. His first act was to telephone her anxiously to find out if she were well—as if her absence had exposed her to terrible unknown dangers. His official day with its various duties was a torment. He positively galloped home to lunch in order to see her again. In all justice I must say that his attachment was fully reciprocated for all that their relationship was like that of two elderly retired pensioners in its purity. If he were kept late at an official dinner she would work herself into a fever of apprehension. ("No, it is not his fidelity that worries me, it is his safety. He drives so carelessly, as you know.") Fortunately during this period the nightly bombardment of the harbour acted upon social activities almost like a curfew, so that it was possible to spend almost every evening together, playing chess or cards, or reading aloud. Fosca I found to be a thoughtful, almost intense young woman, a little lacking in humour but devoid of the priggishness which I had been inclined to suspect from Pombal's own description of her when first we met. She had a keen and mobile face whose premature wrinkles suggested that perhaps she had been marked by her experiences as a refugee. She never laughed aloud, and her smile had a touch of reflective sadness in it. But she was wise, and always had a spirited and thoughtful answer ready—indeed the quality of *esprit* which the French so rightly prize in a woman. The fact that she was nearing the term of her pregnancy only seemed to make Pombal more attentive and

161

adoring—indeed he behaved with something like complacence about the child. Or was he simply trying to suggest that it was his own: as a show of face to a world which might think that he was "unmanned"? I could not decide. In the summer afternoons he would float about the harbour in his cutter while Fosca sat in the stern trailing one white hand in the sea. Sometimes she sang for him in a small true voice like a bird's. This transported him, and he wore the look of a good *bourgeois papa de famille* as he beat time with his finger. At night they sat out the bombardment for preference over a chess board—a somewhat singular choice; but as the infernal racket of gunfire gave him nervous headaches he had skilfully constructed ear plugs for them both by cutting the filter-tips from cigarettes. So they were able to sit, concentrating in silence!

But once or twice this peaceful harmony was overshadowed by outside events which provoked doubts and misgivings understandable enough in a relationship which was so nebulous—I mean so much *discussed* and anatomised and not acted out. One day I found him padding about in a dressing-gown and slippers looking suspiciously distraught, even a little red-eyed. "Ah, Darley!" he sighed gustily, falling into his gout chair and catching his beard in his fingers as if he were about to dismantle it completely. "We will never understand them, never. Women! What bad luck. Perhaps I am just stupid. Fosca! Her husband!"

"He has been killed?" I asked.

Pombal shook his head sadly. "No. Taken prisoner and sent to Germany."

"Well why the fuss?"

"I am ashamed, that is all. I did not fully realise until this news came, neither did she, that we were really *expecting* him to be killed. Unconsciously, of course. Now she is full of self disgust. But the whole plan for *our* lives was unconsciously built upon the notion of him surrendering his own. It is monstrous. His death would have freed us; but now the whole problem is deferred perhaps for years, perhaps forever. . . ."

He looked quite distracted and fanned himself with a newspaper, muttering under his breath. "Things take the strangest turns" he went on at last. "For if Fosca is too honourable to confess the truth to him while he is at the front, she would equally never do it to a poor prisoner. I left her in tears. Everything is put off till the *end of the war*."

He ground his back teeth together and sat staring at me. It was difficult to know what one could say by way of consolation.

"Why doesn't she write and tell him?"

"Impossible! Too cruel. And with the child coming on? Even I, Pombal, would not wish her to do such a thing. Never. I found her in *tears*, my friend, holding the telegram. She said in tones of anguish: 'O Georges-Gaston for the first time I feel ashamed of my love, when I realise that we were wishing him to die rather than get captured this way.' It may sound complicated to you, but her emotions are so fine, her sense of honour and pride and so on. Then a queer thing happened. So great was our mutual pain that in trying to console her I slipped and we began to make real love without noticing it. It is a strange picture. And not an easy operation. Then when we came to ourselves she began to cry all over again and said: 'Now for the first time I have a feeling of hate for you, Georges-Gaston, because now our love is on the same plane as everyone else's. We have cheapened it.' Women always put you in the wrong somehow. I was so full of joy to have at last. . . . Suddenly her words plunged me into despair. I rushed away. I have not seen her for *five hours*. Perhaps this is the end of everything? Ah but it could have been the beginning of something which would at least sustain us until the whole problem sees the light of day."

"Perhaps she is too stupid."

Pombal was aghast. "How can you say that! All this comes from her exquisite finesse of spirit. That is all. Don't add to my misery by saying foolish things about one so fine."

"Well, telephone her."

"Her phone is out of order. Aie! It is worse than toothache.

I have been toying with the idea of suicide for the first time in my life. That will show you to what a point I've been driven."

But at this moment the door opened and Fosca stepped into the room. She too had been crying. She stopped with a queer dignity and held out her hands to Pombal who gave an inarticulate growling cry of delight and bounded across the room in his dressing-gown to embrace her passionately. Then he drew her into the circle of his arm and they went slowly down the corridor to his room together and locked themselves in.

Later that evening I saw him coming down Rue Fuad towards me, beaming. "Hurrah!" he shouted and threw his expensive hat high into the air. "*Je suis enfin là*"!

The hat described a large parabola and settled in the middle of the road where it was immediately run over by three cars in rapid succession. Pombal clasped his hands together and beamed as if the sight gave him the greatest joy. Then he turned his moon-face up into the sky as if searching for a sign or portent. As I came abreast of him he caught my hands and said: "Divine logic of women! Truly there is nothing so wonderful on earth as the sight of a woman thinking out her feelings. I adore it. I adore it. Our love. . . . Fosca! It is complete now. I am so astonished, truthfully, I am *astonished*. I would never have been able to think it out so accurately. Listen, she could not bring herself to deceive a man who was in hourly danger of death. Right. But now that he is safely behind bars it is different. We are free to normalise ourselves. We will not, of course, hurt him by telling him as yet. We will simply help ourselves from the pantry, as Pursewarden used to say. My dear friend, isn't it wonderful? Fosca is an angel."

"She sounds like a woman after all."

"A Woman! The word, magnificent as it is, is hardly enough for a spirit like hers."

He burst into a whinny of laughter and punched me affectionately on the shoulder. Together we walked down the long street. "I am going to Pierantoni to buy her an expensive present . . . I, who never give a woman presents, never in my life. It always seemed absurd. I once saw a film of penguins in the mating season. The male penguin, than which nothing could more ludicrously resemble man, collects stones and places them before the lady of his choice when he proposes. It must be seen to be appreciated. Now I am behaving like a male penguin. Never mind. Never mind. Now our story cannot help but have a happy ending."

Fateful words which I have so often recalled since, for within a few months Fosca was to be a problem no more.

o   o   o   o   o

IV

For some considerable time I heard nothing of Purse-warden's sister, though I knew that she was still up at the summer legation. As for Mountolive, his visits were recorded among the office memoranda, so that I knew he came up from Cairo for the night about every ten days. For a while I half expected a signal from him, but as time wore on I almost began to forget his existence as presumably he had forgotten mine. So it was that her voice, when first it floated over the office telephone, came as an unexpected intrusion—a surprise in a world where surprises were few and not unwelcome. A curiously disembodied voice which might have been that of uncertain adolescence, saying: "I think you know of me. As a friend of my brother I would like to talk to you." The invitation to dinner the following evening she described as "private, informal and unofficial" which suggested to me that Mountolive himself would be present. I felt the stirring of an unusual curiosity as I walked up the long drive with its very English hedges of box, and through the small coppice of pines which encircled the summer residence. It was an airless hot night—such as must presage the gathering of a *khamseen* somewhere in the desert which would later roll its dust clouds down the city's streets and squares like pillars of smoke. But as yet the night air was harsh and clear.

I rang the bell twice without result, and was beginning to think that perhaps it might be out of order when I heard a soft swift step inside. The door opened and there stood Liza with an expression of triumphant eagerness on her blind face. I found her extraordinarily beautiful at first sight, though a little on the short side. She wore a dress of some dark soft stuff with a collar cut very wide, out of which her slender throat and head rose as if out of the corolla of a flower. She stood before me with her face thrown upwards, forwards—with an air of spectral bravery —as if presenting her lovely neck to an invisible executioner. As I uttered my own name she smiled and nodded and repeated it back to me in a whisper tense as a thread. "Thank goodness, at last you have come" she said, as though she had lived in the expectation of my visit for years! As I stepped forward she added quickly "Please forgive me if I. . . . It is my only way of knowing." And I suddenly felt her soft warm fingers on my face, moving swiftly over it as if spelling it out, I felt a stirring of some singular unease, composed of sensuality and disgust, as these expert fingers travelled over my cheeks and lips. Her hands were small and well-shaped; the fingers conveyed an extraordinary impression of delicacy, for they appeared to turn up slightly at the ends to present their white pads, like antennae, to the world. I had once seen a world-famous pianist with just such fingers, so sensitive that they appeared to grow into the keyboard as he touched it. She gave a small sigh, as if of relief, and taking me by the wrist drew me across the hall and into the living-room with its expensive and featureless official furniture where Mountolive stood in front of the fireplace with an air of uneasy concern. Somewhere a radio softly played. We shook hands and in his handclasp I felt something infirm, indecisive which was matched by the fugitive voice in which he excused his long silence. "I had to wait until Liza was ready" he said, rather mysteriously.

Mountolive had changed a good deal, though he still bore all the marks of the superficial elegance which was a prerequisite for his work, and his clothes were fastidiously chosen—for even (I thought grimly) informal undress is still a uniform for a diplomat. His old kindness and attentiveness were still there. Yet he had aged. I noticed that he now needed reading-glasses, for they lay upon a copy of *The Times* beside the sofa. And he had grown a moustache which he did not trim and which had altered the shape of his mouth, and emphasised a certain finely bred feebleness of feature. It did not seem possible to imagine him ever to have been in the grip of a passion strong enough to qualify the standard responses of an education so definitive as his. Nor now, looking from one to the other, could I credit the suspicions which Clea had voiced about his love for this strange blind witch who now sat upon the sofa staring sightlessly at me, with her hands folded in her lap—those rapacious, avaricious hands of a musician. Had she coiled herself, like a small hateful snake, at the centre of his peaceful life? I accepted a drink from his fingers and found, in the warmth of his smile, that I remembered having liked and admired him. I did so still.

"We have both been eager to see you, and particularly Liza, because she felt that you might be able to help her. But we will talk about all that later." And with an abrupt smoothness he turned away from the real subject of my visit to enquire whether my post pleased me, and whether I was happy in it. An exchange of courteous pleasantries which provoked the neutral answers appropriate to them. Yet here and there were gleams of new information. "Liza was quite determined you should stay here; and so we got busy to arrange it!" Why? Simply that I should submit to a catechism about her brother, who in truth I could hardly claim to have known, and who grew more and more mysterious to me every day—less important as a personage, more and more so as an artist? It was clear that I must wait until she chose to speak her mind. Yet it was baffling to idle away the time in the exchange of superficialities.

Yet these smooth informalities reigned, and to my surprise the girl herself said nothing—not a word. She sat there on the sofa, softly and attentively, as if on a cloud. She wore, I noticed, a velvet ribbon on her throat. It occurred to me that her pallor, which had so much struck Clea, was probably due to not being able to make-up in the mirror. But Clea had been right about the shape of her mouth, for once or twice I caught an expression, cutting and sardonic, which was a replica of her brother's.

Dinner was wheeled in by a servant, and still exchanging small talk we sat down to eat it; Liza ate swiftly, as if she were hungry, and quite unerringly, from the plate which Mountolive filled for her. I noticed when she reached for her wineglass that her expressive fingers trembled slightly. At last, when the meal was over, Mountolive rose with an air of scarcely disguised relief and excused himself. "I'm going to leave you alone to talk shop to Liza. I shall have to do some work in the Chancery this evening. You will excuse me won't you?" I saw an apprehensive frown shadow Liza's face for a moment, but it vanished almost at once and was replaced by an expression which suggested something between despair and resignation. Her fingers picked softly, suggestively at the tassel of a cushion. When the door had closed behind him she still sat silent, but now preternaturally still, her head bent downwards as if she were trying to decipher a message written in the palm of her hand. At last she spoke in a small cold voice, pronouncing the words incisively as if to make her meaning plain.

"I had no idea it would be difficult to explain when first I thought of asking your help. This book. . . ."

There was a long silence. I saw that little drops of perspiration had come out on her upper lip and her temples looked as if they had tightened under stress. I felt a certain compassion for her distress and said: "I can't claim to have known him well, though I saw him quite frequently. In truth, I don't think we liked each other very much."

"Originally" she said sharply, cutting across my vagueness with impatience "I thought I might persuade you to do the book about him. But now I see that you will have to know everything. It is not easy to know where to begin. I myself doubt whether the facts of his life are possible to put down and publish. But I have been driven to think about the matter, first because his publishers insist on it—they say there is a great public demand; but mostly because of the book which this shabby journalist is writing, or has written. Keats."

"Keats" I echoed with surprise.

"He is here somewhere I believe; but I do not know him. He has been put up to the idea by my brother's wife. She hated him, you know, after she found out; she thought that my brother and I had between us ruined her life. Truthfully I am afraid of her. I do not know what she has told Keats, or what he will write. I see now that my original idea in having you brought here was to get you to write a book which would . . . disguise the truth somehow. It only became clear to me just now when I was confronted by you. It would be inexpressibly painful to me if anything got out which harmed my brother's memory."

Somewhere to the east I heard a grumble of thunder. She stood up with an air of panic and after a moment's hesitation crossed to the grand piano and struck a chord. Then she banged the cover down and turned once more to me, saying: "I am afraid of thunder. Please may I hold your hand in a firm grip." Her own was deathly cold. Then, shaking back her black hair she said: "We were lovers, you know. That is really the meaning of his story and mine. He tried to break away. His marriage foundered on this question. It was perhaps dishonest of him not to have told her the truth before he married her. Things fall out strangely. For many years we enjoyed a perfect happiness, he and I. That it ended tragically is nobody's fault I suppose. He could not free himself from my inside hold on him, though he tried and struggled. I could not free myself from him, though truthfully I never wished to until . . . until the day arrived which he had predicted so many years before when the man he always called 'the dark stranger' arrived. He saw him so clearly when he gazed into the fire. It was David Mountolive. For a little while I did not tell him that I had fallen in love, the fated love. (David would not let me. The only person we told was Nessim's mother. David asked my permission.) But my brother knew it quite unerringly and wrote after a long silence asking me if the stranger had come. When he got my letter he

170

seemed suddenly to realise that our relationship might be endangered or crushed in the way his had been with his wife—not by anything we did, no, but by the simple fact of my existence. So he committed suicide. He explained it all so clearly in his last letter to me. I can recite it by heart. He said: 'For so many years I have waited in anguished expectation for your letter. Often, often I wrote it for you in my own head, spelling it out word by magical word. I knew that in your happiness you would at once turn to me to express a passionate gratitude for what I had given you—for learning the meaning of all love through mine: so that when the stranger came you were ready. . . . And today it came! this long-awaited message, saying that he had read the letters, and I knew for the first time a sense of inexpressible relief as I read the lines. And joy—such joy as I never hoped to experience in my life—to think of you suddenly plunging into the full richness of life at last, no longer tied, manacled to the image of your tormented brother! Blessings tumbled from my lips. But then, gradually, as the cloud lifted and dispersed I felt the leaden tug of another truth, quite unforeseen, quite unexpected. The fear that, so long as I was still alive, still somewhere existing in the world, you would find it impossible truly to escape from the chains in which I have so cruelly held you all these years. At this fear my blood has turned chill—for I know that truthfully something much more definitive is required of me if you are ever to renounce me and start living. I must really abandon you, really remove myself from the scene in a manner which would permit no further equivocation in our vacillating hearts. Yes, I had anticipated the joy, but not that it would bring with it such a clear representation of certain death. This was a huge novelty! Yet it is the completest gift I can offer you as a wedding present! And if you look beyond the immediate pain you will see how perfect the logic of love seems to one who is ready to die for it.' "

She gave a short clear sob and hung her head. She took the handkerchief from the breast pocket of my coat and pressed it

171

to her trembling lip. I felt stupefied by the sad weight of all this calamitous information. I felt, in the ache of pity for Pursewarden, a new recognition of him growing up, a new enlightenment. So many things became clearer. Yet there were no words of consolation or commiseration which could do justice to so tragic a situation. She was talking again.

"I will give you the private letters to read so that you can advise me. These are the letters which I was not to open but was to keep until David came. He would read them to me and we would destroy them—or so he said. Is it strange—his certainty? The other ordinary letters were of course read to me in the usual way; but these private letters, and they are very many, were all pierced with a pin in the top left-hand corner. So that I could recognise them and put them aside. They are in that suitcase over there. I would like you to take them away and study them. O Darley, you have not said a word. Are you prepared to help me in this dreadful predicament? I wish I could read your expression."

"Of course I will help you. But just how and in what sense?"

"Advise me what to do! None of this would have arisen had not this shabby journalist intervened and been to see his wife."

"Did your brother appoint a literary executor?"

"Yes. I am his executor."

"Then you have a right to refuse to allow any of his unsold writings to be published while they're in copyright. Besides, I do not see how such facts could be made public without your own permission, even in an unauthorised biography. There is no cause whatsoever to worry. No writer in his senses could touch such material; no publisher in the world would undertake to print it if he did. I think the best thing I can do is to try and find out something about this book of Keats's. Then at least you will know where you stand."

"Thank you, Darley. I could not approach Keats myself because I knew he was working for her. I hate and fear her—perhaps unjustly. I suppose too that I have a feeling of having

172

wronged her without wishing it. It was a deplorable mistake on
his part not to tell her before their marriage; I think he recognised it, too, for he was determined that I should not make the
same mistake when at last David appeared. Hence the private
letters, which leave no one in doubt. Yet it all fell out exactly
as he had planned it, had prophesied it. That very first night
when I told David I took him straight home to read them. We
sat on the carpet in front of the gas-fire and he read them to me
one by one in that unmistakable voice—the stranger's voice.''

She gave a queer blind smile at the memory and I had a
sudden compassionate picture of Mountolive sitting before the
fire, reading these letters in a slow faltering voice, stunned by
the revelation of his own part in this weird masque, which had
been planned for him years before, without his knowing. Liza
sat beside me, lost in deep thought, her head hanging. Her lips
moved slowly as if she were spelling something out in her own
mind, following some interior recitation. I shook her hand
softly, as if to awaken her. "I should leave you now" I said
softly. "And why should I see the private letters at all? There is
no need."

"Now that you know the worst and best I would like you to
advise me about destroying them. It was his wish. But David
feels that they belong to his writings, and that we have a duty
to preserve them. I cannot make up my mind about this. You
are a writer. Try and read them as a writer, as if you had written
them, and then tell me whether you would wish them preserved
or not. They are all together in that suitcase. There are one or
two other fragments which you might help me edit if you have
time or if you think them suitable. He always puzzled me—
except when I had him in my arms.''

A sudden expression of savage resentment passed across her
white face. As if she had been goaded by a sudden disagreeable
memory. She passed her tongue over her dry lips and as we
stood up together she added in a small husky voice: "There is
one thing more. Since you have seen so far into out lives why

should you not look right to the bottom? I always keep this close to me." Reaching down into her dress she took out a snapshot and handed it to me. It was faded and creased. A small child with long hair done up in ribbons sat upon a park bench, gazing with a melancholy and wistful smile at the camera and holding out a white stick. It took me a moment or so to identify those troubling lines of mouth and nose as the features of Pursewarden himself and to realise that the little girl was blind.

"Do you see her?" said Liza in a thrilling whisper that shook the nerves by its strange tension, its mixture of savagery, bitterness and triumphant anguish. "Do you see her? She was our child. It was when she died that he was overcome with remorse for a situation which had brought us nothing but joy before. Her death suddenly made him guilty. Our relationship foundered there; and yet it became in another way even more intense, closer. We were united by our guilt from that moment. I have often asked myself why it should be so. Tremendous unbroken happiness and then . . . one day, like an iron shutter falling, *guilt.*"

The word dropped like a falling star and expired in the silence. I took this unhappiest of all relics and pressed it into her cold hands.

"I will take the letters" I said.

"Thank you" she replied with an air now of dazed exhaustion. "I knew we had a friend in you. I shall count on your help."

As I softly closed the front-door behind me I heard a chord struck upon the piano—a single chord which hung in the silent air, its vibrations diminishing like an echo. As I crossed among the trees I caught a glimpse of Mountolive sneaking towards the side door of the house. I suddenly divined that he had been walking up and down outside the house in an agony of apprehension, with the air of a schoolboy waiting outside his housemaster's study to receive a beating. I felt a pang of sympathy for him, for his weakness, for the dreadful entanglement in which he had found himself.

I found to my surprise that it was still early. Clea had gone to Cairo for the day and was not expected back. I took the little suitcase to her flat and sitting on the floor unpacked it.

In that quiet room, by the light of her candles, I began to read the private letters with a curious interior premonition, a stirring of something like fear—so dreadful a thing is it to explore the inmost secrets of another human being's life. Nor did this feeling diminish as I proceeded, rather it deepened into a sort of terror, almost a horror of what might be coming next. The letters! Ferocious, sulky, brilliant, profuse—the torrent of words in that close hand flowed on and on endlessly, studded with diamond-hard images, a wild self-analytical frenzy of despair, remorse and passion. I began to tremble as one must in the presence of a great master, to tremble and mutter. With an interior shock I realised that there was nothing in the whole length and breadth of our literature with which to compare them! Whatever other masterpieces Pursewarden may have written these letters outshone them all in their furious, unpremeditated brilliance and prolixity. Literature, I say! But these were life itself, not a studied representation of it in a form —life itself, the flowing undivided stream of life with all its pitiable will-intoxicated memories, its pains, terrors and submissions. Here illusion and reality were fused in one single blinding vision of a perfect incorruptible passion which hung over the writer's mind like a dark star—the star of death! The tremendous sorrow and beauty which this man expressed so easily—the terrifying abundance of his gifts—filled me with helpless despair and joy at once. The cruelty and the richness! It was as if the words poured from every pore in his body— execrations, groans, mixed tears of joy and despair—all welded to the fierce rapid musical notation of a language perfected by its purpose. Here at last the lovers confronted one another, stripped to the bone, stripped bare.

175

In this strange and frightening experience I caught a glimpse, for a moment, of the true Pursewarden—the man who had always eluded me. I thought with shame of the shabby passages in the Justine manuscript which I had devoted to him—to my image of him! I had, out of envy or unconscious jealousy, invented a Pursewarden to criticise. In everything I had written there I had accused him only of my own weaknesses—even down to completely erroneous estimates of qualities like social inferiorities which were mine, had never been his. It was only now, tracing out the lines written by that rapid unfaltering pen, that I realised that poetic or transcendental knowledge somehow cancels out purely relative knowledge, and that his black humours were simply ironies due to this enigmatic knowledge whose field of operation was above, beyond that of the relative fact-finding sort. There *was* no answer to the questions I had raised in very truth. He had been quite right. Blind as a mole, I had been digging about in the graveyard of relative fact piling up data, more information, and completely missing the mythopoeic reference which underlies fact. I had called this searching for truth! Nor was there any way in which I might be instructed in the matter—save by the ironies I had found so wounding. For now I realised that his irony was really tenderness turned inside out like a glove! And seeing Pursewarden thus, for the first time, I saw that through his work he had been seeking for the very tenderness of logic itself, of the Way Things Are; not the logic of syllogism or the tide-marks of emotions, but the real essence of fact-finding, the *naked* truth, the *Inkling* . . . the whole pointless Joke. Yes, Joke! I woke up with a start and swore.

If two or more explanations of a single human action are as good as each other then what does action mean but an illusion —a gesture made against the misty backcloth of a reality made palpable by the delusive nature of human division merely? Had any novelist before Pursewarden considered this question? I think not.

And in brooding over these terrible letters I also suddenly stumbled upon the true meaning of my own relationship to Pursewarden, and through him to all writers. I saw, in fact, that we artists form one of those pathetic human chains which human beings form to pass buckets of water up to a fire, or to bring in a lifeboat. An uninterrupted chain of humans born to explore the inward riches of the solitary life on behalf of the unheeding unforgiving community; manacled together by the same gift.

I began to see too that the real "fiction" lay neither in Arnauti's pages nor Pursewarden's—nor even my own. It was life itself that was a fiction—we were all saying it in our different ways, each understanding it according to his nature and gift.

It was now only that I began to see how mysteriously the configuration of my own life had taken its shape from the properties of those elements which lie outside the relative life—in the kingdom which Pursewarden calls the "heraldic universe". We were three writers, I now saw, confided to a mythical city from which we were to draw our nourishment, in which we were to confirm our gifts. Arnauti, Pursewarden, Darley—like Past, Present and Future tense! And in my own life (the staunchless stream flowing from the wounded side of Time!) the three women who also arranged themselves as if to represent the moods of the great verb, Love: Melissa, Justine and Clea.

And realising this I was suddenly afflicted by a great melancholy and despair at recognising the completely limited nature of my own powers, hedged about as they were by the limitations of an intelligence too powerful for itself, and lacking in sheer word-magic, in propulsion, in passion, to achieve this other world of artistic fulfilment.

I had just locked those unbearable letters away and was sitting in melancholy realisation of this fact when the door opened and Clea walked in, radiant and smiling. "Why, Darley, what are you doing sitting in the middle of the floor in that rueful attitude? And my dear there are tears in your eyes." At once she was down beside me on her knees, all tenderness.

"Tears of exasperation" I said, and then, embracing her, "I have just realised that I am not an artist at all. There is not a shred of hope of my ever being one."

"What on earth have you been up to?"

"Reading Pursewarden's letters to Liza."

"Did you see her?"

"Yes. Keats is writing some absurd book——"

"But I just ran into him. He's back from the desert for the night."

I struggled to my feet. It seemed to me imperative that I should find him and discover what I could about his project. "He spoke" said Clea "about going round to Pombal's for a bath. I expect you'll find him there if you hurry."

Keats! I thought to myself as I hurried down the street towards the flat; he was also to play his part in this shadowy representation, this tableau of the artist's life. For it is always a Keats that is chosen to interpret, to drag his trail of slime over the pitiful muddled life out of which the artist, with such pain, recaptures these strange solitary jewels of self-enlightenment. After those letters it seemed to me more than ever necessary that people like Keats should if possible be kept away from interfering in matters beyond their normal concerns. As a journalist with a romantic story (suicide is the most romantic act for an artist) he doubtless felt himself to be in the presence of what he, in the old days, would have called "A stunner. A Story in a Million". I thought that I knew my Keats—but of course once more I had completely forgotten to take into account the operations of Time, for Keats had changed as we all had, and my meeting with him turned out to be as unexpected as everything else about the city.

I had mislaid my key and had to ring for Hamid to open the door for me. Yes, he said, Mr. Keats was there, in the bath. I traversed the corridor and tapped at the door behind which came the sound of rushing water and a cheerful whistling. "By God, Darley, how splendid" he shouted in answer to my call. "Come in while I dry. I heard you were back."

Under the shower stood a Greek god! I was so surprised at the transformation that I sat down abruptly on the lavatory and studied this . . . apparition. Keats was burnt almost black, and his hair had bleached white. Though slimmer, he looked in first-class physical condition. The brown skin and ashen hair had made his twinkling eyes bluer than ever. He bore absolutely *no resemblance* to my memories of him! "I just sneaked off for the night" he said, speaking in a new rapid and confident voice. "I'm developing one of those blasted desert sores on my elbow, so I got a chit and here I am. I don't know what the hell causes them, nobody does; perhaps all the tinned muck we eat up there in the desert! But two days in Alex and an injection and presto! The bloody thing clears up again! I say, Darley, what fun to meet again. There's so much to tell you. This war!" He was bubbling over with high spirits. "God, this water is a treat. I've been revelling."

"You look in tremendous shape."

"I am. I am." He smacked himself exuberantly on the buttocks. "Golly though, it is good to come into Alex. Contrasts make you appreciate things so much better. Those tanks get so hot you feel like frying whitebait. Reach my drink, there's a good chap." On the floor stood a tall glass of whisky and soda with an ice cube in it. He shook the glass, holding it to his ear like a child. "Listen to the ice tinkling" he cried in ecstasy. "Music to the soul, the tinkle of ice." He raised his glass, wrinkled up his nose at me and drank my health. "You look in quite good shape, too" he said, and his blue eyes twinkled with a new mischievous light. "Now for some clothes and then . . . my dear chap, I'm rich. I'll give you a slap-up dinner at the Petit Coin. No refusals, I'll not be baulked. I particularly wanted to see you and talk to you. I have news."

He positively skipped into the bedroom to dress and I sat

on Pombal's bed to keep him company while he did so. His high spirits were quite infectious. He seemed hardly able to keep still. A thousand thoughts and ideas bubbled up inside him which he wanted to express simultaneously. He capered down the stairs into the street like a schoolboy, taking the last flight at a single bound. I thought he would break into a dance along Rue Fuad. "But seriously" he said, squeezing my elbow so hard that it hurt. "*Seriously*, life is wonderful" and as if to illustrate his seriousness he burst into ringing laughter. "When I think how we used to brood and worry." Apparently he included me in this new euphoric outlook on life. "How slowly we took everything, I feel ashamed to remember it!"

At the Petit Coin we secured a corner table after an amiable altercation with a naval lieutenant, and he at once took hold of Menotti and commanded champagne to be brought. Where the devil had he got this new laughing authoritative manner which instantly commanded sympathetic respect without giving offence?

"The desert!" he said, as if in answer to my unspoken question. "The desert, Darley, old boy. That is something to be seen." From a capacious pocket he produced a copy of the *Pickwick Papers*. "Damn!" he said. "I mustn't forget to get this copy replaced. Or the crew will bloody well fry me." It was a sodden, dog-eared little book with a bullet hole in the cover, smeared with oil. "It's our only library, and some bastard must have wiped himself on the middle third. I've sworn to replace it. Actually there's a copy at the flat. I don't suppose Pombal would mind my pinching it. It's absurd. When there isn't any action we lie about reading it aloud to one another, under the stars! Absurd, my dear chap, but then everything is more absurd. More and more absurd every day."

"You sound so happy" I said, not without a certain envy.

"Yes" he said in a smaller voice, and suddenly, for the first time, became relatively serious. "I am. Darley, let me make you a confidence. Promise not to groan."

"I promise."

He leaned forward and said in a whisper, his eyes twinkling, "I've become a writer at last!" Then suddenly he gave his ringing laugh. "You promised not to groan" he said.

"I didn't groan."

"Well, you looked groany and supercilious. The proper response would have been to shout 'Hurrah!' "

"Don't shout so loud or they'll ask us to leave."

"Sorry. It came over me."

He drank a large bumper of champagne with the air of someone toasting himself and leaned back in his chair, gazing at me quizzically with the same mischievous sparkle in his blue eyes.

"What have you written?" I asked.

"Nothing" he said, smiling. "Not a word as yet. It's all up here." He pointed a brown finger at his temple. "But now at least I know it is. Somehow whether I do or don't actually write isn't important—it isn't, if you like, the whole point about becoming a writer at all, as I used to think."

In the street outside a barrel organ began playing with its sad hollow iteration. It was a very ancient English barrel organ which old blind Arif had found on a scrap heap and had fixed up in a somewhat approximate manner. Whole notes misfired and several chords were hopelessly out of tune.

"Listen" said Keats, with deep emotion, "just listen to old Arif." He was in that delicious state of inspiration which only comes when champagne supervenes upon a state of fatigue—a melancholy tipsiness which is wholly inspiriting. "Gosh!" he went on in rapture, and began to sing in a very soft husky whisper, marking time with his finger, '*Taisez-vous petit babouin*'. Then he gave a great sigh of repletion, and chose himself a cigar from Menotti's great case of specimens, sauntering back to the table where he once more sat before me, smiling rapturously. "This war" he said at last, "I really must tell you. . . . It is quite different to what I imagined it must be like."

181

Under his champagne-bedizened tipsiness he had become relatively grave all at once. He said: "Nobody seeing it for the first time could help crying out with the whole of his rational mind in protest at it: crying out 'It must stop!' My dear chap, to see the ethics of man *at his norm* you must see a battlefield. The general idea may be summed up in the expressive phrase: 'If you can't eat it or **** it, then **** on it.' Two thousand years of civilisation! It peels off in a flash. Scratch with your little finger and you reach the woad or the ritual war paint under the varnish! Just like that!" He scratched the air between us languidly with his expensive cigar. "And yet—you know what? The most unaccountable and baffling thing. It has made a man of me, as the saying goes. More, a writer! My soul is quite clear. I suppose you could regard me as permanently disfigured! I have begun it at last, that bloody joyful book of mine. Chapter by chapter it is forming in my old journalist's noddle—no, not a journalist's any more, a *writer's*." He laughed again as if at the preposterous notion. "Darley when I look around that . . . battlefield at night, I stand in an ecstasy of shame, revelling at the coloured lights, the flares wallpapering the sky, and I say: 'All this had to be brought about so that poor Johnny Keats could grow into a man.' That's what. It is a complete enigma to me, yet I am absolutely certain of it. No other way would have helped me because I was too damned *stupid*, do you see?" He was silent for a while and somewhat distrait, drawing on his cigar. It was as if he were going over this last piece of conversation in his mind to consider its validity, word by word, as one tests a piece of machinery. Then he added, but with care and caution, and a certain expression of bemused concentration, like a man handling unfamiliar terms: "The man of action and the man of reflection are really the same man, operating on two different fields. But to the same end! Wait, this is beginning to sound silly," He tapped his temple reproachfully and frowned. After a moment's thought he went on, still frowning: "Shall I tell you my notion about it . . . the war? What I have come to believe? I believe the desire for war was first lodged in the instincts as a biological shock-mechanism to precipitate a spiritual crisis which couldn't be done any other how in limited people. The less sensitive among us can hardly visualise death, far less live joyfully with it. So the powers that arranged things for us felt they must concretise it, in order to lodge death in the actual present. Purely helpfully, if you see what I mean!" He laughed again, but ruefully this time. "Of course it is rather different now that the bystander is getting hit harder than the front-line bloke. It is unfair to the men of the tribe who would like to leave the wife and kids in relative safety before stumping off to this primitive ordination. For my part I think the instinct has somewhat atrophied, and may be on the way out altogether; but what will they put in its place—that's what I wonder? As for me, Darley, I can only say that no half-dozen French mistresses, no travels round the globe, no adventures in the peace-time world we knew could have grown me up so thoroughly in half the time. You remember how I used to be? Look, I'm really an adult now—but of course ageing fast, altogether too fast! It will sound damn silly to you, but the presence of death out there as a normal feature of life—only in full acceleration so to speak—has given me an inkling of Life Everlasting! And there was no other way I could have grasped it, damn it. Ah! well, I'll probably get bumped off up there in full possession of my imbecility, as you might say."

He burst out laughing once more, and gave himself three noiseless cheers, raising his cigar-hand ceremoniously at each cheer. Then he winked carefully at me and filled his glass once more, adding with an air of vagueness the coda: "Life only has its full meaning to those who co-opt death!" I could see that he was rather drunk by now, for the soothing effects of the hot shower had worn off and the desert-fatigue had begun to reassert itself.

"And Pursewarden?" I said, divining the very moment at

which to drop his name, like a hook, into the stream of our conversation.

"Pursewarden!" he echoed on a different note, which combined a melancholy sadness and affection. "But my dear Darley, it was something like this that he was trying to tell me, in his own rather bloody way. And I? I still blush with shame when I think of the questions I asked him. And yet his answers, which seemed so bloody enigmatic then, make perfect sense to me *now*. Truth is double-bladed, you see. There is no way to express it in terms of language, this strange bifurcated medium with its basic duality! Language! What is the writer's struggle except a struggle to use a medium as precisely as possible, but knowing fully its basic imprecision? A hopeless task, but none the less rewarding for being hopeless. Because the task itself, the act of wrestling with an insoluble problem, grows the writer up! This was what the old bastard realised. You should read his letters to his wife. For all their brilliance how he whined and cringed, how despicably he presented himself—like some Dostoievskian character beset by some nasty compulsion neurosis! It is really staggering what a petty and trivial soul he reveals there." This was an amazing insight into the tormented yet wholly complete being of the letters which I myself had just read!

"Keats" I said, "for goodness' sake tell me. Are you writing a book about him?"

Keats drank slowly and thoughtfully and replaced his glass somewhat unsteadily before saying: "No." He stroked his chin and fell silent.

"They say you are writing something" I persisted. He shook his head obstinately and contemplated his glass with a blurred eye. "I wanted to" he admitted at last, slowly. "I did a long review of the novels once for a small mag. The next thing I got a letter from his wife. *She* wanted a book done. A big raw-boned Irish girl, very hysterical and sluttish: handsome in a big way, I suppose. Always blowing her nose in an old envelope.

Always in carpet slippers. I must say I felt for him. But I tumbled straight into a hornets' nest there. She *loathed* him, and there seemed to be plenty to loathe, I must say. She gave me a great deal of information, and simply masses of letters and manuscripts. Treasure trove all right. But, my dear chap, I couldn't use this sort of stuff. If for no other reason than that I respect his memory and his work. No. No. I fobbed her off. Told her she would never get such things published. She seemed to want to be publicly martyred in print just to get back at him—old Pursewarden! I couldn't do such a thing. Besides the material was quite hair-raising! I don't want to talk about it. Really, I would never repeat the truth to a soul."

We sat looking thoughtfully, even watchfully at each other, for a long moment before I spoke again.

"Have you ever met his sister, Liza?"

Keats shook his head slowly. "No. What was the point? I abandoned the project right away, so there was no need to try and hear her story. I know she has a lot of manuscript stuff, because the wife told me so. But. . . . She is here isn't she?" His lip curled with the faintest suggestion of disgust. "Truthfully I don't want to meet her. The bitter truth of the matter seems to me that the person old Pursewarden most loved—I mean purely spiritually—did not at all understand the state of his soul, so to speak, when he died: or even have the vaguest idea of the extent of his achievement. No, she was busy with a vulgar intrigue concerned with legalising her relations with Mountolive. I suppose she feared that her marriage to a diplomat might be imperilled by a possible scandal. I may be wrong, but that is the impression I gathered. I believe she was going to try and get a whitewashing book written. But now, in a sense, I have my own Pursewarden, my own copy of him, if you like. It's enough for me. What do the details matter, and why should I meet his sister? It is his work and not his life which is necessary to us—which offers one of the many meanings of the word with four faces!"

I had an impulse to cry out "Unfair", but I restrained it. It is impossible in this world to arrange for full justice to be done to everyone. Keats's eyelids drooped. "Come" I said, calling for the bill, "it's time you went home and got some sleep."

"I do feel rather tired" he mumbled.

"Avanti."

There was an old horse-drawn gharry in a side-street which we were glad to find. Keats protested that his feet were beginning to hurt and his arm to pain him. He was in a pleasantly exhausted frame of mind, and slightly tipsy after his potations. He lay back in the smelly old cab and closed his eyes. "D'you know, Darley" he said indistinctly, "I meant to tell you but forgot. Don't be angry with me, old fellow-bondsman, will you. I know that you and Clea. . . . Yes, and I'm glad. But I have the most curious feeling that one day I am going to marry her. Really. Don't be silly about it. Of course I would never breathe a word, and it would happen years after this silly old war. But somewhere along the line I feel I'm bound to hitch up with her."

"Now what do you expect me to say?"

"Well, there are a hundred courses open. Myself I would start yelling and screaming at once if you said such a thing to me. I'd knock your block off, push you out of the cab, anything. I'd punch me in the eye."

The gharry drew up with a jolt outside the house. "Here we are" I said, and helped my companion down into the road. "I'm not as drunk as all that" he cried cheerfully, shaking off my help, "'tis but fatigue, dear friend." And while I argued out the cost of the trip with the driver he went round and held a long private confabulation with the horse, stroking its nose. "I was giving it some maxims to live by" he explained as we wound our weary way up the staircase. "But the champagne had muddled up my quotation-box. What's that thing of Shakespeare's about the lover and the cuckold all compact, seeking the bubble reputation e'en in the cannon's mouth." The last phrase he pronounced in the strange (man-sawing-wood) delivery of Churchill. "Or something about swimmers into cleanness leaping—a pre-fab in the eternal mind no less!"

"You are murdering them both."

"Gosh I'm tired. And there seems to be no bombardment tonight."

"They are getting less frequent."

He collapsed on his bed fully dressed, slowly untying his suède desert boots and wriggling with his toes until they slid slowly off and plopped to the floor. "Did you ever see Purse-warden's little book called *Select Prayers for English Intellectuals*? It was funny. 'Dear Jesus, please keep me as eighteenth century as possible—but without the c*******d. . . .' " He gave a sleepy chuckle, put his arms behind his head and started drifting into smiling sleep. As I turned out the light he sighed deeply and said: "Even the dead are overwhelming us all the time with kindnesses."

I had a sudden picture of him as a small boy walking upon the very brink of precipitous cliffs to gather seabirds' eggs. One slip. . . .

But I was never to see him again. *Vale!*

o   o   o   o   o

V

Ten thirsty fingers of my blind Muse
Confer upon my face their sensual spelling

The lines ran through my head as I pressed the bell of the summer residence the following evening. In my hand I held the green leather suitcase which contained the private letters of Pursewarden—that brilliant sustained fusillade of words which still exploded in my memory like a firework display, scorching me. I had telephoned to Liza from my office in the morning to make the rendezvous. She opened the door and stood before me with a pale graven expression of expectancy. "Good" she whispered as I murmured my name and "Come". She turned and walked before me with a stiff upright expressive gait which reminded me of a child dressed up as Queen Elizabeth for a charade. She looked tired and strained, and yet in a curious way proud. The living-room was empty. Mountolive, I knew, had returned to Cairo that morning. Rather surprisingly, for it was late in the year, a log-fire burned in the chimney-piece. She took up her stand before it, arching her back to the warmth, and rubbing her hands as if she were chilled.

"You have been quick, very quick" she said, almost sharply, almost with a hint of implied reproach in her tone. "But I am glad." I had already told her by telephone the gist of my conversation with Keats about the non-existent book. "I am glad, because now we can decide something, finally. I couldn't sleep last night. I kept imagining you reading them, the letters. I kept imagining him writing them."

"They are marvellous. I have never read anything like them in my whole life." I felt a note of chagrin in my own tones.

188

"Yes" she said, and fetched a deep sigh. "And yet I was afraid you would think so; *afraid* because you would share David's opinion of them and advise me that they should be preserved *at all costs*. Yet *he* expressly told me to burn them."

"I know."

"Sit down, Darley. Tell me what you really think."

I sat down, placing the little suitcase on the floor beside me, and said: "Liza, this is not a literary problem unless you choose to regard it as one. You need take nobody's advice. Naturally nobody who has read them could help but regret the loss."

"But Darley, if they had been yours, written to someone you . . . loved?"

"I should feel relief to know that my instructions had been carried out. At least I presume that is what *he* would feel, wherever he might be now."

She turned her lucid blind face to the mirror and appeared to explore her own reflection in it earnestly, resting the tips of her frilly fingers on the mantelpiece. "I am as superstitious as he was" she said at last. "But it is more than that. I was always obedient because I knew that he saw farther than I and understood more than I did."

> *This caged reflection gives her nothing back*
> *That women drink like thirsty stags from mirrors*

How very much of Pursewarden's poetry became crystal-clear and precise in the light of all this new knowledge! How it gathered consequence and poignance from the figure of Liza exploring her own blindness in the great mirror, her dark hair thrown back on her shoulders!

At last she turned back again, sighing once more, and I saw a look of tender pleading on her face, made the more haunting and expressive by the empty sockets of her eyes. She took a step forward and said: "Well, then, it is decided. Only tell me you will help me burn them. They are very many. It will take a little time."

"If you wish."

"Let us sit down beside the fire together."

So we sat facing each other on the carpet and I placed the suitcase between us, pressing the lock so that the cover released itself and sprang up with a snap.

"Yes" she said. "This is how it must be. I should have known all along that I must obey him." Slowly, one by one I took up the pierced envelopes, unfolded each letter in turn and handed it to her to place upon the burning logs.

"We used to sit like this as children with our playbox between us, before the fire, in the winter. So often, and always together. You would have to go back very far into the past to understand it all. And even then I wonder if you would understand. Two small children left alone in an old rambling farmhouse among the frozen lakes, among the mists and rains of Ireland. We had no resources except in each other. He converted my blindness into poetry, I saw with his brain, he with my eyes. So we invented a whole imperishable world of poetry together—better by far than the best of his books, and I have read them all with my fingers, they are all at the institute. Yes I read and re-read them looking for a clue to the guilt which had transformed everything. Nothing had affected us before, everything conspired to isolate us, keep us together. The death of our parents happened when we were almost too small to comprehend it. We lived in this ramshackle old farmhouse in the care of an eccentric and deaf old aunt who did the work, saw that we were fed, and left us to our own devices. There was only one book there, a Plutarch, which we knew by heart. Everything else he invented. This was how I became the strange mythological queen of his life, living in a vast palace of sighs— as he used to say. Sometimes it was Egypt, sometimes Peru, sometimes Byzantium. I suppose I must have known that really it was an old farmhouse kitchen, with shabby deal furniture and floors of red tile. At least when the floors had been washed with carbolic soap with its peculiar smell I *knew*, with half my mind, that it was a farmhouse floor, and not a palace with magnificent tessellated floors brilliant with snakes and eagles and pygmies. But at a word he brought me back to reality, as he called it. Later, when he started looking for justifications for our love instead of just simply being proud of it, he read me a quotation from a book. 'In the African burial rites it is the sister who brings the dead king back to life. In Egypt as well as Peru the king, who was considered as God, took his sister to wife. But the motive was ritual and not sexual, for they symbolised the moon and the sun in their conjunction. The king marries his sister because he, as God the star, wandering on earth, is immortal and may therefore not propagate himself in the children of a strange woman, any more than he is allowed to die a natural death.' That is why he was pleased to come there to Egypt, because he felt, he said, an interior poetic link with Osiris and Isis, with Ptolemy and Arsinoë—the race of the sun and the moon!''

Quietly and methodically she placed letter after letter on the burning pyre, talking in a sad monotone, as much to herself as to me.

"No it would not be possible to make it all comprehensible to those who were not of our race. But when the guilt entered the old poetic life began to lose its magic—not for me: but for him. It was he who made me dye my hair black, so that I could pretend to be a step-sister of his, not a sister. It hurt me deeply to realise suddenly that he was guilty all of a sudden; but as we grew up the world intruded more and more upon us, new lives began to impinge on our solitary world of palaces and kingdoms. He was forced to go away for long periods. When he was absent I had nothing whatsoever except the darkness and what my memory of him could fill it with; somehow the treasures of his invention went all lustreless until he came back, his voice, his touch. All we knew of our parents, the sum of our knowledge, was an old oak cupboard full of their clothes. They seemed enormous to us when we were small—the clothes of

191

giants, the shoes of giants. One day he said they oppressed him, these clothes. We did not need parents. And we took them out into the yard and made a bonfire of them in the snow. We both wept bitterly, I do not know why. We danced round the bonfire singing an old hunting song with savage triumph and yet weeping."

She was silent for a long moment, her head hanging in profound concentration over this ancient image, like a soothsayer gazing fixedly into the dark crystal of youth. Then she sighed and raised her head, saying: "I know why you hesitate. It is the last letter, isn't it? You see I counted them. Give it to me, Darley."

I handed it to her without a word and she softly placed it in the fire saying: "It is over at last."

o   o   o   o   o

BOOK III

I

As the summer burned away into autumn, and autumn into winter once more we became slowly aware that the war which had invested the city had begun slowly to ebb, to flow gradually away along the coast-roads fringing the desert, releasing its hold upon us and our pleasures. For receding like a tide it left its strange coprolitic trophies along the beaches which we had once used, finding them always white and deserted under the flying gulls. War had denied them to us for a long time; but now, when we rediscovered them, we found them littered with pulped tanks and twisted guns, and the indiscriminate wreckage of temporary supply harbours abandoned by the engineers to rot and rust under the desert sun, to sink gradually into the shifting dunes. It gave one a curious melancholy reassurance to bathe there now—as if among the petrified lumber of a Neolithic age: tanks like the skeletons of dinosaurs, guns standing about like outmoded furniture. The minefields constituted something of a hazard, and the Bedouin were often straying into them in the course of pasturing; once Clea swerved—for the road was littered with glistening fragments of shattered camel from some recent accident. But such occasions were rare, and as for the tanks themselves, though burned out they were tenantless. There were no human bodies in them. These had presumably been excavated and decently buried in one of the huge cemeteries which had grown up in various unexpected corners of the western desert like townships of the dead. The city, too, was finding its way back to its normal habits and rhythms, for the bombardments had now ceased altogether and the normal night-life of the Levant had begun once more to flower. And though uniforms were less abundant the bars and night clubs still plied a splendid trade with servicemen on leave.

My own eventless life, too, seemed to have settled itself into a natural routine-fed pattern, artificially divided by a private life which I had surrendered to my complete absorption in Clea, and an office life which, though not onerous, had little meaning to me. Little had changed: but yes, Maskelyne had at last managed to break his bonds and escape back to his regiment. He called on us, resplendent in uniform, to say goodbye, shyly pointing—not his pipe but a crisp new swagger-stick—at his tail-wagging colleague. "I told you he'd do it" said Telford with a triumphant sadness in his voice. "I always knew it." But Mountolive stayed on, apparently still "frozen" in his post.

From time to time by arrangement I revisited the child at Karm Abu Girg to see how she was faring. To my delight I found that the transplantation, about which I had had many misgivings, was working perfectly. The reality of her present life apparently chimed with the dreams I had invented for her. It was all as it should be—the coloured playing-card characters among whom she could now number herself! If Justine remained a somewhat withdrawn and unpredictable figure of moods and silences it only added, as far as I could see, to the sombre image of a dispossessed empress. In Nessim she had realised a father. His image had gained definition by greater familiarity because of his human tendernesses. He was a delightful companion-father now, and together they explored the desert lands around the house on horseback. He had given her a bow and arrows, and a little girl of about her own age, Taor, as a body-servant and *amah*. The so-called palace, too, which we had imagined together, stood the test of reality magnificently. Its labyrinth of musty rooms and its ramshackle treasures were a perpetual delight. Thus with her own horses and servants, and a private palace to play in, she was an Arabian Nights queen indeed. She had almost forgotten the island now, so absorbed was she among these new treasures. I did not see Justine during these visits, nor did I try to do so. Sometimes however Nessim was there, but he never accompanied us on our walks or rides, and usually the child came to the ford to meet me with a spare horse.

In the Spring Balthazar, who had by now quite come to himself and had thrown himself once more into his work, invited Clea and myself to take part in a ceremony which rather pleased his somewhat ironic disposition. This was the ceremonial placing of flowers on Capodistria's grave on the anniversary of the Great Porn's birthday. "I have the express authority of Capodistria himself" he explained. "Indeed he himself always pays for the flowers every year." It was a fine sunny day for the excursion and Balthazar insisted that we should walk. Though somewhat hampered by the nosegay he carried he was in good voice. His vanity in the matter of his hair had become too strong to withstand, and he had duly submitted to Mnemjian's ministrations, thus "rubbing out his age", as he expressed it. Indeed the change was remarkable. He was now, once more, the old Balthazar, with his sapient dark eyes turned ironically on the doings of the city. And no less on Capodistria from whom he had just received a long letter. "You can have no idea what the old brute is up to over the water. He has taken the Luciferian path and plunged into Black Magic. But I'll read it to you. His graveside is, now I come to think of it, a most appropriate place to read his account of his experiments!"

The cemetery was completely deserted in the sunshine. Capodistria had certainly spared no expense to make his grave imposing and had achieved a fearsome vulgarity of decoration which was almost mind-wounding. Such cherubs and scrolls, such floral wreaths. On the slab was engraved the ironic text: "Not Lost But Gone Before". Balthazar chuckled affectionately as he placed his flowers upon the grave and said "Happy Birthday" to it. Then he turned aside, removing coat and hat for the sun was high and bright, and together we sat on a bench under a cypress tree while Clea ate toffees and he groped in his pockets for the bulky typewritten packet which contained

Capodistria's latest and longest letter. "Clea" he said, "you must read it to us. I've forgotten my reading glasses. Besides, I would like to hear it through once, to see if it sounds less fantastic or more. Will you?"

Obediently she took the close-typed pages and started reading.

"My dear M.B."

"The initials" interposed Balthazar "stand for the nickname which Pursewarden fastened on me—Melancholia Borealis, no less. A tribute to my alleged Judaic gloom. Proceed, my dear Clea."

The letter was in French.

"I have been conscious, my dear friend, that I owed you some account of my new life here, yet though I have written you fairly frequently I have got into the habit of evading the subject. Why? Well, my heart always sank at the thought of your derisive laugh. It is absurd, for I was never a sensitive man or quick to worry about the opinion of my neighbours. Another thing. It would have involved a long and tiresome explanation of the unease and unfamiliarity I always felt at the meetings of the Cabal which sought to drench the world in its abstract goodness. I did not know then that my path was not the path of Light but of Darkness. I would have confused it morally or ethically with good and evil at that time. Now I recognise the path I am treading as simply the counterpoise—the bottom end of the see-saw, as it were—which keeps the light side up in the air. Magic! I remember you once quoting to me a passage (quite nonsensical to me then) from Paracelsus. I think you added at the time that even such gibberish must mean something. It does! 'True Alchemy which teaches how to make (or ☉ out of the five imperfect metals, requires no other materials but only the metals. The perfect metals are made out of the imperfect metals, through them and with them alone; for with other things is *Luna* (phantasy) but in the metals is *Sol* (wisdom).'

"I leave a moment's pause for your peculiar laugh, which in

198

the past I would not have been slow to echo! What a mountain of rubbish surrounding the idea of the *tinctura physicorum*, you would observe. Yes but. . . .

"My first winter in this windy tower was not pleasant. The roof leaked. I did not have my books to solace me as yet. My quarters seemed rather cramped and I wondered about extending them. The property on which the tower stands above the sea had also a straggle of cottages and outbuildings upon it; here lodged the ancient, deaf couple of Italians who looked after my wants, washed and cleaned and fed me. I did not want to turn them out of their quarters but wondered whether I could not convert the extra couple of barns attached to their abode. It was then that I found, to my surprise, that they had another lodger whom I had never seen, a strange and solitary creature who only went abroad at night, and wore a monk's cassock. I owe all my new orientation to my meeting with him. He is a defrocked Italian monk, who describes himself as a Rosicrucian and an alchemist. He lived here among a mountain of masonic manuscripts—some of very great age—which he was in the process of studying. It was he who first convinced me that this line of enquiry was (despite some disagreeable aspects) concerned with increasing man's interior hold on himself, on the domains which lie unexplored within him; the comparison with everyday science is not fallacious, for the form of this enquiry is based as firmly on method—only with different premises! And if, as I say, it has some disagreeable aspects, why so has formal science—vivisection for instance. Anyway, here I struck up a rapport, and opened up for myself a field of study which grew more and more engrossing as the months went by. I also discovered at last something which eminently fitted my nature! Truthfully, everything in this field seemed to nourish and sustain me! Also I was able to be of considerable practical assistance to the Abbé F. as I will call him, for some of these manuscripts (stolen from the secret lodges on Athos I should opine) were in Greek, Arabic and Russian—languages which he did not know well. Our friendship ripened into a partnership. But it was many months before he introduced me to yet another strange, indeed formidable figure who was also dabbling in these matters. This was an Austrian Baron who lived in a large mansion inland and who was busy (no, do not laugh) on the obscure problem which we once discussed—is it in *De Natura Rerum*? I think it is—the *generatio homunculi?* He had a Turkish butler and famulus to help him in his experiments. Soon I became *persona grata* here also and was allowed to help them to the best of my ability.

"Now this Baron—whom you would certainly find a strange and imposing figure, heavily bearded and with big teeth like the seeds of a corn-cob—this Baron had . . . ah! my dear Balthazar, had *actually produced* ten homunculi which he called his 'prophesying spirits'. They were preserved in the huge glass canisters which they use hereabouts for washing olives or to preserve fruit, and they lived in water. They stood on a long oaken rack in his studio or laboratory. They were produced or 'patterned', to use his own expression, in the course of five weeks of intense labour of thought and ritual. They were exquisitely beautiful and mysterious objects, floating there like sea-horses. They consisted of a king, a queen, a knight, a monk, a nun, an architect, a miner, a seraph, and finally a blue spirit and a red one! They dangled lazily in these stout glass jars. A tapping fingernail seemed to alarm them. They were only about a span long, and as the Baron was anxious for them to grow to a greater size, we helped him to bury them in several cartloads of horse-manure. This great midden was sprinkled daily with an evil-smelling liquid which was prepared with great labour by the Baron and his Turk, and which contained some rather disgusting ingredients. At each sprinkling the manure began to steam as if heated by a subterranean fire. It was almost too hot to place one finger in it. Once every three days the Abbé and the Baron spent the whole night praying and fumigating the midden with incense. When at last the Baron deemed this process complete the bottles were carefully removed and returned to the laboratory shelves. All the homunculi had grown in size to such an extent that the bottles were now hardly big enough for them, and the male figures had come into possession of heavy beards. The nails of their fingers and toes had grown very long. Those which bore a human representation wore clothes appropriate to their rank and style. They had a kind of beautiful obscenity floating there with an expression on their faces such as I have only once seen before—on the face of a Peruvian pickled human head! Eyes turned up into the skull, pale fish's lips drawn back to expose small perfectly formed teeth! In the bottles containing respectively the red and blue spirit there was nothing to be seen. All the bottles, by the way, were heavily sealed with oxbladders and wax bearing the imprint of a magic seal. But when the Baron tapped with his fingernail on the bottles and repeated some words in Hebrew the water clouded and began to turn red and blue respectively. The homunculi began to show their faces, to develop cloudily like a photographic print, gradually increasing in size. The blue spirit was as beautiful as any angel, but the red wore a truly terrifying expression.

"These beings were fed every three days by the Baron with some dry rose-coloured substance which was kept in a silver box lined with sandalwood. Pellets about the size of a dried pea. Once every week, too, the water in the bottles had to be emptied out; they had to be refilled (the bottles) with fresh rainwater. This had to be done very rapidly because during the few moments that the spirits were exposed to the air they seemed to get weak and unconscious, as if they were about to die like fish. But the blue spirit was never fed; while the red one received once a week a thimbleful of the fresh blood of some animal—a chicken I think. This blood disappeared at once in the water without colouring or even troubling it. As soon as this bottle was opened it turned turbid and dark and gave off the odour of rotten eggs!

"In the course of a couple of months these homunculi reached their full stature, the stage of prophecy—as the Baron calls it; then every night the bottles were carried into a small ruined chapel, situated in a grove at some distance from the house, and here a service was held and the bottles 'interrogated' on the course of future events. This was done by writing questions in Hebrew on slips of paper and pressing them to the bottle before the eyes of the homunculus; it was rather like exposing sensitized photographic paper to light. I mean it was not as if the beings read but divined the questions, slowly, with much hesitation. They spelled out their answers, drawing with a finger on the transparent glass, and these responses were copied down immediately by the Baron in a great commonplace book. Each homunculus was only asked questions appropriate to his station, and the red and blue spirits could only answer with a smile or a frown to indicate assent or dissent. Yet they seemed to know everything, and any question at all could be put to them. The King could only touch on politics, the monk religion . . . and so on. In this way I witnessed the compilation of what the Baron called 'the annals of Time' which is a document at least as impressive as that left behind him by Nostradamus. So many of these prophecies have proved true in these last short months that I can have little doubt about the rest also proving so. It is a curious sensation to peer thus into the future!

"One day, by some accident, the glass jar containing the monk fell to the stone flags and was broken. The poor monk died after a couple of small painful respirations, despite all the efforts made by the Baron to save him. His body was buried in the garden. There was an abortive attempt to 'pattern' another monk but this was a failure. It produced a small leech-like object without vitality which died within a few hours.

"A short while afterwards the King managed to escape from his bottle during the night; he was found sitting upon the bottle containing the Queen, scratching with his nails to get the seal away! He was beside himself, and very agile, though weakening desperately from his exposure to the air. Nevertheless he led us quite a chase among the bottles—which we were afraid of overturning. It was really extraordinary how nimble he was, and had he not become increasingly faint from being out of his native element I doubt whether we could have caught him. We did however and he was pushed, scratching and biting, back into his bottle, but not before he had severely scratched the Abbé's chin. In the scrimmage he gave off a curious odour, as of a hot metal plate cooling. My finger touched his leg. It was of a wet and rubbery consistency, and sent a shiver of apprehension down my spine.

"But now a mishap occurred. The Abbé's scratched face became inflamed and poisoned and he went down with a high fever and was carried off to hospital where he lies at present, convalescing. But there was more to follow, and worse; the Baron, being Austrian, had always been something of a curiosity here, and more especially now when the spy-mania which every war brings has reached its height. It came to my ears that he was to be thoroughly investigated by the authorities. He received the news with despairing calmness, but it was clear that he could not afford to have unauthorised persons poking about in his laboratory. It was decided to 'dissolve' the homunculi and bury them in the garden. In the absence of the Abbé I agreed to help him. I do not know what it was he poured into the bottles but all the flames of hell leaped up out of them until the whole ceiling of the place was covered in soot and cobwebs. The beings shrank now to the size of dried leeches, or the dried navel-cords which sometimes village folk will preserve. The Baron groaned aloud from time to time, and the sweat stood out on his forehead. The groans of a woman in labour. At last the process was complete and at midnight the bottles were taken out and interred under some loose flags in the little chapel where, presumably, they must still be. The Baron has been interned, his books and papers sealed by the Custodians of Property. The Abbé lies, as I said, in hospital. And I? Well, my

Greek passport has made me less suspect than most people hereabouts. I have retired for the moment to my tower. There is still the mass of masonic data in the barns which the Abbé inhabited; I have taken charge of these. I have written to the Baron once or twice but he has not, perhaps out of tact, replied to me; believing perhaps that my association with him might lead to harm. And so . . . well, the war rolls on about us. Its end and what follows it—right up to the end of this century—I know: it lies here beside me as I write, in question and answer form. But who would believe me if I published it all—and much less you, doctor of the empiric sciences, sceptic and ironist? As for the war—Paracelsus has said: 'Innumerable are the *Egos* of man; in him are angels and devils, heaven and hell, the whole of the animal creation, the vegetable and mineral kingdoms; and just as the little individual man may be diseased, so the great universal man has his diseases, which manifest themselves as the ills which affect humanity as a whole. Upon this fact is based the prediction of future events.' And so, my dear friend, I have chosen the Dark Path towards my own light. I know now that I must follow it wherever it leads! Isn't that something to have achieved? Perhaps not. But for me it truthfully seems so. But I hear that laughter!

"Ever your devoted Da Capo".*

"Now" said Clea "oblige with the laughter!"

"What Pursewarden" I said, "called 'the melancholy laughter of Balthazar which betokens solipsism'."

Balthazar did indeed laugh now, slapping his knee and doubling himself up like a jack knife. "That damned rogue, Da Capo" he said. "And yet, *soyons raisonnables* if that is indeed the expression—he wouldn't tell a pack of lies. Or perhaps he might. No, he wouldn't. Yet can you bring yourself to believe in what he says—you two?"

"Yes" said Clea, and here we both smiled for her bondage to the soothsayers of Alexandria would naturally give her a predisposition towards the magic arts. "Laugh" she said quietly.

"To tell the truth" said Balthazar more soberly, "when one casts around the fields of so-called knowledge which we have partially opened up one is conscious that there may well be whole areas of darkness which may belong to the Paracelsian regions—the submerged part of the iceberg of knowledge. No, dammit, I must admit that you are right. We get too certain of ourselves travelling backwards and forwards along the tram-lines of empirical fact. Occasionally one gets hit softly on the head by a stray brick which has been launched from some other region. Only yesterday, for example, Boyd told me a story which sounded no less strange: about a soldier who was buried last week. I could, of course, supply explanations which might fit the case, but not with any certainty. This young boy went on a week's leave to Cairo. He came back having had an enjoyable time, or so he said. Next he developed an extraordinary intermittent fever with simply huge maximum temperatures. Within a week he died. A few hours before death a thick white cataract formed over his eyeballs with a sort of luminous red node over the retina. All the boy would repeat in the course of his delirium was the single phrase: *She did it with a golden needle.* Nothing but these words. As I say one could perhaps strap the case down clinically with a clever guess or two but . . . had I to be honest I would be obliged to admit that it did not exactly fit within an accepted category that I knew. Nor, by the way, did the autopsy give one anything more to go on: blood tests, spinal fluid, stomach etc. Not even a nice, familiar (yet itself perhaps inexplicable) meningeal disturbance. The brain was lovely and fresh! At least so Boyd says, and he took great pleasure in thoroughly exploring the young man. Mystery! Now what the devil could he have been doing on leave? It seems quite impossible to discover. His stay is not recorded at any of the hotels or army transit hostels. He spoke no language but English. Those few days spent in Cairo are completely missing from the count. And then the woman with the golden needle?"

"But in truth it is happening all the time, and I think you

are right" (this to Clea) "to insist obstinately on the existence of the dark powers and the fact that some people do scry as easily as I gaze down the barrel of my microscope. Not all, but some. And even quite stupid people, like your old Scobie, for example. Mind you, in my opinion, that was a rigmarole of the kind he produced sometimes when he was tipsy and wanted to show off—I mean the stuff supposedly about Narouz: that was altogether too dramatic to be taken seriously. And even if some of the detail were right he *could* have had access to it in the course of his duties. After all Nimrod did the *procès verbal* and that document must have been knocking around."

"What about Narouz?" I asked curiously, secretly piqued that Clea had confided things to Balthazar which she had kept from me. It was now that I noticed that Clea had turned quite white and was looking away. But Balthazar appeared to notice nothing himself and went plunging on. "It has the ingredients of a novelette—I mean about trying to drag you down into the grave with him. Eh, don't you think? And about the weeping you would hear." He broke off abruptly, noticing her expression at last. "Goodness, Clea my dear" he went on in self-approach, "I hope I am not betraying a confidence. You suddenly look upset. Did you tell me not to repeat the Scobie story?" He took both her hands and turned her round to face him.

A spot of red had appeared in both her cheeks. She shook her head, though she said nothing, but bit her lips as if with vexation. At last "No" she said, "there is no secret. I simply did not tell Darley because . . . well, it is silly as you say: anyway he doesn't believe in that sort of rubbish. I didn't want to seem stupider than he must find me." She leaned to kiss me apologetically on the cheek. She sensed my annoyance, as did Balthazar who hung his head and said: "I've talked out of turn. Damn! Now he will be angry with you."

"Good heavens, no!" I protested. "Simply curious, that is all. I had no intention of prying, Clea."

She made a gesture of anguished exasperation and said: "Very

206

well. It is of no importance. I will tell you the whole thing." She started speaking hastily, as if to dispose of a disagreeable and time-wasting subject. "It was during the last dinner I told you about. Before I went to Syria. He was tipsy, I don't deny it. He said what Balthazar has just told you, and he added a description of someone who suggested to me Nessim's brother. He said, marking the place with his thumbnail on his own lips: 'His lips are split here, and I see him covered in little wounds, lying on a table. There is a lake outside. He has made up his mind. He will try and drag you to him. You will be in a dark place, imprisoned, unable to resist him. Yes, there is one near at hand who might aid you if he could. But he will not be strong enough.' " Clea stood up suddenly and brought her story to an end with the air of someone snapping off a twig. "At this point he burst into tears" she said.

It was strange what a gloom this nonsensical yet ominous recital put over our spirits; something troubling and distasteful seemed to invade that brilliant spring sunshine, the light keen air. In the silence that followed Balthazar gloomily folded and refolded his overcoat on his knee while Clea turned away to study the distant curve of the great harbour with its flotillas of cubist-smeared craft, and the scattered bright petals of the racing dinghies which had crossed the harbour boom, threading their blithe way towards the distant blue marker buoy. Alexandria was virtually at norm once more, lying in the deep backwater of the receding war, recovering its pleasures. Yet the day had suddenly darkened around us, oppressing our spirits—a sensation all the more exasperating because of its absurd cause. I cursed old Scobie's self-importance in setting up as a fortune-teller.

"These gifts might have got him a bit further in his own profession had they been real" I said peevishly.

Balthazar laughed, but even here there was a chagrined doubt in his laughter. His remorse at having stirred up this silly story was quite patent.

"Let us go" said Clea sharply. She seemed slightly annoyed as well, and for once disengaged her arm when I took it. We found an old horse-drawn gharry and drove slowly and silently into town together.

"No damn it!" cried Balthazar at last. "Let us go down and have a drink by the harbour at least." And without waiting for answer from us he redirected the jarvey and set us mutely clip-clopping down the slow curves of the Grande Corniche towards the Yacht Club in the outer harbour of which was now to befall something momentous and terrible for us all. I remember it so clearly, this spring day without flaw; a green bickering sea lighting the minarets, softly spotted here and there by the dark gusts of a fine racing wind. Yes, with mandolines fretting in the Arab town, and every costume glowing as brightly as a child's coloured transfer. Within a quarter of an hour the magnificence of it was to be darkened, poisoned by unexpected—completely unmerited death. But if tragedy strikes suddenly the actual moment of its striking seems to vibrate on, extending into time like the sour echoes of some great gong, numbing the spirit, the comprehension. Suddenly, yes, but yet how *slowly* it expands in the understanding—the ripples unrolling upon the reason in ever-widening circles of fear. And yet, all the time, outside the centre-piece of the picture, so to speak, with its small tragic anecdote, normal life goes on unheeding. (We did not even hear the bullets, for example. Their sullen twang was carried away on the wind.)

Yet our eyes were drawn, as if by the lines-of-force of some great marine painting, to a tiny clutter of dinghies snubbing together in the lee of one of the battleships which hovered against the sky like a grey cathedral. Their sails flapped and tossed, idly as butterflies contending with the breeze. There was some obscure movement of oars and arms belonging to figures too small at this range to distinguish or recognise. Yet this tiny commotion had force to draw the eye—by who knows what interior premonition? And as the cab rolled silently along the rim of the inner harbour we saw it unroll before us like some majestic seascape by a great master. The variety and distinction of the small refugee craft from every corner of the Levant—their differing designs and rigs—gave it a brilliant sensuality and rhythm against the glittering water. Everything was breath-taking yet normal; tugs hooted, children cried, from the cafés came the rattle of the *trictrac* boards and the voices of birds. The normality of an entire world surrounded that tiny central panel with its flicking sails, the gestures we could not interpret, the faint voices. The little craft tilted, arms rose and fell.

"Something has happened" said Balthazar with his narrow dark eye upon the scene, and as if his phrase had affected the horse it suddenly drew to a halt. Besides ourselves on the dockside only one man had also seen; he too stood gazing with curious open-mouthed distraction, aware that something out of the ordinary was afoot. Yet everywhere people bustled, the chandlers cried. At his feet three children played in complete absorption, placing marbles in the tramlines, hoping to see them ground to powder when the next tram passed. A water carrier clashed his brass mugs, crying: "Come, ye thirsty ones." And unobtrusively in the background, as if travelling on silk, a liner stole noiselessly down the green thoroughfare towards the open sea.

"It's Pombal" cried Clea at last, in puzzled tones, and with a gesture of anxiety put her arm through mine. It was indeed Pombal. What had befallen them was this. They had been drifting about the harbour in his little dinghy with their customary idleness and inattention and had strayed too near to one of the French battleships, carried into its lee and off their course by an unexpected swoop of the wind. How ironically it had been planned by the invisible stage-masters who direct human actions, and with what speed! For the French ships, though captive, had still retained both their small-arms and a sense of shame, which made their behaviour touchy and unpredictable. The sentries they mounted had orders to fire a warning shot across the bows of any craft which came within a dozen metres of any battleship. It was, then, only in response to orders that a sentry put a bullet through Pombal's sail as the little dinghy whirled down on its rogue course towards his ship. It was merely a warning, which intended no deliberate harm. And even now this might have . . . but no: it could not have fallen out otherwise. For my friend, overcome with rage and mortification, at being treated thus by these cowards and lack-bones of his own blood and faith, turned purple with indignation, and abandoned his tiller altogether in order to stand precariously upright and shake his huge fist, screaming: *"Salauds!"* and *"Espèces de cons!"* and—what was perhaps the definitive epithet—*"Lâches!"*

Did he hear the bullets himself? It is doubtful whether in all the confusion he did, for the craft tilted, gybed, and turned about on another course, toppling him over. It was while he was lying there, recovering the precious tiller, that he noticed Fosca in the very act of falling, but with infinite slowness. Afterwards he said that she did not know she had been hit. She must have felt, perhaps, simply a vague and unusual dispersion of her attention, the swift anaesthesia of shock which follows so swiftly upon the wound. She tilted like a high tower, and felt the sternsheets coming up slowly to press themselves to her cheek. There she lay with her eyes wide open, plump and soft as a wounded pheasant will lie, still bright of eye in spite of the blood running from its beak. He shouted her name, and felt only the immense silence of the word, for the little freshet had sharpened and was now rushing them landward. A new sort of confusion supervened, for other craft, attracted as flies are by wounds, began to cluster with cries of advice and commiseration. Meanwhile Fosca lay with vague and open eyes, smiling to herself in the other kind of dream.

And it was now that Balthazar suddenly awoke from his trance, struggled out of the cab without a word and began his queer lurching, traipsing run across the dock to the little red field-ambulance telephone with its emergency line. I heard the small click of the receiver and the sound of his voice speaking, patient and collected. The summons was answered, too, with almost miraculous promptness, for the field-post with its ambulances was only about fifty yards away. I heard the sweet tinkle of the ambulance's bell, and saw it racing along the cobbles towards us. And now all faces turned once more towards that little convoy of dinghies—faces on which was written only patient resignation or dread. Pombal was on his knees in the sheets with bent head. Behind him, deftly steering, was Ali the boatman who had been the first to comprehend and offer his help. All the other dinghies, flying along on the same course, stayed grouped around Pombal's as if in active sympathy. I could read the name *Manon* which he had so proudly bestowed upon it, not six months ago. Everything seemed to have become bewildering, shaken into a new dimension which was swollen with doubts and fears.

Balthazar stood on the quay in an agony of impatience, urging them in his mind to hurry. I heard his tongue clicking against the roof of his mouth *teck tsch*, clicking softly and reproachfully; a reproach, I wondered, directed against their slowness, or against life itself, its unpremeditated patterns?

At last they were on us. One heard quite distinctly the sound of their breathing, and our own contribution, the snap of stretcher-thongs, the tinkle of polished steel, the small snap of heels studded with hobnails. It all mixed into a confusion of activity, the lowering and lifting, the grunts as dark hands found purchase on a rope to hold the dinghy steady, the sharp serrated edges of conflicting voices giving orders. "Stand by" and "Gently now" all mixed with a distant foxtrot on a ship's radio. A stretcher swinging like a cradle, like a basket of fruit upon the dark shoulders of an Arab. And steel doors opening on a white throat.

Pombal wore an air of studied vagueness, his features all dispersed and quite livid in colour. He flopped on to the quay as if he had been dropped from a cloud, falling to his knees and recovering. He wandered vaguely after Balthazar and the stretcher-bearers bleating like a lost sheep. I suppose it must have been her blood splashed upon the expensive white *espadrilles* which he had bought a week before at Ghoshen's Emporium. At such moments it is the small details which strike one like blows. He made a vague attempt to clamber into the white throat but was rudely ejected. The doors clanged in his face. Fosca belonged now to science and not to him. He waited with humbly bent head, like a man in church, until they should open once more and admit him. He seemed hardly to be breathing. I felt an involuntary desire to go to his side but Clea's arm restrained me. We all waited in great patience and submissiveness like children, listening to the vague movements within the ambulance, the noise of boots. Then at long last the doors opened and the weary Balthazar climbed down and said: "Get in and come with us." Pombal gave one wild glance about him and turning his pain-racked countenance suddenly upon Clea and myself, delivered himself of a single gesture—spreading his arms in uncomprehending hopelessness before clapping a fat hand over each ear, as if to avoid hearing something. Balthazar's voice suddenly cracked like parchment. "Get in" he said roughly, angrily, as if he were speaking to a criminal; and as they climbed into the white interior I heard him add in a lower voice, "She is dying." A clang of iron doors closing, and I felt Clea's hand turn icy in my own.

So we sat, side by side and speechless on that magnificent spring afternoon which was already deepening into dusk. At last I lit a cigarette and walked a few yards along the quay among the chaffering Arabs who described the accident to each other in yelping tones. Ali was about to take the dinghy back to its moorings at the Yacht Club; all he needed was a light for his cigarette. He came politely towards me and asked if he might light up from me. As he puffed I noticed that the flies had already found the little patch of blood on the dinghy's floorboards. "I'll clean it up" said Ali, noticing the direction of my glance; with a lithe cat-like leap he jumped aboard and unloosed the sail. He turned to smile and wave. He wanted to say "A bad business" but his English was inadequate. He shouted "Bad poison, sir." I nodded.

Clea was still sitting in the gharry looking at her own hands. It was as if this sudden incident had somehow insulated us from one another.

"Let's go back" I said at last, and directed the driver to turn back into the town we had so recently quitted.

"Pray to goodness she will be all right" said Clea at last. "It is too cruel."

"Balthazar said she was dying. I heard him."

"He may be wrong."

"He may be wrong."

But he was not wrong, for both Fosca and the child were dead, though we did not get the news until later in the evening. We wandered listlessly about Clea's rooms, unable to concentrate on anything. Finally she said: "You had better go back and spend the evening with him, don't you think." I was uncertain. "He would rather remain alone I imagine."

"Go back" she said, and added sharply, "I can't bear you hanging about at a time like this. . . . O, darling, I've hurt you. I'm sorry."

"Of course you haven't, you fool. But I'll go."

All the way down Rue Fuad I was thinking: such a small displacement of the pattern, a single human life, yet it had power to alter so much. Literally, such an eventuality had occurred to none of us. We simply could not stomach it, fit it into the picture which Pombal himself had built up with such care. It poisoned everything this small stupid fact—even almost our affection for him, for it had turned to horror and sympathy! How inadequate as emotions they were, how powerless to be of use. My own instinct would have been to keep away altogether! I felt as if I never wanted to see him again—in order not to shame him. Bad poison, indeed. I repeated Ali's phrase to myself over and over again.

Pombal was already there when I got back, sitting in his gout-chair, apparently deep in thought. A full glass of neat whisky stood beside him which he did not seem to have touched. He had changed, however, into the familiar blue dressing-gown with the gold peacock pattern, and on his feet were his battered old Egyptian slippers like golden shovels. I went into the room quite quietly and sat down opposite him without a word. He did not appear to actually look at me, yet somehow I felt that he was conscious of my presence; yet his eye was vague and dreamy, fixed on the middle distance, and his fingers softly played a five-finger exercise on each other. And still looking at the window he said, in a squeaky little voice—as if the words had power to move him although he did not quite know their meaning: "She's dead, Darley. They are both dead." I felt a sensation of a leaden weight about my heart. *"C'est pas juste"* he added absently and fell to pulling his side-beard with fat fingers. Quite unemotional, quite flat—like a man recovering from a severe stroke. Then he suddenly took a gulp of whisky and started up, choking and coughing. "It is neat" he said in surprise and disgust, and put the glass down with a long shudder. Then, leaning forward he began to scribble, taking up a pencil and pad which were on the table—whorls and lozenges and dragons. Just like a child. "I must go to confession to-morrow for the first time for ages" he said slowly, as if with infinite precaution. "I have told Hamid to wake me early. Will you mind if *Cléa* only comes?" I shook my head. I understood that he meant to the funeral. He sighed with relief. *"Bon"* he said, and standing up took the glass of whisky. At that moment the door opened and the distraught Pordre appeared. In a flash Pombal changed. It was the presence of someone of his race perhaps. He gave a long chain of deep sobs. The two men embraced muttering incoherent words and phrases, as if consoling

214

each other for a disaster which was equally wounding to both. The old diplomat raised his white womanish fist in the air and said suddenly, fatuously: "I have already protested strongly." To whom, I wondered? To the invisible powers which decree that things shall fall out this way or that? The words sputtered out meaninglessly on the chill air of the drawing-room. Pombal was talking.

"I must write and tell him everything" he said. "Confess everything."

"Gaston" said his Chief sharply, reprovingly, "you must not do any such thing. It would increase his misery in prison. *C'est pas juste.* Be advised by me: the whole matter must be forgotten."

"Forgotten!" cried my friend as if he had been stung by a bee. "You do not understand. Forgotten! He must know for *her* sake."

"He must never know" said the older man. "Never."

They stood for a long while holding hands and gazing about them distractedly through their tears; and at this moment, as if to complete the picture, the door opened to admit the porcine outlines of Father Paul—who was never to be found far from the centre of any scandal. He paused inside the doorway with an air of unction, with his features composed around an air of gluttonous self-satisfaction. "My poor boy" he said, clearing his throat. He made a vague gesture of his paw as if scattering Holy Water over us all and sighed. He reminded me of some great hairless vulture. Then surprisingly he clattered out a few phrases of consolation in Latin.

I left my friend among these elephantine comforters, relieved in a way that there was no place for me in all this incoherent parade of Latin commiserations. Simply pressing his hand once I slipped out of the flat and directed my thoughtful footsteps in the direction of Clea's room.

The funeral took place next day. Clea came back, looking pale and strained. She threw her hat across the room and shook out her hair with an impatient gesture—as if to expel the whole distasteful memory of the incident. Then she lay down ex-exhaustedly on the sofa and put her arm over her eyes.

"It was ghastly" she said at last, "really ghastly, Darley. First of all it was a *cremation*. Pombal insisted on carrying out her wishes despite violent protests from Father Paul. What a beast that man is. He behaved as though her body had become Church property. Poor Pombal was furious. They had a terrible row settling the details I hear. And then . . . I had never visited the new Crematorium! It is unfinished. It stands in a bit of sandy waste-land littered with straw and old lemon-ade bottles, and flanked by a trash heap of old car-bodies. It looks in fact like a hastily improvised furnace in a concentration camp. Horrid little brick-lined beds with half-dead flowers sprouting from the sand. And a little railway with runners for the coffin. The ugliness! And the faces of all those consuls and acting consuls! Even Pombal seemed quite taken aback by the hideousness. And the heat! Father Paul was of course in the foreground of the picture, relishing his rôle. And then with an incongruous squeaking the coffin rolled away down the garden path and swerved into a steel hatch. We hung about, first on one leg then on the other; Father Paul showed some inclination to fill this awkward gap with impromptu prayers but at that moment a radio in a nearby house started playing Viennese waltzes. Attempts were made by various chauffeurs to locate and silence it, but in vain. Never have I felt unhappier than standing in this desolate chicken run in my best clothes. There was a dreadful charred smell from the furnace. I did not know then that Pombal intended to scatter the ashes in the desert, and that he had decided that I alone would accompany him on this journey. Nor, for that matter, did I know that Father Paul —who scented a chance of more prayers—had firmly made up his mind to do so as well. All that followed came as a surprise.

"Well finally the casket was produced—and what a casket! That was a real poke in the eye for us. It was like a confectioner's triumphant effort at something suitable for inexpensive chocolates. Father Paul tried to snatch it, but poor Pombal held on to it firmly as we trailed towards the car. I must say, here Pombal showed some backbone. 'Not you' he said as the priest started to climb into the car. 'I'm going alone with Clea.' He beckoned to me with his head.

" 'My son' said Father Paul in a low grim voice, 'I shall come too.'

" 'You won't' said Pombal. 'You've done your job.'

" 'My son, I am coming' said this obstinate wretch.

"For a moment it seemed that all might end with an exchange of blows. Pombal shook his beard at the priest and glared at him with angry eyes. I climbed into the car, feeling extremely foolish. Then Pombal pushed Father Paul in the best French manner—hard in the chest—and climbed in, banging the door. A susurrus went up from the assembled consuls at this public slight to the cloth, but no word was uttered. The priest was white with rage and made a sort of involuntary gesture—as if he were going to shake his fist at Pombal, but thought better of it.

"We were off; the chauffeur took the road to the eastern desert, acting apparently on previous instructions. Pombal sat quite still with this ghastly *bonvonnière* on his knees, breathing through his nose and with half-closed eyes. As if he were recovering his self composure after all the trials of the morning. Then he put out his hand and took mine, and so we sat, silently watching the desert unroll on either side of the car. We went quite far out before he told the chauffeur to stop. He was breathing rather heavily. We got out and stood for a desultory moment at the roadside. Then he took a step or two into the sand and paused, looking back. 'Now I shall do it' he said, and broke into his fat shambling run which carried him about twenty yards into the desert. I said hurriedly to the chauffeur, 'Drive on for five minutes, and then come back for us.' The sound of the car starting did not make Pombal turn round. He had slumped down on his knees, like a child playing in a sand-pit; but he stayed quite still for a long time. I could hear him talking in a low confidential voice, though whether he was praying or reciting poetry I could not tell. It felt desperately forlorn on that empty desert road with the heat shimmering up from the tarmac.

"Then he began to scrabble about in the sand before him, to pick up handfuls like a Moslem and pour it over his own head. He was making a queer moaning noise. At last he lay face downwards and quite still. The minutes ticked by. Far away in the distance I could hear the car coming slowly towards us— at a walking pace.

" 'Pombal' I said at last. There was no reply. I walked across the intervening space, feeling my shoes fill up with the burning sand, and touched him on the shoulder. At once he stood up and started dusting himself. He looked dreadfully old all of a sudden. 'Yes' he said with a vague, startled glance all round him, as if for the first time he realised where he was. 'Take me home, Clea.' I took his hand—as if I were leading a blind man —and tugged him slowly back to the car which by now had arrived.

"He sat beside me with a dazed look for a long time until, as if suddenly touched to the quick by a memory, he began to howl like a little boy who has cut his knee. I put my arms round him. I was so glad you weren't there—your Anglo-Saxon soul would have curled up at the edges. Yet he was repeating: 'It must have looked ridiculous. It must have looked ridiculous.' And all of a sudden he was laughing hysterically. His beard was full of sand. 'I suddenly remembered Father Paul's face' he explained, still giggling in the high hysterical tones of a schoolgirl. Then he suddenly took a hold on himself, wiped his eyes, and sighing sadly said: 'I am utterly washed out, utterly exhausted. I feel I could sleep for a week.'

"And this is presumably what he is going to do. Balthazar has given him a strong sleeping draught to take. I dropped him at his flat and the car brought me on here. I'm hardly less exhausted than he. But thank God it is all over. Somehow he will have to start his life all over again.''

As if to illustrate this last proposition the telephone rang and Pombal's voice, weary and confused, said: ''Darley, is that you? Good. Yes, I thought you would be there. Before I went to sleep I wanted to tell you, so that we could make arrangements about the flat. Pordre is sending me into Syria *en mission*. I leave early in the morning. If I go this way I will get allowances and be able to keep up my part of the flat easily until I come back. Eh?''

''Don't worry about it'' I said.

''It was just an idea.''

''Sleep now.''

There was a long silence. Then he added: ''But of course I will write to you, eh? Yes. Very well. Don't wake me if you come in this evening.'' I promised not to.

But there was hardly any need for the admonition for when I returned to the flat later that night he was still up, sitting in his gout-chair with an air of apprehension and despair. ''This stuff of Balthazar's is no good'' he said. ''It is mildly emetic, that is all. I am getting more drowsy from the whisky. But somehow I don't want to go to bed. Who knows what dreams I shall have?'' But I at last persuaded him to get into bed; he agreed on condition that I stayed and talked to him until he dozed off. He was relatively calm now, and growing increasingly drowsy. He talked in a quiet relaxed tone, as one might talk to an imaginary friend while under anaesthetic.

''I suppose it will all pass. Everything does. In the very end, it passes. I was thinking of other people in the same position. But for some it does not pass easily. One night Liza came here. I was startled to find her on the doorstep with those eyes which give me the creeps—like an eyeless rabbit in a poultry shop. She wanted me to take her to her brother's room in the Mount Vulture Hotel. She said she wanted to 'see' it. I asked what she would see. She said, with anger, 'I have my own way of seeing.' Well I had to do it. I felt it would please Mountolive perhaps. But I did not know then that the Mount Vulture was no longer a hotel. It had been turned into a brothel for the troops. We were half-way up the stairs before the truth dawned on me. All these naked girls, and half-dressed sweating soldiers with their hairy bodies; their crucifixes tinkling against their identity discs. And the smell of sweat and rum and cheap scent. I said we must get out, for the place had changed hands, but she stamped her foot and insisted with sudden anger. Well, we climbed the stairs. Doors were open on every landing, you could see everything. I was glad she was blind. At last we came to his room. It was dark. On his bed there lay an old woman asleep with a hashish pipe beside her. It smelt of drains. She, Liza, was very excited. 'Describe it' she told me. I did my best. She advanced towards the bed. 'There is a woman asleep there' I said, trying to pull her back. 'This is a house of ill fame now, Liza, I keep telling you.' Do you know what she said? '*So much the better.*' I was startled. She pressed her cheek to the pillow beside the old woman, who groaned all at once. Liza stroked her forehead as if she were stroking a child and said 'There now. Sleep.' Then she came slowly and hesitantly to my hand. She gave a curious grin and said: 'I wanted to try and take his imprint from the pillow. But it was a useless idea. One must try everything to recover memory. It has so many hiding-places.' I did not know what she meant. We started downstairs again. On the second landing I saw some drunken Australians coming up. I could see from their faces that there was going to be trouble. One of their number had been cheated or something. They were terribly drunk. I put my arms around Liza and pretended we were making love in a corner of the landing until they passed us safely. She was trembling, though whether from fear or emotion I could not tell. And she said 'Tell me about his women. What were they like?' I gave her a good hard shake. 'Now you are being banal' I said. She stopped trembling and went white with anger. In the street she said 'Get me a taxi. I do not like you.' I did and off she went without a word. I regretted my rudeness afterwards, for she was suffering; at the time things happen too fast for one to take them into account. And one never knows enough about people and their sufferings to have the right response ready at the moment. Afterwards I said many sympathetic things to her in my mind. But too late. Always too late."

A slight snore escaped his lips and he fell silent. I was about to switch off his bedside lamp and tip-toe from his room when he continued to speak, only from far away, re-establishing the thread of his thought in another context: "And when Melissa was dying Clea spent all day with her. Once she said to Clea: 'Darley made love with a kind of remorse, of despair. I suppose he imagined Justine. He never excited me like other men did. Old Cohen, for example, he was just dirty-minded, yet his lips were always wet with wine. I liked that. It made me respect him for he was a man. But Pursewarden treated me like precious china, as if he were afraid he might break me, like some precious heirloom. How good it was for once to be at rest!' "

So the year turned on its heel, through a winter of racing winds, frosts keener than grief, hardly preparing us for that last magnificent summer which followed the spring so swiftly. It came curving in, this summer, as if from some long-forgotten latitude first dreamed of in Eden, miraculously rediscovered among the slumbering thoughts of mankind. It rode down upon us like some famous snow-ship of the mind, to drop anchor before the city, its white sails folding like the wings of a seabird. Ah! I am hunting for metaphors which might convey something of the piercing happiness too seldom granted to those who love; but words, which were first invented against despair, are too crude to mirror the properties of something so profoundly at peace with itself, at one with itself. Words are the mirrors of our discontents merely; they contain all the huge unhatched eggs of the world's sorrows. Unless perhaps it were simpler to repeat under one's breath some lines torn from a Greek poem, written once in the shadow of a sail, on a thirsty promontory in Byzantium. Something like . . .

> Black bread, clear water, blue air.
> Calm throat incomparably fair.
> Mind folded upon mind
> Eyes softly closed on eyes.
> Lashes a-tremble, bodies bare.

But they English badly; and unless one hears them in Greek falling softly, word by word, from a mouth made private and familiar by the bruised endearments of spent kisses they must remain always simply charmless photographs of a reality which overreaches the realm of the poet's scope. Sad that all the brilliant plumage of that summer remains beyond capture—for one's old age will have little but such memories upon which to found its regretful happinesses. Will memory clutch it—that incomparable pattern of days, I wonder? In the dense violet shadow of white sails, under the dark noon-lantern of figs, on the renowned desert roads where the spice caravans march and the dunes soothe themselves away to the sky, to catch in their dazed sleep the drumming of gulls' wings turning in spray? Or in the cold whiplash of the waters crushing themselves against the fallen pediments of forgotten islands? In the night-mist falling upon deserted harbours with the old Arab seamarks pointing eroded fingers? Somewhere, surely, the sum of these things will still exist. There were no hauntings yet. Day followed day upon the calendar of desire, each night turning softly over in its sleep to reverse the darkness and drench us once more in the royal sunlight. Everything conspired to make it what we needed.

It is not hard, writing at this remove in time, to realise that it had all *already happened*, had been ordained in such a way and in no other. This was, so to speak, only its "coming to pass'— its stage of manifestation. But the scenario had already been devised somewhere, the actors chosen, the timing rehearsed down to the last detail in the mind of that invisible author— which perhaps would prove to be only the city itself: the Alexandria of the human estate. The seeds of future events are carried within ourselves. They are implicit in us and unfold according to the laws of their own nature. It is hard to believe, I know, when one thinks of the perfection of that summer and what followed it.

Much had to do with the discovery of the island. The island! How had it eluded us for so long? There was literally not a corner of this coast which we did not know, not a beach we had not tried, not an anchorage we had not used. Yet it had been there, staring us in the face. "If you wish to hide something" says the Arabic proverb "hide it in the sun's eye." It lay, not hidden at all, somewhat to the west of the little shrine of Sidi El Agami—the white scarp with the snowy butt of a tomb emerging from a straggle of palms and figlets. It was simply an upshouldered piece of granite pushed up from the seabed by an earthquake or some submarine convulsion in the distant past. Of course, when the sea ran high it would be covered; but it is curious that it remains to this day unmarked on the Admiralty charts, for it would constitute quite a hazard to craft of medium draught.

It was Clea who first discovered the little island of Narouz. "Where has this sprung from?" she asked with astonishment; her brown wrist swung the cutter's tiller hard over and carried us fluttering down into its lee. The granite boulder was tall enough for a windbreak. It made a roundel of still blue water in the combing tides. On the landward side there was a crude N carved in the rock above an old eroded iron ring which, with a stern anchor out to brace her, served as a secure mooring. It would be ridiculous to speak of stepping ashore for the "shore" consisted of a narrow strip of dazzling white pebbles no larger than a fireplace. "Yes, it is, it is Narouz' island" she cried, beside herself with delight at the discovery—for here as last was a place where she could fully indulge her taste for solitude. Here one would be as private as a seabird. The beach faced landward. One could see the whole swaying line of the coast with its ruined Martello towers and dunes travelling away to ancient Taposiris. We unpacked our provisions with delight for here we could swim naked and sunbathe to our heart's content without interruption.

Here that strange and solitary brother of Nessim had spent his time fishing. "I always wondered where it could be this island of his. I thought perhaps it lay westerly beyond Abu El Suir. Nessim could not tell me. But he knew there was a deep rock-pool with a wreck."

"There is an N carved here."

Clea clapped her hands with delight and struggled out of her bathing costume. "I'm sure of it. Nessim said that for months he was fighting a duel with some big fish he couldn't identify.

That was when he gave me the harpoon-gun which Narouz owned. Isn't it strange? I've always carried it in the locker wrapped in an oilskin. I thought I might shoot something one day. But it is so heavy I can't manage it under water."

"What sort of fish was it?"

"I don't know."

But she scrambled back to the cutter and produced the bulky package of greased rags in which this singular weapon was wrapped. It was an ugly-looking contrivance, a compressed-air rifle no less, with a hollow butt. It fired a slim steel harpoon about a metre and a half in length. It had been made to specifications for him in Germany. It looked deadly enough to kill quite a large fish.

"Pretty horrible looking" she said, eating an orange.

"We must try it."

"It's too heavy for me. Perhaps you will manage it. I found that the barrel lagged in the water. I couldn't bring it to bear properly. But he was a marksman, so Nessim said, and shot a lot of quite large fish. But there was one, a very big one, which made infrequent appearances. He watched and waited in ambush for it for months. He had several shots at it but always missed. I hope it wasn't a shark—I'm scared of them."

"There aren't many in the Mediterranean. It is down the Red Sea that you get them in numbers."

"Nevertheless I keep a sharp eye out."

It was too heavy an instrument, I decided, to lug about under water; besides I had no interest in shooting fish. So I wrapped and stowed it once more in the cutter's ample locker. She lay there naked in the sunlight, drowsing like a seal, to smoke a cigarette before exploring further. The rock-pool glowed beneath the glimmering keel of the boat like a quivering emerald, the long ribbons of milky light penetrating it slowly, stealing down like golden probes. About four fathoms, I thought, and drawing a deep breath rolled over and let my body wangle downwards like a fish, not using my arms.

225

Its beauty was spell-binding. It was like diving into the nave of a cathedral whose stained-glass windows filtered the sunlight through a dozen rainbows. The sides of the amphitheatre —for it opened gradually towards the deep sea—seemed as if carved by some heartsick artist of the Romantic Age into a dozen half-finished galleries lined with statues. Some of these were so like real statuary that I thought for a moment that I had made an archaeological find. But these blurred caryatids were wave-born, pressed and moulded by the hazard of the tides into goddesses and dwarfs and clowns. A light marine fucus of brilliant yellow and green had bearded them—shallow curtains of weed which swung lightly in the tide, parting and closing, as if to reveal their secrets suggestively and then cover them again. I pushed my fingers through this scalp of dense and slippery foliage to press them upon the blind face of a Diana or the hooked nose of a mediaeval dwarf. The floor of this deserted palace was of selenite plastic clay, soft to the touch and in no way greasy. Terra-cotta baked in a dozen hues of mauve and violet and gold. Inside close to the island it was not deep— perhaps a fathom and a half—but it fell away steeply where the gallery spread out to the sea, and the deeper lining of water faded from emerald to apple green, and from Prussian blue to black, suggesting great depth. Here, too, was the wreck of which Clea had spoken. I had hopes of finding perhaps a Roman amphora or two, but it was not alas a very old ship. I recognised the flared curve of the poop as an Aegean design— the type of caique which the Greeks call 'trechandiri'. She had been rammed astern. Her back was broken. She was full of a dead weight of dark sponges. I tried to find the painted eyes on the prow and a name, but they had vanished. Her wood was crawling with slime and every cranny winked full of hermit crabs. She must have belonged to sponge fishers of Kalymnos I thought, for each year their fleet crosses to fish the African coast and carry its haul back for processing in the Dodecanese Islands.

A blinding parcel of light struck through the ceiling now and down flashed the eloquent body of Clea, her exploding coils of hair swerved up behind her by the water's concussion, her arms spread. I caught her and we rolled and sideslipped down in each other's arms, playing like fish until lack of breath drove us upwards once more into the sunlight. To sit at last panting in the shallows, gazing with breathless delight at each other.

"What a marvellous pool." She clapped her hands in delight.

"I saw the wreck."

And climbing back to the little sickle of beach with its warm pebbles with her drenched thatch of hair swinging behind her she said: 'I've thought of another thing. This must be Timonium. I wish I could remember the details more clearly.'

"What is that?"

"They've never found the site, you know. I am sure this must be it. O let us believe that it is, shall we? When Antony came back defeated from Actium—where Cleopatra fled with her fleet in panic and tore open his battle-line, leaving him at the mercy of Octavian; when he came back after that unaccountable failure of nerve, and when there was nothing for them to do but to wait for the certain death which would follow upon Octavian's arrival—why he built himself a cell on an islet. It was named after a famous recluse and misanthrope— perhaps a philosopher?—called Timon. And here he must have spent his leisure—*here*, Darley, going over the whole thing again and again in his mind. That woman with the extraordinary spells she was able to cast. His life in ruins! And then the passing of the God, and all that, bidding him to say goodbye to her, to Alexandria—a whole world!"

The brilliant eyes smiling a little wistfully interrogated mine. She put her fingers to my cheek.

"Are you waiting for me to say that it is?"

"Yes."

"Very well. It is."

"Kiss me."

"Your mouth tastes of oranges and wine."

It was so small, the beach—hardly bigger than a bed. It was strange to make love thus with one's ankles in blue water and the hot sun blazing on one's back. Later we made one of many desultory attempts to locate the cell, or something which might correspond to her fancy, but in vain; on the seaward side lay a tremendous jumble of granite snags, falling steeply into black water. A thick spoke of some ancient harbour level perhaps which explained the wind-and-sea-break properties of the island. It was so silent, one heard nothing but the faint stir of wind across our ears, distant as the echo of some tiny seashell. Yes, and sometimes a herring gull flew over to judge the depth of the beach as a possible theatre of operations. But for the rest the sun-drunk bodies lay, deeply asleep, the quiet rhythms of the blood responding only to the deeper rhythms of sea and sky. A haven of animal contents which words can never compass.

It is strange, too, to remember what a curious sea-engendered *rapport* we shared during that memorable summer. A delight almost as deep as the bondage of kisses—to enter the rhythm of the waters together, responding to each other and the play of the long tides. Clea had always been a fine swimmer, I a poor one. But thanks to my period spent in Greece I too was now expert, more than a match for her. Under water we played and explored the submarine world of the pool, as thoughtlessly as fishes of the fifth day of the Creation. Eloquent and silent water-ballets which allowed us to correspond only by smile and gesture. The water-silences captured and transformed everything human in movement, so that we were like the coloured projections of undines painted upon these brilliant screens of rock and weed, echoing and copying the water-rhythms. Here thought itself perished, was converted into a fathomless content in physical action. I see the bright figure travelling like a star across this twilit firmament, its hair combed up and out in a rippling whorl of colour.

But not only here, of course. When you are in love with one

of its inhabitants a city can become a world. A whole new geography of Alexandria was born through Clea, reviving old meanings, renewing ambiences half forgotten, laying down like a rich wash of colour a new history, a new biography to replace the old one. Memory of old cafés along the seafront by bronze moonlight, their striped awnings a-flutter with the midnight sea-breeze. To sit and dine late, until the glasses before one had brimmed with moonlight. In the shadow of a minaret, or on some strip of sand lit by the twinkle of a paraffin lamp. Or gathering the masses of shallow spring blossom on the Cape of Figs—brilliant cyclamen, brilliant anemone. Or standing together in the tombs of Kom El Shugafa inhaling the damp exhalations of the darkness which welled out of those strange subterranean resting-places of Alexandrians long dead; tombs carved out of the black chocolate soil, one upon the other, like bunks in a ship. Airless, mouldy and yet somehow piercingly cold. ("Hold my hand.") But if she shivered it was not then with the premonitions of death, but with the sheer weight of the gravid earth piled above us metre upon metre. Any creature of the sunlight would shiver so. That brilliant summer frock swallowed by the gloom. "I'm cold. Let us go." Yes, it was cold down there. But with what pleasure one stepped from the darkness into the roaring, anarchic life of the open street once more. So the sun-god must have risen, shaking himself free from the damp clutch of the soil, smiling up at the printed blue sky which spelt travel, release from death, renewal in the life of common creatures.

Yes, but the dead are everywhere. They cannot be so simply evaded. One feels them pressing their sad blind fingers in deprivation upon the panels of our secret lives, asking to be remembered and re-enacted once more in the life of the flesh— encamping among our heartbeats, invading our embraces. We carry in ourselves the biological trophies they bequeathed us by their failure to use up life—alignment of an eye, responsive curve of a nose; or in still more fugitive forms like someone's dead laugh, or a dimple which excites a long-buried smile. The simplest of these kisses we exchanged had a pedigree of death. In them we once more befriended forgotten loves which struggled to be reborn. The roots of every sigh are buried in the ground.

And when the dead invade? For sometimes they emerge in person. That brilliant morning, for example, with everything so deceptively normal, when bursting from the pool like a rocket she gasped, deathly pale: *"There are dead men down there"*: frightening me! Yet she was not wrong, for when I mustered the courage to go down myself and look—there they were in very truth, seven of them, sitting in the twilight of the basin with an air of scrupulous attention, as if listening to some momentous debate which would decide everything for them. This conclave of silent figures formed a small semicircle across the outer doorway of the pool. They had been roped in sacks and leadweighted at the feet, so that now they stood upright, like chess pieces of human size. One has seen statues covered in this way, travelling through a city on a lorry, bound for some sad provincial museum. Slightly crouched, responding to the ligatures which bound them, and faceless, they nevertheless stood, flinching and flickering softly like figures in an early silent film. Heavily upholstered in death by the coarse canvas wrappers which bound them.

They turned out to be Greek sailors who had been bathing from their corvette when, by some accident, a depth-charge had been detonated, killing them instantly by concussion. Their unmarked bodies, glittering like mackerel, had been harvested laboriously in an old torpedo net, and laid out upon dripping decks to dry before burial. Flung overboard once more in the traditional funeral dress of mariners the curling tide had brought them to Narouz' island.

It will sound strange, perhaps, to describe how quickly we got used to these silent visitants of the pool. Within a matter of days we had accommodated them, accorded them a place of their own. We swam between them to reach the outer water, bowing ironically to their bent attentive heads.

It was not to flout death—it was rather that they had become friendly and appropriate symbols of the place, these patient, intent figures. Neither their thick skin-parcels of canvas, nor the stout integuments of rope which bound them showed any sign of disintegration. On the contrary they were covered by a dense silver dew, like mercury, which heavily proofed canvas always collects when it is immersed. We spoke once or twice of asking the Greek naval authorities to remove them to deeper water, but by long experience I knew that we should find them un-co-operative if we tried, and the subject was dropped by common consent. Once I thought I saw the flickering shadow of a great catfish moving among them but I must have been mistaken. We even thought later of giving them names, but were deterred by the thought that they must already have names of their own—the absurd names of ancient sophists and generals like Anaximander, Plato, Alexander. . . .

So this halcyon summer moved towards its end, free from omens—the long sunburnt ranks of marching days. It was, I think, in the late autumn that Maskelyne was killed in a desert sortie, but this was a passing without echoes for me—so little substance had he ever had in my mind as a living personage. It was, in very truth, a mysterious thing to find Telford sitting red-eyed at his desk one afternoon repeating brokenly: "The old Brig's copped it. The poor old Brig" and wringing his purple hands together. It was hard to know what to say. Telford went on, with a kind of incoherent wonder in his voice that was endearing. "He had no-one in the world. D'you know what? He gave me as his next-of-kin." He seemed immeasurably touched by this mark of friendship. Nevertheless it was with a reverent melancholy that he went through Maskelyne's exiguous personal effects. There was little enough to inherit save a few civilian clothes of unsuitable size, several campaign medals and stars, and a credit account of fifteen pounds in the Tottenham Court Road Branch of Lloyds Bank. More interesting relics to me were those contained in a little leather wallet—the tattered pay-book and parchment certificate of discharge which had belonged to his grandfather. The story they told had the eloquence of a history which unfolded itself within a tradition. In the year 1861 this now forgotten Suffolk farm-boy had enlisted at Bury St. Edmunds. He served in the Coldstream Guards for thirty-two years, being discharged in 1893. During his service he was married in the Chapel of the Tower of London and his wife bore him two sons. There was a faded photograph of him taken on his return from Egypt in 1882. It showed him dressed in white pith helmet, red jacket and blue serge trousers with smart black leather gaiters and pipe-clayed cross belts. On his breast was pinned the Egyptian War Medal with a clasp for the battle of Tel-el-Kebir and the Khedive's Star. Of Maskelyne's own father there was no record among his effects.

"It's tragic" said little Telford with emotion. "Mavis couldn't stop crying when I told her. She only met him twice. It shows what an effect a man of character can have on you. He was always the perfect gentleman, was the Brig." But I was brooding over this obscure faded figure in the photograph with his grim eyes and heavy black moustache, with the pipe-clayed cross belts and the campaign medals. He seemed to lighten the picture of Maskelyne himself, to give it focus. Was it not, I wondered, a story of success—a success perfectly complete within the formal pattern of something greater than the individual life, a tradition? I doubted whether Maskelyne himself could have wanted things to fall out otherwise. In every death there is the grain of something to be learned. Yet Maskelyne's quiet departure made little impact on my feelings, though I did what I could to soothe the forlorn Telford. But the tide-lines of my own life were now beginning to tug me invisibly towards an unforeseeable future. Yes, it was this beautiful autumn, with its torrent of brass brown leaves showering down from the trees in the public gardens, that Clea first became a matter of concern to me. Was it, in truth, because she heard the weeping? I do not know. She never openly admitted it. At times I tried to imagine that I heard it myself—this frail cry of a small child, or a pet locked out: but I knew that I heard nothing, absolutely nothing. Of course one could look at it in a matter-of-fact way and class it with the order of natural events which time revises and renews according to its own caprices. I mean love can wither like any other plant. Perhaps she was simply falling out of love? But in order to record the manner of its falling out I feel almost compelled to present it as something else—preposterous as it may sound—as a visitation of an agency, a power initiated in some uncommon region beyond the scope of the ordinary imagination. At any rate its onset was quite definitive, marked up like a date on a blank wall. It was November the fourteenth, just before dawn. We had been together during the whole of the previous day, idling about the city, gossiping and shopping. She had bought some piano music, and I had made her a present of a new scent from the Scent Bazaar. (At the very moment when I awoke and saw her standing, or rather crouching by the window, I caught the sudden breath of scent from my own wrist which had been dabbed with samples from the glass-stoppered bottles.) Rain had fallen that night. Its delicious swishing had lulled our sleep. We had read by candle-light before falling asleep.

But now she was standing by the window listening, her whole body stiffened into an attitude of attentive interrogation so acute that it suggested something like a crisis of apprehension. Her head was turned a little sideways, as if to present her ear to the uncurtained window behind which, very dimly, a rain-washed dawn was beginning to break over the roofs of the city. What was she listening for? I had never seen this attitude before. I called to her and briefly she turned a distraught and unseeing face to me—impatiently, as if my voice had ruptured the fine membrane of her concentration. And as I sat up she cried, in a deep choked voice: "O *no!*", and clapping her hands over her ears fell shuddering to her knees. It was as if a bullet had been fired through her brain. I heard her bones creak as she hung crouching there her features contorted into a grimace. Her hands were locked so tightly over her ears that I could not disengage them, and when I tried to lift her by her wrists she simply sank back to her knees on the carpet, with shut eyes, like a dement. "Clea, what on earth is it?" For a long moment we knelt there together, I in great perplexity. Her eyes were fast shut. I could feel the cool wind from the window pouring into the room. The silence, save for our exclamations, was complete. At last she gave a great sigh of relaxation, a long sobbing respiration, and unfastened her ears, stretched her limbs slowly, as if unbinding them from painful cramps. She shook her head at me as if to say that it was nothing. And walking like a drunkard to the bathroom she was violently sick in the washbasin. I stood there like a sleep-walker; feeling as if I had been uprooted. At last she came back, got into bed and turned her face to the wall. "What is it, Clea?" I asked again, feeling foolish and importunate. Her shoulders trembled slightly under my hand, her teeth chattered lightly from cold. "It is nothing, really nothing. A sudden splitting headache. But it has gone. Let me sleep now, will you?"

In the morning she was up early to make the breakfast. I thought her exceptionally pale—with the sort of pallor that might come after a long and agonising toothache. She complained of feeling listless and weary.

"You frightened me last night" I said, but she did not answer, turning away evasively from the subject with a curious look of anxiety and distress. She asked to be allowed to spend the day alone painting, so I took myself off for a long walk across the town, teased by half-formulated thoughts and premonitions which I somehow could not make explicit to myself. It was a beautiful day. High seas were running. The waves flailed the Spouting Rocks like the pistons of some huge machine. Immense clouds of spray were flung high into the air like the explosion of giant puff-balls only to fall back in hissing spume upon the crown of the next wave. I stood watching the spectacle for a long time, feeling the tug of the wind at the skirt of my overcoat and the cool spray on my cheeks. I think I must have known that from this point onward everything would be subtly changed. That we had entered, so to speak, a new constellation of feelings which would alter our relationship.

One speaks of change, but in truth there was nothing abrupt, coherent, definitive about it. No, the metamorphosis came about with comparative slowness. It waxed and waned like a tide, now advancing now retreating. There were even times when, for whole weeks, we were apparently completely restored to our former selves, reviving the old raptures with an intensity born now of insecurity. Suddenly for a spell we would be once more completely identified in each other, inseparable: the shadow had lifted. I tell myself now—and with what truth I still do not know—that these were periods when for a long time she had not heard the weeping which she once long ago described as belonging to a she-camel in distress or some horrible mechanical toy. But what could such nonsense really mean to anyone—and how could it elucidate those other periods when she fell into silence and moroseness, became a nervous and woebegone version of her old self? I do not know. I only know that this new personage was subject to long distracted silences now, and to unusual fatigues. She might, for example, fall asleep on a sofa in the middle of a party and begin to snore: as if overcome with weariness after an immensely long vigil. Insomnia too began to play its part, and she resorted to relatively massive doses of barbiturates in order to seek release from it. She was smoking very heavily indeed.

"Who is this new nervy person I do not recognise?" asked Balthazar in perplexity one evening when she had snapped his head off after some trivial pleasantry and left the room, banging the door in my face.

235

"There's something wrong" I said. He looked at me keenly for a moment over a lighted match. "She isn't pregnant?" he asked, and I shook my head. "I think she's beginning to wear me out really." It cost me an effort to bring out the words. But they had the merit of offering something like a plausible explanation to these moods—unless one preferred to believe that she were being gnawed by secret fears.

"Patience" he said. "There is never enough of it."

"I'm seriously thinking of absenting myself for a while."

"That might be a good idea. But not for too long."

"I shall see."

Sometimes in my clumsy way I would try by some teasing remark to probe to the sources of this disruptive anxiety. "Clea, why are you always looking over your shoulder—for what?" But this was a fatal error of tactics. Her response was always one of ill-temper or pique, as if in every reference to her distemper, however oblique, I was in some way mocking her. It was intimidating to see how rapidly her face darkened, her lips compressed themselves. It was as if I had tried to put my hand on a secret treasure which she was guarding with her life.

At times she was particularly nervous. Once as we were coming out of a cinema I felt her stiffen on my arm. I turned my eyes in the direction of her gaze. She was staring with horror at an old man with a badly gashed face. He was a Greek cobbler who had been caught in a bombardment and mutilated. We all knew him quite well by sight, indeed Amaril had repaired the damage as well as he was able. I shook her arm softly, reassuringly and she suddenly seemed to come awake. She straightened up abruptly and said "Come. Let us go." She gave a little shudder and hurried me away.

At other such times when I had unguardedly made some allusion to her inner preoccupations—this maddening air of always *listening* for something—the storms and accusations which followed seriously suggested the truth of my own hypothesis—namely that she was trying to drive me away: "I am no good for you, Darley. Since we have been together you haven't written a single line. You have no plans. You hardly read any more." So stern those splendid eyes had become, and so troubled! I was forced to laugh, however. In truth I now knew, or thought I did, that I would never become a writer. The whole impulse to confide in the world in this way had foundered, had guttered out. The thought of the nagging little world of print and paper had become unbearably tedious to contemplate. Yet I was not unhappy to feel that the urge had abandoned me. On the contrary I was full of relief—a relief from the bondage of these forms which seemed so inadequate an instrument to convey the truth of feelings. "Clea, my dear" I said, still smiling ineffectually, and yet desiring in a way to confront this accusation and placate her. "I have been actually meditating a book of criticism."

"Criticism!" she echoed sharply, as if the word were an insult. And she smacked me full across the mouth—a stinging blow which brought tears to my eyes and cut the inside of my lip against my teeth. I retired to the bathroom to mop my mouth for I could feel the salty taste of the blood. It was interesting to see my teeth outlined in blood. I looked like an ogre who had just taken a mouthful of bleeding flesh from his victims. I washed my mouth, furiously enraged. She came in and sat down on the *bidet*, full of remorse. "Please forgive me" she said. "I don't know what sort of impulse came over me. Darley, please forgive" she said.

"One more performance like this" I said grimly "and I'll give you a blow between those beautiful eyes which you'll remember."

"I'm sorry." She put her arms round my shoulders from behind and kissed my neck. The blood had stopped. "What the devil is wrong?" I said to her reflection in the mirror. "What has come over you these days? We're drifting apart, Clea."

"I know."

"Why?"

"I don't know." But her face had once more become hard and obstinate. She sat down on the *bidet* and stroked her chin thoughtfully, suddenly sunk in reflection once more. Then she lit a cigarette and walked back into her living-room. When I returned she was sitting silently before a painting gazing at it with an inattentive malevolent fixity.

"I think we should separate for a while" I said.

"If you wish" she rapped out mechanically.

"Do you wish it?"

Suddenly she started crying and said "O stop questioning me. If only you would stop asking me question after question. It's like being in court these days."

"Very well" I said.

This was only one of several such scenes. It seemed clear to me that to absent myself from the city was the only way to free her—to give her the time and space necessary to . . . what? I did not know. Later that winter I thought that she had begun running a small temperature in the evenings and incurred another furious scene by asking Balthazar to examine her. Yet despite her anger she submitted to the stethoscope with comparative quietness. Balthazar could find nothing physically wrong, except that her pulse rate was advanced and her blood pressure higher than normal. His prescription of stimulants she ignored, however. She had become much thinner at this time.

By patient lobbying I at last unearthed a small post for which I was not unsuitable and which somehow fitted into the general rhythm of things—for I did not envisage my separation from Clea as something final, something in the nature of a break. It was simply a planned withdrawal for a few months to make room for any longer-sighted resolutions which she might make. New factors were there, too, for with the ending of the war Europe was slowly coming accessible once more—a new horizon opening beyond the battle-lines. One had almost stopped dreaming of it, the recondite shape of a Europe hammered flat

238

by bombers, raked by famine and discontents. Nevertheless it was still there. So it was that when I came to tell her of my departure it was not with despondency or sorrow—but as a matter-of-fact decision which she must welcome for her own part. Only the manner in which she pronounced the word "Away" with an indrawn breath suggested for a brief second that perhaps, after all, she might be afraid to be left alone. "You are going away, after all?"

"For a few months. They are building a relay station on the island, and there is need for someone who knows the place and can speak the language."

"Back to the island?" she said softly—and here I could not read the meaning of her voice or the design of her thought.

"For a few short months only."

"Very well."

She walked up and down the carpet with an air of perplexity, staring downwards at it, deep in thought. Suddenly she looked up at me with a soft expression that I recognised with a pang— the mixture of remorse and tenderness at inflicting unwitting sorrow upon others. It was the face of the old Clea. But I knew that it would not last, that once more the peculiar shadow of her discontent would cast itself over our relationship. There was no point in trusting myself once more to what could only prove a short respite. "O Darley" she said, "when do you go, my dear?" taking my hands.

"In a fortnight. Until then I propose not to see you at all. There is no point in our upsetting each other by these wrangles."

"As you wish."

"I'll write to you."

"Yes of course."

It was a strange listless way of parting after such a momentous relationship. A sort of ghostly anaesthesia had afflicted our emotions. There was a kind of deep ache inside me but it wasn't sorrow. The dead handshake we exchanged only ex- pressed a strange and truthful exhaustion of the spirit. She sat

239

in a chair, quietly smoking and watching me as I gathered my possessions together and stuffed them into the old battered briefcase which I had borrowed from Telford and forgotten to return the summer before. The toothbrush was splayed. I threw it away. My pyjamas were torn at the shoulder but the bottom half, which I had never used, were still crisp and new. I assembled these objects with the air of a geologist sorting specimens of some remote age. A few books and papers. It all had a sort of unreality, but I cannot say that a single sharp regret was mixed with it.

"How this war has aged and staled us" she said suddenly, as if to herself. "In the old days one would have thought of going away in order, as we said, to get away from oneself. But to get away from *it*. . . ."

Now, writing the words down in all their tedious banality, I realise that she was really trying to say goodbye. The fatality of human wishes. For me the future lay open, uncommitted; and there was no part of it which I could then visualise as not containing, somehow, Clea. This parting was . . . well, it was only like changing the bandages until a wound should heal. Being unimaginative, I could not think definitively about a future which might make unexpected demands upon me; as something entirely new. It must be left to form itself upon the emptiness of the present. But for Clea the future had already closed, was already presenting a blank wall. The poor creature was afraid!

"Well, that's everything" I said at last, shoving the brief-case under my arm. "If there's anything you need, you have only to ring me. I'll be at the flat."

"I know."

"I'm off then for a while. Goodbye."

As I closed the door of the little flat I heard her call my name once—but this again was one of those deceptions, those little accesses of pity or tenderness which deceive one. It would have been absurd to pay any attention to it, to return on my tracks, and open a new cycle of disagreements. I went on down the stairs, determined to let the future have every chance to heal itself.

It was a brilliantly sunny spring day and the streets looked washed with colour. The feeling of having nowhere to go and nothing to do was both depressing and inspiriting. I returned to the flat and found on the mantelpiece a letter from Pombal in which he said that he was likely to be transferred to Italy shortly and did not think he would be able to keep the flat on. I was delighted as this enabled me to terminate the lease, my share of which I would soon not be able to afford myself.

It was at first somewhat strange, even perhaps a little numbing, to be left entirely to my own devices, but I rapidly became accustomed to it. Moreover there was quite a lot of work to be done in winding up my censorship duties and handing over the post to a successor while at the same time collecting practical information for the little unit of technicians which was to install the radio post. Between the two departments with their different needs I was kept busy enough. During these days I kept my word and saw nothing of Clea. The time passed in a sort of limbo pitched between the world of desire and of fare-well—though there were no emotions in very clear definition for me: I was not conscious of regrets or longings.

So it was that when at last that fatal day presented itself, it did so under the smiling guise of a spring sunshine hot enough to encourage the flies to begin hatching out upon the window-panes. It was their buzzing which awoke me. Sunlight was pouring into the room. For a moment, dazzled by it, I hardly recognised the smiling figure seated at the foot of my bed, waiting for me to open my eyes. It was the Clea of some for-gotten original version, so to speak, clad in a brilliant summer frock of a crisp vine-leaf pattern, white sandals, and with her hair arranged in a new style. She was smoking a cigarette whose smoke hung in brilliant ash-veined whorls in the sunlight above us, and her smiling face was completely relaxed and un-

241

shadowed by the least preoccupation. I stared, for she seemed so precisely and unequivocally the Clea I should always have remembered; the mischievous tenderness was back in the eyes. "Well" I said in sleepy amazement. "What . . . ?" and I felt her warm breath on my cheek as she leaned down to embrace me.

"Darley" she said, "I suddenly realised that it's tomorrow you are leaving; and that today is the Mulid of El Scob. I couldn't resist the idea of spending the day together and visiting the shrine this evening. O say you will! Look at the sunshine. It's warm enough for a bathe, and we could take Balthazar."

I was still not properly awake. I had completely forgotten the Name Day of the Pirate. "But it's long past St. George's Day" I said. "Surely that's at the end of April."

"On the contrary. Their absurd method of lunar calendar reckoning has turned him into a movable feast like all the others. He slides up and down the calendar now like a domestic saint. In fact it was Balthazar who telephoned yesterday and told me or I would have missed it myself." She paused to puff her cigarette. "We shouldn't miss it, should we?" she added a little wistfully.

"But of course not! How good of you to come."

"And the island? Perhaps you could come with us?"

The time was just ten o'clock. I could easily telephone to Telford to make some excuse for absenting myself for the day. My heart leaped.

"I'd love to" I said. "How does the wind sit?"

"Calm as a nun with easterly freshets. Ideal for the cutter I should say. Are you sure you want to come?"

She had a wicker-covered demijohn and a basket with her. "I'll go on and provision us up; you dress and meet me at the Yacht Club in an hour."

"Yes." It would give me ample time to visit my office and examine the duty mail. "A splendid idea."

242

And in truth it was, for the day was clear and ringing with a promise of summer heat for the afternoon. Clip-clopping down the Grande Corniche I studied the light haze on the horizon and the flat blue expanse of sea with delight. The city glittered in sunshine like a jewel. Brilliantly rode the little craft in the inner basin, parodied by their shining reflections. The minarets shone loudly. In the Arab quarter the heat had hatched out the familiar smells of offal and drying mud, of carnations and jasmine, of animal sweat and clover. In Tatwig Street dark gnomes on ladders with scarlet flower-pot hats were stretching strings of flags from the balconies. I felt the sun warm on my fingers. We rolled past the site of the ancient Pharos whose shattered fragments still choke the shallows. Toby Mannering, I remembered, had once wanted to start a curio trade by selling fragments of the Pharos as paperweights. Scobie was to break them up with a hammer for him and he was to deliver them to retailers all over the world. Why had the scheme foundered? I could not remember. Perhaps Scobie found the work too arduous? Or perhaps it had got telescoped with that other scheme for selling Jordan water to Copts at a competitive price? Somewhere a military band was banging away.

They were down on the slip waiting for me. Balthazar waved his stick cheerfully. He was dressed in white trousers and sandals and a coloured shirt, and sported an ancient yellowing Panama hat.

"The first day of summer" I called cheerfully.

"You're wrong" he croaked. "Look at that haze. It's altogether too hot. I've betted Clea a thousand piastres we have a thunderstorm by this afternoon."

"He's always got something gloomy to say" smiled Clea.

"I know my Alexandria" said Balthazar.

And so amidst these idle pleasantries we three set forth, Clea at the tiller of her little craft. There was hardly a breath of wind inside the harbour and she lagged somewhat, only gathering way by the momentum of the currents which curved down

243

towards the harbour entrance. We stole past the battleships and
liners, breasting the choppy main-channel hesitantly, the main-
sail hardly drawing as yet, until at last we reached the huddle of
grey forts which marked the main harbour entrance. Here there
was always a bundle of choppy water piled up by the tide and
we wallowed and yawed for a while until suddenly she heeled
and threaded herself upon the wind and settled her bowsprit
true. We began to hiss through the sea like a flying fish, as if
she were going to impale a star. I lay in the sheets now, staring
up at the gold sun shining through the sails, hearing the smat-
tering of the wavelets on the elegant prow of the cutter. Balthazar was humming an air. Clea's brown wrist lay upon the
tiller with a deceptive soft negligence. The sails were stiff.
These are the heart-lifting joys of small sailing-craft in ideal
weather. A speechless delight held me, a mixture of luxuries
born of the warm sun, the racing wind, and the light cool
touches of spray which dashed our cheeks from time to time.
We went far out on an easterly course in order to come about
and tack inshore. By now we had performed this manœuvre so
often that it had become second nature to Clea: to ride down
upon the little island of Narouz and to judge the exact
moment at which to turn into the eye of the wind and hang,
fluttering like an eyelash, until I had run the sail in and
scrambled ashore to make fast. . . .

"Smart work indeed" said Balthazar approvingly as he
stepped into the water; and then "By God! it is quite fantastically warm."

"What did I tell you?" said Clea busy in the locker.

"It only proves my point about a thunderstorm."

And curiously enough, at this moment, there came a distinct rumble of thunder out of that cloudless sky. "There" said
Balthazar in triumph. "We will get a fine soaking and you
will owe me some money, Clea."

"We'll see."

"It was a shore battery" I said.

"Rubbish" said Balthazar.

So we secured the cutter and carried our provisions ashore. Balthazar lay on his back with his hat over his nose in the best of humours. He would not bathe, pleading the indifference of his swimming, so Clea and I dived once more into the familiar pool which we had neglected all winter long. Nothing had changed. The sentinels were still there, grouped in silent debate, though the winter tides had altered their dispositions somewhat, grouping them a little nearer to the wreck. Ironically yet respectfully we greeted them, recognising in these ancient gestures and underwater smiles a familiar happiness growing up in the sheer act of swimming once more together. It was as if the blood had started to flow again in veins long withered from disuse. I caught her by the heel and rolled her in a long somersault towards the dead mariners, and turning expertly she repaid the debt by coming up behind me to drag me down by the shoulders and climb surfacewards before I could retaliate. It was here, spiralling up through the water with her hair coiled out behind her, that the image of Clea was restored once more. Time had rendered her up, whole and intact again—'natural as a city's grey-eyed Muse'—to quote the Greek poem. Swiftly, precisely the fingers which pressed upon my shoulder re-evoked her as we slid through the silent pool.

And then: to sit once more in the simple sunlight, sipping the red wine of St. Menas as she broke up the warm brown loaf of French bread, and hunted for a particular cheese or a cluster of dates: while Balthazar talked discursively (half asleep) of the Vineyard of Ammon, the Kings of the Harpoon Kingdom and their battles, or of the Mareotic wine to which, not history, but the gossiping Horace once attributed Cleopatra's distempers of mind . . . ("History sanctions everything, pardons everything —even what we do not pardon ourselves.")

So the warm noon drew on as we lay there on the hot pebbles: and so at last—to Balthazar's great delight and Clea's discomfiture—the predicted thunderstorm made its appearance, heralded by a great livid cloud which rolled up from the east and squatted over the city, bruising the sky. So suddenly too—as when an ink-squid in alarm puffs out its bag and suddenly fogs clear water in a cloud of black—rain flowed down in glittering sheets, thunder bellowed and insisted. At each peal Balthazar clapped his hands with delight—not only to be proved right, but also because here we were sitting in full sunlight, fully at our ease, eating oranges and drinking wine beside an untroubled blue sea.

"Stop crowing" said Clea severely.

It was one of those freak storms so prevalent in the early spring with its sharp changes of temperature born of sea and desert. They turned the streets to torrents in the twinkling of an eye, yet never endured above half an hour. Suddenly the cloud would be whisked away by a scrap of wind, utterly to disappear. "And mark me now" said Balthazar, inebriated by the success of his prediction. "By the time we get back to harbour everything will be dry again, dry as a bone."

But now the afternoon brought us another phenomenon to delight us—something rarely seen in summer in the waters of Alexandria, belonging as it did to those days preceding winter storms when the glass was falling steeply. The waters of the pool darkened appreciably, curdled, and then became phosphorescent. It was Clea who first noticed. "Look" she cried with delight crushing her heels down in the shallows to watch the twinkling prickling light spark from them. "Phosphorus!" Balthazar started saying something learned about the organism which causes this spectacle but unheeding we plunged side by side and ranged down into the water, transformed into figures of flame, the sparks flashing from the tips of our fingers and toes with the glitter of static electricity. A swimmer seen underwater looks like an early picture of the fall of Lucifer, literally on fire. So bright was the electrical crackle that we could not help wondering how it was that we were not scorched by it. So we played, glittering like comets, among the quiet mariners who sat, watching us perhaps in their thoughts, faintly echoing the twitching of the tide in their canvas sacks.

"The cloud's lifting already" cried Balthazar as I surfaced at last for air. Soon even the fugitive phosphorescence would dwindle and vanish. For some reason or other he had climbed into the stern of the cutter, perhaps to gain height and more easily watch the thunderstorm over the city. I rested my fore-arms on the gunwale and took my breath. He had unwrapped the old harpoon gun of Narouz and was holding it negligently on his knee. Clea surfaced with a swish of delight and pausing just long enough to cry: "The fire is so beautiful" doubled her lithe body back and ducked downward again.

"What are you doing with that?" I asked idly.

"Seeing how it works."

He had in fact pushed the harpoon to rest in the barrel. It had locked with the spring. "It's cocked" I said. " Have a care."

"Yes, I'm going to release it."

Then Balthazar leaned forward and uttered the only serious remark he had made all that day. "You know" he said, "I think you had better take her with you. I have a feeling you won't be coming back to Alexandria. Take Clea with you!"

And then, before I could reply, the accident happened. He was fumbling with the gun as he spoke. It slipped from be-tween his fingers and fell with a crash, the barrel striking the gunwale six inches from my face. As I reared back in alarm I heard the sudden cobra-like hiss of the compressor and the leaden twang of the trigger-release. The harpoon whistled into the water beside me rustling its long green line behind it. "For Christ's sake" I said. Balthazar had turned white with alarm and vexation. His half-muttered apologies and expressions of horrid amazement were eloquent. "I'm terribly sorry." I had heard the slight snick of steel settling into a target, somewhere down there in the pool. We stayed frozen for a second for something else had occurred simultaneously to our minds. As I

saw his lips starting to shape the word "Clea" I felt a sudden
darkness descending on my spirit—a darkness which lifted and
trembled at the edges; and a rushing like the sough of giant
wings. I had already turned before he uttered the word. I
crashed back into the water, now following the long green
thread with all the suspense of Ariadne; and to it added the
weight of slowness which only heartsick apprehension brings.
I knew in my mind that I was swimming vigorously—yet it
seemed like one of those slow-motion films where human
actions, delayed by the camera, are drawn unctuously out to
infinity, spooled out like toffee. How many light-years would
it take to reach the end of that thread? What would I find at
the end of it? Down I went, and down, in the dwindling phosphorescence, into the deep shadowed coolness of the pool.

At the far end, by the wreck, I distinguished a convulsive,
coiling movement, and dimly recognised the form of Clea. She
seemed intently busy upon some childish underwater game of
the kind we so often played together. She was tugging at something, her feet braced against the woodwork of the wreck, tugging and relaxing her body. Though the green thread led to her
I felt a wave of relief—for perhaps she was only trying to extri-
cate the harpoon and carry it to the surface with her. But no,
for she rolled drunkenly. I slid along her like an eel, feeling
with my hands. Feeling me near she turned her head as if to
tell me something. Her long hair impeded my vision. As for
her face I could not read the despairing pain which must have
been written on it—for the water transforms every expression
of the human features into the goggling imbecile grimace of
the squid. But now she arched out and flung her head back so
that her hair could flow freely up from her scalp—the gesture of
someone throwing open a robe to exhibit a wound. And I saw.
Her right hand had been pierced and nailed to the wreck by
the steel arrow. At least it had not passed through her body,
my mind cried out in relief, seeking to console itself; but the
relief turned to sick malevolent despair when, clutching the

248

steel shaft, I myself braced my feet against the wood, tugging until my thigh muscles cracked. It would not be budged by a hair's breadth. (No, but all this was part of some incomprehensible dream, fabricated perhaps in the dead minds of the seven brooding figures which attended so carefully, so scrupulously to the laboured evolutions we now performed—we no longer free and expeditious as fish, but awkward, splayed, like lobsters trapped in a pot.) I struggled frantically with that steel arrow, seeing out of the corner of my eye the long chain of white bubbles bursting from the throat of Clea. I felt her muscles expending themselves, ebbing. Gradually she was settling in the drowsiness of the blue water, being invaded by the watersleep which had already lulled the mariners to sleep. I shook her.

I cannot pretend that anything which followed belonged to my own volition—for the mad rage which now possessed me was not among the order of the emotions I would ever have recognised as belonging to my proper self. It exceeded, in blind violent rapacity, anything I had ever before experienced. In this curious timeless underwater dream I felt my brain ringing like the alarm bell of an ambulance, dispelling the lulling languorous ebb and flow of the marine darkness. I was suddenly rowelled by the sharp spur of terror. It was as if I were for the first time confronting myself—or perhaps an alter ego shaped after a man of action I had never realised, recognised. With one wild shove I shot to the surface again, emerging under Balthazar's very nose.

"The knife" I said sucking in the air.

His eyes gazed into mine, as if over the edge of some sunken continent, with an expression of pity and horror; emotions preserved, fossilised, from some ice age of human memory. And native fear. He started to stammer out all the questions which invaded his mind—words like "what" "where" "when" "whither"—but could achieve no more than a baffled "wh——": a vague sputtering anguish of interrogation.

249

The knife which I had remembered was an Italian bayonet which had been ground down to the size of a dirk and sharpened to razor keenness. Ali the boatman had manufactured it with pride. He used it to trim ropes, for splicing and rigging. I hung there for a second while he reached out for it, eyes closed, lungs drinking in the whole sky it seemed. Then I felt the wooden haft in my fingers and without daring to look again at Balthazar I turned my toes to heaven and returned on my tracks, following the green thread.

She hung there limp now, stretched languorously out, while her long hair unfurled behind her; the tides rippled out along her body, passing through it, it seemed like an electric current playing. Everything was still, the silver coinage of sunlight dappling the floor of the pool, the silent observers, the statues whose long beards moved slowly, unctuously to and fro. Even as I began to hack at her hand I was mentally preparing a large empty space in my mind which would have to accommodate the thought of her dead. A large space like an unexplored sub-continent on the maps of the mind. It was not very long before I felt the body disengage under this bitter punishment. The water was dark. I dropped the knife and with a great push sent her reeling back from the wreck: caught her under the arms: and so rose. It seemed to take an age—and endless progression of heartbeats—in that slow-motion world. Yet we hit the sky with a concussion that knocked the breath from me—as if I had cracked my skull on the ceiling of the universe. I was standing in the shallows now rolling the heavy sodden log of her body. I heard the crash of Balthazar's teeth falling into the boat as he jumped into the water beside me. We heaved and grunted like stevedores until she was out on the pebbles, Balthazar meanwhile scrabbling about to grasp that injured hand which was spouting. He was like an electrician trying to capture and insulate a high-tension wire which had snapped. Grabbing it, he held on to it like a vice. I had a sudden picture of him as a small child holding his mother's hand nervously

250

among a crowd of other children, or crossing a park where the
boys had once thrown stones at him. . . . Through his pink
gums he extruded the word "Twine"—and there was some
luckily in the cutter's locker which kept him busy.

"But she's dead" I said, and the word altered my heartbeats,
so that I felt about to faint. She was lying, like a fallen seabird,
on the little spit of pebbles. Balthazar squatted almost in the
water, holding frenziedly on to the hand at which I could
hardly bear to look. But again this unknown alter ego whose
voice came from far away helped me to adjust a tourniquet,
roll a pencil in it and hand it to him. With a heave now I
straightened her out and fell with a thump upon her, crashing
down as if from a very great height upon her back. I felt the
soggy heavy lungs bounce under this crude blow. Again and
again, slowly but with great violence I began to squeeze them
in this pitiful simulacrum of the sexual act—life saving, life-
giving. Balthazar appeared to be praying. Then came a small
sign of hope for the lips of that pale face opened and a little sea
water mixed with vomit trickled from them. It meant nothing,
of course, but we both cried out at the omen. Closing my eyes
I willed my wrists to seek out those waterlogged lungs, to
squeeze and void them. Up and down, up and down in this
slow cruel rhythm, I pumped at her. I felt her fine bones creaking under my hands. But still she lay lifeless. But I would not
accept the thought that she was dead, though I knew it with
one part of my mind. I felt half mad with determination to
disprove it, to overthrow, if necessary, the whole process of
nature and by an act of will force her to live. These decisions
astonished me, for they subsisted like clear and sharply defined
images underneath the dazed physical fatigue, the groan and
sweat of this labour. I had, I realised, decided either to bring
her up alive or to stay down there at the bottom of the pool
with her; but where, from which territory of the will such a
decision had come, I could not guess! And now it was hot. I
was pouring with sweat. Balthazar still sat holding the hand,

251

the painter's hand, humbly as a child at its mother's knee. Tears trickled down his nose. His head went from side to side in that Jewish gesture of despairing remorse and his toothless gums formed the sound of the old Wailing Wall "Aiee, Aiee". But very softly, as if not to disturb her.

But at last we were rewarded. Suddenly, like a spout giving in a gutter under the pressure of rain, her mouth opened and expelled a mass of vomit and sea-water, fragments of breadsoak and orange. We gazed at this mess with a lustful delight, as if at a great trophy. I felt the lungs respond slowly to my hand. A few more strokes of this crude engine and a secondary ripple seemed to stir in the musculature of her body. At almost every downward thrust now the lungs gave up some water, reluctantly, painfully. Then, after a long time, we heard a faint whimper. It must have hurt, as the first few breaths hurt a newly born child. The body of Clea was protesting at this forcible rebirth. And all of a sudden the features of that white face moved, composed themselves to express something like pain and protest. (Yes, but it *hurts* to realise.)

"Keep it up" cried Balthazar in a new voice, shaky and triumphant. There was no need to tell me. She was twitching a little now, and making a soundless whimpering face at each lunge. It was like starting a very cold diesel engine. Finally yet another miracle occurred—for she opened very blue sightless unfocused eyes for a second to study, with dazed concentration, the stones before her nose. Then she closed them again. Pain darkened her features, but even the pain was a triumph—for at least they expressed living emotions now—emotions which had replaced the pale set mask of death. "She's breathing" I said. "Balthazar she's breathing."

"She's breathing" he repeated with a kind of idiotic rapture.

She was breathing, short staggering inspirations which were clearly painful. But now another kind of help was at hand. We had not noticed, so concentrated were we on this task, that a vessel had entered the little harbour. This was the Harbour

Patrol motorboat. They had seen us and guessed that something was wrong. "Merciful God" cried Balthazar flapping his arms like an old crow. Cheerful English voices came across the water asking if we needed help; a couple of sailors came ashore towards us. "We'll have her back in no time" said Balthazar, grinning shakily.

"Give her some brandy."

"No" he cried sharply. "No brandy."

The sailors brought a tarpaulin ashore and softly we baled her up like Cleopatra. To their brawny arms she must have seemed as light as thistledown. Their tender clumsy movements were touching, brought tears to my eyes. "Easy up there, Nobby. Gently with the little lady." "That tourniquet will have to be watched. You go too, Balthazar."

"And you?"

"I'll bring her cutter back."

We wasted no more time. In a few moments the powerful motors of the patrol vessel began to bustle them away at a good ten knots. I heard a sailor say: "How about some hot Bovril?"

"Capital" said Balthazar. He was soaked to the skin. His hat was floating in the water beside me. Leaning over the stern a thought suddenly struck him.

"My teeth. Bring my teeth!"

I watched them out of sight and then sat for a good while with my head in my hands. I found to my surprise that I was trembling all over like a frightened horse with shock. A splitting headache assailed me. I climbed into the cutter and foraged for the brandy and a cigarette. The harpoon gun lay on the sheets. I threw it overboard with an oath and watched it slowly crawling downwards into the pool. Then I shook out the jib, and turning her through her own length on the stern anchor pressed her out into the wind. It took longer than I thought, for the evening wind had shifted a few points and I had to tack widely before I could bring her in. Ali was waiting for me. He had already been apprised of the situation, and carried a message from Balthazar to the effect that Clea had been taken up to the Jewish hospital.

I took a taxi as soon as one could be found. We travelled across the city at a great pace. The streets and buildings passed me in a sort of blur. So great was my anxiety that I saw them as if through a rain-starred window-pane. I could hear the metre ticking away like a pulse. Somewhere in a white ward Clea would be lying drinking blood through the eye of a silver needle. Drop by drop it would be passing into the median vein heart-beat by heart-beat. There was nothing to worry about, I told myself; and then, thinking of that shattered hand, I banged my fist with rage against the padded wall of the taxi.

I followed a duty nurse down the long anonymous green corridors whose oil-painted walls exuded an atmosphere of damp. The white phosphorescent bulbs which punctuated our progress wallowed in the gloom like swollen glow-worms. They had probably put her, I reflected, in the little ward with the single curtained bed which in the past had been reserved for critical cases whose expectation of life was short. It was now the emergency casualty ward. A sense of ghostly familiarity was growing upon me. In the past it was here that I had come to see Melissa. Clea must be lying in the same narrow iron bed in the corner by the wall. ("It would be just like real life to imitate art at this point.")

In the corridor outside, however, I came upon Amaril and Balthazar standing with a curious chastened expression before a trolley which had just been wheeled to them by a duty nurse. It contained a number of wet and glistening X-ray photographs, newly developed and pegged upon a rail. The two men were studying them anxiously, gravely, as if thinking out a chess problem. Balthazar caught sight of me and turned, his face lighting up. "She's all right" he said, but in rather a broken voice, as he squeezed my hand. I handed him his teeth and he blushed, and slipped them into his pocket. Amaril was wearing horn-rimmed reading glasses. He turned from his intent study of those dripping dangling sheets with an expression of utter rage. "What the bloody hell do you expect me to do with this mess?" he burst out waving his insolent white hand in the direction of the X-rays. I lost my temper at the implied accusation and in a second we were shouting at each other like fishmongers, our eyes full of tears. I think we would have come to blows out of sheer exasperation had not Balthazar got between us. Then at once the rage dropped from Amaril and he walked round Balthazar to embrace me and mutter an apology. "She's all right" he murmured, patting me consolingly on the shoulder. "We've tucked her up safely."

"Leave the rest to us" said Balthazar.

"I'd like to see her" I said enviously—as if, in bringing her to life, she had become in a way my own property too. "Could I?"

As I pushed open the door and crept into the little cell like a miser I heard Amaril say peevishly: "It's all very well to talk about surgical repair in that glib way——"

It was immensely quiet and white, the little ward with its tall windows. She lay with her face to the wall in the uncomfortable steel bed on castors of yellow rubber. It smelt of flowers, though there were none to be seen and I could not identify the odour. It was perhaps a synthetic atomiser spray— the essence of forget-me-nots? I softly drew up a chair beside the bed and sat down. Her eyes were open, gazing at the wall with the dazed look which suggested morphia and fatigue combined. Though she gave no sign of having heard me enter she said suddenly:

"Is that you Darley?"

"Yes."

Her voice was clear. Now she sighed and moved slightly, as if with relief at my coming. "I'm so glad." Her voice had a small weary lilt which suggested that somewhere beyond the confines of her present pain and drowsiness a new self-confidence was stirring. "I wanted to thank you."

255

"It is Amaril you're in love with" I said—rather, blurted out. The remark came as a great surprise to me. It was completely involuntary. Suddenly a shutter seemed to roll back across my mind. I realised that this new fact which I was enunciating was one that I had always known, but without *being aware of the knowing!* Foolish as it was the distinction was a real one. Amaril was like a playing card which had always been there, lying before me on the table, face downwards. I had been aware of its existence but had never turned it over. Nor, I should add, was there anything in my voice beyond genuine scientific surprise; it was without pain, and full of sympathy only. Between us we had never used this dreadful word—this synonym for derangement or illness—and if I deliberately used it now it was to signify my recognition of the thing's autonomous nature. It was rather like saying "My poor child, you have got cancer!"

After a moment's silence she said: "Past tense now, alas!" Her voice had a puzzled drawling quality. "And I was giving you good marks for tact, thinking you had recognised him in my Syrian episode! Had you really not? Yes, Amaril turned me into a woman I suppose. O isn't it disgusting? When will we all grow up? No, but I've worn him out in my heart, you know. It isn't as you imagine it. I know he is not the man for me. Nothing would have persuaded me to replace Semira. I know this by the fact of having made love to him, been in love with him! It's odd, but the experience prevented me from mistaking him for the other one, the once for aller! Though who and where he is remains to discover. I haven't really affronted the real problems yet, I feel. They lie the other side of these mere episodes. And yet, perverse as it is, it is nice to be close to him —even on the operating-table. How is one to make clear a single truth about the human heart?"

"Shall I put off my journey?"

"But no. I wouldn't wish it at all. I shall need a little time to come to myself now that at last I am free from the horror.

256

That at least you have done for me—pushed me back into midstream again and driven off the dragon. It's gone and will never come back. Put your hand on my shoulder and squeeze, instead of a kiss. No. Don't change plans. Now at last we can take things a bit easily. Unhurriedly. I shall be well cared for here as you know. Later when your job is done we shall see, shall we? Try and write. I feel perhaps a pause might start you off."

"I will." But I knew I wouldn't.

"Only one thing I want you to do. Please visit the Mulid of El Scob tonight so that you can tell me all about it; you see it is the first time since the war that they are allowing the customary lighting in that *quartier*. It should be fun to see. I don't want you to miss it. Will you?"

"Of course."

"Thank you, my dear."

I stood up and after a moment's pause said: "Clea what exactly *was* the horror?"

But she had closed her eyes and was fading softly into sleep. Her lips moved but I could not catch her answer. There was the faintest trace of a smile at the corners of her mouth.

A phrase of Pursewarden's came into my mind as I softly closed the door of the ward. "The richest love is that which submits to the arbitration of time."

o   o   o   o   o

It was already late when at last I managed to locate a gharry to take me back to the town. At the flat I found a message to say that my departure had been put forward by six hours; the motor-launch would be leaving at midnight. Hamid was there, standing quite still and patient, as if he already knew the contents of the message. My luggage had been collected by an Army truck that afternoon. There was nothing left to do except kill the time until twelve, and this I proposed to do in the fashion suggested by Clea: by visiting the Mulid of El Scob. Hamid still stood before me, gravid with the weight of another parting. "You no come back this time, sir" he said blinking his eye at me with sorrow. I looked at the little man with emotion. I remembered how proudly he had recounted the saving of this one eye. It was because he had been the younger and uglier brother of the two. His mother had put out his brother's two eyes in order to prevent him from being conscripted; but he Hamid, being puny and ugly—he had escaped with one. His brother was now a blind *muezzin* in Tanta. But how rich he was, Hamid, with his one eye! It represented a fortune to him in well-paid work for rich foreigners.

"I come to you in London" he said eagerly, hopefully.

"Very well. I'll write to you."

He was all dressed up for the Mulid in his best clothes—the crimson cloak and the red shoes of soft morocco leather; in his bosom he had a clean white handkerchief. It was his evening off I remembered. Pombal and I had saved up a sum of money to give him as a parting present. He took the cheque between finger and thumb, inclining his head with gratitude. But self-interest could not buoy him up against the pain of parting from us. So he repeated "I come to you in London" to console himself; shaking hands with himself as he said the words.

"Very well" I said for the third time, though I could hardly see one-eyed Hamid in London. "I will write. Tonight I shall visit the Mulid of El Scob."

"Very good." I shook him by the shoulders and the familiarity made him bow his head. A tear trickled out of his blind eye and off the end of his nose.

"Goodbye ya Hamid" I said, and walked down the stairs, leaving him standing quietly at the top, as if waiting for some signal from outer space. Then suddenly he rushed after me, catching me at the front door, in order to thrust into my hand, as a parting present, his cherished picture of Melissa and myself walking down Rue Fuad on some forgotten afternoon.

III

The whole quarter lay drowsing in the umbrageous violet of approaching nightfall. A sky of palpitating *velours* which was cut into by the stark flare of a thousand electric light bulbs. It lay over Tatwig Street, that night, like a velvet rind. Only the lighted tips of the minarets rose above it on their slender invisible stalks—appeared hanging suspended in the sky; trembling slightly with the haze as if about to expand their hoods like cobras. Drifting idly down those remembered streets once more I drank in (forever: keepsakes of the Arab town) the smell of crushed chrysanthemums, ordure, scents, strawberries, human sweat and roasting pigeons. The procession had not arrived as yet. It would form somewhere beyond the harlots' quarter, among the tombs, and wind its slow way to the shrine, geared to a dancing measure; calling on the way at each of the mosques to offer up a verse or two of the Book in honour of El Scob. But the secular side of the festival was in full swing. In the dark alleys people had brought their dinner tables into the street, candlelit and decked with roses. So sitting they could catch the chipped headtones of the girl singers who were already standing on the wooden platforms outside the cafés, piercing the heavy night with their quartertones. The streets were beflagged, and the great framed pictures of the circumcision doctors rippled on high among the cressets and standards. In a darkened yard I saw them pouring the hot sugar, red and white, into the little wooden moulds from which would emerge the whole bestiary of Egypt—the ducks, horsemen, rabbits, and goats. The great sugar figurines too of the Delta folklore—Yuna and Aziz the lovers interlocked, interpenetrated—and the bearded heroes like Abu Zeid, armed and mounted among his brigands. They were splendidly obscene—surely the stupidest word in our language?—and brilliantly coloured before being dressed in their garments of paper, tinsel, and spangled gold, and set up on display among the Sugar Booths for the children to gape at and buy. In every little square now the coloured marquees had been run up, each with its familiar sign. The Gamblers were already busy—Abu Firan, the Father of Rats, was shouting cheerfully for customers. The great board stood before him on trestles, each of the twelve houses marked with a number and a name. In the centre stood the live white rat which had been painted with green stripes. You placed your money on the number of a house, and won, if the rat entered it. In another box the same game was in play, but with a pigeon this time; when all the bets were laid a handful of grain was tossed into the centre and the pigeon, in eating it, entered one of the numbered stalls.

I bought myself a couple of sugar figurines and sat down outside a café to watch the passing show with its brilliant pristine colour. These little "arusas" or brides I would have liked to keep, but I knew that they would crumble or be eaten by ants. They were the little cousins of the *santons de Provence* or the *bonhommes de pain d'épices* of the French country fair: of our own now extinct gilt gingerbread men. I ordered a spoon of mastika to eat with the cool fizzing sherbet. From where I sat at an angle between two narrow streets I could see the harlots painting themselves at an upper window before coming down to set up their garish booths among the conjurers and tricksters; Showal the dwarf was teasing them from his booth at ground level and causing screams of laughter at his well-aimed arrows. He had a high tinny little voice and the most engaging of acrobatic tricks despite his stunted size. He talked continuously even when standing on his head, and punctuated the point of his patter with a double somersault. His face was grotesquely farded and his lips painted in a clown's grin. At the other corner under a hide curtain sat Faraj the fortune-teller with his instruments of divination—ink, sand, and a curious hairy ball like a bull's testicles only covered in dark hair. A radiantly beautiful prostitute squatted before him. He had filled her palm with ink and was urging her to scry.

Little scenes from the street life. A mad wild witch of a woman who suddenly burst into the street, foaming at the lips and uttering curses so terrible that silence fell and everyone's blood froze. Her eyes blazed like a bear's under the white matted hair. Being mad she was in some sort holy, and no-one dared to face the terrible imprecations she uttered which, if turned on him, might spell ill luck. Suddenly a grubby child darted from the crowd and tugged her sleeve. At once calmed she took his hand and turned away into an alley. The festival closed over the memory of her like a skin.

I was sitting here, drunk on the spectacle, when the voice of Scobie himself suddenly sounded at my elbow. "Now, old man" it said thoughtfully. "If you have Tendencies you got to have Scope. That's why I'm in the Middle East if you want to know. . . ."

"God, you gave me a start" I said, turning round. It was Nimrod the policeman who had been one of the old man's superiors in the Police Force. He chuckled and sat down beside me, removing his tarbush to mop his forehead. "Did you think he'd come to life?" he enquired.

"I certainly did."

"I know my Scobie, you see."

Nimrod laid his flywhisk before him and with a clap of his hands commanded a coffee. Then giving me a sly wink he went on in the veritable voice of the saint. "The thing about Budgie was just that. In Horsham there's no Scope. Otherwise I would have joined him years ago in the earth-closet trade. The man's a mechanical genius I don't mind admitting. And not having any income except what the old mud-slinger—as he laughingly calls it—brings him in, he's stymied. He's in baulk. Did I ever tell you about the Bijou Earth Closet? No? Funny I thought I did.

Well, it was a superb contrivance, the fruit of long experiment. Budgie is an F.R.Z.S. you know. He got it by home study. That shows you what a brain the man has. Well it was a sort of lever with a trigger. The seat of the closet was on a kind of spring. As you sat down it *went* down, but when you got up it sprang up of its own accord and threw a spadeful of earth into the bin. Budgie says he got the idea from watching his dog clear up after himself with his paws. But how he adapted it I just can't fathom. It's sheer genius. You have a magazine at the back which you fill with earth or sand. Then when you get up the spring goes bang and presto! He's making about two thousand a year out of it, I don't mind admitting. Of course it takes time to build up a trade, but the overheads are low. He has just one man working for him to build the box part, and he buys the springs—gets them made to specification in Hammer-smith. And they're very prettily painted too, with astrology all round the rim. It looks queer, I admit. In fact it looks arcane. But it's a wonderful contrivance the little Bijou. Once there was a crisis while I was home on leave for a month. I called in to see Budgie. He was almost in tears. The chap who helped, Tom the carpenter, used to drink a bit and must have misplaced the sprockets on one series of Bijous. Anyway complaints started to pour in. Budgie said that his closets had gone mad all over Sussex and were throwing earth about in a weird and unwholesome way. Customers were furious. Well, there was nothing for it but to visit all his parishioners on a motor-bike and adjust the sprockets. I had so little time that I didn't want to miss his company—so he took me along with him. It was quite an adventure I don't mind telling you. Some of them were quite mad with Budgie. One woman said the sprocket was so strong her closet threw mud the length of the drawing-room. We had a time quietening her down. I helped by lending a soothing influence I don't mind admitting, while Budgie tinkered with the spring. I told stories to take their minds off the unhappy business. But finally it got straightened out. And now it's a profitable industry with members everywhere."

Nimrod sipped his coffee reflectively and cocked a quizzical eye in my direction, proud of his mimicry. "And now" he said, throwing up his hands, "El Scob. . . ."

A crowd of painted girls passed down the street, brilliant as tropical parrots and almost as loud in their chattering and laughing. "Now that Abu Zeid" said Nimrod "has taken the Mulid under his patronage it's likely to grow into a bit of headache for us. It's such a crowded quarter. This morning he sent a whole string of he-camels on heat into the town with *bercim* clover. You know how horrible they smell. And when they're in season they get that horrible jelly-like excrescence on their necks. It must irritate them or suppurate or something for they're scratching their necks the whole time on walls and posts. Two of them had a fight. It took hours to untangle the affair. The place was blocked."

Suddenly a series of bangs sounded from the direction of the harbour and a series of bright coloured rockets traced their splendid grooves across the night, drooping and falling away with a patter and a hiss. "Aha!" said Nimrod with self-satisfaction. "There goes the Navy. I'm glad they remembered."

"Navy?" I echoed as another long line of rockets tossed their brilliant plumage across the soft night.

"The boys of H.M.S. *Milton*" he chuckled. "I happened to dine on board last night. The wardroom was much taken by my story of an old Merchant Seaman who had been beatified. I naturally did not tell them very much about Scobie; least of all about his death. But I did hint that a few fireworks would be appropriate as coming from British mariners, and I also added that as a political gesture of respect it would earn them good marks with the worshippers. The idea caught on at once, and the Admiral was asked for permission. And there we go!"

We sat for a while in companionable silence watching the fireworks and the highly delighted crowd which saluted each salvo with long quivering exclamations of pleasure. "All—ah!

All—ah!'' Finally Nimrod cleared his throat and said: "Darley, can I ask you a question? Do you know what Justine is up to?" I must have looked very blank for he went on at once without hesitation. "I only ask you because she rang me yesterday and said that she was going to break parole today, come into town deliberately, and that she wanted me to arrest her. It sounds quite absurd—I mean to come all the way into town to give herself up to the Police. She said she wanted to force a personal interview with Memlik. It had to be me as reports from the British officers on the force would carry weight and draw Memlik's attention. It sounds a bit of a rigmarole doesn't it? But I've got a date with her at the Central Station in half an hour."

"I know nothing about the matter."

"I wondered if you did. Anyway keep it under your hat."

"I will."

He stood up and held out his hand to say goodbye. "You're off tonight I gather. Good luck." As he stepped down from the little wooden platform he said: "By the way, Balthazar is looking for you. He's somewhere down at the shrine—what a word!" With a brief nod his tall figure moved away into the brilliant swirling street. I paid for my drink and walked down towards Tatwig Street, bumped and jostled by the holiday crowd.

Ribbons and bunting and huge coloured gonfalons had been hung from every balcony along the street. The little piece of waste land under the arched doors was now the most sumptuous of saloons. Huge tents with their brilliant embroidered designs had been set up creating a ceremonial parade ground where the dancing and chanting would be held when the procession reached its destination. This area was crowded with children. The drone of prayers and the shrill tongue-trills of women came from the shrine which was dimly lit. The suppliants were invoking fruitfulness of Scobie's bath-tub. The long quavering lines of the Suras spun themselves on the night in a web of melodious sound. I quested round a bit among the crowd like a gun-dog, hunting for Balthazar. At last I caught sight of him sitting somewhat apart at an outdoor café. I made my way to his side. "Good" he said. "I was on the look out for you. Hamid said you were off tonight. He telephoned to ask for a job and told me. Besides I wanted to share with you my mixture of shame and relief over this hideous accident. Shame at the stupidity, relief that she isn't dead. Both mixed. I'm rather drunk with relief, and dazed with the shame." He was indeed rather tipsy. "But it will be all right, thank God!"

"What does Amaril think?"

"Nothing as yet. Or if he does he won't say. She must have a comfortable twenty-four hours of rest before anything is decided. Are you really going?" His voice fell with reproof. "You should stay, you know."

"She doesn't want me to stay."

"I know. I was a bit shocked when she said she had told you to go; but she said 'You don't understand. I shall see if I can't will him back again. We aren't quite ripe for each other yet. It will come.' I was amazed to see her so self-confident and radiant again. Really amazed. Sit down, my dear chap, and have a couple of stiff drinks with me. We'll see the procession quite well from here. No crowding." He clapped his hands rather unsteadily and called for more mastika.

When the glasses were brought he sat for a long while silent with his chin on his hands, staring at them. Then he gave a sigh and shook his head sadly.

"What is it?" I said, removing his glass from the tray and placing it squarely before him on the tin table.

"Leila is dead" he said quietly. The words seemed to weight him down with sorrow. "Nessim telephoned this evening to tell me. The strange thing is that he sounded exhilarated by the news. He has managed to get permission to fly down and make arrangements for her funeral. D'you know what he said?" Balthazar looked at me with that dark all-comprehending eye and went on. "He said: 'While I loved her *and all that*, her death has

265

freed me in a curious sort of way. A new life is opening before me. I feel years younger.' I don't know if it was a trick of the telephone or what but he sounded younger. His voice was full of suppressed excitement. He knew, of course, that Leila and I were the oldest of friends but not that all through this period of absence she was writing to me. She was a rare soul, Darley, one of the rare flowers of Alexandria. She wrote: 'I know I am dying, my dear Balthazar, but all too slowly. Do not believe the doctors and their diagnoses, you of all men. I am dying of heartsickness like a true Alexandrian.' " Balthazar blew his nose in an old sock which he took from the breast-pocket of his coat; carefully folded it to resemble a clean handkerchief and pedantically replaced it. "Yes" he said again, gravely, "what a word it is—'heartsickness'! And it seems to me that while (from what you tell me) Liza Pursewarden was administering her death-warrant to her brother, Mountolive was giving the same back-hander to Leila. So we pass the loving-cup about, the poisoned loving-cup!" He nodded and took a loud sip of his drink. He went on slowly, with immense care and effort, like someone translating from an obscure and recondite text. "Yes, just as Liza's letter to Pursewarden telling him that at last the stranger had appeared was his *coup de grâce* so to speak, so Leila received, I suppose, exactly the same letter. Who knows how these things are arranged? Perhaps in the very same words. The same words of passionate gratitude: 'I bless you, I thank you with all my heart that through you I am at last able to receive the precious gift which can never come to those who are ignorant of its powers.' Those are the words of Mountolive. For Leila quoted them to me. All this was after she went away. She wrote to me. It was as if she were cut off from Nessim and had nobody to turn to, nobody to talk to. Hence the long letters in which she went over it all, backwards and forwards, with that marvellous candour and clear-sightedness which I so loved in her. She refused every self-deception. Ah! but she fell between two stools, Leila, between two lives, two loves. She said

266

something like this in explaining it to me: 'I thought at first when I got his letter that it was just another attachment—as it was in the past for his Russian ballerina. There was never any secret between us of his loves, and that is what made ours seem so truthful, so immortal in its way. It was a love without reserves. But this time everything became clear to me when he refused to tell me her name, to share her with me, so to speak! I knew then that everything was ended. Of course in another corner of my mind I had always been waiting for this moment; I pictured myself facing it with magnanimity. This I found, to my surprise, was impossible. That was why for a long time, even when I knew he was in Egypt, and anxious to see me, I could not bring myself to see him. Of course I pretended it was for other reasons, purely feminine ones. But it was not that. It wasn't lack of courage because of my smashed beauty, no! For I have in reality the heart of a man.' "

Balthazar sat for a moment staring at the empty glasses with wide eyes, pressing his fingers softly together. His story meant very little to me—except that I was amazed to imagine Mountolive capable of any very deep feeling, and at a loss to imagine this secret relationship with the mother of Nessim.

"The Dark Swallow!" said Balthazar and clapped his hands for more drink to be brought. "We shall not look upon her like again."

But gradually the raucous night around us was swelling with the deeper rumour of the approaching procession. One saw the rosy light of the cressets among the roofs. The streets, already congested, were now black with people. They buzzed like a great hive with the contagion of the knowledge. You could hear the distant bumping of drums and the hissing splash of cymbals, keeping time with the strange archaic peristaltic rhythms of the dance—its relatively slow walking pace broken by queer halts, to enable the dancers, as the ecstasy seized them, to twirl in and out of their syncopated measures and return once more to their places in the line of march. It pushed its way through the narrow funnel of the main street like a torrent whose force makes it overleap its bed; for all the little side streets were full of sightseers running along, keeping pace with it.

First came the grotesque acrobats and tumblers with masks and painted faces, rolling and contorting, leaping in the air and walking on their hands. They were followed by a line of carts full of candidates for circumcision dressed in brilliant silks and embroidered caps, and surrounded by their sponsors, the ladies of the harem. They rode proudly, singing in juvenile voices and greeting the crowd: like the bleating of sacrificial lambs. Balthazar croaked: "Foreskins will fall like snow tonight, by the look of it. It is amazing that there are no infections. You know, they use black gunpowder and lime-juice as a styptic for the wound!"

Now came the various orders with their tilting and careening gonfalons with the names of the holy ones crudely written on them. They trembled like foliage in the wind. Magnificently robed sheiks held them aloft walking with difficulty because of their weight, yet keeping the line of the procession straight. The street-preachers were gabbling the hundred holy names. A cluster of bright braziers outlined the stern bearded faces of a cluster of dignitaries carrying huge paper lanterns, like balloons, ahead of them. Now as they overran us and flowed down the length of Tatwig Street in a long ripple of colour we saw the various orders of Dervishes climb out of the nether darkness and emerge into the light, each order distinguished by its colour. They were led by the black-capped Rifaia—the scorpion-eaters of legendary powers. Their short barking cries indicated that the religious ecstasy was already on them. They gazed around with dazed eyes. Some had run skewers through their cheeks, others licked red-hot knives. At last came the courtly figure of Abu Zeid with his little group of retainers on magnificently caparisoned ponies, their cloaks swelling out behind them, their arms raised in salutation like knights embarking on a tournament. Before them ran a helter skelter collection of male prostitutes with powdered faces and long flowing hair, chuckling and ejaculating like chickens in a farm-yard. And to all this queer discontinuous and yet somehow congruent mass of humanity the music lent a sort of homo-geneity; it bound it and confined it within the heart-beats of the drums, the piercing skirl of the flutes, the gnashing of the cymbals. Circling, proceeding, halting: circling, proceeding, halting, the long dancing lines moved on towards the tomb, bursting through the great portals of Scobie's lodgings like a tide at full, and deploying across the brilliant square in clouds of dust.

And as the chanters moved forward to recite the holy texts six Mevlevi dervishes suddenly took the centre of the stage, expanding in a slow fan of movement until they had formed a semicircle. They wore brilliant white robes reaching to their green slippered feet and tall brown hats shaped like huge *bombes glacées*. Calmly, beautifully, they began to whirl, these "tops spun by God", while the music of the flutes haunted them with their piercing quibbles. As they gathered momen-tum their arms, which at first they hugged fast to their shoulders, unfolded as if by centrifugal force and stretched out to full reach, the right palm turned upward to heaven, the left downward to the ground. So, with heads and tall rounded hats tilted slightly, like the axis of the earth, they stayed there miraculously spinning, their feet hardly seeming to touch the floor, in this wonderful parody of the heavenly bodies in their perpetual motion. On and on they went, faster and faster, until the mind wearied of trying to keep pace with them. I thought of the verses of Jalaluddin which Pursewarden used sometimes to recite. On the outer circles the Rifaia had begun their display of self-mutilation, so horrible to behold and yet so apparently harmless. The touch of a sheik's finger would heal all these wounds pierced in the cheeks and breasts. Here a dervish drove a skewer through his nostrils, there another fell

269

upon the point of a dirk, driving it up through his throat into his skull. But still the central knot of dancers continued its unswerving course, spinning in the sky of the mind.

"My goodness" said Balthazar at my elbow, with a chuckle, "I thought he was familiar. There's the Magzub himself. The one at the further end. He used to be an absolute terror, more than half mad. The one who was supposed to have stolen the child and sold it to a brothel. Look at him."

I saw a face of immense world-weary serenity, the eyes closed, the lips curved in a half-smile; as the dancer spun slowly to a halt this slender personage, with an air of half-playful modesty, took up a bundle of thorns and lighting it at a brazier thrust the blazing mass into his bosom against the flesh, and started to whirl once more like a tree in flames. Then as the circle came to a swaying halt he plucked it out once more and gave the dervish next to him a playful slap upon the face with it.

But now a dozen dancing circles intervened and took up the measure and the little courtyard overflowed with twisting turning figures. From the little shrine came the steady drone of the holy word, punctuated by the shrill tongue trills of the votaries.

"Scobie's going to have a heavy night" said Balthazar with irreverence. "Counting foreskins up there in the Moslem heaven."

Somewhere far away I heard the siren of a ship boom in the harbour, recalling me to my senses. It was time to be going. "I'll come down with you" said Balthazar, and together we started to push and wriggle our way down the crowded street towards the Corniche.

We found a gharry and sat silent in it, hearing the music and drumming gradually receding as we traversed the long rolling line of the marine parade. The moon was up, shining on the calm sea, freckled by the light breeze. The palms nodded. We clip-clopped down the narrow twisted streets and into the commercial harbour at last with its silent ghostly watercraft. A few lights winked here and there. A liner moved out of its berth and slid softly down the channel—a long glittering crescent of light.

The little launch which was to carry me was still being loaded with provisions and luggage.

"Well" I said, "Balthazar. Keep out of mischief."

"We'll be meeting again quite soon" he said quietly. "You can't shake me off. The Wandering Jew, you know. But I'll keep you posted about Clea. I'd say something like 'Come back to us soon', if I didn't have the feeling that you weren't going to. I'm damned if I know why. But that we'll meet again I'm sure."

"So am I" I said.

We embraced warmly, and with an abrupt gesture he climbed back into the gharry and settled himself once more.

"Mark my words" he said as the horse started up to the flick of a whip.

I stood, listening to the noise of its hooves until the night swallowed them up. Then I turned back to the work in hand.

IV

Dearest Clea:

Three long months and no word from you. I would have been very much disquieted had not the faithful Balthazar sent me his punctual postcard every few days to report so favourably on your progress: though of course he gives me no details. You for your part must have grown increasingly angry at my callous silence which you so little deserve. Truthfully, I am bitterly ashamed of it. I do not know what curious inhibition has been holding me back. I have been unable either to analyse it or to react against it effectively. It has been like a handle of a door which won't turn. Why? It is doubly strange because I have been deeply conscious of you all the time, of you being actively present in my thoughts. I've been holding you, metaphorically, cool against my throbbing mind like a knife-blade. Is it possible that I enjoyed you better as a thought than as a person alive, acting in the world? Or was it that words themselves seemed so empty a consolation for the distance which has divided us? I do not know. But now that the job is nearly completed I seem suddenly to have found my tongue.

Things alter their focus on this little island. You called it a metaphor once, I remember, but it is very much a reality to me —though of course vastly changed from the little haven I knew before. It is our own invasion which has changed it. You could hardly imagine that ten technicians could make such a change. But we have imported money, and with it are slowly altering the economy of the place, displacing labour at inflated prices, creating all sorts of new needs of which the lucky inhabitants were not conscious before. Needs which in the last analysis will destroy the tightly woven fabric of this feudal village with its tense blood-relationships, its feuds and archaic festivals. Its wholeness will dissolve under these alien pressures. It was so tightly woven, so beautiful and symmetrical like a swallow's nest. We are picking it apart like idle boys, unaware of the damage we inflict. It seems inescapable the death we bring to the old order without wishing it. It is simply done too—a few steel girders, some digging equipment, a crane! Suddenly things begin to alter shape. A new cupidity is born. It will start quietly with a few barbers' shops, but will end by altering the whole architecture of the port. In ten years it will be an un-recognisable jumble of warehouses, dance-halls and brothels for merchant sailors. Only give us enough time!

The site which they chose for the relay station is on the mountainous eastward side of the island, and not where I lived before. I am rather glad of this in an obscure sort of way. I am sentimental enough about old memories to enjoy them—but how much better they seem in the light of a small shift of gravity; they are renewed and refreshed all at once. Moreover this corner of the island is unlike any other part—a high wine-bearing valley overlooking the sea. Its soils are gold, bronze and scarlet—I suppose they consist of some volcanic marl. The red wine they make is light and very faintly *pétillant*, as if a volcano still slumbered in every bottle. Yes, here the mountains ground their teeth together (one can *hear* them during the frequent tremors!) and powdered up these metamorphic rocks into chalk. I live in a small square house of two rooms built over a wine-magazine. A terraced and tiled courtyard separates it from several other such places of storage—deep cellars full of sleeping wine in tuns.

We are in the heart of the vineyards; on all sides, ruled away on the oblong to follow the spine of the blue hill above the sea, run the shallow canals of humus and mould between the sym-metrical vines which are now flourishing. Galleries—no, bowling-alleys of the brown ashy earth, every mouthful finger-and-fist-sifted by the industrious girls. Here and there figs and

273

olives intrude upon this rippling forest of green, this vine-carpet. It is so dense that once you are in it, crouched, your field of visibility is about three feet, like a mouse in the corn. As I write there are a dozen invisible girls tunnelling like moles, turning the soil. I hear their voices but see nothing. Yes, they are crawling about in there like sharpshooters. They rise and start work before dawn. I wake and hear them arriving often, sometimes singing a snatch of a Greek folk-song! I am up at five. The first birds come over and are greeted by the small reception committee of optimistic hunters who pot idly at them and then pass up the hill, chattering and chaffing each other.

Shading my terrace stands a tall tree of white mulberries, with the largest fruit I have ever seen—as big as caterpillars. The fruit is ripe and the wasps have found it and are quite drunk on the sweetness. They behave just like human beings, laughing uproariously about nothing, falling down, picking fights. . . .

The life is hard, but good. What pleasure to actually sweat over a task, actually use one's hands! And while we are harvesting steel to raise, membrane by membrane, this delicate mysterious ex-voto to the sky—why the vines are ripening too with their reminder that long after man has stopped his neurotic fiddling with the death-bringing tools with which he expresses his fear of life, the old dark gods are there, underground, buried in the moist humus of the chthonian world (that favourite word of P's). They are forever sited in the human wish. They will never capitulate! (I am talking at random simply to give you an idea of the sort of life I lead here.)

The early hill-barley is being gathered. You meet walking haystacks—haystacks with nothing but a pair of feet below them trudging along these rocky lanes. The weird shouts the women give, either at cattle or calling to one another from hillside to hillside. *"Wow" "hoosh" "gnaiow"*. This barley is laid upon the flat roofs for threshing out the chaff which they do with sticks. Barley! hardly is the word spoken before the ant-processions begin, long chains of dark ants trying to carry it away to their private storehouses. This in turn has alerted the yellow lizards; they prowl about eating the ants, lying in ambush winking their eyes. And, as if following out the octave of causality in nature, here come the cats to hunt and eat the lizards. This is not good for them, and many die of a wasting disease attributed to this folly. But I suppose the thrill of the chase is on them. And then? Well, now and then a viper kills a cat stone dead. And the man with his spade breaks the snake's back. And the man? Autumn fevers come on with the first rain. The old men tumble into the grave like fruit off a tree. *Finita la guerra!* These people were occupied by Italians and quite a few learned the language which they speak with a Sienese accent.

In the little square is a fountain where the women gather. They proudly display their babies, and fancy them as if they were up for sale. This one is fat, that one thin. The young men pass up and down the road with hot shy glances. One of them sings archly *"Solo, per te, Lucia"*. But they only toss their heads and continue with their gossip. There is an old and apparently completely deaf man filling his pitcher. He is almost electrocuted by the phrase "Dmitri at the big house is dead." It lifts him off the ground. He spins round in a towering rage. "Dead? Who's dead? Eh? What?" His hearing is much improved all at once.

There is a little acropolis now called Fontana, high up there in the clouds. Yet it isn't far. But a steep climb up clinker-dry river-beds amid clouds of black flies; you come upon herds of rushing black goats like satans. There is a tiny hospice on the top with one mad monk; built as if on a turntable like a kiln of rusk. From here you can drink the sweet indolent misty curves of the island to the west.

And the future?

Well, this is a sketch of a nearly ideal present which will not last forever; indeed has almost expired, for within another month or so my usefulness will come to an end, and with it presumably the post upon which I depend for my exiguous livelihood. I have no resources of my own and must consider ways and means. No, the future rolls about inside me with every roll of the ship, so to speak, like a cargo which has worked loose. Were it not to see you again I doubt if I could return again to Alexandria. I feel it fade inside me, in my thoughts, like some valedictory mirage—like the sad history of some great queen whose fortunes have foundered among the ruins of armies and the sands of time! My mind has been turning more and more westward, towards the old inheritance of Italy or France. Surely there is still some worthwhile work to be done among their ruins—something which we can cherish, perhaps even revive? I ask myself this question, but it really addresses itself to you. Uncommitted as yet to any path, nevertheless the one I would most like to take leads westward and northward. There are other reasons. The terms of my contract entitle me to free "repatriation" as they call it; to reach England would cost me nothing. Then, with the handsome service gratuity which all this bondage has earned me, I think I could afford a spell in Europe. My heart leaps at the thought.

But something in all this must be decided for me; I have a feeling, I mean, that it is not I who shall decide.

Please forgive me my silence for which I cannot offer any excuse and write me a line.

Last Saturday I found myself with a free day and a half, so I walked across the island with a pack to spend a night in the little house where I lived on my previous visit. What a contrast to this verdant highland it was to strike that wild and windy promontory once more, the acid green seas and fretted coastlines of the past. It was indeed another island—I suppose the past always is. Here for a night and a day I lived the life of an echo, thinking much about the past and about us all moving in it, the "selective fictions" which life shuffles out like a pack of cards, mixing and dividing, withdrawing and restoring. It did not seem to me that I had the right to feel so calm and happy: a sense of Plenitude in which the only unanswered question was the one which arose with each memory of your name.

Yes, a different island, harsher and more beautiful of aspect. One held the night-silence in one's hands; feeling it slowly melting—as a child holds a piece of ice! At noon a dolphin rising from the ocean. Earthquake vapours on the sea-line. The great grove of plane trees with their black elephant hides which the wind strips off in great scrolls revealing the soft grey ashen skin within. . . . Much of the detail I had forgotten.

It is rather off the beaten track this little promontory; only olive-pickers might come here in season. Otherwise the only visitants are the charcoal burners who ride through the grove before light every day with a characteristic jingle of stirrups. They have built long narrow trenches on the hill. They crouch over them all day, black as demons.

But for the most part one might be living on the moon. Slightly noise of sea, the patient stridulation of *cigales* in the sunlight. One day I caught a tortoise at my front door; on the beach was a smashed turtle's egg. Small items which plant themselves in the speculative mind like single notes of music belonging to some larger composition which I suppose one will never hear. The tortoise makes a charming and undemanding pet. I can hear P say: "Brother Ass and his tortoise. The marriage of true minds!"

For the rest: the picture of a man skimming flat stones upon the still water of the lagoon at evening, waiting for a letter out of silence.

o   o   o   o   o

But I had hardly confided this letter to the muleteer-postman who took our mail down to the town before I received a letter with an Egyptian stamp, addressed to me in an unknown hand. It read as follows:

277

"You did not recognise it, did you? I mean the handwriting on the envelope? I confess that I chuckled as I addressed it to you, before beginning this letter: I could see your face all of a sudden with its expression of perplexity. I saw you turn the letter over in your fingers for a moment trying to guess who had sent it!

"It is the first serious letter I have attempted, apart from short notes, with my new hand: this strange accessory-after-the-fact with which the good Amaril has equipped me! I wanted it to become word-perfect before I wrote to you. Of course I was frightened and disgusted by it at first, as you can imagine. But I have come to respect it very much, this delicate and beautiful steel contrivance which lies beside me so quietly on the table in its green velvet glove! Nothing falls out as one imagines it. I could not have believed myself accepting it so completely—steel and rubber seem such strange allies for human flesh. But the hand has proved itself almost more competent even than an ordinary flesh-and-blood member! In fact its powers are so comprehensive that I am a little frightened of it. It can undertake the most delicate of tasks, even turning the pages of a book, as well as the coarser ones. But most important of all—ah! Darley I tremble as I write the words—IT can *paint*!

"I have crossed the border and entered into the possession of my kingdom, thanks to the Hand. Nothing about this was premeditated. One day it took up a brush and lo! pictures of truly troubling originality and authority were born. I have five of them now. I stare at them with reverent wonder. Where did they come from? But I know that the Hand was responsible. And this new handwriting is also one of its new inventions, tall and purposeful and tender. Don't think I boast. I am speaking with the utmost objectivity, for I know that I am not responsible. It is the Hand alone which has contrived to slip me through the barriers into the company of the Real Ones as Pursewarden used to say. Yet it is a bit frightening; the elegant velvet glove guards its secret perfectly. If I wear both gloves a perfect anonymity is preserved! I watch with wonder and a certain distrust, as one might a beautiful and dangerous pet like a panther, say. There is nothing, it seems, that it cannot do impressively better than I can. This will explain my silence and I hope excuse it. I have been totally absorbed in this new hand-language and the interior metamorphosis it has brought about. All the roads have opened before me, everything seems now possible for the first time.

"On the table beside me as I write lies my steamship ticket to France; yesterday I knew with absolute certainty that I must go there. Do you remember how Pursewarden used to say that artists, like sick cats, knew by instinct exactly which herb they needed to effect a cure: and that the bitter-sweet herb of their self-discovery only grew in one place, France? Within ten days I shall be gone! And among so many new certainties there is one which has raised its head—the certainty that you will follow me there in your own good time. I speak of certainty not prophecy—I have done with fortune-tellers once and for all!

"This, then, is simply to give you the dispositions which the Hand has imposed on me, and which I accept with eagerness and gratitude—with resignation also. This last week I have been paying a round of goodbye visits, for I think it will be some long time before I see Alexandria again. It has become stale and profitless to me. And yet how can we but help love the places which have made us suffer? Leave-takings are in the air; it's as if the whole composition of our lives were being suddenly drawn away by a new current. For I am not the only person who is leaving the place—far from it. Mountolive, for example, will be leaving in a couple of months; by a great stroke of luck he has been given the plum post of his profession, Paris! With this news all the old uncertainties seem to have vanished; last week he was secretly married! You will guess to whom.

"Another deeply encouraging thing is the return and recovery of dear old Pombal. He is back at the Foreign Office now in a senior post and seems to have recovered much of his old form

279

to judge by the long exuberant letter he sent me. 'How could I have forgotten' he writes 'that there are no women in the world except French women? It is quite mysterious. They are the most lovely creation of the Almighty. And yet . . . dear Clea, there are *so very many of them*, and each more perfect than the other. What is one poor man to do against so many, against such an army? For Godsake ask someone, anyone, to bring up reinforcements. Wouldn't Darley like to help an old friend out for old times' sake?'

"I pass you the invitation for what it is worth. Amaril and Semira will have a child this month—a child with the nose I invented! He will spend a year in America on some job or other, taking them with him. Balthazar also is off on a visit to Smyrna and Venice. My most piquant piece of news, however, I have saved for the last. *Justine!*

"This I do not expect you to believe. Nevertheless I must put it down. Walking down Rue Fuad at ten o'clock on a bright Spring morning I saw her come towards me, radiant and beautifully turned out in a spring frock of eloquent design: and *flop flop flop* beside her on the dusty pavements, hopping like a toad, the detested Memlik! Clad in elastic-sided boots with spats. A cane with a gold knob. And a newly minted flower-pot on his fuzzy crown. I nearly collapsed. She was leading him along like a poodle. One almost saw the cheap leather leash attached to his collar. She greeted me with effusive warmth and introduced me to her captive who shuffled shyly and greeted me in a deep groaning voice like a bass saxophone. They were on their way to meet Nessim at the Select. Would I go too? Of course I would. You know how tirelessly curious I am. She kept shooting secret sparks of amusement at me without Memlik seeing. Her eyes were sparkling with delight, a sort of impish mockery. It was as if, like some powerful engine of destruction, she had suddenly switched on again. She has never looked happier or younger. When we absented ourselves to powder our noses I could only gasp: 'Justine! Memlik! What

280

on earth?' She gave a peal of laughter and giving me a great hug said: 'I have found his *point faible*. He is hungry for *society*. He wants to move in social circles in Alexandria and meet a lot of *white* women!' More laughter. 'But what is the object?' I said in bewilderment. Here all at once she became serious, though her eyes sparkled with clever malevolence. 'We have started something, Nessim and I. We have made a break through at last. Clea, I am so happy, I could cry. It is something much bigger this time, international. We will have to go to Switzerland next year, probably for good. Nessim's luck has suddenly changed. I can't tell you any details.'

"When we reached the table upstairs Nessim had already arrived and was talking to Memlik. His appearance staggered me, he looked so much younger, and so elegant and self-possessed. It gave me a queer pang, too, to see the passionate way they embraced, Nessim and Justine, as if oblivious to the rest of the world. Right there in the café, with such ecstatic passion that I did not know where to look.

"Memlik sat there with his expensive gloves on his knee, smiling gently. It was clear that he enjoyed the life of high society, and I could see from the way he offered me an ice that he also enjoyed the company of white women!

"Ah! it is getting tired, this miraculous hand. I must catch the evening post with this letter. There are a hundred things to attend to before I start the bore of packing. As for you, wise one, I have a feeling that you too perhaps have stepped across the threshold into the kingdom of your imagination, to take possession of it once and for all. Write and tell me—or save it for some small café under a chestnut-tree, in smoky autumn weather, by the Seine.

"I wait, quite serene and happy, a real human being, an artist at last.

"Clea."

o   o   o   o   o

But it was to be a little while yet before the clouds parted before me to reveal the secret landscape of which she was writing, and which she would henceforward appropriate, brush-stroke by slow brushstroke. It had been so long in forming inside me, this precious image, that I too was as unprepared as she had been. It came on a blue day, quite unpremeditated, quite unannounced, and with such *ease* I would not have believed it. I had been until then like some timid girl, scared of the birth of her first child.

Yes, one day I found myself writing down with trembling fingers the four words (four letters! four faces!) with which every story-teller since the world began has staked his slender claim to the attention of his fellow-men. Words which presage simply the old story of an artist coming of age. I wrote: "Once upon a time . . ."

And I felt as if the whole universe had given me a nudge!

WORKPOINTS

Hamid's story of Darley and Melissa.

o o o

Mountolive's child by the dancer Griskin. The result of the duel. The Russian letters. Her terror of Liza when after her mother's death she is sent to her father.

o o o

Memlik and Justine in Geneva.

o o o

Balthazar's encounter with Arnauti in Venice. The violet sunglasses, the torn overcoat, pockets full of crumbs to feed the pigeons. The scene in Florian's. The shuffling walk of general paralysis. Conversations on the balcony of the little *pension* over the rotting backwater of the canal. Was Justine actually Claudia? He cannot be sure. "Time is memory, they say; the art however is to revive it and yet avoid remembering. You speak of Alexandria. I can no longer even imagine it. It has dissolved. A work of art is something which is more like life than life itself!" The slow death.

o o o

The northern journey of Narouz, and the great battle of the sticks.
Smyrna. The manuscripts, The Annals of Time. The theft.

NOTES

* *Page 140*

CHE FECE . . . IL GRAN RIFIUTO

To some among us comes that implacable day
Demanding that we stand our ground and utter
By choice of will the great Yea or Nay.
And whosoever has in him the affirming word
Will straightway then be heard.
The pathways of his life will clear at once
And all rewards will crown his way.
But he, the other who denies,
No-one can say he lies; he would repeat
His Nay in louder tones if pressed again.
It is his right—yet by such little trifles,
A 'No' instead of 'Yes' his whole life sinks and stifles.

free translation from C. P. Cavafy

* *Page 40*

FAR AWAY

This fugitive memory . . . I should so much
Like to record it, but it's dwindled . . .
Hardly a print of it remaining . . .
It lies so far back, back in my earliest youth,
Before my gifts had kindled.

A skin made of jasmine-petals on a night . . .
An August evening . . . but *was* it August?
I can barely reach it now, barely remember . . .
Those eyes, the magnificent eyes . . .
Or was it perhaps in September . . . in the dog days . . .

Irrevocably blue, yes, bluer than
A sapphire's mineral gaze.

free translation from C. P. Cavafy

* Page 39

THE AFTERNOON SUN

This little room, how well I know it!
Now they've rented this and the next door one
As business premises, the whole house
Has been swallowed up by merchants' offices,
By limited companies and shipping agents . . .

O how familiar it is, this little room!

Once here, by the door, stood a sofa,
And before it a little Turkish carpet,
Exactly here. Then the shelf with the two
Yellow vases, and on the right of them:
No. Wait. Opposite them (how time passes)
The shabby wardrobe and the little mirror.
And here in the middle the table
Where he always used to sit and write,
And round it the three cane chairs.
How many years . . . And by the window over there
The bed we made love on so very often.

Somewhere all these old sticks of furniture
Must still be knocking about . . .

And beside the window, yes, that bed.
The afternoon sun climbed half way up it.

We parted at four o'clock one afternoon,
Just for a week, on just such an afternoon.
I would have never
Believed those seven days could last forever.

free translation from C. P. Cavafy

* *Page 204*
The incidents recorded in Capodistria's letter have been
borrowed and expanded from a footnote in Franz Hart-
mann's *Life of Paracelsus*.

Midnight. A small figure comes flying down the stairs of the Sweeney house in suburban Connecticut, his eyes wide with terror. "Chuong! What is it? *Tell* me!" Ann Sweeney, on her way to bed, grabs her son and holds on tight as he nearly knocks her backward, locked in another of his wrenching night terrors.

Eleven-year-old Chuong is reliving for the thousandth time that day in 1975 in Saigon, when the overcrowded fishing boat he was on unexpectedly pulled away from the crush of people at the dock, leaving behind his frantic mother and father. He never saw them again. Chuong's baby sister Huong was in his arms, little brother Dat was clinging to his leg.

How the three of them come to Connecticut, how Huong (now Hope) and Dat blossom, and how Chuong finally learns to let go of the past by accepting the love of his new family is but one of the fascinating subplots within the larger drama of *Patchwork Clan*, the story of John and Ann Sweeney and their seventeen children.

When Ann Sweeney had a miscarriage while carrying her sixth child, she thought she would never recover from the loss. But when she and John discovered the joys of adoption, a renewed sense of love and commitment came into their lives. First there was Marcus, a delightful redheaded imp — part American Indian, part black, part "something else." This miracle was soon followed by another: at forty-one Ann gave birth to twins! Then the Sweeneys adopted Faith and Terry. Minh, a Vietnamese teenager, followed. Maria, a blind Colombian Indian girl,

Also by Doris Lund
ERIC

PATCHWORK CLAN

PATCHWORK CLAN

How the Sweeney Family Grew

by

DORIS LUND

LITTLE, BROWN AND COMPANY　　BOSTON — TORONTO

Second Printing

Library of Congress Cataloging in Publication Data

Lund, Doris Herold.
  Patchwork clan.

  1. Children, Adopted — United States — Family
relationships.   2. Sweeney, Ann.   3. Mothers —
United States — Biography.   I. Title.
  HV875.L87   362.7'34'0922 [B]   81-19301
  ISBN 0-316-53657-1   AACR2

MV

DESIGNED BY JANIS CAPONE

*Published simultaneously in Canada
by Little, Brown & Company (Canada) Limited*

PRINTED IN THE UNITED STATES OF AMERICA

To my mother, Katherine Herold,
and to Cora Hill,
who were wonderful "other mothers"
to my children

"He who saves a single life, it is as if he has saved the entire world."

— Saying from *The Talmud* tacked up on Ann Sweeney's kitchen bulletin board

Author's Introduction

Authors can be changed by the books they write. I came away from the experience of writing *Patchwork Clan* with a whole new feeling about adoption and a new appreciation of what it's all about. For the first time, I thought of it as something you do from joy — not from desperation.

When I got married, I used to wonder if I'd have the courage to adopt if we couldn't have children of our own. I wanted kids very much, but I was secretly afraid I might not love a baby who was not really mine — who was an unknown quantity. Seeing the Sweeney family up close, week after week, for almost two years taught me what I should have known all along. Loving happens much more easily than some of us might suppose. And every baby born, whether it comes to you from your own womb or from another's through the complicated process of adoption, is sure to be an unknown quantity. The most flawless family tree may produce an imperfect apple — or a prizewinner. But children are not apples, and what's needed to raise children is enormous energy, willingness to do battle for them on all fronts, unflagging optimism in their possibilities for good, and lots of love. Ann and John Sweeney give these things in abundance to all their children.

What they gave me, the writer who wandered into their world, was an uncommonly generous welcome.

It all began one day in early June, 1979, when I got a note from an editor at Little, Brown enclosing a letter she'd received from Ann Sweeney, mother of fifteen children (seven born to her, eight adopted), who thought she had a story to tell. She didn't have time to write it herself, she wrote, because she ran the household and also taught forty-five piano pupils every week. "Doris, would you like to check this out?" was the question put to me by the editor.

Good God, I thought, the mother has to be off the wall. I don't believe a word of this. Fortunately, my writer's curiosity overcame my skepticism. I made an appointment, drove the twenty miles or so to the Sweeney home, and soon found myself in bedlam. The backyard was swarming with children swinging or climbing one of the many jungle gyms, running around the swimming pool, diving in, clambering out, splashing, shouting, laughing, crying. It was terrifying. It was irresistible. This was *one family?* There didn't seem to be a waif or a washout in the crowd. They were all beautiful kids, and as the afternoon wore on, I discovered they were astonishingly normal. I was also relieved to find that their mother, Ann, was not wearing a halo. The chief difference between her and most mothers was that she screamed louder, ran faster, and had the figure of a girl of twenty.

My head was whirling trying to keep all the characters straight as I drove home. I knew there'd be formidable difficulties facing a writer who tried to put together a coherent book about a family so enormous. (And if I'd known the Sweeneys would adopt *two more* during the project, I probably would have fled then and there.) But all I knew was I was in love with the idea.

From the first, the Sweeneys made it easy for me by adopting me, too, into their family. I went to their birthday parties and picnics, attended their holiday celebrations, and also spent plenty of dull rainy Sunday afternoons with them, until I became as familiar as wallpaper. The Sweeney dogs no longer barked but wagged at my arrival. The Sweeney cats sat on my lap — when it wasn't occupied by children — and I was able to write my book from the inside out, from the good knowledge of how it felt to be almost one of them.

The story is as true as I could make it. We have changed a name or two here and there. But everyone was wonderfully open with me. Chuong and Maria told me what they remembered of their early lives. Megan and Jay told me how it was to be part of an ever-expanding family. John generously shared with me his own family history, as well as his view of things in his present position as "Papa."

But, of course, it was Ann who dreamed this book into being. She was the dynamo, rising at five o'clock to do pages of "homework" for me. I gave her lists and lists of questions. "How did you feel when you first saw Marcus?" "Tell me what Chuong looked like the first day you saw him." Somehow she snatched the time before dawn, or waiting in dentists' or doctors' offices, or even standing in line at supermarkets, to give me the answers that fill this book with vitality. Wherever possible, I've used Ann's own words. You can't beat them. The lady has quite a style — and quite a family.

I love them every one, and I give them all my thanks.

Doris Lund
April, 1981

Contents

Illustrations

ONE

1975–1976

ONE

Chuong—Vietnam, 1975

THE WAR WAS up there somewhere. North of the city. Everybody knew it was there. Chuong, who was nine, could not remember a time without talk of war. Without American soldiers around. Planes droning overhead. Everybody just hoped the war would stay up there in the north. Away from *them*.

In the meantime, life went on well for Chuong and his family on the outskirts of Saigon. They were pretty far out. Beyond their street of houses were green farms, fields where fog hung low in the early mornings, and grove after grove of banana trees laden with the rich fruit and chattering birds. A good place. Even so, Chuong liked the excitement of the big city. Once he had been to see a movie. Other times he had gone in with his family to visit relatives. He loved the colorful shop windows, the strange sweets they bought from vendors on the sidewalks. And he couldn't help being impressed with the powerful American trucks and jeeps rumbling impatiently as they tried to push their way through the wooden carts and flimsy taxis clogging Saigon's crowded streets.

Sometimes when he saw an American truck his heart swelled

and he wanted to shout, "Hey — my father has a fine truck, too! A fine, big truck. Almost as big as yours!"

The truck was their life. Because of the truck, their house was the biggest on the street. Chuong's father bought bananas from the surrounding farms and took them into the market. Chuong loved to see the truck piled high with bananas. Short yellow ones, long skinny ones, red bananas, green ones, tiny, sweet bananas as big as your thumb. For a long time Chuong thought that bananas must be the most important thing that grew in all of Vietnam. That was why his father always came home with money, why he was able to buy Chuong a bicycle when he was very small. And when Chuong kept on growing, his father bought him another bigger one with shining silver wheels. There was also plenty of good food, too. Chuong's mother did not scold if he sometimes took rice from the pot to use for paste when he made a kite. There was enough. And he didn't have to work like many of the other children. His family thought going to school was important. Still, he had time to fly his kite or squat in the dirt playing marbles with his friends on the long, hot afternoons when school was out.

The change in their lives, when it came, was like a strange cloud that kept getting bigger, coming closer. Heavy and dark, even though the sky itself stayed the same. It was odd, that sky, staying light as always, while the darkness kept growing and growing all around them like the feeling before a storm. The grownups became shrill and excitable, scolding the children for nothing, standing and talking when they usually were working.

"We began to see people from another place moving along our road," says Chuong remembering that time. "And for five days we just stayed there and watched as more and more of them kept going by. They were carrying everything they could. Some of them had carts piled high with things — baskets and clothes and cooking pots. Every day there were more people and they were walking faster. My father didn't go into the city. Bananas were rotting on the ground. But all the time we kept thinking *we* would be all right because we had the truck. . . .

"Then on the fifth day, people weren't walking anymore. They were running. And when some of them got tired they just lay down by the side of the road. Often they didn't get up again. My mother was getting very frightened. At last my father decided we must all go fast. Our whole family, my brothers, my sisters, my mother, the baby, and I got in the truck and my father started the motor. My mother was crying because she had to leave her house. We couldn't take half of what we wanted. I looked back as we went away and I saw my bicycle lying on the ground. . . ."

Saigon was, in fact, in a state of panic. As the North Vietnamese troops neared the city, rumors of terrible deeds began to spread like wildfire. Every man began to see his house in flames, his womenfolk raped, his children murdered. Driven frantic by the desire to escape, everyone began to move faster, to run, eventually to trample anyone who got in the way. In that instant, friends became foes, and it seemed that only those would survive who were very strong, who cared nothing for others.

Chuong's family abandoned their truck when they got to the waterfront and almost instantly found themselves swept along in a tide of people all clamoring, shouting, and shoving as they tried to board an ancient fishing vessel. The boat, jammed to overflowing, sat there in the harbor for a whole day before the frantic passengers finally realized its engines were useless. Totally dead. Then came the sudden rush to abandon that ship and find another.

"This time we all managed to get on a very big boat," Chuong remembers. "It was long and flat, sort of like a tanker. Square on the ends. There was more room but more and more people kept crowding on, too. We stayed there for three days. But the boat didn't move. We had used up most of our food. Then they told us it wouldn't go either, like the first boat. And we believed them. So lots of us got off.

Suddenly right after we left, we saw the boat pulling away from the dock very fast with just a few people on board! It was a trick! Now everybody went wild they were so angry. This huge crowd of screaming, angry people began moving like a wave to get on another boat. People were in such a hurry and pushing so hard, some fell down and others ran right over them. We were trying to stay together. I was very scared. Some people fell in the water screaming and nobody stopped or tried to pull them out. My mother was right behind me then. 'Take Huong!' she cried. 'Here!'

"She shoved the baby in my arms. I held her close and bent down. Then I crawled very fast between a man's legs and the next thing I knew this crowd of people carried me up onto the boat. It was a big fishing boat, the kind they use to go out and catch the big fish like tuna. There were nets all over, and so many people coming and coming. I was afraid I'd get pushed off the other end. But this time the boat started to go very soon. There were maybe a thousand people. Maybe more, I don't know. I thought my mother, my father, my brothers and sisters were there, too. I was sure I would find them soon. I could see lots of people still yelling and waving and crying down on the dock as the boat went away and left them. I held onto the baby very hard."

Chuong searched through the tightly packed crowd on board the fishing boat all throughout the next day. He finally found his three-year-old brother, Dat, huddled, wailing, in a corner. He found some friends of the family's. But he never saw his mother, his father, or his other brothers and sisters again.

The boat drifted for three days.

"That first day we had only a little water," Chuong says. "Then the second day there was none. By afternoon it was very bad. The sun came down on us so hard, so hard. People said we should put salt water on our bodies so we wouldn't dry out. So they let down buckets over the side about twenty feet. Then they pulled them up full. I put salt water on my head and my arms and legs. I was putting some on Huong when I saw Dat *drinking* the salt water! I screamed at him. 'NO! Dat! Stop that!' But it was too late. He drank lots of salt water before I could stop him.

"That night was terrible. Dat screamed and screamed. Lots of people were sick. But a woman gave milk to Huong, my baby. She nursed her after she nursed her own baby. Huong was very little then, maybe nine months old. That woman kept my baby alive.

"I don't remember how long it was to Hong Kong. Once we got very scared. We saw this boat with guns coming at us. It was smaller but we were afraid they would start shooting. We didn't know it was empty, just drifting. It ran right into us! Then it turned over. We saw the bottom, then it sank."

Somehow the fishing boat reached Hong Kong. It may have been the evening of the third day. By this time Chuong had lost track of days and hours. Many of the passengers were more dead than alive. All were suffering from heat exhaustion and raging thirst. Their skin was burned raw. Their mouths were cracked and bleeding, their tongues swollen. They were loaded in trucks like so much cargo and taken to a huge, already-overcrowded camp for refugees.

"There we had water. It was hard to swallow. And we had a little food," Chuong says. "The food was disgusting, but I ate it anyway because I was so hungry."

Chuong, Dat, and baby Huong stayed in the camp for perhaps four or five months. Time ceased to have meaning for Chuong. He did not know if it was months or a year that passed. All he knew was that his good other life was Before. This was an endless dreadful Now. Sometimes he felt sorry for Dat, who cried all the time. Sometimes the little boy's crying enraged Chuong, and he would hit him in desperation to make him stop. "What do you want me to do?" he would scream. Then he would pick up Huong, who rarely cried anymore, who just lay passive like a tiny dog in his arms, and he would walk and walk until his anger cooled.

He tried not to think about his family. There was a time during the first weeks in the camp when Chuong saw a picture in a newspaper. A picture someone had taken of the people left behind, waving and crying on that dock in Saigon. "It was a very small picture," he says. "I looked at it over and over. I couldn't be sure, but I think I saw them there. A man, a woman waving in the crowd. My father and mother there on the dock."

In November of 1975 an American sponsor was finally found for the three children who had been swept by the panic of war from their home in South Vietnam. Chuong, Dat, and little Huong then set out on the long journey to still another camp somewhere in the United States.

TWO

✍§ ξ❧

Ann—Connecticut, 1976

AT 6:15, AS SHE DID every weekday evening, Ann Sweeney
rolled the black cover gently down over the keys of her
Yamaha baby grand. Then she got up slowly, stretching and
rubbing her arms, which always got cold and stiff from her
sitting in the library teaching all afternoon. The front door
closed. Glancing out the window, she watched her last pupil
trudging up the driveway through dirty end-of-February
snow. She gave a sudden shiver. Freezing out there! But the
child didn't have far to go, just across the street, and her own
were all gathered in safe and sound, thank goodness. Then
she saw a sled left across the far end of the drive. A pucker of
annoyance darted across her brow.

"Jay?" She went out in the hall. "Jay, where are you?
Jay!"

Her eight-year-old finally surfaced from the sun room,
where he'd been sprawled on a beanbag in front of t.v. "Yes,
Mom?"

"I want you to go out right now and move that sled out of
the driveway. Papa will be coming in from the train. How
many times do I have to tell you to put things away?"

Jay cast an experienced eye out the window at the offending sled. "That's Marcus's. Mine *is* put away."

Ann sighed. "Marcus is taking a bath —"

"*I'll* get it, Mom." Jay knew when to be generous. He didn't have to fight for justice in this house. He was the oldest resident son since Randy was off working and Chris had just got his own pad. He sure missed them. But being top man next to Pop carried its privileges. Life generally treated him pretty fine, Jay had to admit.

"Thanks, Jay." Ann gave him a grateful hug. "Here — take this. It's freezing out." She thrust a jacket at him. "And put *it* away when you come back."

Jay grimaced, thrust an arm in, went off. The door shuddered half shut behind him. Nothing was square in this big old house. Hinges groaned, windows had to be tugged open all summer, then coaxed shut all fall. They'd never been able to afford storm windows downstairs, since every one would have to be custom-made. With the house kept at 58° day and night all winter to save money and fuel, Ann was always freezing, though she had to admit John and the kids didn't seem to mind the cold. Just the same, Ann loved every nook and cranny of this place, which had bought them — not the other way around — the first time they'd seen it four years ago. They'd outgrown their smaller house in a nearby suburb one memorable day in March, 1972, when Ann gave birth to twins. Once Paddy and Timmy joined the six other kids in the family, the Sweeneys' walls immediately began to bulge.

House-hunting in those days wasn't such a dreadful, expensive hassle. Still, it wasn't easy to come up with a suitable place for a family of moderate means who had eight children, going on nine. (They'd started proceedings to adopt infant Faith a few months after Paddy and Timmy arrived.) Many buyers might have regarded the huge fieldstone and shingle dwelling on Old Mill Road simply as a friendly white elephant. But Ann and John had been immediately intrigued.

Built around 1900, the house suffered from a pleasantly split personality. The grounds were generous and well landscaped. The main-floor rooms were spacious and elegant, with fireplaces, double doors, and nicely detailed molding. And of course the indoor swimming pool (a luxurious afterthought tacked onto one side by the most recent owner) was an irresistible asset. But once you moved on to kitchen, sun porch, bedrooms, and baths, you were looking at old-fashioned problems. Paint was peeling, linoleum curling, and ceilings showed imminent signs of falling. Never mind, thought Ann. Possibilities of rescue always stimulated her. She felt a surge of energy just at the thought of what might be done. As for John, he was relieved and delighted to find a house with eight bedrooms for his growing brood — there was even a spare he could use as an office. Moreover the price was ridiculously low considering that the house was right at the edge of the most exclusive waterfront section in town. The Sweeneys bought it on sight.

The four years since they moved in had flown by quickly. The family first expanded, then contracted. Faith arrived practically in the middle of the move. Terry, a black child just her age, was adopted the following year, while Minh, a sixteen-year-old Vietnamese refugee, had joined the clan only recently. Meanwhile the Sweeney's oldest three, Randy, Lynn, and Chris, had moved out to begin lives of their own. The total count of resident kids was down to a mere eight the night Ann sent Jay out to retrieve the sled.

She watched him run up the drive, then bent to gather up several little jackets, a flock of wet, woolly mittens, a handful of blocks, and a plastic car. There! She stood for a minute in the shining, polished hallway savoring this brief moment when all was well and under control, the day's chores and piano lessons over, the children all fed, getting ready for baths, the good evening coming up when she and John could relax over a glass of wine while the last of the casserole waited in the oven.

The place was really shaping up at last. Just look at the way that amber porch light, coming in softly through the beautiful leaded windowpanes, was glowing on her two pine church benches. What a steal they'd been! Absolutely perfect, too, for that corner where her pupils waited every day for their lessons to begin. Ann was a passionate bargain-hunter. No garage or tag sale escaped her sharp eye. Nearly every stick of furniture in the house, including the huge round bed where she and John slept — often with two or three stow-away children snuggled in beside them — had been bought secondhand for a song. Now if she could just pick up a good-looking sofa for the living room . . .

At that particular moment Ann Sweeney, mother of eleven children, looked serenely happy and much younger than her forty-five years. Her figure was trim and lithe, her auburn hair swept back in a becoming ponytail. From across the hall she might have been a teenager in her close-fitting corduroy jeans and turtleneck sweater. Soon enough, how-ever, the characteristic little frown returned between her intense brown eyes. Serenity would never be Ann's style. Her cup was full to overflowing with children, husband, home, and a nearly full-time career teaching piano and play-ing cello in occasional concerts. Yet the impression she gave was of being in mid-chase after something that still eluded her. She might have been a racehorse stamping at a starting gate instead of the contented winner of so many races. People meeting her for the first time, knowing something about the size of the family, were always startled. This was no placid earth mother. She was attractively restless, very sure of her-self and unsure all at one. What did she really want? What was behind all that drive? You found yourself wondering what sort of life Ann Sweeney had had as a little girl. . . .

Bathtime! She stepped deftly over Woof, the big black dog, who for some reason always elected to sleep in the one spot where he completely blocked the stairs. Then she ran quickly up to the second floor. Squeals, shouts, loud sounds of splashing water were rising from three different tubs. On the landing, Wendy, the baby-sitter, was trying to zip her jacket while keeping an eye on developing situations. "Paddy! Stop that splashing! You're getting water all over the rug —"

"Everybody's started," said Wendy. "The little boys aren't really washed yet, though. Megan's in your tub. And Minh's helping Faith and Terry in the pink bathroom."

"Thank God for *that!*" Ann rummaged in her purse, thrust some bills at the girl, and gave her a quick hug. "Thanks, Wendy. I couldn't live without you."

"See you tomorrow." Wendy started down the stairs. "Oh — you'd better get Megan out pretty soon," she added. "She's been in there over half an hour —"

Ann nodded. "She'll keep. First things first —" She marched into the little boys' bathroom and began vigorous scrubbing of various faces, hands, and feet belonging to the three small occupants of the tub. "Now! Stand up, Paddy —"

She always tackled this three-year-old imp first. Paddy, younger by one minute than his twin, Timmy, was nevertheless bigger, stronger, and twenty times more likely to create interesting trouble. The experienced mother found it desirable to get Paddy out of the way and into his pajamas before the others. "Rub-a-dub-dub, three boys in a tub!" she sang, lathering Paddy's slender ivory back. Quickly she rinsed him off, swung him out, and handed him a towel. "Dry yourself!" she commanded.

But Paddy, not to be disposed of so lightly, hopped up on the toilet seat and began dancing around waving his towel, chanting, "See! See me! See me!" As usual he succeeded in mesmerizing Timmy, who lay back in the tub entranced waiting to see what Paddy might do next. This action somewhat squashed his older brother, Marcus, a four-year-old redhead who was trying to sail a plastic boat in the lee of Timmy's back. "Quit it!" he yelled. "Timmy! Look out —" On second thought, Marcus saw that it was Paddy who really deserved his outrage. These two frequently fought over who should have the limelight. Now, deciding that Paddy had been on-stage long enough, Marcus snatched up a washcloth and lobbed it with excellent aim. He caught Paddy right in the eye.

It was at this precise moment that the hall telephone began to ring.

Ten-year-old Megan, floating serenely alone in her mother's bathtub, surrounded by seven cages of guinea pigs, gerbils, and mice of assorted colors, heard it vaguely as if from a great distance. The ring did not really penetrate her dream. Lanky, long, and already aristocratic in every bone of her body, Megan was engaged in deciding what animal she absolutely had to have next. She didn't allow herself to reach for the impossible, a horse of her very own. That was reserved for some beautiful time in the future. A Persian cat with a pedigree, Megan decided. A cat with cool blue eyes. And fur like a cloud of snow. Yes, that was what she had to have! Failing that, though, she really ought to be able to demand a rat. Anybody could get a rat. And they were so interesting. Her mother would see it her way. She wondered if she could convince her father that she needed a rat.

The telephone rang on.

In the pink bathroom Minh heard it clearly and paid no attention. For the moment it pleased her to play at bathing three-year-old Faith. She was spreading soapy bubbles under Faith's coffee-colored chin. Faith, attempting to pin Minh's hand to her breastbone, was giving out loud squeals of pain and pleasure. "OOOh, Minh! It tickles! *Don't!*" A born prima donna, Faith was the one child out of eleven who could not only laugh and cry simultaneously, but also manage to calculate the effect of her actions on an attentive audience.

"Minh? I hear the phone —" Small black Terry, trying in his gentle way to be helpful, touched Minh's arm. Although Faith and Terry were the same age and had been raised as twins ever since Terry's adoption, the two could hardly have been more different. Faith, round, glamorous, demanding. Terry, slim, shy, accommodating. Now, while he sat quietly

Jay, 1976

The Sweeneys' house

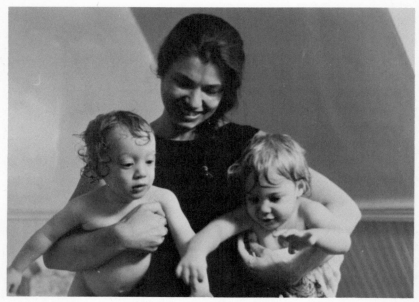

Ann with twins Timmy and Paddy

The Sweeney children, soon after Faith's adoption. Left to right: Jay, Paddy, Megan, Faith (on Megan's lap), Timmy, and Marcus

Minh (taken at school in cooking class)

Terry

Marcus

enough in the water, his sense of order was disturbed by the unanswered phone. "Minh — it's ringing."

Minh exclaimed in irritated Vietnamese, brushing off his small black hand. She didn't like to answer phones. English was still a foreign language and she found it difficult to take messages. At sixteen she had known all too much of the world's work. As a small child in Saigon she'd been sent off to an employer who fed and housed her. But her wages always returned to her mother. When she joined the American family in September as an adopted daughter, she had bravely determined to make life better for herself. Yet how to do this was not at all clear. Minh hadn't been lucky enough to have any education. Now, when it was at last possible, she found it hard to study. At times she plunged into housework, for it was one thing she understood and could do beautifully. But there were other times when she longed for something more and rejected the whole idea. The truth was that Minh was still searching, trying to find her way in a new land.

The phone rang on. "Jesus Christ!" said Ann under her breath. Her use of language was carefully controlled for the benefit of all the little people she was trying to raise; she was much more skilled in the use of profanity than anyone would have supposed. But what would become of her hopes and aspirations that all her children be accepted and successful in the world if she blew her cool and cussed every time she felt like it? Still, the phone could not possibly have picked a more goddamned inconvenient time to ring.

She gave Paddy a swat on the behind. "*You* get dry! Put your pajamas on. And *you*," she said, flinging the washcloth at Marcus, "had better wash yourself well or I'll drown you myself the minute I get back."

Timmy was beginning to shiver. The last thing she needed was another round of sore throats for these twins. For the past year both had been on preventive penicillin. Now Ann plucked Timmy out of the tub, wound him quickly in a big towel, balanced him on her hip and rushed out to the hall table, where the phone was shrilly uttering its sixth ring.

"Hello?"

"Mrs. Sweeney?" The caller identified himself as a member of a local committee interested in placing Vietnamese children with American families. He remembered the party Ann and John had given for Minh to help her find contacts in the neighborhood when she came to live with the Sweeneys. "What I'm calling about," said the voice, "is that we have three other children. Two brothers and a baby sister. They are really very much in need of a good home. Chuong, the oldest, is ten. Dat, the little brother, is nearly four. And Huong, the baby girl, is about a year-and-a-half, we think. What we'd like to know is, would you and your husband be willing to take Dat? The four-year-old boy?"

Standing there in the hall, a wet, shivering twin in her arms, Ann felt her answer rising like a burst in her throat. Yes, Yes, *Yes*! She put down the feeling, knowing that, after all, John would have to agree. It was not her nature to hang back in caution. Generally she went all out when, as she said, God clearly meant for her to make a move. Now, trying her best to sound thoughtful, she said, "Well, of course I'll have to ask my husband. I expect he'll be coming in in just a few minutes. Can I have your number and we'll call you back?"

During the next twenty minutes Ann Sweeney finished the bathing and supervising of her brood with uncharacteristic detachment. Calmly she washed little bottoms, toweled little arms and legs, coaxed little characters along until they were all dried off and snug in pajamas. But underneath her unfurrowed brow her thoughts raced ahead in joyful plotting and planning. One more little boy! One of the three who needed to be rescued.

When John walked in, she gave him the facts as simply, bluntly as they'd been given to her. Then she said, "They want to know if we'll take the four-year-old. Dat?"

John paused in the act of removing his coat, a tall, thoughtful, imposing figure with his snow-white beard, penetrating dark eyes. "Good heavens! One more little boy!" he said quietly. Paused again. Then he turned to Ann. "What would you say to taking all three?"

What would she say! She'd wanted all three from the moment she'd first heard about them. How could she resist children in need? And clearly it would be better if they weren't separated. But she wanted John to be for it as strongly as she was, since the hard work of getting them adjusted to the family would certainly involve him, too.

No more than forty minutes could have elapsed from the first ring to the moment now when Ann went to the phone and dialed the number she'd been given to return the call. "We'd like to take all three children," she said.

It was decided that Chuong, Dat, and Huong would be brought for a weekend in the near future. Ann would send driving directions. The committee would get back to her with a firm date. Ann said good-bye, put down the phone and looked at John. "My God, where are we going to put those kids? We're almost out of bedrooms!"

But her voice held not the slightest hint of regret. Already she was moving ahead into another of those exciting times, the very best times in her life with John, when their thoughts and hopes converged and ran happily in the same direction. This strong desire they both had to care for children was perhaps the deepest thing they shared, the cornerstone of their marriage. Children born to them and the world's children who somehow found their way to their doorstep needing love and shelter were one and the same. To *nurture* was both a need and an enormous satisfaction for Ann and John Sweeney.

"Well," said John now, in his calm, deliberate way, "The little girl can go in with Faith, of course."

"Of course!" Ann could see them now in twin beds in a room all pretty and pink and totally little-girl. Faith, half-black, 100 percent seductive and feminine, had been adopted when she was just six weeks old. "The most fun baby anyone ever had!" as she'd said many times. Ann had been wanting another little girl for a long time. In fact she and John had started proceedings over six months ago to take a nine-year-old Colombian Indian child, Maria, from an institution in Bogotá. The delays had been many and correspondence with the nuns in Bogotá so confusing that the Sweeneys had begun to despair of ever seeing Maria. The little girl was blind, a handicap that did not deter the family. However, there were many preparations one had to make for a blind child: specially built large shelves to hold Braille books, and so on. Ann had been anxious to get started. But she wanted to know definitely if and when Maria was coming before redoing a corner of Faith's room to hold all the things she'd need. Now, in a matter of minutes, she'd been presented with an opportunity to have a baby girl from the other side of the world. Vietnam! Would she be a delicate, lovely little creature? Or would she be sturdy, short, and square of build like Minh?

While Ann dreamed on about daughters, John, busily working a stubborn cork out of a bottle of white wine, planned for sons. "The smaller boy, Dat — is that his name? — can go in with Terry and the twins."

"But what about Marcus? *He's* in there now —"

"You know, I've been thinking," said John. "Marcus would really be better off in that little room up on the third floor next to Jay. He's two years older than Terry and the twins. But the longer he stays in with them, the more he tends to stay on their level. It's just making for trouble."

"I'll say!" Ann sighed, shook her head, smiling. "Marcus, Marcus!" The most enchanting, infuriating kid. "I never know whether to strangle him or hug him —" she said.

"So you do both," John smiled, pouring to the rim of the glass she held out. "One after the other."

"You'll say, 'Marcus, did you pick up your room, did you put away the Big Wheel, did you do this, did you do that?' He looks right at you, with those sparkly dark eyes. 'Yes,

Mom!' And he hasn't done a thing! But it isn't lying, you see, because he has every intention of doing it and he doesn't want to upset you. Only then he forgets —"

Ann and John clinked glasses gently. "Yes, I think you're right. Marcus should move upstairs. He won't like it, but he'll have Jay next door. Maybe that'll help —"

"That leaves the older boy unaccounted for," said John.

"You mean the ten-year-old, Chuong." Ann suddenly had a thought. "My, won't Jay be excited at having a big brother again!" Jay especially had missed Chris when he moved out. It was a funny thing about big families. You'd think there'd be so many characters around, nobody'd ever have a chance to get lonely. Not so. Each person played a special role, so when that person left, everybody felt it in different ways. Would Chuong help fill the empty spot in Jay's heart?

"Let's hope it works out," said John thoughtfully. He was thinking of the distance, greater than all the thousands of miles, between the war-torn city and the untouched comfort of a Connecticut suburb. "That boy must have been through a lot," he said.

"But where *are* we going to put him?" worried Ann, back, as usual, to the practicalities of life.

"Oh, we'll fit him in somehow. We can always divide my office if it comes to that. And temporarily we can put him in a bed in the big hall upstairs with some screens around it for privacy." As casually as that, John took the first step toward cutting his own space in half to share it with a ten-year-old Vietnamese boy he'd never laid eyes on. That was the sort of man he was. And Ann, his wife, said immediately, "Oh, that's a good idea!" She considered it settled from that moment. That's the sort of woman she was.

They might have been any handsome Connecticut couple lingering over their wine on a winter evening. The man, distinguished-looking with his white beard and courteous, almost grave, manner. The woman, sitting on the edge of her chair, brown eyes alive and happy now, her small frown gone, her body almost vibrating with excitement. They might have been discussing some new upper-echelon success in the business world, a triumphant merger, a clever bit of maneuvering down at the bank. Or perhaps the wife's hope for them to go to Paris on their anniversary. For such is the talk of many husbands and wives under many gleaming candelabra in the dining rooms of well-to-do sections of towns all across the country. Instead, these two people were talking about making a commitment that would involve their energy and their fortune, such as it was, in helping three young children for many, many years. There was not a shred of argument. The matter was considered settled almost from the moment it arose. Emotionally it had taken but a few seconds for them to expand their family of children from eleven to fourteen.

How did these two remarkable people ever find each other? What had led Ann and John Sweeney to make parenting the first and foremost career of their lives?

Katherine Ann Taylor Sweeney was born into a world without children. It was the strange, often stimulating world of a small traveling man's hotel: the Hotel Jefferson in Flint, Michigan. At the time Ann, as she was called, was born to Mary and Harry Embrey Taylor, the hotel was owned and operated by Ann's maternal grandmother and her third husband. Over the years the Hotel Jefferson would actually shelter four family generations within its old-fashioned corridors.

For her first three years, Ann, a chubby little girl with big brown eyes, was the adored only child in this family of many adults, and the darling of the hotel staff. Where most children grow up with memories of early social life in the sandbox, Ann remembers a hotel desk where Mac, the clerk, who was her best friend, greeted strangers who came in carrying suitcases. Instead of a backyard tree, she had a potted palm. And instead of learning about life from watching the neighbors, she watched the happenings in the hotel lobby with its dark woodwork, red velvet walls, smell of cigars, and the two brass cuspidors that fascinated but repelled her.

The Depression soon caught up with the Hotel Jefferson. Many of its fifty rooms often went empty. Ann's mother, Mary, sighs, remembering. "There's nothing more perishable than a hotel room. If you don't sell it, *that* night is gone forever. Harry got a job on the Detroit *Times* as soon as he could. We moved into our own house. Then before you know it, the hotel was lost and both sets of parents, aunts and uncles, too, moved in with us!"

Ann's happy but overprotected childhood might have flowed into more normal channels with the family move, if she hadn't soon gotten serious ear infections, which led to operations for double mastoiditis. She was in bed so long she had to be taught to walk all over again at three years of age. The little girl was lonely during those long months with only her dolls for young companionship. She dressed, undressed them, bossed them, scolded them. The family of dolls kept growing till there were eighteen or twenty.

"In the beginning my favorites always had golden curls," says Ann. "I had straight brown hair then and was already thinking of myself as ugly. It was a Mexican souvenir doll that first gave me any confidence in being dark. She was pretty and vivid — and she had dark hair!" The integration of Ann's doll family was thus established early. Far from being inferior, this dark-haired, dark-skinned new "baby" was a reassuring addition to the circle. The world apparently had room for all kinds. You didn't have to be a blue-eyed blond.

But there was another sort of discrimination waiting for young Ann Taylor. By the time she went to school, she didn't talk or behave like the other kids. Living with adults, playing mommy to doll children, she'd become a miniature adult. Her classmates, with that sense of the kill children have for anyone "different," did not make her welcome. She was lonely but even so, she seems to have had a sense of her destiny. When a newspaper told of the little Peruvian miracle girl who'd startled the world by giving birth to a baby when she herself was only five years old, Ann, then age six, mourned, "And I'm not even pregnant yet!"

At nine, Ann had double mastoiditis all over again, missing all but twelve days of school that semester. The pattern of illness and isolation continued, with only her dolls and lots of reading to help pass the time. When she was twelve, her father joined the navy during World War II, and the family moved to California to be near his station. On the West Coast, Ann finally got to play with a real live baby — the son of an officer on her father's ship. "I willingly carried him, fed him, was wet on, changed him, and played with him every chance I got," she remembers. "It was great!" But before long, Ann and her mother went back to Mt. Clemens, Michigan, Harry's hometown, to wait out the war.

In Mt. Clemens Ann started to make a few friends, but her real love was music. Through the high school years she poured her energy into piano and cello lessons, performing in school concerts and soon finding herself in demand in local orchestra and solo performances. She was good. The next move to Oberlin College with its famous conservatory seemed logical. But even then she wasn't your stereotyped dedicated student of the music world. There were other things in the world. Dating, for one thing. She thought she might be in love. Instead of moving on into her junior year, however, she went to Paris for a year, where she lived alone and studied the cello.

"I discovered I didn't want a concert career. A boy I'd known since high school begged me to marry him before he was sent overseas with the Army of Occupation. So I came home, married, and Randy was born on the day I would have graduated from Oberlin. I'd hoped he'd be born in Germany, where my husband had been sent. I'd planned to join him as soon as he found us a place. But I was threatened with placenta praevia, and spent the pregnancy home in bed. He returned when Randy was four months old. We bought a house, Lynn was born thirteen months after Randy, and two years later Chris." But the young parents found they were growing in different directions. By the time she was twenty-five, Ann was a divorcee with three small children and a very necessary career teaching piano six days a week. Looking back is not Ann's style. She regrets nothing ."And I wouldn't have missed having those three kids for anything."

Before long Ann found herself in love again, this time with a handsome orchestra conductor. But while Ann occupied an important chair playing cello in John Sweeney's orchestra, she was by no means sure she occupied first place in his affections. "Oh, God, I was jealous!" Ann moans, remembering. "Here I was with three little kids — not exactly the greatest inducement to a committed bachelor to give up his freedom. And here *he* was going out with other girls! We'd have a big date planned, one of the kids would run a high fever, I'd have to call it off. I knew I wanted to marry John — but he had to take my children along with me. I mean take them to heart — not just put up with them. I almost gave up hope —"

For some years John Sweeney had thought he'd never marry, let alone assume responsibility for raising children. Wedded to music at an early age, he was making brilliant solo appearances with symphony orchestras by the time he was seventeen. And by 1950 he was giving recitals in Paris and London. Tragedy struck. Polio. At twenty-four he was left with a partially withered arm. He finally made a good recovery, and strangers meeting him today would never realize he was incapacitated. But muscles had been damaged. The hand, the arm knew what they could not do. John knew his concert days were over. He could still play a piano, but not on the stage of his early dreams. After a year or so of newspaper work, he turned to conducting, first studying in his hometown Detroit, then Munich and Vienna. He conducted successfully throughout the Midwest, then finally came to Mt. Clemens hoping to organize an orchestra there.

It was a newspaper friend who'd been covering the town's musical activities for years who introduced him to Ann Taylor. "So we organized the Mt. Clemens orchestra together," Ann says, "and for the next few years I played cello in cities nearby wherever John conducted."

When John finally decided to return to Europe for more study, however, Ann was sure all was lost. With his fluent command of French, German, Italian, and Spanish, John would surely be sweeping females off their feet in four languages. She never dreamed he'd be willing to part with his independence. "One Sunday after John left, I really hit bottom," Ann remembers. "I was moping in my parents' backyard while the kids played around. Suddenly Mother shouted out the kitchen window. 'Ann! John is on the phone — calling from Vienna!'"

"I nearly fainted when he asked me to marry him. He took the next boat home." The informal wedding took place immediately. John Sweeney, confirmed bachelor-musician, found himself overnight a family man with three children. He soon discovered he liked his new life. The next years were busy, happy, full of travel. The Sweeneys decided to add to their clan. "But when we didn't get pregnant right away," Ann recalls, laughing, "Randy thought we must be doing something wrong. He offered to help us out with any information we needed —"

Apparently the parents didn't need his advice. Ann became pregnant with Megan while the family lived in Washington one year while John conducted the National Ballet. At the end of the season, however, the Sweeneys decided they'd like to live in Connecticut, where John had friends. More conducting jobs followed. But when Mills Music offered John the position of manager of their classical music division, he decided the time had come to settle down.

John Scripps Sweeney IV, who would be called Jay, had joined the clan two years after Megan. John now had five

*Ann and John on their
wedding day*

John Sweeney

small reasons to give up the peripatetic life of a conductor. Both he and Ann were contentedly going against the trend of the times and hoped to continue adding to their already-big family. But in 1976 not even the cosmopolitan John or the passionately acquiring mother, Ann, could ever have imagined themselves ready to become the instant parents of three small Oriental refugee children on but a moment's notice.

THREE

The Meeting

WHEN THE CARS carrying members of the Vietnamese committee and the three refugee children swung off the turnpike and began following the small road map that Ann herself had drawn and sent to the man in charge, the two youngest, Dat and Huong, did not stir. Much of their lives in the past months had been spent half-asleep, huddled in corners. Instinctively they shut themselves away at any sign of change, for with change came pain.

Chuong, on the other hand, still had much of the curiosity of a normal ten-year-old faced with any new situation. The incredible stream of cars and thundering trailer trucks was now left behind. This meant they were probably coming to a place people lived. The living habits of Americans wherever he encountered them still left Chuong dazzled. He sat up straight and began to look around. Big, big houses. Fine snow-covered grounds spreading out very far all around. It would take many gardeners to keep those lawns green and smooth in summer, Chuong thought. The father of one of his friends had been such a gardener for a big estate outside Saigon. But in Vietnam, one had flowering trees and bushes to care for all year long. What did a gardener do in the American winter, Chuong wondered. Perhaps he shoveled snow from the driveways or polished the beautiful cars? Chuong longed to own an elegant car someday, one he could drive up a driveway as long as a street, paved silky smooth all the way. And his driveway would have tall black trees rising on either side, too, like these. Ah! They were turning in. Chuong broke off his daydream abruptly at the sight of the huge white wood and stone house. *This* driveway sloped down a hill and carried them through a wonderful arch of stone all covered with green ivy. The arch, which had great pillars, swept out from the house like a bridge over their car. Chuong loved the look of this place at once. The entrance was like a castle! "They must be millionaires," he said to himself. The very idea made his heart pound because he didn't know what this meant for *him.* Good? Bad? Maybe they had taken him to do the hard work? Carry out garbage, sweep the halls? Would they give him enough to eat?

Food was number one on the list of things Chuong worried about. In the long months, almost a year now, since he had left his homeland, Chuong had learned painfully what many an exile had learned before him. As the everyday comforts and little privileges which have always been taken for granted begin disappearing one after another, life finally reduces itself to the first, most important human right of all — the right to eat. Only the raw hunger of those days in the open boat could have prepared Chuong to accept the disgusting food of that Hong Kong camp. At home he would have shoved it aside instantly! Of course, when he and Dat and Huong were finally airlifted to the barracks provided for Vietnamese refugees in Arkansas, the food did improve. But to Chuong it was still tasteless. Sometimes he dreamed of the cucumber and ginger soup of home, or the good spicy smells rising from the kettle of garlic, green peppers, and small sausages his mother used to cook to go with their rice. Dreaming was not Chuong's way, however. He ate the army food in Arkansas, complaining less than many of the soldiers who had occupied those barracks long before him. It was not too bad.

Still, his hopes rose foolishly when it was finally decided that the three children were to go and live with a Vietnamese family somewhere in New York State. One of the family members was a second cousin of Chuong's father and had volunteered to accept the children. It was hardly a close connection, but in Oriental life such ties have weight. Unfortunately for Chuong, it turned out that there were several families crowded in one house. These people were also recent refugees, having all the problems of learning a new language and earning money that always beset new arrivals. The women, overburdened with children of their own and cupboards that were too often bare, were not delighted to see three more faces at the kitchen table. Custom forbade them to throw these children out, but custom also allowed that they be fed only after all others had been satisfied. Small wonder that anger flashed. Frequently Chuong and his brother and sister sat down to scraps, odds and ends nobody else would touch. Sometimes there was nothing. Nothing! Then he shouted and screamed because he was so furious that this should happen to him, to Dat and Huong, who were not growing the way they should. He could see his own ribs sticking out. His stomach often growled at night, keeping him awake.

Sometimes he thought of running away, stealing out in the night and running, running until he ran far enough to find a good life again. He was only a boy but he could do many things; he was strong and smart. At other times, though, he was overwhelmed by fears of the unknown. The world seemed to be full of flames, enemies, and gunfire around the next corner. His imagination had a tendency to run wild once it got started. Even when his fear passed and a sort of dull peace replaced it, he knew he could not abandon Dat and

Huong. They must all stay together. This shelter, which was poor enough, was still better than the streets. At ten, Chuong was already wary and full of survival knowledge. You did not leap from one boat until you knew for sure that the next would not sink under you.

Now, climbing out of the car in the Sweeneys' driveway, Chuong caught sight of a shining blue-green pool through big windows in a wing of the house there off to the right. A swimming pool! *Inside* the house! They were millionaires for sure. He was staring at the pool with wild hope and despair when Ann and John came down the stone stairs to greet the party. Only the very rich had such pools in Vietnam, and never had Chuong seen one inside a private house before. Would he ever be allowed to swim in that shimmering blue water? Or would they set him to work wiping the slime from the bottom when it had to be cleaned? It was in such a mood of wonder and deep worry that he looked up to see the two people who had asked him and Dat and Huong to come here. The lady from the committee had told him only that Mr. and Mrs. Sweeney wanted them to come and live with them. "Why?" he wanted to shout. "Tell me why right now? Why do you want us?"

Ann had never seen anything like these children. The baby girl in the arms of one of the Vietnamese women looked more like a bedraggled Pekingese puppy than a real child. The little boy, Dat, was so frail he looked as if he might break. They had said he was probably four years old. He looked barely two. But it was Chuong who truly frightened Ann. One glance told her that he was terrified, angry, maybe even capable of violence. As for his physical appearance, Ann recalls, "If it was ever possible for Chuong not to be handsome it was then. His haircut was the most obvious flaw, the back rising straight up, the front hanging down over his eyes. He always appeared to have his head bent and to be looking up at you with violent, angry eyes through that black hair.

Those eyes were never still! They darted around looking, looking — for what? I wondered if maybe he was looking for a way to escape? Obviously he didn't trust us."

This preliminary visit of children and prospective parents had been planned for just a weekend. Ann was surprised that six Vietnamese adults had turned up to escort three little children on such an expedition from a city hours away in another state. But obviously the thing to do was invite everybody inside and make them warm and comfortable as soon as possible. March was certainly coming on lion-strong with a raw and blustery wind. Her own kids were used to playing outside in anything short of a blizzard or a flood, and right now the sun was shining although clouds were scudding across the sky. But the Vietnamese children, with so little meat on their bones, dressed only in thin, shabby jackets, were shivering.

"Please everybody, come in, come in!" Anne said with her best company smile. "I think we all need some hot tea."

"Yes, do come in," said John, a tall and imposing host.

Nods, smiles, and a flow of incomprehensible Vietnamese followed. From this jabber, however, a woman's voice rose in flawless, weclome English. A small well-dressed Vietnamese lady stepped forward. "Thank you very much for your hospitality," she said to Ann, taking her hand. "We are delighted to be invited to your home." She went up the stone steps and everyone followed.

The Sweeneys were immediately impressed with this charming little person. She was not a member of the household that had been caring for the children, she told Ann and John. But the priest of the Catholic church the Vietnamese attended had arranged for her to accompany the group to be their interpreter. Tea was soon served, along with cookies and soft drinks for the youngsters. Minh had been eyeing the proceedings from a distance. Now, however, she joined the visitors, who were conversing among themselves in Vietnamese, and soon was talking away in her home language. One of the women was still holding the baby, Huong, but Minh made no attempt to take her. What interested her was this smalltalk in Vietnamese. It had been a long time since she'd enjoyed anything resembling backyard gossip. Glancing over at Minh, Ann thought how pretty she looked, relaxed but animated and happy to be back among her countrymen.

After finishing their snack, Paddy, Timmy, Terry, and Marcus got out their little cars and plastic trucks and began racing them in the hallway. Tiny Dat immediately slipped off a lap and ran to join them. Frail he might be, but Ann was pleased to see he was certainly friendly and outgoing. "He didn't have any trouble fitting right in," she remembers now. "And it's been that way from the first day."

Chuong, on the other hand, remained standing almost stiffly to one side with his ever-watchful eyes. He did not want tea. He accepted fruit juice and cookies with a blank-faced nod of thanks. But so far he hadn't uttered a single sound. Definitely, Ann realized, Chuong was the one who was going to need all her help. "And no doubt he'll resist accepting it every step of the way," she thought. It was children like Chuong who tried a parent's soul, who left you praying for guidance and racking your brains at the end of every day. She saw it all, with the experience that comes only from mothering twelve different children of widely assorted talents and temperaments, not to mention different capacities for throwing tantrums. But knowing the path she would have to travel with Chuong didn't make her hesitate. His stubbornness, his anger, his proud aloofness were the very qualities that had brought him through. How rewarding it would be to make possible the rescue of a strong-minded child like Chuong. She could hardly wait to begin. Anyone could feed starving bodies. It was much harder, as Ann very well knew, to reach a starving heart.

At that moment, with Chuong still frozen in mistrust, with Ann still unsure how to approach him in the midst of this noisy, somewhat awkward tea party, it was Jay who came to the rescue. "Mom," he said, "how about if Chuong and I take a bike ride over to the Baileys' on Possum Lane? They've got some Vietnamese kids staying with them. Maybe we could find someone for Chuong to talk to. . . ."

"Bless you, Jay!" Ann thought, rising quickly. "Would you like to go, Chuong? You can take Chris's bike — it's still in the basement."

A bike! How long ago it had been, that day when he had had to leave his own bike behind in that yard outside Saigon. At the memory, Chuong's eyes showed pain, fear, despair, while Ann held her breath, not knowing what to think. Maybe he was terrified at the thought of leaving his brother and sister? Oh God, would she ever, ever get behind that wall and know what was going on in his head? Unaccountably, Chuong relaxed in the next moment and suddenly gave Jay a smile. "Okay," he said. "Let's go —"

He actually *smiled!* He said *"Okay!"* "A good American omen if ever I heard one," thought Ann, almost limp with relief. "Jay," she said, "take a sweater from the hall closet for Chuong. He'll need one under his jacket if you're going bike-riding in all that wind —"

"Okay, Mom."

Ann could feel her breath expire slowly, her limbs beginning to relax. "Does Chuong speak English well, then?" she asked the interpreter.

"Very well," the lady assured her with a charming smile. "Chuong is extremely bright. He is in his proper grade in school, which is remarkable considering what he has been through." She then told Ann and John as much as she knew of the children's past history. "Right now Dat is the one who needs immediate attention. That's why we wanted you to take *him* when we first called. He's a beautiful child, as you can see, but physically he's in much worse shape than the other two. Perhaps it's that his constitution is really more delicate to begin with; I don't know. . . ."

As if on cue, Dat drifted in from the hallway then, although the other little boys were still racing their cars and building

tunnels of blocks. His eyes seemed dazed with fatigue. A lot
had happened in a very short time, and Dat, as usual, was
looking for a warm place to curl up and withdraw. Ann held
out her arms, and he came right to her.

She would never in her life forget that first moment when
she held Dat. "In less than thirty seconds," as she says, "he
melted down the front of me. He had the feel of a *baby!* He
slipped around inside his skin just the way Timmy had when
he was tiny —"

(Timmy, the smaller of Ann's four-year-old twins, had
spent three weeks in a heated Isolette after his birth by
cesarean section.)

"— Dat's head was on my shoulder and his body shaped to
mine all in less time than it takes to tell. I held him and held
him, and I was so grateful that someone else must have held
him tenderly a long time ago. Whatever had happened to him,
he knew what it was to be loved and to love back, and that
was so reassuring. I just knew we could save this one!

"— But when he opened his mouth," Ann remembers next,
"it was a disaster area! There was nothing but brown stumps
of all his baby teeth. And the most awful smell!"

The appalling condition of Dat's mouth might have repelled
a less experienced mother. For Ann, it only intensified her
desire to do something quickly. She held the frail little boy
close. He snuggled against her drowsily, restoring and rebuilding himself for a little time while the grown-ups conversed
politely over his head. The snuggling nourished Ann even as
it satisfied Dat's deep need for love and comfort. She savored
the moment, wishing it could go on and on. No sooner had
she wished it than life reasserted itself and Dat suddenly sat
up. The little boys in the front hall were building a bridge of
blocks to carry their cars and trucks. "Not *that* way, Paddy!"
Marcus was shouting. "Like this — see?"

Dat wanted to see, too. He wriggled off Ann's lap and ran
back to the action. The small Vietnamese lady smiled at Ann.
"I can see things are going very well," she said, standing up.

"We must be getting on our way. We are going into the city for the weekend, and we will stop by to pick up the children on Sunday evening. Will six o'clock be all right?"

"Fine. I'll give them an early supper so they won't get hungry on the way home." The word *home* jumped out at Ann the minute she said it. It was wrong! Already she knew that "home" for these children had to be here with her, with John. Smiling a bit nervously, she said quickly, "Of course you know we're hoping this will be home. We want Dat. We want them all — very much."

"You are very kind," said the interpreter noncommittally. The good-byes were formal. Another flurry of Vietnamese, stiff bows, and wide smiles from the rest of the party. One of the women placed the baby girl in Ann's arms. They were gone.

If Dat had felt exactly like Ann's own baby the first moment she held him, little Huong was a totally different story. She curled in upon herself like some small animal carved out of wood. Ann tried putting her over the shoulder, rubbing her bony little back gently in the classic manner of mother comforting baby. It was no good. Huong's knees remained drawn up tight, her tiny arms would not go around Ann's neck; they stayed clutched across her own small chest.

"What have we here?" said John kindly, peering down at the strange little creature.

"I don't know," said Ann, "but it sure doesn't feel like a *baby*."

"Shall I try?"

"By all means," said Ann passing Huong to John. "Maybe what she needs is Papa's magic touch."

John walked up and down the big living room, a tall, white-bearded man crooning softly to the rigid Vietnamese child in his arms. His deep eyes tried to look into the tiny, dull black eyes, to catch some hint of her need and perhaps reach the spirit within. Nothing! She gave no response. The feeblest kitten, the most neglected puppy in the pound was a bundle of action compared to Huong.

"I'm a failure," he said, disappointed, giving her back to Ann.

"Maybe she's scared. Maybe she just needs time to get to know us," said Ann. She had to admit her heart sank a bit at the prospect of making something of this unlovely, dejected scrap of humanity. How would Huong ever be able to compete with Faith's golden good looks? Faith, the royal beauty, with her great, glowing eyes, sculptured brow, and elegant eyebrows, had been conquering hearts for every moment of her three years in the Sweeney household. Strangers on the street couldn't resist stopping to admire her. "Did you ever see such eyelashes!" "Such a gorgeous smile!" Faith was a year and a half older than hopeless Huong. The comparison was going to be unavoidable and unfortunate.

"Even your name's hopeless," sighed Ann, hugging the sad baby girl on her lap. Pronounced "Hung," her name would make her become an easy target for teasing the minute she grew up enough to go out and play. "Hopeless, hopeless, hopeless Huong," sang Ann, trying to rock the little stone figure.

"Come now —" said John. "We'll have to do better than that. At least we can be hope*ful*." Without anyone thinking about it, Huong found her new name during that first weekend at the Sweeneys'. She began to be Huong-Hope. Later she was just Hope. Or Hopeful when her mother was trying to get her to do something. During those first days and hours, however, Hope gave no hint of the person hidden in her unyielding small body. But if her spirit could not be reached, her body's needs demanded to be taken care of. Ann was still trying to rock her when a sudden warmth spread over her lap. In another second the baby was soaking wet and she herself was very damp.

"Hey!" she cried, jumping up. "What's going on here?" She carried the baby quickly upstairs, laid her down on the bedroom carpet. It was then she discovered that Huong-Hope had been sent off for a weekend's visit wearing no underwear. Her thin, faded outer clothing was little better than rags. (Dat, too, Ann was to find out, was similarly dressed — or, you could say, "undressed." So the minute either one of them was wet, a small accident became a big one.) Saddest of all was Ann's discovery that Hope was wearing two left shoes!

It was almost a relief to be able to do *something* for this child since she would not allow herself to be comforted. Ann gave Huong-Hope a bath, put her in Pampers, then took out a pretty dress that Faith had long ago outgrown. She found some tiny sneakers the right size. (There was a heap of outgrown spare pairs in the laundry room. When the kids got wet feet or lost a sneaker, they usually could find others here with which to make do.) Then she brushed the little girl's hair till it was smooth and shining. "At least her hair's nice and thick," Ann thought.

"See!" she said then, holding Huong-Hope up to the big bedroom mirror. "*Now* you look pretty! There's Huong — in the mirror. Doesn't Huong look pretty?"

Huong-Hope stared at herself unblinking, unsmiling. God, she doesn't even cry! Ann realized. It was chilling to try to care for a child so turned off, so totally indifferent. "I'd far rather she screamed," Ann thought, carrying her back downstairs. But before she had time to dwell on what might be ahead for this strange, unpromising baby, there was plenty that had to be done here and now for everybody.

"Mom — I'm starving!" "Mom! Can we have something to eat?"

"I've started chicken soup with noodles," John said, poking his head out of the kitchen. "All right?"

"Wonderful," said Ann. I'll be right there —" She went out in the hall calling, "Minh? Minh?"

"She can't hear you, Mom," said Megan. "She's locked in her room playing records. I'll watch Huong for you —"

Megan at ten was just beginning to extend her passionate interest in animals to small human creatures.

"Oh, thanks," sighed Ann putting Huong-Hope down on the sunroom floor. "At least she won't fall off anything here. But watch her —" Huong, could, in fact, walk. Most of the time she chose to sit or huddle in a little ball. But who knew when this unpredictable baby might scuttle away, hurt herself? Now Ann plunged quickly into lunch-making to back up John. Crackers, small slices of cheese, cut up apples, milk. *Twelve* glasses again! She hadn't had twelve children under her roof since Randy, Lynn, and Chris had grown and gone. How good, how right it felt. But where were Jay and Chuong?

Apples had been eaten, cookies fought over, milk spilled by the time the two older boys came in. John was patiently trying to coax Huong-Hope into eating her lunch. She drank little milk, spat out everything else except bits of cookie. Ann was already familiar with the Vietnamese sweet tooth and dislike of milk. Now she watched Chuong shake his head no, as Jay passed him a glass. "You got Coke?" he asked hoarsely. At least he was talking! Jay looked at his mother questioningly.

"All right, just this once," Ann said, guilt washing over her. Bribery! That's what it was. Well, at least the little kids were all outside, all except Dat, who was slowly making his way peacefully through his third bowl of chicken soup. "And I promise you, God, I'll fight the good fight against Coca-Cola tomorrow," Ann vowed. The important thing was to get these kids eating and feeling at home. The chicken soup was a hit. Chuong ate two bowls rapidly, without saying a word. Jay tried to keep up. Soon the two boys had left the table. Ann was about to help little Dat down from his place when he turned his round face questioningly to hers and pointed to the empty bowl. He said a Vietnamese word she had never heard. She knew what it was in an instant. "More?" It had the same sound all over the world no matter how you spelled it. Children had been saying it for hundreds of years.

"John!" she cried in excitement and delight. "Look! Dat wants *more* of your chicken soup! And he's already had three bowls —" She took Huong-Hope from John, preparing to put her down in the little girls' room for a nap.

"He wants more?" John pretended surprise. "Why, certainly, Oliver. You may have more," he said gravely. "You may have all you want —" He took a pot from the stove and carefully ladled some golden broth and noodles into Dat's bowl. Dat's big black eyes never left John's hands as he worked. Ann had seen the same look on small, hungry animals waiting with keen eyes and panting tongue for any crumb that might fall their way in a kitchen. Now she felt a stab of pain to think that Dat, too, must have waited in a crowded kitchen with just such a look. "But you're *not* a mutt or a stray cat," she thought sadly.

Dat ate five bowls of chicken soup before he finally left the Sweeney lunch table that memorable day. Ann could hardly believe there was room for so much in his tiny frame. This was more than ordinary hunger. Dat was by far the skinniest of the three children. Perhaps Huong had fared better because she was a baby and less active. Or perhaps she simply had a different metabolism. Some of Ann's kids gained more easily than others even though they didn't overeat. As for Chuong, he was thin but definitely husky. No doubt he'd also been better able to fight for what he needed. Poor little Dat had lost out as the frail one of a litter often loses. Now, worried for fear he might have overeaten and might be sick as a result, Ann held him again, rocking gently, before letting him run out to join the others. Again, she marveled at how easily he molded to her body.

"Oliver here seems to be doing fine," observed John, looking down at the comfortable twosome. "We've passed the test with *him* anyway —"

Ann laughed happily, dropping a kiss on top of Dat's coarse

shining black hair. "Wonder what Dickens would have thought of an Oriental Oliver Twist with shiny black bangs?" she said.

"He'd have understood, of course," said John. "Good Lord, if there was one thing Dickens understood it was the marvelous differences in people. Think of all his characters —"

"Think of all *ours!*" said Ann, suddenly amazed at the richness, the diversity of her family. The patchwork family, as she often called it, made up of beautiful, different-colored pieces, woven and sewed together with love. Several piercing screams from the backyard brought her reverie to a quick close. "What in God's name is going on out there?"

John peered out the kitchen window. "Paddy wants to go down the slide. Marcus won't get out of the way. Nothing unusual."

"They're *not* supposed to do that. Someone could get hurt." Ann eased Dat gently off her lap. "Marcus! Paddy! Off the slide this minute!" she screamed out the sun porch door. "I'll hang you up by your earlobes if you try anything like that again —"

Ann Sweeney's use of hyperbole occasionally startled her friends and neighbors. Her children, however, understood their mother perfectly. She was not likely to hang one of her valuable children up by the earlobes, cut their arms off at the shoulders, or grind their bones. But if she started to count in a certain tone of voice, "ONE — TWO — THREE — FOUR —" any Sweeney child who knew what was good for him would certainly stop doing what he was doing before his mother ever reached FIVE. This sytem of discipline might not win Ann high praise from all child psychologists, but somehow it worked. Now, her irritation, once unbottled and sprayed at the offenders, vanished as quickly as it had come. "The sun's out! The last snow's melting fast. Would you believe it's March?" she said sweetly to John. She took a small jacket from the pile in the corner, put it on Dat. "Let's go out and see all the things we've got to play on." Dat put a small hand trustingly in hers. "Listen for the baby, will you, John? If she wakes, I don't want to leave her crying too long. . . ."

But no sooner had Ann stepped outside than Jay came up to her with a serious face. "Mom — I don't know where Chuong is. I think maybe he ran away."

"Jay!" Ann felt real fear. "Which way did he go?"

"I don't know. That's just it. We were riding the bike and then the Big Wheel down the driveway. Chuong was shouting and yelling real loud. I thought he was having fun. Suddenly he got off and went by me with this awful funny look on his face. He ran off around the house. I looked for him. I can't find him —"

"Watch the little ones. Stay right here —" Ann ran all around the house. Up the driveway. Out to the road. It was not a highway but cars came very fast down the long straight stretch. People were always in a hurry to get into town. As far as she could see in either direction there was nothing. Not a car, not a bicycle, not a person. "Oh dear Jesus! Let him be all right!" she prayed. "What if he's gone as far as the railroad tracks? What if he's already lost?"

At that moment Chuong had indeed embarked on a long and terrible journey. A journey of many thousands of miles, one that he had made many times before inside his head, one that he dreaded. And yet he seemed to have no control over the forces which swept down upon him like a black wind, from time to time, whirling him back to his native land even as the black winds of war had gathered those last five days before the storm broke, before his other life had been washed away. Sometimes he was on the boat, tossing and clinging to the rail, screaming for help. Sometimes he found himself running, running with his breath like a bursting pain in his throat, while soldiers in trucks with raised guns chased him down the streets of his childhood. People were falling, dying, yelling all around him. Where could he go? Where was the way home? Chuong lay in bed, the sofa bed in John's office on the third floor of the Sweeney house, while the war raged inside his head. He lay very still, shivering. The covers were pulled up above his eyes. But he could not shut it out.

Ann couldn't help herself, she began running down the road in near panic. There was something about the boy that made her deeply uneasy. He reminded her of an animal looking for a way out of a trap. He might just take off before she or John could ever get close enough to help him. But maybe he was just around the next corner, maybe she could catch him before he got lost or in trouble. There was a stitch in her side. She stopped for a minute. This was crazy! She'd lost her head. Eight-year-old Jay was too young to be left watching all those little kids in the yard. She'd have to get John; they'd have to decide together what to do. She started back.

In the kitchen John had just finished putting lunch dishes in the dishwasher. From time to time he glanced out back at the slide and the swings. Plenty of noise. No tears. Things seemed to be under control. Was that a wail from upstairs? Better check. He stepped over Woof lying across the bottom landing, and started up. On the second floor he listened carefully for a few minutes at the closed door of Faith's pink room, where they'd set up a crib for the new little visitor. Not a sound. Let sleeping babies lie was John's motto. Relieved, he decided to run up to the office to get some of the work he'd brought home for the weekend. With Chuong in there for the night, he'd have to work in the library. A hungry cat passed him on the stairway, braiding her protest around his ankles. "*That's* what I heard," he thought. "Oddipuss!" he scolded her mildly. "It's not dinnertime yet. Be off!"

The office door was closed. He opened it and was startled to see Chuong lying rigidly straight on the sofa bed, covers pulled high over his head. Only the top of his short black hair stuck out.

"Chuong? Are you all right?"

There was no answer. John lifted the sheet gently just an inch or two. "Chuong — can I help you?"

Two wild, terrified black eyes stared up at him.

"John! Where are you?"

Ann was running up to the second floor when she met John coming down. "Oh, John —" she gasped. "Chuong's run away! We've got to find him!"

"Chuong's right here. In my office," said John calmly. "He's gone to bed."

"Bed! What's the matter with him? Is he sick?"

"I'm not sure. He won't talk to me."

"Chuong? May I come in?" Ann kept her voice soft, tip-toed into John's office, knelt down by the covered-up boy. "I just want to see if you're all right —"

She slipped a knowledgeable hand under the sheet to feel his forehead. No fever, thank goodness. And he'd eaten well. Then suddenly she knew what it had to be. She remembered his eyes the first time she'd ever seen them. They held all the horror of the past. She had no idea of what he must have lived through. But Chuong had the marks of trauma on him as clearly as if he'd been severely burned. Yet his straight back, proud carriage, and the fact that he'd come this far told her also what great strength lay in this child. How could she reassure him, let him know there was no longer anything to fear? For *him*, the unknown must still look very frightening. Well, trust wasn't won in a day. She would have to be patient, not rush him. . . .

She sat there quietly beside him for several minutes. Just to let him know she would be *there* — if he wanted her. "Chuong," she said at last, "Pop's going to take Jay and the bigger kids for a swim in our pool this afternoon. You can swim, too, if you'd like to. I'll lend you a swimsuit of Jay's. You can think about it."

The boy still said nothing. But he lowered the covers just a bit to look at her. Did she mean it?

Ann left the room, found a swimsuit, and left it on his bed without another word.

Half an hour later Ann was changing Huong-Hope's pants in the children's bathroom when she looked up to see Chuong standing in the doorway. He was wearing Jay's bathing suit. While his face was impassive, his black eyes now looked bright, interested. "He wants to swim!" she thought, pleased. The next moment, however, when he saw what she was doing, his eyes clouded with fear. "No! NO!" he cried, putting a hand on her arm. "I do! I do!"

When Ann got to her feet, astonished, leaving Huong-Hope spread out on the bathroom rug, Chuong actually put up an elbow as if to shield his face. At the same time he looked strong, determined. My God, this has been *his* job! Ann suddenly understood. And it looks as if somebody got very angry if he didn't do it. But that's not the point, either. He's *willing* to do it. He knows how to take care! All of these thoughts rushing into her head at once gave her her first real insight into everything that this remarkable boy had been doing to protect himself and his little family. She felt warm tears in her eyes.

"Chuong, this is *my* job," she said gently. "I'm the mother. I'm the one who should do this — and I want to do it. Your job right now is to have fun. To go swimming! I think Pop's already in the pool. You go downstairs and wait in the kitchen. I'll show you how to get down there as soon as I'm finished with Huong —"

Chuong stared at her. His look seemed to say, "This is a crazy woman. Here she is, lady of this big, fancy house, so what's she doing down on her knees with a baby with dirty pants?" He stared a moment longer to see if she really meant it.

"Go on —" said Ann, reading him. "I really do mean it. You go have some fun —"

He didn't smile, he didn't really understand, but he saw his chance and vanished.

Back down on her knees, Ann sighed, suddenly weary. "It isn't the drudgery that exhausts mothers; it's the fact that we have to *think* so hard," she thought wryly. "This job is worse than being a Supreme Court Justice or a bank president. It's almost as bad as being an ambassador to the U.N. And not so different," she laughed suddenly, remembering the circle of different-colored faces straining to read each other across the chamber, with all the difficulties of strange languages, customs, and traditions going back thousands of years getting in the way. At least they had translators! But who could "translate" this odd, unlovely baby girl who lay before her now so passively? Remembering the vigorous struggles she had had with other babies trying to catch them and put them into Pampers, this limp cooperation frightened Ann. Huong-Hope allowed her to unfold her arms and her legs and place them wherever she wanted as if she were a card table.

When Ann left Chuong downstairs at the edge of the Sweeney swimming pool, he stood, straight as an arrow, on the cold tiles, not quite believing what he saw. Boys much younger than he were throwing themselves easily off the side of the pool, diving down, surfacing again, and swimming up and down as easily as fishes. He saw Marcus's red curls bobbing happily out there in the very middle where the water was deep, and Marcus was one of the little kids. Even Paddy, one of the twins, was paddling from one side to the other at the shallow end while John stood nearby supervising, looking rather like a tall, white-bearded crane standing in a marsh.

"Hey, Chuong! Come on in! It's not cold —" yelled Jay. Jay climbed out, came over to Chuong. "Let's go, man" said Jay. He threw himself into a back dive, narrowly missing

Megan, who was swimming with long, graceful strokes up and down the length of the pool. Chuong, who loved sports, had to admit Megan was a beautiful swimmer. She was also, he'd learned, almost exactly his age — and a girl!

John swung Paddy up on the edge of the pool. "You go up and get dry. It's Timmy's turn now. Tell Mama to send him down —" John had learned early that you don't teach twins to swim at the same time. Now he waded over to the Vietnamese boy standing so straight and aloof on the wet tiles. "Do you swim, Chuong?" he inquired politely.

"Yes! I swim — I swim good!" Chuong said in his loud, hoarse voice. With that, he dove in head first and sank promptly to the bottom of the pool. John, looking on, first with interest — was the boy showing how long he could stay underwater? — then with alarm, finally swooped down and managed to fish Chuong out. There was a great deal of sputtering and coughing, during which Chuong could not find his voice, which was just as well for he was mortified and could think of nothing to say. He was not in the least afraid, however. As soon as he could breathe again, he got up, went down to the shallow end, walked in up to his waist and began to get the feel of the water.

"You'll be swimming in no time," John reassured him. "It helps if you learn how to float first —" He demonstrated, holding the side of the pool and letting his long legs float up lightly to the surface.

"Yeah, I see —" said Chuong, wasting no time. If he was, indeed, going to be allowed to swim in this glamorous green pool, the thing to do was master the art immediately. Soon he was floating with ease, and before the session was over Chuong was closer to real swimming than many a child is after half a summer. The same agility that had helped him survive the panic of the crowds attempting to rush that fishing boat in Vietnam, to dodge, to wriggle between a man's legs carrying his baby sister and to get on board where so many others had failed was now coming to his aid in a Connecticut swimming pool. John, looking at Chuong, thought, "He's a natural athlete. Wait'll he gets on the school team! Never mind what the sport is, if Chuong likes it he'll play it, and play it well."

Upstairs, tending the flock of little ones, Ann was watching Faith's first encounter with the green-eyed goddess, Jealousy. Faith had been raised from the start with other babies, all little boys. For a time she'd been penned in with the three youngest Sweeneys in a folding, circular play fence, which was placed just under the kitchen window so Ann could keep an eye on things as she tackled dishes. "That was *some* time in our lives," says Ann. "Four babies in Pampers — and four bottles! The bottles were interchangeable — I never knew who drank how much." Later, when the fence was outgrown, John had a small stockade built on the same spot so the toddlers wouldn't wander off.

Faith had enjoyed this tumbling about with little brothers and she'd also enjoyed a special closeness with one of them, her adopted "twin," Terry. Small black Terry joined the family a year after Faith. But since the two were only three weeks apart in age, the Sweeneys elected to bring them up as twins. Paddy and Timmy were nearly a year older, and by this time Ann and John certainly knew the ropes as far as twins were concerned.

"We really stopped traffic whenever we went to town with our twin strollers," Ann recalls, "one holding Paddy and Timmy, 'the vanilla twins,' and the other holding Faith and Terry, 'the chocolate twins.' Nobody could believe they were all ours."

And of course Faith, the baby Queen Bee in this court of small males, had always found it easy to draw the greatest applause from any crowd that gathered. But it wasn't long before Faith began to discover on her own some of the conventional advantages of being feminine. She adored pretty dresses. She loved watching Mama get fixed up for a party, too. She'd sit on the edge of the bed while Ann brushed out her everyday ponytail, then swept her auburn locks up high in a lovely swirl.

"Mama, do *my* hair!" Soon Faith's brown-gold Afro was swept up high, too, and it was so becoming it finally became her regular style. She always insisted on a dab of Ann's best perfume and begged to play with her sparkly jewelry.

Now, at three-and-a-half, Faith was definitely ready to forget little boys and move on to playing with girls. She had overheard talk about a new little sister. But was this funny-looking baby a sister? She didn't *do* anything but sit. And what was worse, right now Huong-Hope was sitting on Mama's lap. Faith tried to crowd the intruder off. She stuck a book under Ann's nose, demanding to be read to. She whined and twined herself around Ann's shoulders and knees. "Mommy, I want a cookie! Mommy, please —"

"Thank God the cookie break is as established in the home as the coffee break in the office," thought Ann. Having just run out of options, as one did eventually with so many kids, she gave in and headed for the cookie jar in the kitchen. The bigger kids who'd been swimming were just dripping their way up the basement staircase and emerging in the pantry, where they, too, began to hop around, shouting and demanding their fair share of the cookies.

Ann began to shout. "You're leaving puddles on my nice clean floor! *Upstairs* this minute! Every one of you! Marcus! Timmy! Jay! Nobody gets any cookies and nobody gets any dinner if I have to mop this floor —"

Chuong, coming up then, was just in time to hear this last. Ann, overacting as she frequently did for the benefit of a young and extremely inattentive audience, seemed truly blazing with fury, her brown eyes snapping, her voice rising. His stomach knotted in fear. What could he do? His feet *were* wet. Would he have to go without dinner? How could he get upstairs to his clothes without going through the kitchen?

At that same moment, John, right behind him, put a friendly hand on his shoulder. "Chuong did very well for a first time,"

Megan

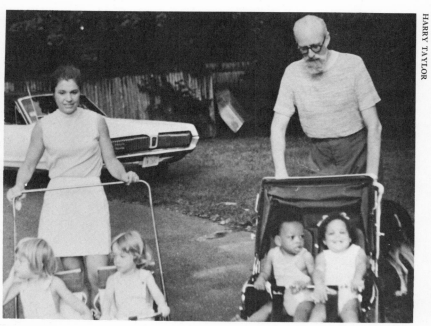

Ann wheels the "vanilla twins," Paddy and Timmy, while John pushes the "chocolate twins," Terry and Faith, in their strollers.

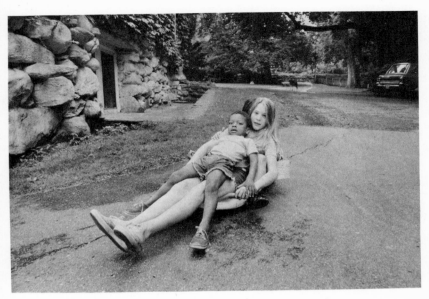

Megan and Terry coasting on the Sweeney driveway

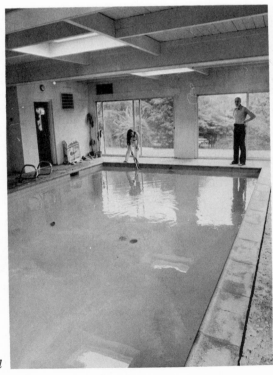

The Sweeneys' pool

he told Ann, saving for a later, private conversation the fact that he'd had to rescue Chuong from the bottom of the pool. "I think he's going to make an excellent swimmer —"

"Why, Chuong, that's wonderful!" said Ann giving him her warmest smile. "How did you like our pool?"

Chuong, still frozen in place, managed to nod. "Okay," he said. "I like —"

"He doesn't *look* as if he liked it," Ann thought, wishing she could get behind his Oriental mask. "How am I ever going to understand him and know what he's really feeling?"

"Who could understand this wild lady," wondered Chuong, "when one minute she is yelling and next minute she is smiling? How can I know what to do next?"

John solved the problem for all of them. He went around Chuong, leaving a few large, damp footprints, and headed for the stairs. "I don't know about you, Chuong, but I'm getting dressed. There's something in that oven for supper that smells awfully good."

Chuong wheeled after him gratefully and vanished.

Later he ate two helpings of everything at dinner. Just to be on the safe side.

That night he slept deeply without dreams. But when he awoke the next morning he felt a moment's panic. Where was he? In the long, troubled time since leaving his homeland, Chuong had rarely slept in a good bed. There had been the crowded decks of boats, the straw matting of the refugee camps, the uncomfortable seats of various planes, and often the floor when there was no place else. As for Dat and Huong, they'd spent most of their nights curled up in corners on old blankets. Maybe this was a good place? Maybe they would get to stay? Chuong thought of yesterday's sunlight shining through big windows into the swimming pool. The water flickered and danced like a summer stream. It was warm as summer, too. Yet outside Chuong could see patches of snow on the ground even as he stood there in the shallow end of the pool. Now he felt his heart stir with eagerness. That ignominious sinking to the bottom was forgotten. Chuong put failure behind him quickly and moved on to the next job in life. Today he would learn to swim! If only he could live here in this house and dive into that bright green water every day —

But then he put that thought aside, too. Chuong had learned not to live on hope. It weakened you to hope for things too much. Take life as it came. You found yourself in a place. Maybe you never wanted to be there. But you looked around. You saw who was in charge, who had the power, and who was the person to watch out for. The person who maybe was going to do something to hurt you. Then, quick as a cat, you tried to jump out of the way before the blow fell! At ten, Chuong had already become a very practical man. But he'd forgotten something. He'd forgotten what it was to like to have good things coming to you not because you'd scratched and fought hard for them, but simply because love had brought them to you.

It was barely light. No clock in this room. But Chuong had slept himself out. So now he got up, put on his clothes, and went down the stairs from John's third-floor office determined to wrest everything he could from this one last day in the rich people's house with its big yard, big pool, big meals.

He met Ann, looking very distressed, on the stairs. She was still in nightgown and robe. "Oh, Chuong! I was coming to get you —"

His heart lurched slightly. What was wrong?

"It's Dat," she said. "He's crying and saying some word over and over. I don't understand him —"

Dat was, indeed, standing in a crib John had set up in the little boys' room. His round, golden face crumpled, tear-stained, and he was wailing something over and over.

"What's he saying?"

"Bathroom," said Chuong.

"My God, of course!" thought Ann. She'd been sleeping

when she heard the little boy's cries. Overanxious because of his frailty, she'd jumped to the conclusion that he must be sick or have a pain somewhere. "Chuong," she said, smiling now, "you're going to have to be my interpreter."

The snow was melting fast. The children rushed outdoors to play as soon as they'd finished breakfast. "Mud season, here we come," thought Ann wryly, watching her troop from the kitchen window. Good-bye, clean floors! Everytime one of her kids came to the door he brought half the yard with him. She passed out cookies, drinks, and comfort for bumped heads or skinned knuckles all morning long, punctuating every word with "Wipe your feet!" It was a refrain that usually drove her crazy, yet Ann felt a curious peace and happiness watching the children that day. She saw Chuong actually *playing*, behaving like the child he was instead of some suspicious enemy. He dashed around shouting, and screaming louder than any of them. He tried to show Jay and Megan, too, how to play soccer, but of course the little kids got in the way. Just the same, Chuong was having a good time, so it came as a painful surprise when everything blew up.

Ann was in the library arranging music for the following week's lessons when she heard angry screams in the kitchen. They got angrier still. She went to take a look, and Chuong went past her, eyes blazing, and raced up the stairs. Ann didn't follow or try to intervene. She was beginning to understand his pattern. He retreated to bed the way a snarling, injured animal might go back to his cave. "Let him be for a while," she thought. Then she went to see what had happened.

Minh, nearly as angry as Chuong, was waving a mop. "He bring in mud! I clean kitchen, he bring in mud!"

"Oh, Minh — I know, and I'm sorry," Ann tried to soothe her, laughing at herself a little bit. Who was she to be on the side of a mud-bringer! "Well, my kitchen is going to have a hard day, let's face it —" "*My* kitchen!" Minh glared at her. "I clean up dishes — my kitchen."

Ann sighed. This was where she'd often come in. She'd hoped that having a Vietnamese daughter already in the house might smooth the way for Chuong. Apparently nothing was going to be that easy. Chuong had too many rough, hurting edges to be easily smoothed. And Minh had her own problems. While she'd been quickly and easily adopted by the Sweeneys the previous September, she'd never really had the experience of being anyone's "daughter." Sent off to work away from home in the big city of Saigon at the age of nine, Minh had very early developed a kind of harsh independence. Independence was a great thing, Ann often reflected, until it spilled over into bossiness. You couldn't blame Minh. She knew but two roles in life, that of worker or boss. Having worked so long, she was anxious to be the one who gave orders. Now, when she cleaned a kitchen — and she knew how to do it beautifully — it became *hers*. And woe to anyone who put an unlucky foot in her domain. What made Ann sad was that so far she had been unsuccessful in opening other doors for Minh. She longed to give her the advantages of being a daughter, not just an underling. Both she and John had tried to get this idea across by actions and in conversation. Not an easy thing to do, for Minh's grasp of English was limited. Unlike Chuong, she'd had little or no education. Sometimes she'd even resorted to pidgin English and to acting things out. Putting one arm around Megan and another around Minh, Ann had said, "Same-same! You are *both* my daughters — same-same. You understand?"

Minh had grinned. And later that day they'd gone on a mother-daughter shopping trip with Minh signaling and pointing, trying to get Ann to understand that what she wanted was a pair of *platform* shoes. At last the shoes had been found and purchased. It had been a step in the right direction, but there were so many others to be taken. How much easier it would have been if she'd had a chance to help Minh when she was a little girl! Realizing all this made Ann all the more determined to rescue the three new Vietnamese children as quickly as possible.

Hunger brought Chuong down from the bedroom in time for lunch. What with twelve children all trying to talk and eat and squawk when anyone got a bigger piece of *anything*, Ann had little time to give special attention to his recent withdrawal. The storm seemed to have passed. She did notice with pleasure Chuong and Jay talking almost as friends — and talking English. She also noticed Minh watching, saying nothing. Later she heard Minh begin a conversation with Chuong in rapid Vietnamese. It was almost as if she wanted to siphon him off, instead of joining him and the others. "We'll see," thought Ann.

The day was balmy enough for John to propose a walk around the neighborhood of Old Mill Road after lunch so the newcomers could get a look at the area. Dat held John's hand for a while, then let go and ran ahead to join the other little boys. Chuong could not believe the houses. Great stone mansions, tremendous white houses with porches and thousands of windows. One house was as big as a palace! Another had six chimneys. Yes, he would like to live in such a place as this and maybe visit people in these houses. The Sweeneys' house, he saw now, was much less grand than many of the others. Still, it was grand enough, and besides there was the pool. Now he turned to John. "We go swimming this afternoon?" he said hopefully.

"We certainly shall," said John. "In fact, I'm ready for a swim right now. Let's go back —"

Chuong learned many things that afternoon. How to go under water, then push himself up, how to float on his back, how to swim almost all the way across the shallow end of the pool. "He's ready for anything," John thought, "once he learns how to breathe and swim at the same time. What a marvelous boy!" Like Ann, he felt a great urge to help him, bring him along without wasting any more time. This young life was too precious to be put on hold while someone in an office somewhere shuffled papers, trying to decide his fate. Chuong must be *here!* Dat and Hope, too.

"Get out the scrapbook while I go get hamburgers," he said to Ann. "You can show Chuong the beach where we all go to swim in the summer —"

"Hamburgers? You go to *McDonald's?*" interrupted Chuong.

John laughed. "Hamburgers across the sea!" he thought. "Yes, we go to McDonald's," he said. "It's a family ritual every Sunday night to save Mom from cooking."

"Yay!" "Pop, can I go?" "Me, too, Pop!" "Pop, can I have a cheeseburger?" "Let's go, Pop —"

"No, everybody stay here with me this time," Ann said. "Papa has to hurry. The kids are to be picked up at six tonight, remember?"

John took orders for the crew. "I'll be right back —" he reassured Ann.

It was the one certain peaceful moment of the weekend. The little kids ranged themselves along the picnic table in the sun room and munched almost silently on the chosen food of America's children. Chuong and Dat, eating right along with the others, suddenly seemed to blend in and lose their difference. Little Oliver with the black bangs, and Big Oliver with his sometimes angry almond eyes, now happy in his concentration on a Big Mac. Even little Huong-Hope, sitting on her new mother's lap, was tentatively chewing on a small bite of Ann's hamburger. Now she put out a tiny claw of a hand and pulled at the bun. She, too, wanted more! Ann felt quick tears in her eyes. "Thank God for junk food, the bridge over troubled waters," she wept, laughing at herself. "Maybe we'll even be able to make *you* happy, too —" she whispered in the baby girl's delicate ear. A wave of joy washed over her at the thought of all the wonderful possibilities that might lie ahead for all of them together. The words from *Oliver*, the musical that more than any other touched their family heart, rang in her ears. "Consider yourself at home. . . . Consider yourself one of the family. . . ." "So be it," she prayed.

When the party of Vietnamese adults came to pick up the children, she went down the stone steps with John to help settle the children in the car and say good-bye. It was hard to see them go. She began to cry as the car drove off. Then she saw Chuong, seated in back, turn and give a small wave. "It's a good omen," she thought. "He'll be back!"

There was no way she could have known that Chuong's return would test her courage and strength as a mother beyond anything she had ever lived through in all the days of her life before.

FOUR

❦ ❦

A Memorable May

THAT SPRING LYNN, the Sweeneys' second child and oldest daughter, told her parents some happy news. She wanted to be married. Ann and John were hardly surprised. The refrain, "Mom! Pop! Lynn and Gary are here," called up the stairs by whatever child happened to answer the door, had become a familiar part of family background music that winter. Lynn, living in a nearby town, had often brought her young man over for Saturday afternoon or Sunday dinner.

It would be the first wedding for any of her children. Ann leaped forward eagerly to play the role of mother of the bride as if she'd rehearsed for it all her life. In a way she had. Some of those dolls Ann had played with during long childhood illnesses had been pretend brides. She was a realist, a clever bargainer, an extremely practical woman in everyday life. Underneath it all she was a romantic.

Both Ann and Lynn would have enjoyed the traditional big wedding with pictures by Bachrach, caterers, and canopies on the lawn, a host of bridesmaids and flower girls. But the dollar-and-cents realities soon pulled them back to earth. Lynn finally decided to have only her ten-year-old sister, Megan, for a bridesmaid. There would be a church wedding, but the reception would be at home with maybe 150 guests.

"If we wait till things warm up, maybe people can be out on the terrace," she said.

"Honey, I'd rather it doesn't get into June," Ann said. "There's the recital, and I'm always on the rack till that's over. We can't have both things going on at once." Ann's many piano students usually performed during the second week in June before everyone in town took off for the summer holidays. A date was set for May eighth. Mother and daughter agreed to prepare the hors d'oeuvres themselves. Ann's mother volunteered to come from Michigan to help get the house in shape, polishing silver, brass, and crystal.

It was just as well Ann had something to keep her busy that April. Something had gone awry in the business of getting the Vietnamese children. Both she and John had expected all three to be under their roof by now. The adoption of Minh had been one of the swiftest in their experience. Things had looked equally promising for the new children. New York State case workers had inspected their house. They'd been told John would have to divide his office. They would also have to install a fire escape up to the third floor.

"It's all right with the government if you burn up children born to you," Ann observed acidly. "But when you put children from the state on a third floor you have to obey fire laws."

She railed at the thought of an ugly, tenementlike staircase running up the outside of her house. But still she and John both got busy seeing if they could get a $5,000 loan to cover costs. The bank approved. So now, they told the state, tell us when the children are coming and we'll sign for the loan and start construction. *That* was the moment when things bogged down. Ann, calling the Department of Social Services each day, would get the run-around. "This is Mrs. John Sweeney calling about the three Vietnamese children who were —"

"Just a minute," a voice would interrupt. "Would you hold, please?"

Minutes would crawl by.

"I'm sorry, Mrs. Sweeney, we don't have any record of —"

"Yes, you do," Ann would say. "It's all there. We've been inspected and cleared and told to build a fire escape. We will, too — but not until we know the children *are* coming."

"I'll have to look into this and call you back."

A day or two later, when her call had not been returned, Ann would start all over, get a new person on the phone who'd never heard of the problem. Angry as this made her, she knew it was all the fault of the damn system. The system was a people-eater. She'd always found good people up and down the line. The trouble was the best ones moved up fast. Or else they got so frustrated they quit and took jobs in private industry.

"The state is so interested in paperwork, it loses track of real, live children!" Ann moaned to John. "There should be a law requiring every official who shuffles papers to spend the same amount of time with the child those papers represent."

John tried to comfort her. The next day Ann would start pushing again. And sometimes she wept thinking of Huong-Hope, who'd forgotten how to smile or cry, and Dat, whose little arms and legs were like a stick-figure drawing of a child. But when she thought of Chuong, she felt real fear. Would his strength hold? Or would he lose control and go under with a rush of dark memories some night before they could help him?

In the meantime, she was rich in children growing up under her feet, children flying off to go their own ways. One and all clamored for attention. If the spotlight was on Lynn that spring more than the others, well, it was *her* time. The short, magical time of the bride-to-be. Mother and daughter talked menus. They would have a curried crab dip. Ann's "poor man's liver pâté." Lynn's cherry tomatoes stuffed with chopped spinach and sour cream. Her friend Susie offered to make Swedish meatballs. Everybody got ravenous discussing recipes and tried not to eat too much standing around the kitchen. Ann was sure she was *pounds* overweight.

One day Lynn disappeared to shop for her gown. She returned several hours later, excited, telling of a lovely embroidered Mexican wedding dress she'd seen in a nearby town. Ann and John drove up the next day to take a look. They thought another might be more becoming, more suitable, or more something. For a moment it looked as if the stormy weather everyone always worries about during weddings was about to break then and there and cloud the event before it even got underway. Lynn's choice prevailed, however. The gown was exactly right, everyone decided at last.

May eighth dawned, and no one can tell you now if it was balmy or rainy, for of course it was beautiful. A beautiful wedding and a beautiful bride. In the church, Ann, brimming with tears as the organ struck up the mighty chords of celebration after the deed was done, didn't know if she cried from joy or pride. It could hardly be loss, for Lynn had already been off working on her own, and wasn't moving any farther away. "It's partly because things are always *changing*," she wept, "and I'm so terrible at letting go." She wanted all of her children to stay babies forever. She also did everything in her power to help them grow up and get on with their lives, do the things they wanted to do. "I can't have it both ways. I'm not in charge, either." She wished she were. She cried a little more at the paradox, then stopped just as suddenly. John took her arm, they moved down the aisle. They were trailed by all their many-splendored children of all sizes and colors, and surrounded by admiring friends. For that moment Ann was completely and totally happy.

Ann woke early the day after Lynn's wedding and immediately began to fret. Worries that had been holding and circling during the wedding preparations suddenly came in to land.

A few hundred miles away three Vietnamese children still needed a home. Had she done everything she could to blast through the mountains of bureaucracy? Maybe not. Those kids were still in limbo. She twisted, she turned. No chance to grab another few minutes sleep now. She was wide awake and angry. She sprang out of bed, slipped on a swimsuit, and crept downstairs to the pool for her daily 40 laps. Swimming kept Ann sane. It also kept her a trim 116-pound size 8, in spite of her recurrent fears of being too fat.

When she climbed out of the pool 20 minutes later, she felt much better. She also had a plan. At that moment, John appeared in a blue swimsuit. "I wish it weren't Sunday," she greeted him absently.

John was profoundly glad that it was Sunday, since it gave him a day of rest from his duties as father-of-the-bride and host to over a hundred guests before he had to plunge back into the world of music publishing. "And why is that?" he inquired politely.

"Because I want to call up the governor," she said. "And I'll have to wait till Monday."

In fact, Ann did not actually manage to communicate with New York's governor in person. But on Monday morning, true to her word, she began to lay siege to the governor's office with tales of a promised placement of three needy Vietnamese refugee children who were still languishing without proper food and medical care, while here were the Sweeneys who'd been waiting weeks now to give these waifs the good home they deserved. Ann in full voice, starring in the drama of motherhood denied, was a force to make the most sluggish official begin to quake. "Who is in charge of *you?*" she would demand. "I'd like to speak to your superior —"

"The trick is," says Ann, explaining her strategy, "to keep threatening to move on up. Take your case higher. Never mind whether you're really going to be able to do this, *say* you're going to — and then try it, if all else fails."

No one knew just when the first chink appeared in the wall

of confusion surrounding the case of Chuong, Dat, and Huong. But suddenly people were calling the Sweeneys back. The tone of phone conversations moved from murky to somewhat encouraging. Then on a memorable morning during the third week in May Ann picked up the receiver and heard some beautiful words. "The Vietnamese children will be coming on the ninth of June. Can you be ready for them?"

"Oh yes! Thank you!" cried Ann. She was standing in the messy sun room, vacuum cleaner in hand, staring into her even messier kitchen, when the call came through. Suddenly everything looked marvelous. Good news, the greatest decorator of all, had transformed her whole world in one minute. She took down all the information, assured the official they would indeed be ready, then hung up and immediately dialed John's office in New York. "We won! They're coming!" she told him. "Chuong, Dat, and Huong-Hope will be here on the ninth of June."

After securing their loan, Papa and Mamma went out to buy a fire escape the following day. Ordinarily Ann shopped eagerly, pursuing tag or garage sales like a knowledgeable bloodhound in order to furnish her home elegantly on a shoestring. But now the thought of having to spend $5,000 on a fire escape, when there were holes in her stair carpeting, springs giving way in her sofa, and ominous noises coming from her washing machine, was particularly infuriating.

"Please don't put it where people can see it —" Ann begged the manager of Amalgamated Iron Works.

The manager sighed. "Ma'am, we'll do what we can but this fire escape has a job to do —"

Men came, stood around the backyard, climbed the stairs inside again and again. They finally sent for Inspector Fish of the local fire department. There was no way, the inspector declared at last, that the fire escape could be put in back and still provide exits for children on two top floors. The north side was best. The stairway would indeed be visible from the road and go right by the library window where Ann taught

The Sweeneys just before Lynn's wedding.

TOP (from left to right): *Lynn and Gary; Mary Taylor, Ann's mother.*

MIDDLE ROW: *John Sweeney, holding Faith; Ann Sweeney, holding Terry; Minh; Megan.*

BOTTOM: *Jay; Marcus; the twins, Paddy and Timmy*

piano every day. "My beautiful library!" she cried. It had just been freshly painted a deep cranberry red with cream woodwork. There were two cream-colored Haitian cotton sofas (snatched up on sale, of course), a handsome corner fireplace, the color t.v. and the stereo, too. It was, in fact, the heart of the house, where everyone gathered to be together, whereas the larger, more formal living room usually remained hidden, like a Victorian parlor, behind huge sliding doors. Ann was no Victorian in taste or behavior. She simply knew only too well what a houseful of children equipped with popsicles and pets could do to a room in ten seconds before you even had time to yell, "Get out!"

"Well, so be it," she thought. At least all my children will be much, much safer. The structure would offer escape to little girls in the second floor pink room and to Marcus and Jay on the third floor, as well as Chuong when he came.

It took weeks to design the stairway and more weeks to install it. Ann watched it go up, her face growing longer every day. The sympathetic men from the iron works gave her a decorative railing to cheer her up. This made her laugh and touched her. Inspector Fish came to examine the final structure and smiled with satisfaction. It was, he assured Ann and John, not only a beautiful job, it was the largest noncommercial fire escape in the State of Connecticut.

"Jesus!" said Ann under her breath. She would have been willing to forgo this last honor.

The Sweeneys' new fire escape was not actually in place until some weeks after the three Vietnamese children arrived in June. But once the contract to build it was signed, Ann felt sure, with all conditions having been met, that Chuong, Dat, and Huong-Hope would soon be theirs. What she and John could never have guessed was that in the meantime they would have still another blessed event. After twelve months of delays, a telephone call finally came through from Bogotá, Colombia, on May 20 telling the family that Maria Elsa, the nine-year-old blind child they'd been trying to adopt for so long, was all packed and ready to come. She would be boarding a plane the following day, traveling in the company of a doctor going back to the States, who would see her through customs in Miami, then put her on the connecting flight to Kennedy.

FIVE

❦ ❧

Maria

A COCKTAIL PARTY hum was floating out the open windows of a mansion on Old Mill Road as Ann and John walked down a neighbor's driveway one warm evening in May. Things were already in full swing. The Sweeneys were arriving a bit late, as usual. At the last minute Ann had had to rush Timmy to the doctor's. He needed penicillin. "Why is it somebody's ear always starts to ache the minute I get dressed up to go somewhere?" she wondered. Well, Timmy had been tucked in bed, the others had been kissed and started on their way to teeth brushing. Her mother was there, and they weren't going far, just down the street a few blocks. Ann's daily schedule left almost no time for the lunches and coffees other women enjoyed. Surrounded by little people from dawn to dusk, she was hungry for the company of adults. Just the thought of getting out of the house and going to a party gave her a quick high. She was happy, already flying, as she crossed the threshold in her new high-heeled sandals.

"Ann! John!" Their hostess came to greet them.

"I'm sorry we're late. Timmy had an earache —"

"Oh, what a shame. Well, do come and have a drink —"

It was inevitable. Halfway through the party, Ann was

introduced to someone she'd never met before, a relative newcomer to the community. "Oh," said the woman giving her a look Ann had come to knew well, "I've been hearing about you." She turned to her husband. "Darling, these are the Sweeneys — Ann and John. They're the people who have dozens of children."

The couples exchanged smiles, said, How do you do. Then of course the husband inquired politely, "How many children *do* you have?"

"Only eleven," said Ann modestly. Then she couldn't resist adding, with a slightly wicked smile, "but we're getting four more any day now. So we *will* have fifteen very soon."

"Four more!" the woman gasped. Heads turned. "Ann! Are you kidding?" said a friend who hadn't been able to help overhearing this astonishing bit of news.

Ann found herself center-stage now, surrounded by incredulous faces. Might as well make the most of it. "No," she laughed. "I'm not kidding — it's really true. We've been trying to adopt this little blind girl, Maria Elsa, from a Catholic orphanage in Colombia for almost a year now. We just got word that's she's coming at last. And in the meanwhile we were told about three Vietnamese children who needed a home. They asked us if we'd take the middle child, a four-year-old boy? So — " she took a deep breath and looked at John.

"So we said, 'No — but we'll take all three,'" said John quietly, enjoying the drama. "The oldest is a boy almost eleven. And there's a baby girl."

"My God!" "I don't believe it!" "But Ann — that's wonderful!" Cries of disbelief and friendly amazement rose on all sides. After the hubbub had died down and people began to circulate again, Ann was left with a few earnest ladies who wanted to know more. "You know I admire what you're doing," said one. "But — uh, I guess what I'm trying to ask is, what makes you do it?"

Ann had been here before. "What you really want to know

is, am I saint, or am I crazy?" Her best answer was the honest one. "I feel I'm doing what I was put on earth to do," she said simply. "If a child comes to me, I figure God must want me to take care of it."

"What about John?" said one, with a doubtful look. "She probably thinks I'm doing this to poor John," Ann thought, "and the only reason he goes along is to back me up." Now she said, "I'm really lucky that John feels the same way. He's even been the instigator in several cases when we've adopted. It was his idea to take all three Vietnamese kids. I guess you could say it's our thing, the thing that's brought us the greatest happiness together."

"Isn't that wonderful!" said one woman enthusiastically. "I wish there were more men like John around," she said to the others. "You know, I've watched John Sweeney over the years and he really does have the patience and commitment it takes to be a parent."

As if on cue, John turned and caught Ann's eye over the crowd. "Do you think we ought to be getting back?"

"Oh, I'm afraid so." She turned to the small group apologetically. "One of our twins has an earache. And we left Mother with the rest of the crowd. We'd better get back before they run all over her." They said their good-byes, thanked their hostess, and made their way slowly through the crowd to the front door.

The evening was soft, promising a good spring day tomorrow and the easy living of summer just ahead. Ann had that relaxed, after-the-party feeling. She'd had a good time, yet she was glad John had cut in at the moment he did with the suggestion that they leave. She always felt shy and slightly pretentious when trying to explain her deep feelings about adoption and mothering. She knew that her neighbors were warmhearted in their interest in the family. They often passed on children's books or beautiful toys that their own children had outgrown. And while the wealthy suburb in which they lived had high standards, and high hedges around its big estates, it was not closed-minded. The schools had welcomed all their children and given the new ones a great deal of special help when they needed it. Even townspeople who hardly knew the family intimately were always generous whenever she went shopping up and down Main Street with her brood. There were often free balloons all around, or a discount on new children's shoes. It was as if they were saying, "We know what you're trying to do and we think it's great!"

Yet the subtle changes in your thinking, that gradually became part of you once you'd adopted children, were really hard for people to comprehend. So it was that even well-meaning people occasionally asked Ann, "How many children do you have that are your own?" No matter how it was asked, she always found the question distasteful. "They are *all* my children — our children," she would answer shortly. "There is no difference." When pressed she would admit to having actually given birth to seven, but it was a point she never liked to make.

There was another question that also upset her. "But how do you know you're going to get along with a child you adopt?" "You don't" was her quick answer. "How do you know you're going to get along with a child who's born to you?" Babies didn't come from either the womb or the adoption agency with warranties like washers and dryers. There was only one reason to have a baby or adopt one — for the pure joy of it. But it was hard to explain to anyone who'd never been through an adoption that great wave of thanksgiving you felt when you were finally given a new child to love and care for. There was joy in the rescue, a joy that increased as you saw the child unfold, grow, and respond. *That* was the time, while the hallelujah mood was still on her — on them both — that Ann and John often took their first steps toward getting still another child. The rich satisfaction they experienced from each adopted child led them to want to share their love and their home with more children.

They'd been looking for another little girl when they first heard of Maria Elsa. The news that she was coming after all these months, at nearly the same time as Chuong and his brother and sister, was, for Ann, one more reason to rejoice. Children were her fortune.

As she and John walked up the street after the party, she reflected that her view of wealth was not everyone's. The good people who lived all around them, who were, for the most part, more than comfortably fixed, would have had a hard time understanding how the Sweeneys managed. Many of the families here went en masse to Europe or took the whole brood to the Virgin Islands for school holidays, yet they'd be shocked at our grocery bills, she mused. Between $200 and $300 a week went for groceries, excluding milk (which John carried home himself to save money), which accounted for another $30 to $40. Even so they made do only because Ann shopped so carefully. Just that morning she'd made the rounds of the stores doing what she called her "Give me your tired, your poor" routine. Middle-aged fruit and vegetables, day-old baked goods, damaged, bent cans all found their way into the Sweeney market basket at bargain prices. Of course she also brought specials in quantity, such as 9 boxes of macaroni or 12 rolls of paper towels at one crack.

Mere money and canny shopping didn't tell the whole story, either. There were people in stores all over town helping Ann Sweeney stretch her dollars. That very day she'd struck it rich at the butcher's counter. "For you —" said the butcher when he saw her coming, producing a huge box of frozen meat. She had no idea what was in it, but she asked no questions. Once she got it home she found dozens of shoulder and other lamb chops, 6 pounds of lamb stew meat, 4 pounds of bacon, 6 packages of luncheon meat, and some breakfast sausages — all for a total of $35! Every week her friend in the produce market also delivered huge boxes right to her front porch. The cost? No more than $10 or $20 every second or third week, depending on the season. On occasion her imagination might be taxed trying to use some of this remark-able largesse. One week she'd fallen heir to 25 pounds of green beans — and none of the kids really dug green beans either, but somehow she'd managed to camouflage them in salads and various casseroles until they were finally eaten up. Another time she'd received 47 cucumbers and "enough loose grapes to make the kitchen floor slippery all day long." The bigger kids liked to laugh at "Mom's garbage," but she noticed they were hungry enough to reach for the apples, bananas, and other fruit piled in the big box on the kitchen counter without pausing too long over any bruises.

Despite Ann's careful shopping, the Sweeneys made ends meet only by working very hard every minute. The kids did small chores. Ann had to spend $125 a week for baby-sitters while she taught piano every afternoon and all day Saturday. She spent $45 a week for a cleaning team who came in for a few hours. Outside of that, she did all the cooking, launder-ing, painting of walls and woodwork, and thrift-shopping for house furnishings. She even rented a steam cleaner to clean her own carpets. But she bought her kids the best haircuts in town, and dressed them in clothes from the town's number one store. *That* was where the big bills really added up. Even passing things down from big kids to little, her monthly bill for clothing was always about $250 a month for everybody. And unfortunately nobody in the family had what Ann called a "cheap-shoe foot." The kids' feet were either long and extra narrow, or short and extra wide. This meant she had to spend between $80 to $100 a month on shoes, sneakers, and boots.

The Sweeneys were lucky that none of their children re-quired special schools. The town's public school system was well funded and beautifully set up to provide such things as special reading or math help or speech therapy. Camps were expensive, of course, but here, too, Ann had managed to get scholarship help in some cases. She was able to swing summer activities for all the children for about $2,800.

The family had once bought a brand-new station wagon,

but in general it was their policy to buy secondhand cars and run them till they dropped. By 1980 Ann would be spending $30 a week on gas for her car. John's gas expenses for his are harder to estimate, since he'd made several trips back and forth to Michigan for family reasons. The major household expenses such as mortgage payments of $500 a month, utilities, insurance, and taxes were paid by John, who had an annuity from a small trust fund, as well as his own work.

If John's hair had not been prematurely white already, the energy costs of keeping his large family sheltered and warm might quickly have made it so. Electric bills had soared from $25 a month to $200 or more since they moved in. Even worse, by 1976 the cost of heating his home by gas had more than tripled! There was but one ray of sunshine in this gloomy financial picture of family expenses. Those many lively little deductions went a long way to reducing any income tax bill.

John also paid doctor bills. Fortunately, the state gave financial help to any family taking a child who would otherwise be institutionalized or on welfare. The amount varied depending on the child's status and state of health. It also varied from state to state. Connecticut, for example, granted $150 a month per child in state custody, plus medical and dental subsidies. New York went so far as to grant $233 per month for subsidized adoptions. But there was certainly no way the Sweeney famliy could have raised their large brood on aid from either state alone.

If anyone had dared to ask Ann how much aid she and John received for which children, her answer would have been a terse "No comment." Once a child joined the Sweeney clan, he was no different from any other Sweeney offspring.

Now, however, with Maria, as well as the three Vietnamese children, coming very soon, Ann knew she would have to scratch and scramble, figure and finagle more closely than she ever had before. Wasn't this what mothers always had to do? There would surely be times she'd rail against heaven and wail that she couldn't possibly manage, but all the while she'd

be trying to find a way. For this was Ann's true career —
juggling. Juggling mixed with love so that things worked out
right for all of her kids nearly all the time. It was impossible.
But she tried for it every day.

As a first step in getting ready for Maria Elsa, she got out
all the notes she'd taken after talking with the Braille specialist
months ago when they first thought the little girl might be
arriving soon. They would need a big table for the Brailler,
deep shelves to hold Braille books, a special tape recorder to
play talking books, certain kinds of toys. But most important,
she had to put herself in a blind child's place and try to understand how it would be for her to live in this house. Ann blindfolded her own eyes, then set out to feel her way around. She
learned that going upstairs was easy, coming down dangerous
and difficult. This was because the landing branched as it
reached the front hall. You turned left and went down four
steps to the kitchen, or turned right and went down four into
the big front hall. You were also extremely likely to step on
Woof, who liked to sleep at the bottom. The Sweeney kids
thought Mom blindfolded was playing a marvelous game.
"Can we play?" "Mom, I want *my* eyes tied up!" "Mom,
if Jay gets his eyes blindfolded, then I get to, too —"

"Not in the house," said Ann firmly. You didn't have to
be a genius to see the possibilities in that one. Tipped-over
chairs, smashed plants, broken crockery. "You kids will have
to help Maria get around so she doesn't hurt herself. I want
your eyes open."

"Isn't her name Maria Elsa?" asked Megan.

"In Latin America nearly everybody is Maria something,"
said Ann. "Pop and I thought we'd ask her if she'd like to be
called just Maria, though. Maria Sweeney is prettier than
Elsa Sweeney. What do you think?"

"I like Maria Sweeney," Megan agreed. "And it goes well
with Megan. Like she was really my sister —" Megan was
lonesome. Ever since Lynn had left home she'd missed having
a big sister. Minh was too independent to be very close, and

there was still a language barrier. They couldn't chatter away in English the way sisters usually do. Of course Maria was a few months younger, but maybe they would be friends. "She can keep Elsa for her middle name, can't she?" said Megan.

"*My* name is Faith Mary-Elizabeth," interrupted Faith grandly. She had only recently mastered the entire mouthful and felt now that the talk had been off the subject of interest — which was herself — long enough. "And I'm — I'm — I'm named for my grandmother!" Faith often postponed the conclusion to her sentence in an effort to hang on to the spotlight.

"You certainly are," said her mother, understanding her very well, and stopping to give her a big hug. "Faith Mary-Elizabeth Sweeney." The family made a big deal of bestowing family middle names on new children when they came. It helped take away the newness to give them part of the past. Ann had given Marcus her own name, Taylor, for a second name. Little black Terry had a new middle name — Nathaniel — that was doubly significant. It had been an uncle's name and it also meant "gift of God." As for Minh, they had let her pick out her own. At that time she had been learning to write English, and she particularly like the letter *W*. "It has to start with a *W*," she said. Her new family and their friends had tried hard to make her feel welcome, and so she became Minh Welcome Sweeney.

"Everybody outside now," said Ann. Again she put on the blindfold and realized immediately that the stone front landing, which had no railing, was another danger zone. "Children — here's another place we'll have to watch out for Maria. Put her hand on the banister. We don't want her falling off here." The yard was well protected, with high shrubs along the road edge. Only the driveway entrances could be trouble spots. "Have to get some signs made right away," she thought. "One for each side. Let's see, what should they say? CAUTION BLIND CHILD." Imagining the signs in place gave Ann a nervous shiver of excitement. What a responsibility, but what a challenge! For a moment she was afraid, wondering if she could handle it. In the next she thought of Chuong, and realized that today — the day of getting ready for Maria's arrival tomorrow — was the first day she hadn't had a knot in her stomach thinking about him off and on for all her waking hours. Maria's problem at least had a label and there were specific steps she could take to try to help her. But with Chuong? She felt as if she were groping her way through a dangerous fog. There were all sorts of unknowns. Obviously he was a very strong character. But what had the war done to him, what were the hurts he still carried around? Would they be able to reach him and help him in time? Even the bravest boy might give way to despair if he didn't eventually get the love and care he needed. From despair it was but a step to withdrawal and violence. She wanted to draw him within the circle of the family before it was too late. Oh, she didn't want him to become one of the lost outsiders! "Please, God, give him the strength to hang on, and somehow let him know that help is on its way. . . ."

The little girl in the white chemise dress could not look out of the plane window, for she was blind, but she knew she was flying into a new world — and she was not afraid. She could not remember her parents. They had died or disappeared shortly after she was born. For nearly all of her nine years she had lived in the Institute in Bogotá, cared for by Catholic sisters. They were kind to her. She had also been petted and fussed over by ladies who visited the Institute doing good works. "Maria Elsa, sit here, darling —" Arms would lift her up to silken laps. She smelled the lovely perfumes, felt the cool pearls against her cheek. "Elsa, shall we take a little walk around the garden?" Soft hands would reach out for her small brown one. Elsa, the smallest of all the children, with her black pixie locks and round, smiling face, had won hearts easily and had grown used to being led through her days. It was this very thing, perhaps, that had kept her from learning and applying herself to her schoolwork. One of her admirers, worrying that Elsa was not going anywhere, had initiated the effort to have her adopted. The child was too valuable to be wasted. She was blind, yes, but she was also very intelligent. Once outside the Institute's protective walls, in a big normal family of healthy, active American children, Maria Elsa might wake up and start to use her mind.

She did not know the doctor who was going to travel with her to the United States, but when the sisters kissed her good-bye and placed her hand in the big, firm one, she accepted it without question. She knew where she was going, for Ann Sweeney had written a long, warm letter to the little girl, trying to make the bridge from one life to another easier to walk. "We are a big family," Ann wrote, giving the names and ages of all the children. "You'll be able to tell some of us easily because of the way we feel. I'm Mama and sometimes my hair hangs down in back in a ponytail. Other times I wear it piled on my head. Papa is very tall, and he has a long beard. Your big sister, Minh, has hair that might feel like yours. But Megan, who's just a little older than you, is tall for her age, and her hair is long and silky. You'll know your little sister Faith right away for she has a topknot of wiry hair. . . ." Ann's letter rambled on, trying to describe Maria's new brothers, the big house, the swimming pool, the many cats and all their names, the big, shaggy dog named Woof. One of the sisters had translated the letter into Spanish and read it several times to the little girl in the days before she left.

Now, sitting in the plane, Maria thought about the animals. The Institute had been pleasant. There were sweet-smelling flowers, fruits and vegetables, too, in the big garden. She liked the soft petals, the shapes of things, the lovely sounds the birds made. But everything was the same day after day. Once her half-brother — he was a grown young man — had taken her out for a day's visit to his home somewhere in the jungle. You couldn't get there by car. They'd ridden a horse together! Maria Elsa had never forgotten it. The rich, dark smell of the animal, the feel of his satiny coat, the bumpy, rocking movements of his body carrying them through leaves that brushed her face. The American mama had promised her an animal of her very own when she joined the family. Maria Elsa wondered what it would be.

The whole family went to meet Maria Elsa's plane at Kennedy Airport. This meant that the little kids were kept up 'way past their bedtime. But Ann and John felt it was important for everybody to be in on the arrival of a "new baby" from the very first. The excitement of greeting the newcomer might help dispel any feelings of jealousy or fears of being neglected now that someone else was going to be competing for Mama and Papa's attention. The ceremony of welcoming also reassured the children that they, too, had once been received with open arms and joyful hugs even if it all had happened too long ago for them to have any memory of it.

Megan, who sat in the middle seat of the giant station wagon, had been rehearsing her fledgling Spanish all the way to the airport. "*Gato* is cat. *Perro* is dog. What's the word for *sister*, Pop?"

"*Hermana*," said John, trying to change lanes so as not to miss the turn to the Expressway.

"Mom, how can we talk to Maria if she doesn't speak English?" Jay wanted to know.

"She'll learn," said Ann. "We'll have to be patient. And Papa knows Spanish, so he'll translate for us."

"*I* can speak Spanish," boasted Marcus, letting go a bunch of nonsense syllables at Paddy and Timmy. "How's that?"

"That's *not* Spanish, is it, Pop?" demanded Paddy indignantly.

The traffic was beginning to congeal. Apparently everyone in Connecticut must have decided to drive to Long Island. John was trying to concentrate; Ann felt her irritation beginning to soar. "If you kids don't be quiet I'm going to stuff pillows in your mouths the minute we get home!" What if they got held up, missed connections? She had no real idea what Maria Elsa looked like beyond a few dim snapshots. And she certainly didn't want the little girl to start off lost and frightened the minute she set foot on her new land.

At last they were there. Everybody piled out, while John parked the car, and Ann rushed up to find the gate number for incoming Flight 123 from Miami. But they were stopped at the barricade and told to wait until the flight had unloaded before going farther. "Please — I have to go ahead." Ann cornered a gold-braided official. "I'm meeting a little blind girl and I'm afraid we'll lose each other in the crowd —"

He let her go.

Ann went forward alone, her heart beating hard. Then she saw her. A tiny, gaminlike child, being led by the hand, coming down the ramp slowly. "I couldn't believe how little she was," Ann remembers. "She was almost as small as Faith, who was only three-and-a-half, yet I knew she was close to Megan's age. Her black hair was freshly cut, close to her head, and she looked very pretty in her white knit dress, red coat, and navy blue buckled shoes. I ran up to her and said, 'Hello, Elsa — I'm Mama!' (I knew the sisters had called her Elsa and I thought we'd change to Maria slowly.) We didn't know each other's language, but we didn't have to. The minute I picked her up and hugged her, she was my little girl. It was a very emotional moment, but then childbirth usually is.

"We went together, hand in hand, to meet the rest of the family, and my education began six steps later when we had to go down a long flight of stairs. I'd read everything I could find about blind children in our town library. Still, I saw right away that it was a matter of changing all my habits and trying to be alert to how it was for *her*. I stopped at the top of the stairs. That was her signal. She immediately reached for a wall or a banister. And so it all began. That turned out to be our pattern, Maria next to a wall in any strange place, and I on the outside. I learned quickly that a hesitation on my part was all she needed to alert her to any upcoming change, with no words needed. She could feel, through her guide, whether it was up, down, or turning a corner."

Ann and Maria finally found the rest of the family. Minh, Megan, Jay, Marcus, Paddy, Timmy, Faith, and Terry were edgy with excitement and fatigue, and everyone began talking to Maria at once and trying to touch her so she would know them. Maria laughed and didn't seem to mind the confusion or the babble of strange voices talking a strange language. She began touching the children back, and she recognized Faith and Terry right away by their hair. Then John bent down to greet his new small daughter. "Maria Elsa, *yo soy* Papa," he said. "*Bienvenida a nuestra familia.*" These were the words she'd needed to hear. *Welcome to our family* in her native Spanish. She reached out, felt John's long beard. Yes, this had to be Papa. She remembered the words of Ann's letter. Her arms went around his neck. She held on hard.

Although it was late, Ann and John decided they'd celebrate Maria Elsa's arrival by a stop for hamburgers on the way home. "The local McDonald's — our port in any storm," Ann laughed a bit wryly to her husband. "But let's get them and then go home to eat." She knew some of the little kids wouldn't finish all of theirs. They could be getting into pajamas while the big kids lingered.

Everyone crowded into the sun room and sat down at the big sawbuck table. "Hey, Maria! We're having a picnic in the middle of the night — 'cause you came!" shouted Marcus, grinning around his bun.

Maria Elsa beamed, as if she understood. Ann watching, was happy, thinking, "That's *one* way she'll learn. The kids'll forget she doesn't know English so they'll just rush ahead and talk to her." Maria could certainly understand the spirit of what was said. She was being welcomed! Ann, whose talent for tears had never diminished, felt her eyes brimming. "Our children are so great, the way they help each other. They're generous, they reach out, they really care." Minh had poured some juice for Maria. Megan was guiding her hand to the glass. "I love every one of you!" said Ann to herself. Forgotten were the moments when mud in the front hall, banana peel on the car seat, or water fights in the bathroom had made her swear she would hang them all up by the earlobes.

It was Woof who broke the tender mood. Drawn by the seductive aroma of hamburger, he'd been begging his way around the table. The children all knew better than to give in and feed him. But when he reached Maria, his wet nose nuzzled her bare knee. She gave a little squeal. "It's just Woof," said Paddy who was sitting across from her. "Don't be scared," said Timmy solemnly. "He doesn't bite."

"Woof! Woof!" cried Maria delightedly, getting down to hug the big dog. She'd remembered him from Ann's letter. Now he was licking her face, inspired, no doubt, by the delectable perfume of Medium Rare which clung to her. "*Te quiero! Te quiero*, Woof!" said Maria, nuzzling the furry dog. One of her dreams was coming true. Now she lived in a house where there was a friendly animal.

The children had already begun calling her Maria, forgetting about the Elsa part of her name. This might be confusing for the little newcomer. Although they didn't want to rush her, Ann and John asked Maria Elsa, as they were taking her up to bed, if she would prefer to be called by her second name as she had before? Or would she like to be Maria now? "We thought Maria Sweeney was very pretty. But what do *you* like?" John asked her in Spanish.

The little girl gave them a wide, shy smile. "Maria," she said softly. And so it was settled.

The following morning Ann overslept. She'd been up several times in the night holding Maria's head. Why didn't I remember that hamburgers eaten in excitement, at the end of a long, tiring day, are likely to go down too fast and come back even faster? Now she looked at the clock and groaned.

Maria with John, shortly after her arrival

HARRY TAYLOR

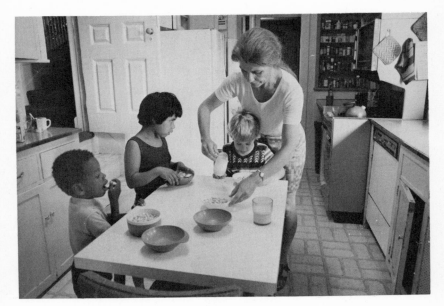

Ann gives some of her children a snack in the kitchen.

"My God, what are all the little people doing for breakfast?" Ann leaped out of bed, tossed on a robe and rushed down-stairs. She left John, whose chances to sleep late were all too rare, to catch up on his rest.

All was well. Someone, probably Minh, had seen that the Rat Pack, as Ann called her smaller kids, were taken care of. Empty cereal bowls and juice glasses lined the trestle table, and now at one end Megan was helping Maria with her break-fast. The little blind girl was neatly dressed, face washed, hair brushed. A full bowl of wheat flakes and milk sat in front of her. "Here's your spoon," said Megan. She spread a napkin on the child's lap. "You okay now?"

As Ann stood in the doorway it suddenly hit her, the dif-ference between these two daughters only six months apart in age! She had hoped, as Megan had hoped, for a sister closeness because of nearness in years. There would be caring, for Megan was a caring person, but the intimacy of equals grow-ing up together and sharing the same aches and pains, fleeting joys or strong, similar needs would never be theirs. Megan was well on her way to being a competent grownup. Maria, physically small, was also lacking in experience. Her blindness had kept her dependent. She was indeed still a little child. "I'm going to have to work hard to help *this* one," Ann thought.

At that moment Megan looked up, saw her mother in the doorway. "Oh, hi!" she said. "When nobody came down I figured I'd better go in and see if Maria needed help. I showed her where the bathroom is and then I helped her get dressed. She's doing pretty well —"

"Megan, Megan!" said Ann, giving her lanky ten-year-old daughter a big hug. "Thank you." She was not even a teenager, yet so many times this child stepped in and saved a situation. Megan showed all the signs of being a true beauty when she was grown up. She was already a beautiful person.

SIX

The Children Come to Stay

IN A CROWDED, steamy room in a small, industrial New York town, a ten-year-old boy lay huddled on the floor on old blankets. Chuong knew it was time for breakfast. His stomach had wakened him early and announced this fact in no uncertain terms. Dinner the night before had been pork bones and a clump of cold rice from someone else's plate. His mind had recoiled at the sight, his body had told him, "Eat!" Now it was sending him the same message. Chuong turned over miserably, wishing he could crawl back into the blackness of sleep, of not-knowing. Right behind him, Dat and Huong still slept on, curled up together on the floor like little animals. Sometimes he thought they slept too much. They should have been running around, playing. Other times he envied their ability to blank out. They had no energy for much of anything. Certainly not for fighting back. And they were much too small anyway. They had no memory of things' ever being any different. But he, Chuong, could remember the sweet bananas, thick stews, and lovely rich soups his mother had served long ago. He had once been very strong for his age before all this trouble began. He could beat his friends when they raced in the cool evenings after supper. And he was one of the fastest in the soccer games at school. He was still strong, strong enough to be very angry, to want to hit someone very hard. But how could he stand up to a whole houseful of people?

That morning Chuong let his thoughts drift back to the big house where he and Dat and Huong had been taken to visit. He'd been told that these rich people were going to bring all of them to live in their home. April had come and gone. May was almost over. On June 8 he would be eleven years old. Yet nothing had happened. For a while he had hoped. Remembering the rich chicken soup, the eggs at breakfast, the Big Mac. They even had cookies and cake almost every day! Now he was angrier than ever because of the trick that had been played on him, the promise that had somehow been broken. Yeah, people were like that. They pretended to care about you, to be friendly because it made them feel good for a few minutes. "Look at me, what a big shot I am!" Then they forget all about it. You couldn't trust anyone. You had to watch out for yourself every minute, not let your guard down. Chuong hardened his heart and vowed he would not be taken in again. He would watch, he would wait, and some day *he* would make things better for himself and his brother and sister. He was the only one who could do it.

All this time while Chuong was feeling abandoned, Ann and John were celebrating the good news that he and his brother and sister would be coming soon. There was also a big social event planned, which would make the perfect occasion not only to welcome Maria, but to announce the imminent "blessed event" of three new Vietnamese children. On the last Sunday of that May the annual interracial picnic was scheduled to take place on the Sweeney lawn.

"Wait'll they hear our news —" Ann said with some glee to John. She had to admit she was shamelessly competitive and greatly enjoyed her position as the mother with the mostest. At the same time she was as supportive and helpful as she could be to others who shared some of the same problems that went with interracial adoptions. The picnic, had, in fact, been born rather spontaneously some years before when Ann ran into someone she knew who had a black-Indian daughter, Dakotah. It turned out they each knew someone else with a mixed family. Before long fifteen or sixteen families were getting together, which meant fifty or sixty grown-ups and children of assorted ages and colors. There were many blacks, a few South Americans, some Korean children, two Alaskan Indians, a child of Mexican-Portuguese origin, and, following the fall of Vietnam, many Oriental babies. As news of the gathering spread, quite a few families who were considering transracial adoption asked if they might come, too, to see mixed families in action.

The picnic that May followed the usual pattern. Everybody parked their cars to the right of the Sweeney driveway, leaving the long, sloping left entrance free for Big Wheels, bikes, and other rolling stock. Each family brought a picnic hamper, while Ann provided sangría for the grown-ups and dessert snacks for the kids. "I know everybody was excited to hear that we had Vietnamese children coming, and they thought Maria was darling, but that's not what I remember that day. All the grownups were standing around up on the terrace drinking wine and trying to pick out each others' kids in the crowd playing down on the lawn. Well, that day nobody could recognize *anybody*. I'd served strawberry popsicles to all the children for dessert. It was an instant equalizer. For the first time *all* our kids were the same color — a violent strawberry pink — and nobody was really sure who was who. *That* was integration!"

One other event had to be attended to before Chuong, Dat, and Huong joined the Sweeney family. On an early June evening, at 7:30 P.M., about ninety parents, grandparents, aunts, and uncles gathered in the hall of the YWCA, where Ann Sweeney's forty-five piano students played the pieces they'd been working on that year. There were a few missed notes, as indeed there are in any recital, but Ann's pupils acquitted themselves well. Their parents exchanged proud glances; their relatives clapped fervently. Then everybody had punch and cookies and went home to wait for next year.

The day after the recital Ann plunged into the pleasant task of getting everything ready for her new Vietnamese children. First she made a quick trip to a budget furniture place in a nearby town, and picked out a second set of bunk beds for the little boys' room. Terry could sleep on top, a spot he'd wanted ever since the twins moved from cribs to the splendor of bunks. Dat, of course, would start off in the bottom bunk, for he'd need more help at first. Then Terry's bed could be set up on the second floor hall for Chuong until the carpenters finished dividing John's office. She prayed this wouldn't take too long. Chuong was the sort of boy who needed to be alone sometimes. She certainly didn't want him to withdraw entirely, but she did want to respect his privacy. The new bunks were installed that afternoon. Terry climbed up and down at least twenty times, shouting at Paddy and Timmy from his new perch, "I'm sleepin' up high! Look at me! I got a bunk, too!" His brothers were not impressed and began to pelt him with stuffed animals in hopes of bringing him down.

"Cut that out — all of you!" Ann was depressed looking at Chuong's bed. It was right in the middle of everything. You couldn't visit the bathroom, work in the laundry room, or make a move without being on top of him. A screen — that would help. She went up to the attic, found one that would do, wrestled it down the stairs with help from Megan and Jay, then turned right around and went back up. Megan's yellow wooden crib, the one they'd bought in Portugal, had caught her eye. She'd never liked that yellow nor the ugly dog's head that was painted on one end. She would do it over right now. She drove to the hardware store, purchased cans of white spray paint, and set herself up in the backyard by the grapestake fence that hid the garbage cans. A perfect place to paint. Ann hung big sheets of plastic over the fence to protect it. The day was bright and breezy, a good drying day. Once the crib was in place she went to work contentedly. Little Hope would have a fresh white crib for her first night in the Sweeneys' house. Ann would buy her a pink flowered spread, too, to go with the pink of the small girls' room. She sprayed vigorously. The spray seemed to fill the air like a snowstorm, but this was certainly faster than old-fashioned brushing by hand.

"Mom, can we go to the beach? When you're through, Mom, take us? *Please?*" The little Rat Pack had come up behind her and was pushing their plan for the afternoon.

She turned around, planning to bargain for time, and was greeted by screams. "MOM!" "Your hair's gone white! Mom, what happened? You're white all over — Mom, even your *glasses* are white!"

Ann had sprayed blissfully onto the plastic behind the crib, proud of her foresight in putting it there. Like a true landlubber she'd forgotten all about wind direction. Three-quarters of the paint had bounced right back at her. "Thank God for latex paint," she remarked to John later. "Otherwise I might be shopping for new glasses — and a wig."

At 1 P.M. on the afternoon of June 9, 1976, John Sweeney assembled the small cast of ambassadors from the family who'd been chosen to go with him and pick up the three new Vietnamese members of the clan. As usual, in a family of this size, there was a head count. "Minh?" Minh was already in the front seat, her chosen spot whenever possible. "Megan?" Megan had been ready since breakfast. Of all the children, it was Megan who had been most upset when the three had had to go back the first time, weeping to see them drive away. "Maria?"

"Right here —" said Ann. Everyone had been surprised at how easily Maria found her way around the house and grounds. On her very first day she had started riding the Big Wheel down the driveway. She was able to sense the change when blacktop gave way to grass. She now also knew the ridge where she must stop when climbing up the hill again. "Never go past here," Ann had explained, showing her how to feel the ridge with her foot, "because this is where the road begins." Now Ann guided her into the car. She still worried that Maria might scrape her short brown legs on the corner of the door or catch her fingers when it was slammed shut. Practically, it might have been a lot easier to leave Maria home. Emotionally, her parents thought it wise to have her go along. Being so new to the family herself, she could have felt threatened by still more kids coming in. But if she got to be in on the welcome, Maria would be in the position of *giving* — not having something taken away.

Jay, of course, was an obvious choice. The oldest boy at home, only two and a half years younger than Chuong, Jay had come closest to breaking through Chuong's reserve and being his friend during the visit back in March. "Jay — where are you?" His father called somewhat impatiently, looking at his watch. John had no way of knowing what difficulties might await him at the other end. The drive would take several hours each way. He certainly hoped they'd manage to get back in time for dinner.

"*Jay!*" Ann's voice, over the years had developed an ability to penetrate attics, locked bathroom doors, basement hiding places, and treetops. It was from the family tree, a giant copper beech, that Jay now answered faintly "Yeah, Mom?"

"Come down here *at once!* Papa's ready to leave —"

"I'm here," announced Faith proudly. She was wearing new white sandals, a pretty sundress, and an expression of triumph, for Faith had been chosen as the delegate of the Rat Pack of little kids.

"Jay — you were clean five minutes ago!" protested his mother angrily as he emerged from the tree at last.

"Does it really matter?" said John, anxious to be off. "We're going right up, and coming right back — I hope."

"I suppose not," Ann sighed. "But don't get out of the car looking like that." A dirty shirt in the backyard was one thing. But in her ideal world, Ann's children never set foot beyond the borders of their home without looking their dazzling best. Someone had once remarked that she, Ann, must have to shop thrift shops or bargain basements to clothe such an enormous cast. "Not on your life," Ann retorted shortly. "You don't buy recycled clothes for recycled kids." This was not to say she didn't appreciate the lovely, hardly worn children's things some of her good friends passed along. But when Ann went out shopping, she bought her kids the best, and if she had to scrimp somewhere else, well that was how it was. She was well aware that there just might be a little discrimination lurking out there somewhere, so when a Sweeney child set out to cross a barrier, he did it in style. "You'd be surprised how much easier it makes everything," Ann had told the person who raised the question. The Sweeney kids were attractive, popular, and got to go all sorts of places. Her most recent shopping expedition with Maria had been a special joy. The salespeople in the town's finest children's store had been entranced with the little blind girl. They'd run around finding this and that, choosing colors and styles to suit Maria's figure and dark coloring. "They cut the prices, too," Ann told John. "People are just wonderful! I love this town. I don't think we could raise this family anywhere else."

John's car was finally loaded with four beautifully dressed daughters and one slightly soiled but cheerful son — the welcoming committee. "See you before dinner, I hope," he called as he put the car in gear.

Ann, watching them all pull out of the driveway, realized she'd have three "new babies" to clothe on the following day. Beyond the need to have her new children look as handsomely turned out as all the other Sweeneys, there was something else at work here.

There is a ritual of adoption every bit as valid and natural as the rituals that go along with pregnancy and childbirth. A mother-to-be often spends nearly nine months getting a beautiful set of baby clothes ready for her expected infant. The baby really becomes totally hers when she finally gets home from the hospital, unwraps her tiny child down to the skin (some hospitals still frown on mothers' "undoing" that wrapped-up baby any sooner), and looks it over from head to toe. The first bath may follow — and then for the new clothes! Of course, the expectant mother took a "going-home" outfit for baby to the hospital in her suitcase, but some nurse probably dressed her child. A baby becomes really yours when you care for it, whether born to you or adopted.

As Ann says, "When I dress my kids in nice new clothes from the skin out, I'm making them really *mine*. It satisfies a deep need. Even if they come pretty well dressed as Maria did, I still have to do this. I also feel that if they look wonderful on the outside, it makes tackling any problems they have on the inside a whole lot easier."

There was no question but what the Vietnamese children were going to need a full-scale renovation. Ann checked the balance outstanding on her charge card. She could probably swing it, and now that they were really coming she could hardly wait to get started.

While John piloted the big station wagon toward the distant town where the Vietnamese children lived, he took the opportunity to tell Maria, first in Spanish and then in English, a little about her new country, the settling of New England by Pilgrims, and the fact that there had once been American Indians all over the place. "Katonah. Lake Mahopac. Those are Indian names," he said, noting exit signs for these towns as they passed them. "And here's another," he said some time later. "Lake Minnewaska. Did you know there were other Indians?" he asked the little Colombian Indian child sitting beside him.

"*No sé,*" said Maria indifferently. No one had been able to give the family any information about Maria's education in Bogotá. She had arrived with no knowledge of English. But school policy was to put her in the mainstream, so it was decided to send her to kindergarten in the mornings and first grade in the afternoons. Maria had already had two weeks of classroom experience by the time the family made its expedition to pick up Chuong, Dat, and Hope.

Two weeks was hardly sufficient time to judge Maria's interest in things intellectual. John felt a passing uneasiness that he wasn't able to excite the little girl's curiosity. But undoubtedly the language barrier was still making things difficult for her. She had adjusted beautifully and quickly in so many ways; they would have to be patient about the places where she seemed indifferent. He was actually more concerned about the situation waiting for him at the end of this road. The drive seemed long. The day was muggy. The children were too listless to chatter or even fight. Maria fell asleep.

By mid-afternoon John had finally found the right street in a rundown section of one of New York's small industrial towns. All the houses looked alike, taller than they were wide, many with roofs slightly askew and cheap asphalt shingles scaling off. "Here it is —" he spotted the number. A house no different from all the rest, the front yard scuffed bare of grass by the trampling of many children's feet. In the weedy vacant lot next door lay a tangle of bicycles. John pulled into the driveway behind a battered pickup truck, and immediately dozens of Oriental heads appeared at every window.

"Minh, you come with me. Children, please stay here." John was hoping to keep the labyrinthine ceremonies of a Vietnamese greeting and departure down to a minimum. By reducing the cast of characters, he might save an hour's time. As it was, he and Minh were greeted with bows and smiles, and an offer of tea the instant they set foot in the house. Tea was an imperative of every Vietnamese occasion. He demurred politely, but there was no way to say no. Behind the smiles, he sensed hostility. Chuong, Dat, and Huong were nowhere to be seen. The room was packed with people of every age and description. Bent, skinny men. Teenage mothers with babies on their hips. A worn older woman hissed repeatedly at the children tussling at John's feet. The room was sparsely furnished, clean, but discarded underwear could be glimpsed in the room beyond. A smell of poverty hung in the air. John was extremely uneasy. "I'm sorry, but we really have to get back right away," he said, addressing the older woman who had pressed tea upon him. "Where are the children? Where is Chuong?"

She grinned but volunteered nothing. Minh had been brought along for just such a moment. "Minh, would you tell her thank you very much for the tea," said John. "And tell her we want to take Chuong, Dat, and Huong with us. We want to get home in time for supper."

Minh, relishing her role as go-between, began a small torrent of Vietnamese. "Ah!" The woman nodded, smiled, bowed, as if the purpose of the meeting had just now dawned on her. She conferred with one of the men in whispers. He scurried out of the room. Came back. More whispers. Then they both left together. About ten minutes later they reappeared with Chuong; Dat and Huong followed. John felt a tremendous sense of relief. The children seemed even smaller than he had remembered. But they were here!

"Hello, Chuong. Do you remember me? I'm Papa. We're going to take all of you to live in our house. Mama will have dinner waiting for us when we get home."

Chuong's eyes were ablaze. He made no move. He stared at John like a cornered animal. Dat clung to his brother's arm looking terrified. Little Huong stood without expression. "At least *she* hasn't changed a bit," John thought wryly. He was sure Chuong understood him. The boy's English had been quite good during the last visit. What then was wrong? He waited a moment. After all, he had known for nearly three weeks that the children were coming to live with them. Hadn't the children been told or prepared?

In truth, that was exactly the case. Or almost. The previous day — it had been Chuong's eleventh birthday — he'd been told the priest was here to see him, just as he was going to bed "You leave here tomorrow," the father had told him. "The Sweeneys are going to take you to live with them."

"Dat? And Huong?" he had cried. "What about them?"

"They'll go, too. You'll like it there, I'm sure."

That was all. He hadn't known if it was really true. Maybe the family here just wanted to be rid of him. Chuong was often screamed at for being a troublemaker, for wanting things he could not have, for protesting unfairness. He felt insecure where he was. But he felt even more afraid of the unknown. Ever since the known, loved world of childhood had vanished when the boat pulled away from the shore of home, each new change had brought pain.

John now decided the time had come to take charge. "Do you have your things ready? We must go, but you can bring anything you like with you —" He put a hand on the boy's shoulder.

"Here! Take!" The woman thrust two paper bags at John. Now that the moment had come, she seemed anxious for it to be over.

"Is that all? Nothing else?" John looked right at Chuong. The boy stared at him defiantly. Shook his head. "So I have nothing. All right, it's true. But that doesn't mean that *I* am nothing." He might have been staring down an enemy. He was only eleven years old, but in some way he was a proud man. Chuong picked up his baby sister and took Dat's hand. Then he followed John out of the house without a word.

They made it home in good time, even with a stop. The new children were so silent John had thought an ice cream break might thaw things a bit. They ate fast, without expression, as if they feared the food might disappear before they'd had their share. They were hungry all right, but they did not smile.

"I love ice cream!" volunteered Faith.

"Yeah, we have it every day," boasted Jay, hoping for a rise out of Chuong. It was not true. But John silently applauded his try. Anything to break the stone wall! "What do you like to eat best, Chuong?" he asked the boy.

Chuong shook his head. The question was beyond him at that moment of emotional turmoil. He understood it well enough. If he had had to reply under torture, he might have shouted, "Food!" Food the way he remembered it, food that was all his own on his own plate. Enough food so he wouldn't have to think about it, ever again.

Although she usually cooked dinner at lunchtime, Ann didn't have dinner ready when they arrived. She had been hesitating between fried chicken and stew but decided the ubiquitous hamburger might be the safest choice. Yet if John were held up leaving, that is exactly what he would probably feed them on the way home. She was caught unprepared. Minh jumped forward to save the situation. "I cook Vietnamese dinner," she said. It was one thing she loved to do and always did very well.

"Thank you!" said Ann fervently. She was feeling exhausted, drained, keyed up, frightened, relieved, and fulfilled — all at once. Somehow each time she received an adopted child Ann managed to run through most of the feelings any woman might experience following a delivery. She remembers nothing of that first dinner or first evening. After all, she had just "given birth" to three Vietnamese children of various sizes, weights, and ages. She was tired.

She knew, instinctively, that Chuong needed structure above all else. And so it was the following day that she called the school principal and told him that Chuong would be coming in that very afternoon, as soon as she had provided him with new clothes from the skin out. Dat and Huong-Hope must be outfitted, too. (All three children had arrived without underwear, and with a scant handful of dirty garments, which Ann promptly threw in the garbage. Chuong, in fact, had come with only the clothes on his back — a ragged sweater and pants with holes in both knees.)

The good man on the other end of the telephone protested a bit. "You brought us Maria just two weeks ago. And now a new boy? School will be closed in another week."

"All the more reason not to waste time," said Ann tartly. "I want him to feel he's settled. It's very important that you find a place for him. He's a bright boy. He's been through a lot. We've got to start helping him right away —"

One of the Sweeneys' cardinal rules with each new adoption was to put that child in school the moment he or she arrived, even if it was only for a few days. "That way you make a connection," said Ann. "They know where they'll be going in the fall — and it's awfully important to have *some* of the pieces in place, because you usually have quite a few that are missing or lost altogether. Helping a kid fit into the puzzle of your family while you're trying to find out who *he* is is quite a job."

The principal sighed. He'd had a good deal of experience with Mrs. Sweeney and all of it had led to a healthy respect. What Ann Sweeney wanted, she usually got. "Does he speak good English?"

"Very good. When he isn't frightened, that is. I don't really care if he opens his mouth; I want him in school for what's left of the year —"

There was no rule that said that a child could not enter school on the last day of the year if his parents felt so inclined. School policy, of course, might suggest that the records, the paperwork, and the convenience of teachers would be better served if the child entered in an orderly manner in September with everybody else. Ann Sweeney's insistence that the school's function was to serve the child now led school policy to pull itself together and do just that. "Very well, bring him over," she was told. "We'll try to make him welcome."

Given the green light for school, Ann now had to work fast. She rounded up Chuong, Dat, and Hope and headed for her favorite department store. The two little ones were easy. She tackled them first while Chuong eyed the racks of new shirts and pants without changing expression. "Maybe he'll find something he loves," she thought. Dat, meanwhile was pleased with his new T-shirt and patted the stripes on his stomach as he looked down, trying to see them. "Here — in the mirror, Dat," she said, propelling the little boy to a full-length glass. Dat was amazed at himself and a smile spread over his wide golden face. "Dat!" he cried, laughing. Was it possible he'd never seen himself before? *Anything* was possible where these kids were concerned, she decided. John had told her the Vietnamese house had been furnished with broken odds and ends. Mirrors were expensive. Now Dat came running to hug Ann around the knees. She bent to give him a warm hug and kiss. "Thank God, I can make one of you happy right off," she thought. Baby Hope looked much prettier in a short flowered sundress. But her eyes were dull, not a dancing, shiny black like Dat's just now. "You look like a sick puppy," Ann told her. "But just you wait — we'll put some sparkle in you one of these days."

While the sales force wrapped up new wardrobes for Dat and Hope, she took the small ones by the hand and went across the store to where Chuong stood frowning.

"Well, we'd better get you some good jeans. Two or three pairs to start with —" Ann began.

Chuong's eyes widened in horror. "*Jeans!*" he said, as if she'd suggested dressing him in velvet knee pants. "No jeans," he said hoarsely. Chuong had a voice that carried well. A few suburban shoppers turned to stare in surprise. A boy who didn't like *jeans?*

Once the battle was joined, Chuong's displeasure extended also to sneakers and T-shirts. He wanted black dress shoes, formal white shirts with long sleeves, but no ties. The pants he preferred were shiny navy blue or checked polyester, but the most crucial issue was the fit. They had to be precisely half a size too small. Anything less than wallpaper-tight was nominated for instant rejection. Ann was in despair. Chuong seemed to be striving for an elegant gangster look. But the total effect was of someone untrustworthy. An Oriental pickpocket. "If he demands white socks to go with the black shoes, I'm going to have a fit and froth at the mouth," Ann thought.

Clothes may not make the boy but they describe his image of himself. She knew now, if she did not before, that the Americanization of Chuong was not going to be accomplished simply by pulling out her charge card and carrying home an armload of new clothes. Where now were her brave words and brave thoughts about the *inside* being easier to tackle once you got the outside looking good?

Ann and Chuong struggled together, compromised, and ended up buying things that pleased neither of them. Ann's hopes for helping Chuong melt into the school crowd, and therefore avoid teasing, had long since flown. Chuong's dreams of early glory as a dude-about-town also went down the drain. His frown was so severe that Ann weakened on the way home and stopped at a bicycle shop. She sensed that a bicycle might make an important difference to the boy. "We're going to get you a bike, Chuong," she said. "It won't be a new one." She didn't explain to him that with the number of children in the family the concept of new bicycles for all had long ago been left behind.

She selected a good used Schwinn, a perfectly respectable vehicle of that time and place. One problem. It needed a crossbar to convert it from girl's to boy's bicycle. Unfortunately the proper color wasn't available. Chuong was upset. In the first place, he hadn't yet grasped the fact that his new family was not rich. He saw the big house, the pool, the two cars. He failed to see how many things were in need of repair, how everyone had to make do. Why couldn't he have a new bike right now, the right color all over?

The store owner offered to order a bar to match the Schwinn.

"No! No order!" yelled Chuong, growing more furious by the minute. Any bike was better than none. And who could wait for an order? He might not even be here.

Chuong had not had a bicycle of his own since the one he left behind in his family's yard outside Saigon. Just the memory of that bicycle, bought for him by his father, brought him close to tears. Chuong did not ever cry. So now he screamed when he saw the man who owned the shop putting a crossbar of a different color on his new bicycle. "It looks awful!" he screamed. "I hate it! Why can't you give me the right color?"

"Chuong! He doesn't *have* it! Don't you understand?" said Ann, who by this time was tired of trying to save the world in general, and this child in particular. "I'm sorry —" she said to the shop owner, embarrassed. "He's just come here to join our family. I guess he's a little overexcited —"

The man, sympathetic, said, "Look — here!" He got out a mirror, a shiny horn. He took a long banana seat and said, "What do you think of this, hey?" and began screwing it on Chuong's new bike, replacing the old girl's saddle.

Chuong grudgingly nodded. "Thank you," he said at last. He was not gracious. He felt he was being maneuvered. In truth, he was, because nobody understood his problem or his pain at all.

A week went by. No one came to take him away. No one here had said he must go back. Every morning there was plenty to eat, cereal, eggs, sometimes French toast, even jelly. The food at school was better than at any school he'd ever known. On the first days Chuong had hidden some of the little dessert cakes they called "brownies" in his pockets to take home. There was the chance someone might get angry later and say he couldn't have dinner. It was a pattern he knew well. In the old house where there'd been little food, if someone gave trouble he could easily miss a meal. But as the days passed, it gradually dawned on Chuong that here, no matter what he did, he would still be allowed to eat his usual meal.

One afternoon there was a big fight. He thought sure they'd take away his dinner that night. Not that he was really wrong. He and Jay had been kicking the soccer ball around in the yard with some other kids after school. They got to arguing over a goal. It was dumb, this wasn't even a real field, they were just out front by the driveway. But Jay said, "Hey, that doesn't count — you touched the ball."

"No, I didn't," said Chuong indifferently. He never touched a ball on purpose. Why should he when he could head it or kick it perfectly well?

"Chuong — I *saw* your hand!" Jay was getting all worked up, making a big case out of nothing.

"What do *you* know?" said Chuong. "How long you been playing soccer, hey?"

"I know what *you* told *me* — that I can't touch the ball with my hands. So how come you get to? You're cheating!"

Chuong felt a rush of anger. He was the biggest, oldest boy in the house; they'd even told him he was now a son. So why didn't they give him the respect he deserved? Always, at home, his mother had told him, you must have respect for your elders. You don't question their word. Often he'd gotten into fights with his brother who was two years older, and always the brother had been upheld. That was the law of the land, the way it was. Chuong had understood that, accepted it, but here — a kid like Jay who was two and a half years younger, who didn't know a thing about how to survive in the world, let alone how to play soccer, a little kid was telling him he was wrong. The word *cheating* cut him like a knife. He whirled

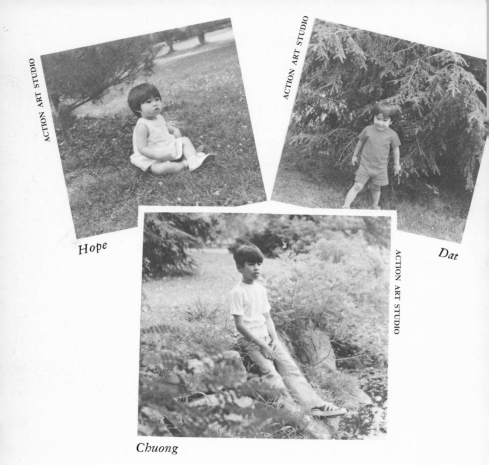

Hope

Dat

Chuong

and gave Jay a crack, knocking him to the ground. He bent down, hitting him some more, and through the blaze of his anger he remembered how it had been when his older brother had had *him* down and he had to take it. Well, maybe Jay would learn how it was, and that would be good.

Jay was yelling, the other kids were screaming, when Ann, leaving her pupil at the piano, came running across the grass and pulled him off. "Chuong! *Stop that! * Don't you dare fight somebody smaller than you are. Go upstairs and you stay there —"

He had gone, but his anger had not cooled. He sat on the bed in his new room made from half of John's office. Unfair,

The expanded Sweeney family. In back (left to right): Ann Sweeney, holding Dat and Terry; John Sweeney, holding Faith; Megan. Front row: Maria; Timmy; Minh, holding Paddy; Jay, holding Hope; Marcus; Chuong, holding Woof

unfair, they didn't understand. This was never going to work out. He was never going to feel at home here —

When her last pupil had gone, Ann came up and found Chuong lying on his bed staring at the ceiling. He didn't look at her. She asked him questions. What had happened? What was the fight about? Why did he have to hit Jay? Her voice was quieter now. She wanted him to tell her all about it, maybe she could help —

Chuong said nothing. There was no use talking to this lady. She couldn't possibly know how he felt. He lay perfectly still, his face wooden; his eyes never met hers.

Ann went downstairs defeated. It was scary trying to deal with a kid who never let you in. Other kids eventually cried, finally told you their side of it, said they were sorry.

She could see that it was going to take a lot of intestinal fortitude to live through this adjustment period. The phrase was apt. Her own bowels tended to get in an uproar when tension between new kids and old gave way to fighting. For a couple of months after Minh arrived, she'd even thought she was developing an ulcer. Come to think of it, there were similarities in the way Minh and Chuong had come on strong with the little kids. Maybe what was going on here was a culture clash rather than a clash of personalities. Maybe it was okay for older kids to swat young ones back in Vietnam.

Minh had taken many a sudden blow at Marcus and Jay and even the twins when they displeased her. On the other hand, she might offer sweets to get them to do things. And in her really generous moods she enjoyed cooking lavish Vietnamese meals to treat the children. Unbeknownst to Ann, Minh was, in fact, already planning a banquet for her new family to celebrate the anniversary of her arrival at the Sweeneys'. It was to be her "thank-you" for giving her a home.

For the most part, however, Ann found herself very confused as to what made for good moods or bad where Minh was concerned. She knew the girl liked to be in charge, a normal feeling for many sixteen-year-olds. But "in charge" was apt to mean almost in military fashion as far as Minh was concerned. Ann would never forget one particular time she'd come home and found all the small children lined up in a row, their arms folded tight, while Minh was scolding them. At the sight of Ann, the littler ones had burst into tears, told of being hit and made to stand in this strange posture for a long time. "Mom, we didn't do anything!" "Mom, make Minh stop —"

Ann tried. "No hitting!" she said forcefully to Minh. "You must not hit the children." But Minh looked blank, and simply retreated behind her Vietnamese wall as if she didn't understand. Her lack of English served her well on occasion. She was a strong survivor; of that there was no doubt. But she wanted to continue to survive on her own terms. Chuong wanted things *his* own way, too. But he was too young and much too disturbed right now to be allowed to run the show.

Thinking of all this, Ann managed to develop a good stomachache by the time John came in. "What can we do?" she said after she'd told him the afternoon's tale of woe. There were times when John's deliberateness annoyed Ann. There were other times when his slower boiling point was a saving grace for everybody. This was one of them. "Chuong and Minh are two very different people," he said now. "Let's not jump to any nervous conclusions. This is one fight on one afternoon. I think we have to expect some trouble at first —"

"But how do we punish him?"

"I think he's been punishing himself up there alone all afternoon. I suggest we invite him down to have dinner and say nothing more —"

Chuong, still staring moodily at the ceiling over his head, had given up any hope of a meal that evening. He was therefore quite surprised to hear the papa's quiet voice and see the tall man standing by his bed. "Chuong? It's time for dinner. Why don't you come down and join the family —"

He couldn't manage a yes or no — he was too astonished and caught off guard. "Uh —" he said.

But that was enough for John. He disappeared. After a few minutes, Chuong sat up. In another minute, his stomach made a simple decision for him. He crept down the stairs and, without looking at anyone, he slipped into a place on the bench at the long children's table. There was good chicken. Hot rice — not cold and gluey. Fresh tomatoes. Sliced bananas and sweet peaches. The sort of meal he really liked, and there was enough for everyone.

The following day Chuong gave up his old practice of hiding food in his pockets to bring home from school, for suddenly it seemed pointless and kind of boring to try to hoard stuff. Ann always saw to it that there was plenty of juice and cookies or something nice every afternoon for all the kids. Even if she was just picking them all up at the beach, she usually had a big box of doughnuts in the car. For Chuong, this largesse meant he finally was able to shake off his constant worries about having enough to eat. For Ann it was a matter of simple sanity. "A full mouth is a quiet mouth," she observed.

Chuong was put into the fourth grade for that last week of the school year, even though he had been in fifth when he left his former school. It was, in a way, school policy's answer to accepting a child without the proper transfer of his records. Ann elected not to fight the move. "Let *them* discover how bright he is," she thought. She herself had no actual proof of Chuong's high I.Q., but look at what he'd already survived! Something besides an agile body had brought him this far. And then there was his good grasp of English — visible only in flashes when he chose to talk, of course, but you knew *he* knew what was going on. He was more interested in learning the language than Minh had been. But there was also an indefinable "something else." When Ann looked into his eyes, beyond the hurt and rage, she glimpsed a strong intelligence at work assessing situations, taking everything in, and trying to make the moves that would make for success. Ann was like that herself. She never knocked the practical. She went after success every time. Right now she would have given odds that come September, after one June week in fourth grade, the school would be more than happy to move this quick Oriental boy into sixth where he belonged. (And, indeed, that turned out to be the case.)

However, the week in fourth grade served another purpose besides giving Chuong a sense of continuity. It freed Ann to tackle what she considered the most pressing problem of her new Vietnamese children — Dat's teeth. The little boy gave off the most awful smell every time he opened his mouth.

"I've got to get that child to the dentist," she said to John.

"Poor fellow!" said John. "You're right, of course. It's got to be done. But it seems a sad way to start your first week in your new home — sitting in a dentist's chair!"

Dat had already shown himself to be warm, trusting, and affectionate with both Ann and John. Little Hope (she had left her old name, Huong, behind now) was another story. Hope still allowed herself to be picked up, put to bed, carried about, or put down almost without change of expression. For the first time, however, she now cried weakly if she was in real discomfort. Ann was glad to see those first small tears. "At least I know *somebody's* there!" she thought. But Dat, when hurt or afraid, came running, arms out, sobbing to be comforted. He was just as responsive to the happy hugs of welcome after short absences, too, and specially loved the long, rocking bedtime hugs. Would this trust be shattered by the dentist's drill? He'd been timid about other people, even the Sweeneys' friends.

To everyone's astonishment Dat, holding tight to Ann's hand, walked into the dentist's office, climbed up in the seat and settled back to enjoy himself. He wasn't put off by the fierce-looking equipment. He accepted the dentist's friendly overtures. Apparently his trust in Ann was now strong enough to carry him across the threshold of this new situation, as long as she stayed close by.

When Dr. Trepp first looked in Dat's mouth he barely suppressed an exclamation of horror. He had never seen a child this age with teeth in such condition before.

"It's a disaster area, isn't it?" said Ann. "But we're sure you can help Dat." "At least let's be positive," she thought.

"Of course I can," said the dentist, smiling reassuringly at Dat.

Dat smiled back, then opened his mouth even wider, all cooperation.

There were eight sessions. Dr. Trepp filled the few teeth that were repairable, pulled what had to be pulled, and ground down the jagged brown stumps of what was left. He could not exactly say whether it was severe malnutrition or an additional cause that had destroyed Dat's teeth. He hoped his permanent teeth had not been impaired. They would have to wait and see. In the meantime, Dat didn't have to wait for the Tooth Fairy to give him the rewards for a six-year-old's toothless grin. Dat got his grin in one week when he was only four years old and came home after each of those eight visits bearing the small rings, sugarless gum, and other trophies with which the dental profession seeks to establish trade relations with the natives of Childhood. Dat's new brothers and sisters were impressed, envious. "Did it hurt?" asked Marcus, who was a sophisticated five and one-half, and rather hoped some price had been paid for all this loot.

"No," Dat shook his head. He was beginning to understand English and to use a few words.

"Dat *liked* going to the dentist, didn't you?" said his mother, who had been amazed by his acceptance of the perilous experience. No one knew why it hadn't hurt, but let's just thank God and move on to the next problem.

"I like," Dat nodded, smiling, flashing his ring like a small gambler and chewing his gum with great enjoyment.

"Gee, Mom," whined Marcus, "when do I get to go to the dentist again?"

"Yeah, Mom — how about me?" This from Paddy.

After that first fight with Jay, Chuong tried hard for a while to be on good behavior. He also began to fill out a bit and lose his hungry look. It pleased him to see his brother and sister eating well at every meal, too. His pleasure was not that of a parent's. It was simple relief that he no longer had to be "father" to these two all the time. He cared about them. But he didn't want them weighing on him; it was too much. The white-bearded papa was a fair and courteous man. He had invited Chuong down to dinner after blows had been struck.

This had gone a long way to help dissipate the boy's total distrust. The mama? Well, Chuong didn't really understand her yet. She was so changeable. Her anger could flash fast as lightning! The next minute she'd be all smiles, offering to do this or that, take you some place, buy you something. Chuong tried to stay ahead of her. He had not yet caught the full force of her anger. But, reluctantly, he had to admit he certainly respected her. This lady, rich as she might be, worked *hard*. She never stopped. Driving, teaching, playing piano in concerts, scrubbing, washing, shopping, carrying. She was crazy, maybe, for in Vietnam a lady like this would have had six people to do all that she did. Still, this mama was really something! Chuong began offering to help carry in the $100 grocery loads Ann brought home in the station wagon every few days. He said, "Hey — you want me to feed the cats? And the dog?" He said, "I can cut lawns real good, too —"

Ann was pleased, though far from over her worry about the boy. She also noticed Chuong's relationship with Jay improving. They were becoming good buddies. There were still plenty of problems everywhere she looked, with a long hot summer ahead, kids out of school with time on their hands, and the four new ones — Maria, Chuong, Dat, and Hope — who had yet to be really assimilated into the family. "Still, maybe we'll be out of the woods by fall," she thought.

Then one evening in late June, she slipped up. The iron works people had been coming every day with huge flatbed trucks, each one carrying a monstrous piece of the fire escape. They'd been trying to assemble the thing like a huge toy Erector Set for giants. Ann had been careful to warn Maria away from the area when the trucks were working. She had also cautioned all the children to watch out for the blind child, who loved to ride the Big Wheel all the way down the driveway until it carried her into the grassy safety of the backyard. As long as the men were working there, play on that side of the driveway was suspended. At the end of a particularly hot afternoon, the men had come in and told Ann they were knocking off; they'd be back next morning. "There's a piece still on the truck. We can't handle it today, so okay if we leave it there, ma'am?"

"Okay," said Ann, who was breathlessly trying to get noodles out of a steaming pot and onto everybody's plate while all twelve children clamored for dinner at once.

She forgot all about the truck with all its wicked metal load sticking out the back end. Always before they had taken the flatbed away each day.

Maria, who ate quickly, finished dinner first. Her English had been coming along, thanks to some friendly neighborhood mothers who had offered to come every day and help the Spanish-speaking child. "Big Wheel," of course, had been one of her first words. Now she said, "Big Wheel, okay? Mama — Big Wheel?"

"All right, Maria," said Ann. The little girl found her way easily down the stone steps and before long Ann noticed the small boys getting down from their places to run and join her.

It was Terry, almost unable to speak, his eyes enormous with fright, who came running in screaming for his mother a moment later. "Maria! Maria! All bloody!" he cried. "*Blood!* Mommy, come quick —"

Ann ran out the front door. Timmy, the gray-eyed twin, was trying to help Maria into the house. Blood was running down one side of her face. "She ran into the thing on the truck. On her Big Wheel," cried Timmy, weeping in sympathy and fear. "Terry shouted, '*Stop!*' but she didn't understand —"

Impossible to say how bad the damage was. At least Maria was *walking.* Ann grabbed a towel from the downstairs bathroom, put the child in the car, and drove as fast as she could to the emergency room. She was shaking with fear and remorse.

The gash, which was over Maria's eyebrow, required stitching up. The injury could have been far worse. Maria was extraordinarily calm and good throughout the ordeal. Ann had the impression that once the original blow and pain were over with, the little girl even enjoyed the tremendous fuss that was being made over her. She had not had this much undivided attention since she'd been the darling of the institute back in Bogotá.

The doctor, however, was furious. "How could you possibly let a blind child ride a Big Wheel down a driveway? You're out of your mind. She's got to be watched *every minute —*"

Ann was indeed sorry. She didn't argue with the man. She had made a serious mistake, but the mistake, she realized, was in forgetting that the truck had been left in a place Maria usually knew to be safe. During the months when she'd been expecting Maria's arrival and doing her homework on how to treat a blind child, she'd learned that both child and parent have to take some risks if life is to be lived at all. The Braille teacher, Dana, who'd been assigned to help Maria at school, had told Ann the same thing. "Better to let her do everything she possibly can than never to chance it," Dana said. "You may have to sew her up a few times — but that's better than sewing her into a straitjacket permanently to try to protect her."

The fire escape was soon in place. Before long Maria was back riding the Big Wheel and Ann was letting her do it. The little girl loved to be active. After a few weeks, using a "bubble," she had begun to swim after a fashion and especially enjoyed jumping into the pool with a tremendous splash. Very soon she also wanted to learn to ride a bike with training wheels. This, too, was encouraged.

To begin with John took her to a large grassy field in a public park. Maria soon got the hang of riding and went wheeling around freely, squealing with delight. "Pop, take little wheels off? Pop, *please?*" Her balance was remarkably good and soon she was riding a regular bicycle much as the other kids did. But when they got back home, John insisted on replacing the training wheels. Maria was tearfully upset. "But Pop — I don't need them. Why?"

"Maria, you go too fast, that's why. You might ride into a car coming in the driveway or run into the house. With the training wheels you can go slowly enough so you know where you are."

Maria didn't like it, but she had to accept it. Soon she was going up and down the driveway with ease. The slope of the hill helped her know when to stop when she got to the top so she didn't go out of bounds.

It was Chuong who now began to go out of bounds emotionally and physically. Ann wondered later if the blood, screams, and terror of Maria's accident had triggered it. At the time he had seemed impassive, withdrawn. But often, where Chuong was concerned, this signaled a return to the horrors of the past.

One Sunday the Sweeneys planned a family trip to a nearby island. An innocent enough adventure, but it nearly carried Chuong over the edge of all control. Ann and John had no idea that anything was wrong at the time. They loaded the wagon with hampers, everyone piled in, and they drove to the dock. The ferryboat was waiting, a double-deck affair, already crowded with people. John parked the station wagon in the lot across from the dock. Ann hopped out, followed by all the kids. "We'll go on ahead," she said. "You catch up. Come on, children — we don't want to miss the boat!"

Chuong's new parents didn't realize what the boy had lived through during the family flight from Saigon. That story was to come out much later. The fact that Chuong was actually able to get on the boat, make the trip to the island, go through the motions of eating a picnic lunch, an afternoon of swimming and play, and then endure a trip back on the ferry tells something of the boys' strength and will. He didn't want to miss an outing, but he was in agony from the moment the boat left the dock. It all came rushing back. The happy shouts of vacationers in Connecticut became the fearful screams of refugees trying to crowd on that fishing boat back in Vietnam. The people waving good-bye from the dock were people who would never be seen again! They grew smaller and smaller. The blue waters of Long Island Sound eddied and whirled like the South China Sea. For the moment Chuong lost his foothold in the here and now.

Ann, busy keeping her younger kids from climbing the rail or running around the deck bumping into other passengers, had just time to catch a glimpse of Chuong's face as he huddled on one of the benches. "He must be seasick," she thought. John was equally busy, answering Jay's questions about how the ferryboat worked, telling Marcus, yes, they would go fishing some time. When he looked at Chuong, as the boat neared its landing — it was a short trip of only about fifteen minutes — John thought, "My God, he has that caged-animal look again! I wonder what's wrong?"

Somehow the family got through the outing without an explosion. Chuong hid his misery and for a time was even able to forget himself in swimming. The beach was sparkling, the tide high and fresh. Chuong, going under water again and again, almost washed himself clean of fear. Swimming always made him feel free and good. But on the homeward trip the same giddying terror overcame him again. He was exhausted but relieved when the family finally got off the dock and everybody piled into the station wagon to go home. Jay and Marcus were the first ones out, and they rushed ahead to get the best spots in the sun room in front of the children's t.v. Chuong, coming in a few moments later, looked at the show they'd picked. A dumb kids' show. He walked up to the set and without a word started switching the dial in search of something more interesting.

"Hey, Chuong — cut it out!" "We got here first —" "I want to watch *that*, Chuong —"

Jay and Marcus scrambled up to argue for their choice and Chuong, emotionally strung out from the afternoon's outing, suddenly lost control. His rights as the Number One Son were once again in dispute. Was he supposed to lie down like a little kid? He swung out, hitting first one, then the other, while the smaller children, who'd just came in, screamed and began to scatter. Marcus howled. But Jay stood smoldering and quiet, then he turned and went outside. By the time Ann and John arrived on the scene, struggling with picnic hampers and half a dozen towels, the moment for simple justice had passed. Chuong was watching a Western while a wailing Marcus and a bunch of excited little kids, all shouting at once, were trying to report a crime.

The scene was repeated, with variations, many times that summer. Whoever crossed Chuong was likely to feel his anger. Anger was one thing, but hitting the other kids was serious. It threatened their sense of security, kept the house in an uproar. They were too small to hit back, and besides, the "eye for an eye" philosophy had never been part of the Sweeney family creed.

Ann racked her brains for ways to improve the situation. "That first summer I had the awful feeling that *he* was in charge," she admits, "and there was nothing I could do about it but stick it out. Fighting was the language he understood, and since I couldn't fight him, I fought *for* the other kids. This really surprised Chuong. He had taken his rage out on the smaller kids because he thought they didn't matter in the hierarchy. I sensed that his rage was really terror turned inside out, so I hoped we could wear it out and win him over. But it wasn't easy to win his trust. Too many really bad things had happened to him. When I began buffering the other children against his anger, I think he began to see that he couldn't just use them as targets — that they were important people to me. By 'buffering,' I mean many things. Sometimes I even put myself between Chuong and whoever was getting the pummeling. Sometimes I removed the other child quickly from the scene. Sometimes I gave the victim some comfort, encouragement. I also tried to give the children who avoided being drawn into a battle an extra treat or added privilege. Chuong *had* to notice this, because he liked treats and privileges, too. It was a long, slow process, believe me. But the point was to make him aware that these were human beings, with feelings, that he was trying to hurt. I had to trust that he was really a good person underneath, a person who wouldn't want to hurt another — if he understood what was happening."

TWO

1977

SEVEN

❧ ⟡ ☙

Good Days—and Bad Dreams

THE OPENING OF SCHOOL in September 1976 took some of the heat off. With the older kids in class all day and plenty of after-school activities, the summer tension that comes from too much time on everybody's hands began to fade away. Chuong did well from the first day. He moved into sixth grade with such ease he might have been an English-speaking suburban kid all his life. His teacher was pleased to see that he was particularly gifted in math. Ann was deeply relieved that whatever problems there had been on the home front, Chuong had not carried them with him to school. They had to be doing something right if he could make this transition so smoothly. There was another thing that made her very happy....

That fall Dat, who was four, was at least strong enough to make his first trip into the big world of American education — nursery school. On a bright September morning, dressed in a new striped shirt and red shorts, he climbed into the family station wagon with Paddy and Timmy, who were also four, and Faith and Terry, who were almost four. Ann reached across the front seat and locked the door beyond Dat.

"Paddy! Timmy! Lock your doors, let me hear the click."

The little boys carried out this order solemnly. "Now, no punching and no screaming —"

"And no pulling my hair!" added Faith, preparing to be aggrieved at the very idea. Her brown-gold topknot of tight curls was too often a target.

"No pulling Faith's hair," echoed Ann mechanically. "Are we ready?" She swung out of the driveway and headed for the Universal Learning Center. Finding this school, which was well off the beaten path of other posh playschools in the area, had been a wonderful bit of serendipity.

Two years earlier, when redheaded Marcus turned three, Ann had enrolled him in a reputable neighborhood nursery school. "I'll never forget the first day," she says. "We drove over to the place, walked in, and there were all these well-behaved little kids sitting there quietly crayoning, with some well-dressed ladies standing around in charge. Marcus immediately began to climb a wall and take the place apart.

"I thought, 'Oh gee, this is *never* going to work. Marcus is not exactly hyperactive, it's just that the ability to sit still was left out of him.' Well, one of the ladies came over very tactfully. She was so nice. She said, 'You know, I'm not sure this is the right place for Marcus. I think he might be much happier in John Fisher's Universal Learning Center.'

"I said, 'Where is it?'

"She said, 'In Chickahominy.' "

Newcomers to the affluent Connecticut town where the Sweeneys live might make the mistake of thinking Chickahominy is on the wrong side of the tracks. While geographically there is some truth to the assumption, emotionally it is far from the mark. The inhabitants of Chickahominy, for the most part proud, independent Italians and blacks, have lived contentedly in their section for many years together. Most own their own homes. Some grow up and go off. But Chickahominy is a family-oriented place, and many people like John Fisher choose to return and work in the neighborhood they love. John had graduated from San Francisco State University with a B.A. in liberal arts. He returned to Connecticut to work on his master's at night, and at the same time opened the day care center in Chickahominy that he called the Universal Learning Center. The center was open from 8 to 6 every weekday, and besides caring for small children, it also offered warm supervision for older kids after school. In a community where many families had two working parents, John Fisher filled a real need. He knew that "latchkey children" running loose in the later afternoons could easily fall into trouble.

Ann, piloting her giant station wagon through the twisting, up-and-down streets of Chickahominy, had no idea what to expect. Universal Learning Center had the grand ring of a mighty complex of white marble buildings spread over a rolling campus. Still, she was not surprised to find herself at last in front of a modest frame building, perched among other houses on top of a steep hill, and protected all around the backyard with high chain link fence. Little kids left their play, ran up and began trying to climb the fence, shouting and squealing in welcome, as Ann, with some difficulty, tried to wedge her wagon into the small parking space. Marcus grinned at them out the window. Moments later a powerfully built black man in bibbed purple overalls emerged from the small house and came toward them. His face was strong with a generous black moustache. "I took one look at John," Ann recalls, "and I knew we'd come to the right place."

The Universal Learning Center, a loose-structured, highly active school, a model of integration, might have been designed by God especially for Marcus Sweeney. Marcus himself was loose, active, and about as integrated as one human being can be. Part black, part American Indian, part Irish or Scotch or German or *something*, Marcus, who was the Sweeney's sixth child — but the first to be adopted — was a small United Nations all by himself. Of all the Sweeney children, it was Marcus who looked most typically "American."

With his merry brown eyes, wide, slightly crooked grin, curly red hair, and sprinkling of freckles, he might easily have popped right out of an old Norman Rockwell *Saturday Evening Post* cover.

Now Marcus had moved on to elementary school and it was time for five more little Sweeneys to have the experience of Universal Learning under John Fisher and the one or two dedicated assistants he was able to afford for his Center. John was standing by the fence to greet them as they all piled out of Ann's car.

"Aren't they something!" she said, trying to line them up to be introduced, and feeling pride about to go off inside her like fireworks. "This is Terry — Faith — Dat, our newest little boy from Vietnam — and our twins, Paddy and Timmy. Children, this is John Fisher, your teacher."

John bent down and greeted each one in a friendly, serious way by name. A person's name was, after all, his first, most important gift. It was not lost on Ann and John that here at this moment, gathered together at the entrance to the Universal Learning Center in Chickahominy, could be seen nearly every shade and flavor in the human race. Terry was a rich chocolate. Faith's lovely skin was coffee with cream. Dat's small, wide face was a bowl of orange-blossom honey. Paddy, nut brown from the sun, was almost exactly like his mother, while Timmy, his twin, had the fair, white skin of his father's side of the family.

"Wow!" said Ann. "They're great, all right," said John, smiling. "Well, kids, let's go see what we can find to do —" Ann followed. She had often taught in nursery schools or played music in order to make it possible for her children to attend. This year she planned to spend one or two mornings a week at the center in return for a break on the tuition. She also wanted to make sure that little Dat could handle the new experience.

While Chuong's turmoil was complex and hard to deal with, Dat's reaction to everything that had happened to him was quite simple. He was afraid. Strange situations made him cling. There had been so much change in his life that now he wanted everything to be *exactly* the same each day. He would refuse to eat breakfast if somebody happened to put his cereal down before they gave him his juice. Juice came first; toast followed cereal. Dat's insistence on ritual drove the other kids mad at times. Ann and John, who understood the little boy's need to order his universe after so much chaos, were able to handle the problem lightly. Compared to many they'd lived through, this was a snap. The children complained that Dat was a slowpoke. Soon they were calling him Pokey. And from that, everyone moved on to giving Dat an affectionate nickname — Polka-Dot. The name suited him, with his round, golden polka-dot face.

"How did it go?" John Sweeney asked after that first day at the Learning Center. "Did Dat hang onto you?"

"He was fine," said Ann. "He moved right in to the place. As a matter of fact he didn't want to sit on my lap once. Of course it helps to have the others going along. I don't think I have to worry at all about the days I don't work there." Of course at home there might be occasional squabbles among so many little kids all the same age. But when they marched out into the world, Faith, Terry, Paddy, and Timmy created a wonderful, close buffer state for themselves — and for Dat.

"The only problem was that Timmy wanted to sit up front with me on the way home. I said yes. And Dat went into a screaming fit. *He* had ridden in front coming over, so *he* should ride in front going home. I thought we might have to call the riot squad. Geez, I'll be glad when that kid gets to be a little more flexible! Well, if anyone can get Dat to relax, it ought to be John Fisher —"

Besides the usual nursery school swing sets and equipment, John had a boat in the backyard for his small pupils to "sail" or steer on delightful imaginary voyages. There was a tree house. There were always a number of things under construction, with John helping little carpenters and painters finish what they started. The classroom was a portable that John had purchased through the town's school system and then fixed up with many built-ins to take care of all sorts of projects. "They do lovely, messy things," Ann told her husband, "like making applesauce. The kids measure and stir and pour — and spill, of course. That's what I like about the place. They *can* spill, and it's okay with John."

Perhaps the triumph of the fall term in the Universal Learning Center was the stuffing of a big turkey at Thanksgiving time. Faith, Terry, Timmy, Paddy, and Dat all helped with the celery, raisins, bread crumbs, and spices. When the turkey was stuffed at last, John Fisher carried it into his house and baked it. The children got to eat the turkey dinner they'd made themselves.

While Ann had been encouraging Dat to make his first small hops into the outside world, John Sweeney had been working gently on a more stubborn problem. It was family custom for both parents to join in the putting-to-bed routine. Ann cajoled the little ones into brushing their teeth, meanwhile picking up toys, putting dirty clothes in hampers, smoothing out beds. She tucked in the boys first, gave them each a kiss, then moved on to the pink room where Faith and Maria were snuggled down into twin beds and Hope lay motionless in a crib. More kisses, more tucking in, then the last thing Ann did was cover up the favorite dolls, who lay in small beds beside their "mothers."

If Ann's style was bright but quick, John's bedtime manner was leisurely and thoughtful. He listened to prayers. He answered last questions. He, too, went first to the boys' room with its two double bunks, for boys were far more apt to pop out of bed again for one last drink of water or some other stall to put off the inevitable. The closing of *their* door was a special blessing for both tired parents. However, John also had another reason for moving slowly into the little girls' room. He had developed a playful ritual. First Faith, and now

Maria, insisted on it each night. He was using it with Hope, too, trying to win some tiny response. The little girl's limp indifference to life troubled John deeply. He had never seen a baby — she was almost two-and-a-half — who was so continually *sad*. It went against everything he knew about children.

And so every night John performed his ritual with Faith, then Maria, then moved over to try to work the same magic on Hope. "I'm going to give you three Nhyt-Nhyts!" he would say in a solemn voice. The tall man, raising one arm straight over his head, would then proceed to point a weaving, wiggling finger at the little girl and bring it slowly down to —? She never knew where! That was the fun of it. Faith would scream with delight as the first "Nhyt-Nhyt" landed on her tummy. Maria would giggle as the second "Nhyt-Nhyt" caught her behind the ear. But it was the third "Nhyt-Nhyt" that traveled around in the air for a long moment of terrible suspense and finally landed under the little girl's chin, the spot most apt to make her laugh. Hope had been deadpan for a month and a half through this evening procedure, never rewarding John with the smallest grin. He didn't give up. Then one night during the sixth week after John's "Nhyt-Nhyt" had landed under her chin, Hope gave a chuckle!

John could hardly believe his ears. He peered down at the child. It was true. Hope's black eyes were shining merrily. She had joined the game at last. "See you in the morning," John said; " —now goodnight."

The following night, Hope rewarded her papa with two chuckles. Before the week was out she was laughing out loud, and it it wasn't long before her smiles and frowns began to be seen during the day as well. A world of emotion had been hidden inside the little girl. Once the flow began, she was hard to stop. Hope turned out to be a true sparkler who wanted to perform every chance she got. "Papa, see me! Mama, look!" Hope, climbing the jungle gym — for she was an agile little monkey — now sought applause. Her papa was proud indeed that his patience had paid off. "I think it was the continuity that did it," he said to Ann. "She'd never had anything she could count on in her life that was fun. She'd been yanked around from here to there. But we did the *same thing* every single night. Well, who knows why — but it worked."

Ann was proud of something else. Little Hope was one very smart baby. Now that her personality had been unlocked, her mind began to work fast. She caught onto English surprisingly quickly and soon was making her wants known with real sentences. The deadpan doll of the early days was gone. Ann found it hard to believe that she'd ever thought Hope was unattractive. Almost overnight she blossomed into an Oriental flower. "All summer long I tried to dress Hope very carefully in nice things so she wouldn't look too drab and awful compared to Faith," Ann remarked to John. "And now look — we've got two beauties on our hands!"

Her little kids were happy. Her bigger ones seemed to be doing well. Though it was still autumn, Ann began making plans for Christmas and looking forward to the time when her older children could be expected home with their mates and their friends. She had actually been wrapping presents since August — a fact which made her friends shriek with dismay. "It's the only way I'll ever make it," she said calmly. "I keep wrapping paper and ribbon in the laundry room, where I also hide presents in a big closet. Then when I'm stoking the washer or waiting to pull things out of the dryer I have something to do." Ann did 35 to 40 laundry loads a week, a job she cordially hated, but presents were her specialty. She loved splurging with the money she made teaching piano. This year she was particularly looking forward to getting Chuong a racing car set. He'd asked for one months ago. He wouldn't be disappointed.

One night Ann stayed up late working on a piano piece she had to play for a school concert the next day. When she started up to bed she fell into planning, rather dreamily, what she might have for Christmas dinner. There were always the traditional pies and Christmas cakes, but didn't it make more sense to have lots of ice cream when that's what little kids really liked best? She didn't have time to bake a lot of stuff and — she stopped in her tracks. There was a figure stumbling, running in panic down the stairs!

"Chuong!" His eyes were wide open, blazing with terror. Instinctively Ann reached out and caught him. He was going so fast he nearly knocked her backward down the stairs. They swayed together, then Chuong fell against the bannister, sat down, and Ann crouched beside him, still holding on tight. "What is it? Tell me —"

He couldn't tell her. He was shouting unintelligibly. The only words Ann could make out were, "No! No! No!" shouted over and over.

"John?" she screamed up the stairs, still afraid to let the boy go for fear he'd hurt himself. "Come quick — help me!"

John, having heard the commotion, was already at the top of the stairs, thrusting a long arm hastily into a bathrobe. "What happened? What's wrong?"

"I don't know. Chuong must be having a nightmare. He keeps screaming something but I can't understand it —"

Both parents held him, then, together. They stayed right there on the stairs, talking softly to the boy. "We're here. It's all right. You're just having a bad dream, Chuong — it'll be over soon." Ann stroked his shoulder gently.

They had no idea how long all three of them were there. Minutes seemed hours. Chuong gradually stopped shouting. He seemed less rigid. His eyes lost their staring look and grew dull. He was not awake, but he allowed them to lead him up to his room to bed. John slept very little that night, staying in his study to be next to Chuong on the third floor. Ann, on the second floor, in their big round double bed, slept not at all until just before daybreak. The minute she awoke, she ran for the phone and put in a call to the doctor's answering service. "Please have Dr. Hecklau call me the minute he comes in." What they had lived through had been no ordinary nightmare. Chuong had never come out of it so they could comfort him. In fact, when he got up, Chuong had no memory at all of having been out of bed.

The doctor agreed that Chuong's experience was something more than your ordinary bad dream. "The open eyes and the inability to wake up all suggest that he must have had a night terror. When children have lived through something terrible like a fire or a bad accident, we see this sort of thing. It has to be worked through, and it's not easy. You did exactly the right thing, holding him and staying with him. Still, I think it would help you to help Chuong if you saw a child psychiatrist. There's nothing wrong with the boy that time won't heal, but we want this to happen as soon as possible."

"I'll say!" said Ann, fervently. "I was scared out of my wits — and I didn't know if I *was* doing the right thing. And how will I know how to handle it if it happens again? The next time might be different —"

"Let's hope there won't *be* a next time," said the doctor. "That's why I'd like you to see Dr. Bartlett. Maybe he can tell you how you and your husband can help head off attacks like this. There may be something that triggers them that you can avoid."

"I'll do anything," said Ann. "I'll call him this morning."

A few days later, after talking with the child psychiatrist, Ann began to see that there was a sort of pattern that might explain what had happened that frightening evening on the stairs. While all the children usually ate together in the sun room at 5:30 (a dinner served by the regular afternoon sitter who took over while Ann taught piano), it was a family custom for older kids to come in and sit with their parents when they finally sat down in the formal dining room around quarter to seven. Megan and Jay would talk about school or their plans for the weekend. Minh, if she sat down, didn't talk much in English. Often she tried to talk to Chuong in Vietnamese. Ann and John were not sure these conversations, which seemed to emphasize a return to the past, were such a good idea, so they tried to draw both Minh and Chuong into their own world. This was not easy to do. Chuong had had very little experience yet of life in America. Any talk at all seemed to overstimulate him, for he was an intelligent boy and proud of his heritage. He would listen to their talk of family. He would hear Ann say, "You know Dra is coming again for Christmas —" ("Dra" being the Sweeney children's name for their grandmother, Mary Taylor, Ann's mother). So then Chuong would have to burst out with, "At *my* grandmother's house we had a big feast when I went to visit. My grandfather had a big farm near Saigon. . . ." And he'd be off and running. Any reminiscing always seemed to escalate. He'd get more and more excited, and soon he'd be talking about the war. But it became hard to tell the difference between horrors he might have seen and horrors he'd heard about or fantasized.

"The soldiers were coming," Chuong would say. "Everybody said they had big trucks, big guns. Out by my grandfather's they shot some people —" Now he had to stand up to show them all how it was. "They were shooting! People tried to run!" Chuong screamed, waving his arms around like a gunner. "The men fell down — they couldn't get up. We were all afraid. I didn't want to see the blood run out —"

Sometimes Minh would join in. She, too, had her share of terrifying memories. "My father — he was killed in the street. One night there was a bad fight —"

"They killed some children!" Chuong, wild-eyed, wanted everyone to listen to him. "We wanted to run away — we didn't know where to go —"

Sitting in a Connecticut dining room, the two young Vietnamese war victims tried to tell their new parents about the nightmare they had lived through. In the beginning, Ann and John had let them both talk as long as they wanted to. They wanted to know what had happened. And with Chuong, especially, they had thought it might help him move on, if he could finally get it all out. The trouble was that the line between what *had* been, and what was going on *right now* always became thinner and thinner.

Now the psychiatrist was able to give Ann some practical help. "I think it would be a good idea to keep things from getting out of hand after dinner. When Chuong starts to get upset about how awful and scary things were, *you* can say, 'Yes, but that's all over now. Isn't it wonderful that that's all in the past? And we have all sorts of good things to look forward to right here and now.' Keep the emotional level down. I don't mean you should shut him up. Just remind him that he's safe now here with you."

"Yes, and there are all sorts of things he can do tomorrow," said Ann, getting the point right away. "He can take drum lessons. He can play soccer. Christmas is coming and we'll have a big tree and a turkey dinner with all the trimmings and three desserts...."

"You've got the idea. But I think I'd like to know how things are going each week." Ann quickly agreed to a weekly appointment until they were out of the woods. She had been nearly as frightened as Chuong was by these waves of remembered terror, which seemed to sweep him away from the reality of life in the Sweeney household. She told John everything the doctor had said, and John, with his calm manner and low-pitched voice, proved an excellent stabilizing force in the Vietnamese boy's life. Chuong had only one other night terror in the weeks that followed. Ann and John had been out to dinner, so had no idea what might have brought it on. Together they were able to hold the boy, gradually quiet him, and then lead him back to bed. Again, they were shocked at the memories of flight and war which still tormented him. In a way it was a blessing that Chuong had no idea what had happened when he got up the next morning.

All the Sweeney kids began to be increasingly keyed up with excitement as Christmas drew near. The girls were easy to please — they all loved clothes, records, animals. Little Hope would have her first doll. Faith had many requests, including one for "real nail polish and lipstick, Mommy!" Ann would have to go around those and come up with a substitute. She could imagine lipstick in the hands of some of her young anarchists, nail polish on the rug. Actually it was the boys whose great expectations worried her. With each day their demands for this or that mounted. Their boasts of achieving superiority in numbers of cars, trucks, or other rolling stock flew back and forth. Then one afternoon Marcus was heard to say, "I'm getting a new bicycle!"

There was immediate pandemonium. Paddy, Timmy, Terry, and Dat all rushed to Ann for confirmation or denial or, better yet, one of the same. Boiled down, what it added up to was "Mom, if Marcus gets a new bike, can I have one, too?"

Ann, feeling as pressured and weary as the mayor of an underfunded city, now had to take a strong stand against the boys' union on this matter. For one thing, she had no intention of rendering Chuong's secondhand bicycle instantly obsolete. He was the oldest resident son, and his position had to be protected. There were also Jay and Megan, older kids, who had transportation needs, and a desire to travel in style. "No," said Ann. "No new bicycles right now." She would stick to family policy, which dictated that secondhand bikes would be purchased when absolutely necessary and shared in a loose, communal manner that, if not ideal, mirrored the state of family finances. New bicycles — if and when — would be reserved for birthdays when equal justice for all was suspended in honor of the event.

Everybody had been sitting around in the library when the matter of the bicycles finally was put to rest. Ann had been making new felt Christmas stockings for the new Sweeney children. She had sewed one for Maria, one for Hope, one for

Dat, and now was working on Chuong's name. He was watching her closely without expression. She finished the final *g* in bright red. "There! Now you can hang up your stocking along with the other kids, Chuong," she said.

"Okay," he said, nodding. He didn't look especially delighted, but then what was a stocking to an eleven-year-old boy? Something was on his mind. "You haven't forgotten? What I wanted? The racing car set —?" he said.

"No, Chuong," Ann laughed, relieved that he had spoken up. It was not the first time he'd mentioned it, either. "You can be sure I haven't forgotten —"

But now Minh began to talk to Chuong in rapid Vietnamese. Ann wished she could understand what they were saying. Actually she wished Minh would practice her English. Of course, she had been fifteen when she arrived in the United States and she would certainly never forget the language of her home. But now the more Minh talked, the more stony-faced Chuong grew. What was she telling him? Ann began to grow very uncomfortable. It could be a perfectly harmless bit of Vietnamese small talk, but Ann's imagination always raced ahead to imagine all sorts of things.

Suddenly Chuong jumped up. He'd been aware of his mother's eyes on him as he listened to Minh. Now he left the room quickly and began to bounce an old tennis ball in the big front hall. Ann leaped to her feet. Rough play of any sort was forbidden in this highly polished, inviting area. For one thing, there was possibility of damage to the lovely leaded windows or crystal chandelier. For another, this hall was the waiting room for Ann's music pupils, and when she taught, behind the closed library doors, she needed peace and quiet. Now her voice came out much more roughly than she intended it to. "Chuong! For God's sake! You *know* you're not allowed to play ball in here —"

Chuong whirled, threw the ball away with such force that it bounced off the bannisters and ricocheted around the room, narrowly missing a tall vase of dried ferns next to the front door. Then before Ann could say another word, he ran up the stairs.

They called him for supper. It was a Sunday evening, John was taking orders for hamburgers and cheeseburgers, but Chuong did not appear. Megan was dispatched to bring him down. "He's not in his room," she reported. "I don't know where he is."

"Oh, Megan —" said her mother exasperated. "He's got to be up there somewhere. He hasn't come down."

"Well, I *looked* and I called all over the place!"

The little children were tugging at John. "Can I go, Pop?" "Please!" He made a quick decision. "I'm going to go ahead," he told Ann. "The natives are restless and want to eat. I'll get an extra hamburger for Chuong." He thought Chuong was probably testing them by refusing to answer. It was something every child has to try once in a while. John had done it himself as a lad. The thing to do now was not to panic or get excited. If he could get his parents in a state of uproar, Chuong would have won the battle.

It was, perhaps, easier for John to remain calm than for volatile Ann. She fumed, she fretted, she went upstairs and down, even to the basement, thinking that maybe he'd slipped past her eagle eye after all and gone down to the playroom off the swimming pool. By 9 o'clock even John was worried and he joined her in a search outdoors around the house. It seemed unlikely that Chuong had slipped out without their seeing him, but the boy was very quick. There were dozens of huge bushes, rhododendrons, hemlocks, all sorts of places a boy might hide if he really wanted to stay out of sight.

"Do you think we ought to call the police? I'm afraid he's run away —" Ann was shivering with fear and cold. A brisk December wind was scouring the sky. Clouds raced across the face of a rising moon.

"Not yet," said John. "I'm not convinced he isn't right here in the house —"

They were met by Megan at the front door. "Mom! I was just coming to get you — he's here!"

"But where was he? Where *was* he?" When Ann was over-wrought she often said the same thing over and over.

"I don't know. He just suddenly appeared in the kitchen and —"

Ann ran across the hall and over the stairs leading to the kitchen. "Chuong!" She could have strangled him but she was so relieved she wanted to put her arms around him. He was not there!

"Chuong went back up the stairs," volunteered Maria. "I hear him go —"

"Yeah," said Terry, who was rather enjoying the excitement because his parents had forgotten to put him to bed yet. "He took some doughnuts."

"He's gone to bed, then," said John. In a sense the boy had won. Well, so be it. John's feeling of relief outweighed everything else. He suddenly felt very tired.

Not so Ann. She was wild. "We have to get him up! He can't *do* this to me! I want to talk to him, make him understand —"

She was saved by all her children, who were still hopping around, still up at 9:30 on a night before school. "Mom — can *we* have doughnuts?" "Chuong took three — I saw him. Mom, can I have just one?"

"You little kids get up the stairs this minute and into your beds. I'm starting to count — ONE — TWO —"

They fled.

When the last child had been tucked in, when Ann had finally realized how tired she was, when John had, indeed, quietly opened the door to Chuong's new room on the third floor and seen just the top of his shiny black head above the covers, the two parents sat down in the library over a night-cap. "I feel he's beaten us," said Ann wearily.

"Yes, in a way. But still, he wasn't in any danger, he *didn't* run away. Not really. And this is one of the first times he didn't take out his anger by trying to beat up on one of the other kids. He's struggling with his feelings in his own way — and I think that's a good sign." John's words were wiser than he knew.

The psychiatrist listened with interest the following week when Ann told him of Chuong's running off to hide. "I can certainly understand why you said what you did. You can't have a front hall full of children playing ball. On the other hand," said the doctor, "Chuong finds it very hard to be under someone else's control. This can be a good quality in the long run, a very good quality. He's a strong person, he's likely to be a real leader. The hard part for you is that in dealing with him, you will have to try to find a way to give him alternatives. If you say flatly, 'No!' he is going to rebel. If you could have said, 'If you want to play ball, go outside —' then maybe he could have accepted it."

"But I was angry!" protested Ann. "I'm a human being, too."

"Of course you are," said Dr. Bartlett. "We all make mistakes, and unfortunately today most mothers are expected to be perfect — or think they are. You reacted quite naturally. All I'm trying to do is help you see a better way to react if you want to make your dealing with Chuong go more smoothly."

Ann sighed. "I'll try, but it certainly isn't my style."

The doctor smiled and stood up, signaling the end of the hour. "Don't feel it's the end of the world if you don't handle every confrontation the way I suggest. I think you and Chuong are both making good progress."

EIGHT

A Test of Wills

Parents and son rocked along during the next few weeks with but a few incidents. It was perhaps easier for John, since he was off to New York on an early train and didn't get home until after the children had had supper. Each time Ann slipped into the instant negative whether it was "No!" or "Don't do that!" or "Stop!" she found Chuong reacted by disappearing quickly. Now that she understood a little better what was going on, she didn't feel quite so threatened by it. She also found it a bit easier to forgive herself. After all, she had to say "Stop!" when one boy was swinging the other's baseball mitt and threatening to throw it through a glass door. She didn't think he'd really do it. But she *had* to set the limits, not only for Chuong but for all the other little kids who were standing around watching. At least she had solved one mystery. Or rather Megan had solved it for her.

"I know where Chuong goes when he runs away in the house," she told her mother one evening. "I saw him this afternoon — after you told him he couldn't go to the Boys' Club till he cleans up the playroom." All of the kids frequently "worked" for Ann for various small sums. It was one way to stretch small allowances and also to involve the whole crew in keeping the ship afloat. Jay, at eight, often vacuumed the sun room where the kids ate and played. Paddy, Terry, and Timmy were already adept at going on small errands to fetch something Ann needed from the other end of the house. Even Dat was beginning to ask, "I help? You give me job, too?" Chuong at first had been slightly disdainful of this activity. Like Minh, he had been afraid he might be taken advantage of. When he saw the real score, however, that everyone pitched in, including the papa, and as his wants grew steadily, he offered his services. "I clean up the playroom, fifty cents?" he had bargained earlier that day.

"Twenty-five cents," Ann had replied. "You made most of the mess." She couldn't be bulldozed into raising everybody's wages just because Chuong had now joined the work force. Inflation had to be fought in the home as well as out.

Chuong hadn't looked pleased. "Okay," he said shortly. But he hadn't gotten around to doing it. Perhaps that was his way of holding firm? Well, Ann had had to hang tough, too. And so she'd vetoed his suggestion that he go down to the Boys' Club at the end of the road to meet some school friends. "The playroom comes first" was all she said. Chuong had stormed off. He'd been late appearing for dinner, but she hadn't realized he'd been hiding again till Megan mentioned it.

Now Megan said, "You know that big closet on the landing where the stairs turn? Where we keep the summer cushions in the winter, and winter clothes in summer? He goes in there —"

Ann laughed. "I used to hide in a closet when I was a little girl, but then I'd get too scared waiting to be found, and I'd have to come out and give myself up —"

"Hey, Mom," said Jay, who'd been listening, "our whole family could hide in *that* closet if the British were coming or something." Jay's fourth grade had been easing into American history. The class had recently gone to see a nearby cannon and some other appropriate relics to help increase their awareness of living in a New England state where battles had once been fought.

"Do we have to hide? Is there gonna be a *war?*" cried Marcus, jumping up from the table, spilling some juice.

Ann handed him a rag. "There's going to be a war if you don't stop moving so fast. That's the fourth glass you've knocked over this week!"

The following day was the first day of Christmas vacation. Twelve children would be underfoot all week tearing up the house if Ann didn't make her stand early. As the last straggler appeared for breakfast, she said, "Kids, I have jobs for every one of you. You can earn some money to buy Christmas presents and then I'll take you shopping later this week. The front steps need sweeping and the front porch, too, so we can put up our little outdoor tree there —"

"Me! Me! I'll do that!" Marcus raised his hand waving violently as if in school.

"I see you, Marcus. And you don't need to yell," said Ann dryly. "Now —" she looked at her list "— Marcus will sweep the porch. Jay, will you take the garage?"

Jay nodded. There were assorted vacuuming jobs for Megan and Minh. "And another thing —" Ann went on. "Everyone who has an animal in my bathroom had better see that those cages are clean or OUT they go!"

"But, Mom — where would the animal go?" asked Terry, full of gentle concern.

"To the city dump! To the river! I don't know, but I mean it," said Ann, trying to sound firm. They knew she was a pushover for animals or she'd never have given in to sharing her bathroom with all those gerbils, mice, and guinea pigs. Long ago John had thrown up his hands and moved his shaving things to the boys' bathroom. "I will *not* start my morning in a zoo!" he declared.

Now the children began to wail and protest on general

principles. But Megan just laughed. "She doesn't mean it."

"Megan," her mother said quietly, "help the little kids, will you? They've got to learn how to clean cages if they want pets." Megan nodded. "I will, Mom. And I'll clean the cat box."

"Maria? What will you do?" Ann asked.

"I don't know." Maria shrugged.

It was not easy to think of things that Maria *could* do. Nevertheless, the little girl could not be allowed to sit there while life went by. "Well, how about straightening all those piles of magazines out in the front hall? And you can pick up your room, too, and see that things are neat in your dresser drawers. Then maybe we'll count the silver together and see if we have enough forks and spoons for Christmas dinner. All right?"

Maria smiled, nodding. "Do I get paid, too?"

"If you do a good job. Of course."

All this time one child had been sitting impassively, saying nothing.

"Chuong?"

He stared at her defiantly.

"What about that playroom job? It's still waiting to be done."

"Fifty cents," said Chuong.

Ann heaved a sigh. "We've already discussed that. I haven't changed my mind." She realized she hadn't given him a face-saving alternative. But how could she? Chuong and Megan were almost the same age, and Jay was certainly as capable. She'd be playing favorites if she raised her rates for one stubborn kid.

Chuong took off. The basement door lurched shut after him. Maybe he was going to do his job, maybe not. Ann didn't care, at that point. The day washed over her with its mountains of laundry, shopping lists, last presents to be wrapped, and all the rest.

When Chuong didn't show up at lunchtime, she sent Jay scouting around the house to find him. He came back breathless. "Can't find him anywhere, Mom. And the playroom's still a mess. So's his room." Jay's halo was showing. He had just pocketed a dollar for polishing off four jobs that morning, and he had the marks of a good kid who comes through pasted all over him. Megan, too, had been patient and resourceful in getting the littler ones to do what had to be done with their bathroom livestock, and on her own she had swabbed down the bathroom floor. Even Maria had managed to finish her small tasks. Ann felt irritation soaring to the bursting point. "Who does he think he is to drop out when everybody else pitches in? Chuong, I won't let you get away with this!" She ran up to the landing on the stairs and opened the door to his recently uncovered hiding place.

"Chuong! Come out of there!" Ann pushed through the green and yellow cushions for the terrace chairs and all the other paraphernalia of summer. The closet ran nearly half the width of the house and was packed tight. Stuffy, too, and dusty overhead. Ann began to sneeze. In times of stress her allergies were apt to surface. She sneezed six or eight times more before she satisfied herself that Chuong was not in the closet. Then she came out, shut the door, and sat down on the stairs feeling very deflated. She'd been so sure she'd find him. But the cupboard was bare of small boys. Oh God, *now* what? Maybe she'd handled the whole thing wrong. But wasn't one of the things she had to get across to this strong-willed child the fact that he couldn't hold up the house every time he didn't get his way? She couldn't redo the rules just because they didn't suit *him*. "Oh, Chuong, where are you? I want to help you!" Worry now replaced anger. Ann huddled on the stairs feeling miserable. If only he'd come back, maybe she could help him understand. Money was important, but being a family was more important.

But Chuong was seeing it differently. He felt he'd been ridiculed. She just didn't understand! He was bigger than all those little kids who got 25 cents for doing their rooms and other dumb jobs. The playroom was a plenty big place, almost half the basement, and everybody used it, too. Jay had been hacking around in there, Marcus, too, when she claimed *he* made the mess. Chuong was determined to make them all sorry. He had begun his strike for more pay by hiding in the same old closet. But the place had lost its glamour. Somehow he wanted to dramatize this particular situation. He was beginning to wonder if they were just keeping him around until he was big enough to do more and more work. They pretended to care, but who could trust anybody? The thing to do now was do something so bold they would all be amazed and impressed. He would go to the Boys' Club just as he had planned! They would see that he was a person who could manage his own affairs. There was a difficulty, though. The club would not be open until later in the day. And now that Chuong had come to a decision, he was much too restless to stay cooped up any longer. Okay then, he would wait for his chance and get out now. Then when no one was looking he would run outside and go down to his favorite tree on Woodland Road. That tree, with huge branches just right for climbing, was a hiding place Chuong really liked. It was only a block from home, but no one had ever seen him there, he was sure. So now he would wait high in the tree until it was time to go to the Boys' Club.

Chuong opened the closet door cautiously. Voices in the kitchen. No one but Woof anywhere in sight. He flew down the stairs and started across the hall. He was almost at the front door when he saw a shadow in the window. Someone was stamping, trying to wipe his feet on the doormat just outside. Someone coming *in*! No good. Too late. Chuong made a dive for the library. He wriggled under a big old-fashioned chair and lay still. His heart was pounding in his chest. Maybe whoever it was would go upstairs. When he heard the stairs stop creaking he could try again. *Damn, hell!* The person was coming in to the library! Chuong was small and slim for eleven. Long experience had taught him how to hide in cramped, out-of-the-way places. Fortunately the chair had a pleated skirt that hung down to the floor. He made sure his feet were not sticking out. Then he recognized the walk, the thump of the briefcase. It was the papa! John Sweeney sat down in the chair.

"John! What are you doing home at this hour?" Ann had heard him come in and followed him into the library.

John was rifling through papers in his briefcase. "Gordon wants me to take the shuttle to Boston and be there in the morning. We have a chance to pick up a manuscript of a concerto he's been after for quite some time. I came home to pack a bag — and leave these." He put aside a pile of papers, snapped his case shut. "Is anything wrong?" He had not missed Ann's concern.

"Oh — Chuong's gone again." She flopped down on the couch and drew her knees up under her chin. "Megan told me he always hides in the big closet on the stairs. But he isn't there! I looked and looked. I'm beginning to be really worried."

"Don't fret," said John. "You know how he is. I'm sure he hasn't gone far. Chuong's just having another of his Oriental tantrums, giving you the silent treatment."

John's quiet acceptance infuriated Ann. "He's not giving it just to me — he's giving it to all of us. Don't you see? He's upsetting the whole house!"

"Then don't let him. We've been all through this before. We've been told that the best thing we can do is to keep calm —" John got up.

"Well, I don't feel calm!" cried Ann. "I'm mad as hell. Just wait'll I find him —" She got up and ran after John. Chuong, somewhat frightened, and yet oddly elated by all

that he'd overheard, lay still under the chair. The front hall
was full of little kids now. "Pop — you're home!" "Hey Pop,
are you going someplace?" "Papa — can you read to me?"
That last was Faith. Chuong groaned. He'd never get out now
to go climb his tree. What should he do? Wait right where he
was, he decided. The best times at the Boys' Club were at
night anyhow. Always before they'd taken him in the car and
picked him up. This time he would go by himself. He was not
afraid; he could find his way in the dark. Maybe when everyone sat down for supper he could make a dash for it. Yes, that
would be a good time. The club, that was the place to go.

But what if they looked for him there? Then what? The
mama was very angry. "Just wait'll I find him!" she'd said.
What would she do? Send him back where he'd been before?
Beat him? He didn't think so, but he couldn't be sure. Whatever happened, the important thing was that Chuong would
not be beaten in his heart. Everyone must understand that.

He moved carefully to get into a more comfortable position
curled up under the chair. There — now he could wait forever. His determination to win this battle made Chuong feel
powerful. He was lying on the floor of the library, hidden
right under their noses by the foolish skirt on this chair, yet
he was feeling a keen excitement. They could do nothing as
long as his will stayed strong.

"I'll leave the car at the airport," said John as he went off,
"then I won't have to wait for the limousine coming home.
Try not to worry, I'll be at the Copley Plaza if you need me."
Ann kissed him good-bye. She spent the next hours after he
left searching the house, sending Megan and Jay to look in
out-of-the-way places. No Chuong. Somehow this disappearance had shaken her more than all the others. Maybe because family unity was threatened. If Chuong split off,
refused to do his part, he set an awful precedent for the other
kids. Everyone had moments when they felt lazy or indiffer-

ent, but part of growing up was learning to overcome this childish self-centeredness.

By mid-afternoon, Ann had run out of steam. She didn't have her usual schedule of piano lessons, since many pupils had gone to visit grandparents for the holidays or take a winter vacation with their families. She was, in fact, so overcome by sudden languor she forgot to turn on the gas under the chicken casserole. Instead, she let the rest of the afternoon drift by while she curled up in the library with a magazine. The truth was, Chuong had her on hold. She couldn't get on with her life until he decided to get on with his. For the moment she couldn't even summon the energy to worry about whether he was all right, for she'd worried through too many crises already. Hours passed.

Ann was half asleep in the dark when she suddenly came to. "My God — the chicken!" At the same moment little kids began swarming all over her. They'd been jumping in piles of wet leaves in the yard. Nobody remembered to call them in when it got dark. It had been a long afternoon of delicious, forbidden play. Their cheeks were flaming with cold, their eyes bright and dancing. Of course they were ravenously hungry. "Mom — when are we gonna eat?" "Mom, what's for dinner?"

What indeed? Megan, who often jumped in to lend a hand when the crowd began to grumble, went out to the kitchen to get things started, but returned almost immediately with the news that the chicken was stone cold. "And it's a quarter to seven," she said. She seemed slightly pleased to be the bearer of such amazing tidings.

Ann just nodded. "I know," she said. "I forgot to turn it on." She had failed in her responsibility to her children. She was an inadequate mother. She was guilty, just as she had suspected all her life. Guilty, and unfit.

For some reason her children all seemed to be delighted at this remarkable turn of events. "Hey, Mom!" cried Jay. "Don't worry — you can go out and get pizzas. It'll be fun —"

"Yeah, Mom!" Marcus seconded the motion lustily. "I want a pizza all-the-way!"

"I want cheese," said Maria.

"I'll wash some lettuce for a salad," said Megan.

The sounds of a family party in the making began to be too much for Chuong. He had withdrawn from the household in order to bring the enemy to terms. But he had ended up being a prisoner under a stuffy chair all afternoon while his mother drowsed on the couch nearby. Somewhere along the line he'd lost the intensity of desire and concentration necessary to pull off his plan to run away to the Boys' Club. At the moment it seemed like rather a dumb idea. He was cold and stiff from not moving around. As the campaign to get pizzas grew stronger, Chuong couldn't resist making a noise of his own. Then he made another, much louder, because they hadn't noticed the first.

"What was that?" said Ann, whose eyes and ears were extraordinarily good from years of being on the lookout for the unexpected.

Jay shrugged. Marcus continued to press for pizzas. "Can we have 'em, Mom? *Can* we?"

The other kids kept up their demands. Hope whispered in her mother's ear, and Faith, not to be outdone, began playing with Ann's ponytail. Paddy wanted to know "Can we swim in the pool after we have pizzas?" This was too much for Chuong. In the end he had to stick a foot out, while giving a great pretend groan.

Everyone found him at once — which, in a sense, saved his pride. He had not been discovered. He could have stayed right where he was for days. He had chosen to rejoin his family, that was all. In the exclamations, the joy, the astonishment that greeted his return, Chuong found himself beginning to feel like a hero.

"Hey, Chuong — that was *neat*! You were right here all the time!" Jay was impressed.

"Chuong!" Dat hugged him around the knees. Chuong tousled the little boy's hair affectionately. "Hey, Dat — cut it out."

Marcus wanted to see if *he* could fit under the chair, Paddy had the same idea; meanwhile Timmy bounced and bounced in the seat until he accidentally kicked Paddy in the nose. Tears! Ann, who was alternating between relief and fury, was spared having to react to Chuong. "Everybody calm down — nobody goes under that chair, do you hear?" She rocked Paddy on her lap and found herself beginning to feel somewhat comforted, too.

It was Megan who managed to have the last word. The afternoon search had been hard on her. Minh had managed to escape from the uproar by busying herself in the kitchen scrubbing everything in sight. Megan, on the other hand, as her mother's deputy, had been ordered around. "Megan, have you looked in the attic?" "Megan, maybe we should try calling up some of Chuong's friends." Megan had done everything she could. She hated to see her mother so upset, and her own nature had made her already very much a caretaker although she was not quite eleven. It was true she bickered with Chuong constantly when he was around, but she really worried whenever he was missing.

Now it was absolutely too much that everyone was making such a fuss over him just because he'd come back. "*You* could hide under a chair, sure," said Megan; "that's because you're still a little kid. You're not even as tall as I am!"

Chuong spun around, ready to defend his eleven-year-old manhood at this unkind thrust. The fact that Nature takes her time most unfairly when it comes to bestowing height on growing males did nothing to ease his outrage.

Ann knew her cue. "If I hear one more word from one more person, that person can go without pizza for dinner," she said. Her words sank home. The entire library rested in peace as she walked briskly across the hall to find her purse.

NINE

꿿 ঽ๏

Breakthrough

IT WAS THE NIGHT before Christmas at last. The first step
in preparing for Santa's traditional visit to the Sweeney house
on Old Mill Road began with a trip by John to the basement.
There he resurrected the round folding fence, which had
once been used to keep two sets of twins from wandering
away in the yard, and carried it upstairs to the library. This
year, when it was finally set up, it would serve, instead of a
mantelpiece, as the Christmas "fence" where fifteen Sweeney
children (and their spouses) hung up holiday stockings. Ann
had added Gary's name to Lynn's stocking after their marriage in May. Randy had married in the fall, a California
wedding, which Ann had been unable to attend because they
didn't want to leave their new adopted children so soon, and
so there was a new name — Vicki — on Randy's stocking.
Chris, too, had a stocking of red felt. But starting with Megan,
who had a green one, the children's stockings ran the gamut
of colors. "It's always been my aim to come out even," Ann
explains. "But each year when I've had a piece of green or
gold felt left over, I think, well — maybe that means another
child is waiting for us."

That Christmas Eve in 1976, all the children were full of
wild ideas of what to expect in their stockings the next morn-

ing. "We always get good stuff to eat," Marcus told Chuong and Dat. "And lots of little cars," said Paddy. "We used to get money," said Jay.

"A hundred dollars?" said Chuong hopefully.

"C'mon," said Jay. "*Nobody* gets a hundred dollars. We used to get a dollar in the toe —"

"No more," said Ann briskly, not wanting to raise hopes. "Hard times, kids. But Santa will do right by you, don't worry."

Chuong tried to stay indifferent. He had been in the United States long enough to have experienced the national Christmas madness, the stores with their overwhelming displays, the promise of too much everything for everyone — everyone but *him*. It had seemed both crazy and tempting. He had not yet been on the receiving end in a big way. In Vietnam, Christmas had been a religious holiday. His family, who were Catholics like many others, had attended church. It was on the lunar New Year, or "Tet," that gifts of money had been exchanged. (Before his arrival, Minh had introduced the Sweeneys to the ceremonies of Tet by giving John and Ann each a dollar. She had then sat back to await a suitable return.)

Now, as Chuong hung up his stocking on a point of the little fence, he had to admit his was as big and as fancy as all the other stockings. Not only that, presents had been coming in from relatives he didn't even know. Some of the gifts under the great tree which stood shimmering and glowing in the hall had his name on them! Chuong could feel himself getting a bit excited. He tried to keep it down. "Wait, wait," he said, guarding against possible disappointment.

But for Maria the stocking was almost the best part of Christmas. While the rest of the kids were busy imagining tomorrow's bulging contents, Maria kept feeling the wonderful soft furry felt. "What's this?" she asked, when her brown fingers ran into the decorations Ann had sewn on.

"Sequins," said Megan.

"Seashells?" said Maria.

The kids laughed. "Why would Mom put *seashells* on a Christmas stocking?"

"They do feel a little like seashells, Maria," said Ann. "But they are *sequins* — little round, shiny things that come sewed together in a rope. I bught them so I could put your name on your stocking. Can you feel 'Maria'?" She helped the child trace her name.

Spelled out this way, her name would not have much meaning for Maria, perhaps, but Ann was grasping at any straw to awaken the girl's interest in words. For the most part, her Braille books had remained unopened. She found studying with her Braille teacher very difficult. This Christmas Ann had bought her Braille checkers and other games, hoping they might turn her on. Now she guided Maria's hands so she could hang her stocking on the last point of the fence. "Okay, kids — time for bed. Everybody upstairs right now!"

This was the one night of the year nobody put up a fight. Every single Sweeney rushed up the stairs and soon was under the covers with eyes shut tight. The sooner they fell asleep, the sooner Christmas would be here.

"Mom? Is it time yet?" "Mom, is Christmas here?" Little shadowy, whispering creatures were crawling under the covers to get into Ann and John's big round bed. The exhausted parents, who had been up till all hours making sure presents for all fifteen children were put where they ought to be under the tree, pretended at first not to hear. Many another American parent was at that very moment playing dead in exactly the same way. But when Marcus Sweeney hopped into the middle of the bed, bruising various occupants and shouting "Merry Christmas, Pop! Merry Christmas, Mom!" they knew the game was lost.

"What time is it?" John asked Ann.

Ann opened an eye and groaned. "Quarter to five."
It had started.

Hours later Ann would try to remember which moments,
out of all the turmoil, were the best of Christmas 1976. There
was the look on Minh's face when she saw that she had what
she wanted — a musical jewel box with a ballerina that
twirled when you lifted the lid. Megan had been given the
exact same box the year before, and Minh had coveted it for
all the 364 days until now. Maria, too, had a jewel box just
like it, as well as records and a zither and a xylophone. But for
Maria, exploring her new treasures was a slow process. Her
fingers gradually "saw" what Christmas had brought her.
With Minh, the flash of satisfaction had been quick, and in
that instant of rare happiness she suddenly became very
pretty.

Faith, who had turned four a few weeks before Christmas,
was already an old hand at tearing into presents. It was
never possible for Faith to be less then beautiful. Sulking, she
was as magnificent as a Babylonian queen. But in joy her
winged eyebrows almost seemed to fly and her gold-brown
eyes grew even more enormous. "Oh!" she cried, "Mom —
look! Mom — look! I got a new doll!"

"Isn't she gorgeous!" said Ann, surprised as if she hadn't
spent forty-five minutes in the doll section of the largest toy
store in town agonizing over all the choices before finally
settling on the charmer that now nestled in Faith's arms. It
was nearly as hard for Ann to pass up a doll as it was for her
to say "no" to a new child. As a little girl, she herself had had
eighteen dolls — all favorites, she insisted, and nearly all of
them named Mary Elizabeth after her mother, with an occasional Patricia thrown in for variety. Where most small
girls usually outgrow playing dolls, Ann simply moved from
dolls to babies, as she says, "almost without missing a beat."
And now the most recent baby, Hope, had joined the family
just in time to remind them all of the miracle of Christmas —

a child is born! In Hope's case, born again. The tiny girl, who had once resembled a miserable little Pekingese, was becoming more lovely every day. "Wonder what's become of our inscrutable, silent baby?" John said to Ann as they watched her.

That Christmas morning Hope's transformation was complete. She was only two and a half, and this must have been the first full-blown Christmas she'd ever seen. The tree with all its twinkling lights turned on in the black dawn, the dazzling sea of presents spread around it left her awestruck. She stood on tiptoe in her long nightie, full mouth open, black eyes holding wonder. "Ohhh!" she breathed softly.

"Hope — open your presents, honey." Ann had to help her. But then as she began to get the idea, when she saw the pretty dolly, when she hugged the soft bear, when she finally realized that all these bright, new toys were really *hers*, she began to run around the room crying, "See! See!" Except that she didn't run, she danced. Ever since she'd come out of her shell, in moments of joy Hope always began to dance. She was so tiny and light, she was able to dance almost on her toes, even without slippers.

Now she tried to get her brother's attention. "Dat — see doll! Dat — look!"

But Dat was methodically lining up his Christmas fleet of tiny cars and trucks. He could not count very far yet in English, but he already had his good, clear eye for justice. "You got blue truck — I got blue truck. You got red car — I got red car," he said in a serious voice to Terry, his bunkmate.

"Dat would make a good lawyer, don't you think?" Ann laughed to John. "Maybe even a judge."

"Too soon to tell," said John. "But Hope is certainly our ballerina."

Hope was now dancing her way through clouds of tissue paper and ribbon to find her other brother. "Chuong — look!" She tugged at his sleeve. Chuong, crouched down in a corner, was staring at something. He put an arm out to hug

Hope absently, but his eyes never left the racing car set, which was spread out on the floor. He was so still that Ann began to worry and quickly went over to him. "Is it the right one? Is it what you wanted, Chuong?"

He looked up at her then. His smile was almost shy. "Just right. Thank you — Mom." Chuong, at that moment, was struggling with complex emotions, some of which he had rarely experienced before. He felt slightly ashamed because he had doubted her. He felt humble and surprised. Life was indeed astonishing. Always before, he'd felt you had to watch out for bad things every minute, and that good things would never come unless you made them happen yourself. Yet here, while he slept through the night, he'd been given a pile of presents with his name on every one — not just something from the church that said, "For a Boy, Merry Christmas." No, every one of these presents had said, "Merry Christmas to Chuong," and there were more than he'd ever had in all his life. Ten! Chuong had counted them carefully several times. He'd watched to see how many Jay had to open, Megan, too. Everybody had ten, not counting the ones from aunts or cousins he didn't even know yet. Chuong began to feel a quiet surge of happiness, not just because of the fine racing car set, or the car which had a wonderful battery-powered motor so you could make it go all over, or any of the other stuff. It was more than that. This family was really fair. And they treated him as if he belonged. Suddenly Chuong jumped up and shouted, "Hey, everybody — Merry Christmas! Hey, everybody — thank you!" Then he sat down quickly and began to arrange the cars on the track with great care and concentration.

The trust that Chuong had begun to feel for his new family for the first time during the Christmas holidays made Ann and John very happy. Chuong's grades for the fall term in his new school were excellent. "Who knows," Ann said to John one evening over their usual wine before dinner, "maybe we're out of the woods. Maybe we're going to get through the spring without any broken heads."

"Or broken spirits," said John, "which is more to the point." In spite of the fact that it was February and freezing, which meant the kids didn't get to blow off their usual steam outdoors, everything was peaceful on the eastern front, where children played on the sun room picnic table after supper.

"Funny, but it always makes me nervous when they're quiet," said Ann. "I wonder if I've left the gas on and asphyxiated everybody."

"Enjoy good fortune," said John, pouring her a little more wine. "You don't have to fret."

At that moment the swinging door to the dining room pushed open. Chuong stood there, waiting politely, for once, to make sure he was not interrupting.

"Everything okay, Chuong?" Ann thought the boy looked rather glum.

"My throat hurts. Real bad. It started in school."

He sounded even more hoarse than usual. *Oh Lord, here we go*, Ann thought. They'd been spared the usual round robin of germs so far. With twelve children and the New England climate to cope with, Ann had often thought of listing her occupation as practical nurse. She was indeed so skilled at diagnosing croup, bronchitis, and several other things that her pediatrician often trusted her enough to prescribe over the phone without demanding to see the child. Now she interrupted dinner to take Chuong's temperature. "A hundred degrees — not too bad," she said. "Take these —" she gave him aspirin. "And don't get up early. I think you'd better stay inside tomorrow. You'll probably be fine."

He didn't even complain. A bad sign, she thought, for Saturdays were big days in his life. He and Jay often talked all week about what they were going to do, although Chuong, typically, refused to be pinned down until the last moment.

Now he simply swallowed the medicine and went up to bed. "Gee — he didn't even want to watch *Star Trek*," she said to John.

"Maybe he's developing some real taste. Did you offer him Channel Thirteen?"

"No, I was glad he went to bed. Maybe the others won't get this one."

Chuong seemed worse the following morning. From feeling his forehead Ann knew the fever was not subsiding, as she'd hoped. The thermometer read only 100.6 degrees, but this was mid-morning, a time when it should have been lower if he were conquering the bug. Even more indicative of trouble was the fact that Chuong made no move to get up but just lay huddled, face to the wall.

"Chuong, I want you to take more aspirin. And I've got juice here I want you to drink."

"Hurts," Chuong groaned, not moving. "Hurts to swallow."

"I know, honey." Ann sat on the edge of his bed, patting his shoulder gently. "But you want to get well as fast as you can. I know it hurts, but I know you're brave —"

Chuong sat up reluctantly and took the glass.

"Now," said Ann when he'd finished, "I want you to get dressed, and be sure to wear a sweater so you stay warm. We're going to the doctor's."

Ed Hecklau, the family's pediatrician, was Ann's Rock of Gibraltar, a man who worked long and hard, always returned your calls, never left you in the lurch. When he'd finished examining Chuong and could find nothing extraordinary, Ann had to accept his word. "So far it just looks like the start of an ordinary old-fashioned bad cold," he told Ann. "The chest is clear. The throat is red, but there's nothing at this point to justify antibiotics."

"Okay," Ann sighed. "If you say so, Ed." She always felt better when there was a shot or a pill that might promise a faster recovery. At the same time, she knew you didn't waste your ammunition on an unidentified enemy.

"Just keep him warm and in bed and —"

"Lots of fluids. Aspirin. And check with you if he doesn't get better," said Ann, reciting the second part of a litany she knew by heart.

Chuong was sleeping when she brought him his tall glass of juice at 4 o'clock. His face was flushed. The thermometer now read 103 degrees. He drank the juice, keeping his eyes closed, trying to hang on to sleep. He made no sound, but he winced with every swallow.

"I don't like this," Ann thought. "He ought to be sneezing and blowing his nose by now if this is a cold." "I want to listen to your chest," she told the boy, who lay, without protesting, while she pulled up his pajama top and put an experienced ear on his rib cage." If something's cooking in there, I can't hear it," she frowned to herself. What the hell was going on here? It was Saturday afternoon, the moment all mothers dread when there's a fever going up and of course you hate to bother a busy doctor on Sunday. "Maybe Ed's still in his office." Ann raced to the hall phone and dialed. She could hear the ring. The nurse was obviously gone. "Oh God," she breathed. Then she heard his voice.

"Ed? I'm so glad I caught you. I really don't like the way Chuong is doing. His fever's up, but no other signs yet —"

"Bring him in. I'll wait for you."

"He's sick all right. But there's still no indication of pneumonia or any other trouble that I can prescribe for. I don't want to give him a drug if what he has is a virus sore throat. I'll do a throat culture. But we still probably aren't going to know much until tomorrow afternoon. These things take twenty-four hours to grow, unfortunately."

"Tell me something I don't know," said Ann, cross with the world of science for failing to make better time when one of her children was involved. "Sorry, Ed, I know you grow them as fast as you can," she said to soften her words.

"Go home. Have a drink," said Ed Hecklau with a small, weary smile. "I won't be on call tomorrow, but of course if things change and something serious comes up, the answering service will call Jack for you."

Ann nodded. She was used to working hand-in-glove with Ed Hecklau, but she also knew his partner and trusted him. "I couldn't raise all these kids without the two of you," she often said. Not many doctors covered their patients as thoroughly as these two.

That night as Ann went down the hall to get Chuong settled for sleeping, she heard a sound before she even reached his door. The sound of a child taking hoarse, raspy breaths. Chuong was half sitting up, his eyes a bit wild when she came in. "Hurts, Mom," he gasped.

"Oh, Chuong, I'm sorry," Ann said. His fever was up, she judged, feeling his forehead once again. When she read the thermometer — close to 105 degrees — she felt her heart lurch. "I'll get something that will help you — I'll be right back." She ran downstairs. "John? Could you give me a hand?"

John, sitting in the library with a book, dropped it quickly and got up.

"Chuong's having trouble breathing. He needs the cold steam vaporizer right away. But I know I'll need a good extension cord to hook it up by his bed. Could you find me one? His temperature is sky-high —"

Quickly the parents set up the vaporizer in Chuong's third-floor room. Soon the comforting hiss of steam was rising like gentle background music in the room. Its familiar sound reminded Ann of another struggle and another time, and suddenly she knew what she had to do. "I'm going to sleep up here with him," she told John.

"There's no room for another bed in here, not even a cot," protested John.

"Remember me?" Ann laughed wryly. "The first two years with the twins I spent more time sleeping on the floor between their cribs than I did in our own bed."

"I do remember," sighed John. "I believe I complained at the time." It had never made sense to him that Ann, who was always shivering with cold, refused even a mattress between her bones and the carpet when she was caring for a child all night. Once the juices of concern started to flow, all thoughts of her own comfort vanished. "Good night, then," said John. "Blessings on you both. I hope you feel better in the morning, Chuong," he added, giving the boy a smile and a pat.

Chuong heard him dimly, through the fever dream that had taken him over. He gave no response, for something was pursuing him, something he would fight off if only he knew what it was. There was a roaring in the forest behind his head, like a wind that carries fire. He was trying to run. Yet each time he opened his eyes the walls of his room were closing him in, he couldn't breathe, they were falling! Chuong tried to run away . . . struggled to get up.

"Just lie still. You'll be all right. I'm going to stay right here with you, Chuong." Ann's voice, often piercing when a crisis was of the spilled milk or lost lunchbox variety, became gentle as whisper when things got really tough. She knew how to hang in, conserving her energy and his for the long night ahead. "The cool mist will help you breathe," she told the boy. "You don't have to worry. Let go . . . go to sleep . . . go to sleep."

Chuong closed his eyes, and drifted away. But Ann, lying on the carpet, her own pillow under her head, a bathrobe and a comforter over her to keep her warm, wanted to stay awake awhile. She didn't like this at all. In spite of aspirin, the boy's fever had shot up ominously. She had just told him the mist would help him breathe. She wished she believed her own words. It was a hope, and hope was often what mothers lived on through the dark hours.

She remembered the months of dark hours before the

twins, Paddy and Timmy, had even been born. To be carrying twins at the age of forty was peril and excitement enough by itself. On top of that was the fact that the babies were lying in a rare and dangerous position usually found but once in 90,000 births. Both heads were on one side. Ann was so uncomfortable she spent most of the last months in bed, which was just as well, for she'd been bleeding on and off almost since the pregnancy began. No one really expected the birth to be full-term or successful. Day after day she had hoped, prayed, pleaded with the Almighty to let the twins be safely born. *Twins!* When the doctor first heard two heartbeats, Ann nearly leaped off the table with joy. But he hadn't minimized the difficulties. A thoughtful man, a good surgeon as well as obstetrician, Dr. Prangley was not surprised when his patient showed small signs of imminent birth a few weeks early. In his opinion a cesarean would seem indicated if the presenting twin appeared in the transverse position. Ann had a history of miscarriages and marginal placenta praevias, in spite of having borne five healthy children. He made his decision and Ann was grateful.

She remembers waking up, with a tube in her throat, just managing to croak, "Alive?"

Dr. Prangley gave her a cocky laugh, which belied the deep concern he'd felt every moment of the delivery. " 'Course they're alive; what did you expect?"

Timmy, one minute older than Paddy, was frail, weighing just 4 pounds. He had had to remain behind in an Isolette for some weeks after his mother and brother went home. Paddy, a dark-eyed imp, almost from the beginning was sturdy and well developed for his 5 pounds, 1 ounce. Yet actually it was Paddy who later became the problem baby of the two in a most surprising way.

Ann had always thought Timmy, who was so little he felt skimpy as a dishrag — "There was nothing you could hold on to" — must be the source of all the infections that struck both twins during their first years. Night after night she had bedded down between them to make sure they breathed — and kept on breathing till dawn. The repeated colds, throat infections that often ended up in serious ear problems, finally led Dr. Hecklau to suggest that they be tested for immunological deficiency. And so the two babies had been taken to the hospital so blood could be drawn from their groins and sent to a California laboratory for analysis. Word finally came back that Paddy was deficient in one gamma globulin factor. "Paddy? I don't believe it," Ann said when she heard the news.

"Neither do I," said Ed Hecklau. "Maybe they got them mixed up somehow. I'm going to rerun the test." He did, and once again, Paddy was found to be ultrasusceptible to pneumonoccus infection because of the missing factor. Fortunately it was a condition that would normally right itself by the time the little boy was five. "Oh, God — I can't wait till *then*," Ann complained. She was wrung out from several years of night-nurse duty by this time.

"You don't have to," said Dr. Hecklau. "I'm going to put the boys on a preventive penicillin compound. I think it may be the answer." The treatment had, indeed, helped a great deal. As they stopped being bombarded by one illness after another, Paddy and Timmy grew sturdier, although Timmy remained the more delicate of the two and never outgrew his infant need to eat every two hours. But they would be six years old before Dr. Hecklau thought it wise to discontinue the medication.

Now, lying in the small third-floor room beside another son, Ann could look back on those frightening times with the twins with a deep gratitude that they had all come through. Much of it had been due to the persistence and wisdom of her doctor. A large part of it had been due to her own strength, a strength very few people would have guessed she possessed. She was slender, high-strung, even nervous on occasion, but underneath she had a fierce doggedness that didn't allow for failure. She fought the germs that threatened her children in much the same way she fought the slothfulness of officials who dragged their feet instead of signing papers she needed to finalize adoptions. She'd learned so much along the way. And now everything she'd learned in saving the twins would be used to help Chuong. His breathing, while still rasping, seemed less labored. He was not choking, he slept. Yes, the steam *was* helping . . . and soothed by its quiet lullabye, Ann went to sleep in spite of herself.

Several times during the long night she roused herself, checked his breathing, felt his skin temperature, sponged off his face. Chuong didn't wake, though he groaned in his sleep. Once she had to go rummage for another blanket. She didn't want the boy to be chilled as the mercury dropped during the night. There was no way to keep this old house stoked with heat during the small hours in winter. Even now a harsh February wind was rattling the loose-fitting window in its sash. Yet in spite of the seriousness of what was happening here, the sick child, the bitter cold, the tiring night watch, Ann felt a curious elation. She was being *used* — and it was a profoundly satisfying feeling to be used in the way Nature had intended her to be. Toward dawn, when she was finally convinced that they were going to make it without having to dash to the hospital, Ann fell into a last comfortable doze.

Morning. The pale light slashing through the gap in the curtains hurt his eyes. Chuong rubbed them, trying to piece together what was happening. He seemed to have been on a long and painful journey. But this was his bed, his room, his window up there, hey — what was *she* doing here? The mother, Ann, was sleeping on the floor! Right beside his bed like a servant. Chuong tried to move, to get out of bed — he fell back. "Aaaahh!" he groaned. His body ached all over, his legs had no strength, he could hardly lift his arms.

At that moment Ann opened her eyes and was instantly awake, responsive to her patient and what he might be needing. "Chuong — how are you feeling?" She was on her feet, putting a hand to his forehead.

"Bad, real bad," he said, and it was true.

But the fact that he could talk without gasping seemed to Ann a good sign. He was terribly weak, but he was in this world.

Chuong's temperature that morning was 104 degrees. Hardly reason to rejoice, but he was in good enough shape, basically, so that his body could put up a fight on its own. Still, Ann would be awfully damn glad when the laboratory report came in and maybe they could give him something. Reinforcements for the battle before they had to go through another night.

With John's help she got Chuong into clean pajamas, changed his bed, gave him a glass of chipped ice — his mouth was sore and cracked — and managed to get him to drink something. Then she got on the phone to prod her pediatrician's partner. "I'll let you know as soon as I've got something" was all he could promise.

It was 4:30 before he called her back. "Bring him in." The man actually sounded elated. "We've got a strep positive here —"

It was out of the question for Chuong to get dressed. Ann wrapped him in a blanket and carried herself to the car. Later, it might surprise them both that she had done this. Chuong seemed older, larger than he actually was. But he was slight for eleven, and at that moment too weak to protest. Ann was amazingly strong. Someone had once asked her the secret of raising such a big family. She had replied tartly, "Get yourself some good gym shoes and learn to run fast." She did indeed run throughout much of her day. That, and the daily conditioning of her 40 laps in the pool, kept her in top shape for emergencies.

"But of course Chuong wasn't really up to par," she told John later. "It only took two of us to hold him down while Jack gave him the penicillin shot."

Ann would spend one more night on the floor beside Chuong, just to be on the safe side. By morning, however, the drug had obviously begun to take hold. Chuong's fever was down to 100.6 degrees. He was pale, exhausted, but he knew where he was and what he wanted. "T.v., Mom?"

Ann laughed with relief. "After a little breakfast," she said.

They propped him up in an old chair on the second-floor hall in front of the upstairs t.v., wrapped in quilts and lots of warm wishes from the passing crowd. Dat and Paddy and Timmy and Terry came to stare at this big brother covered up like a baby. They had never seen Chuong quiet before. They were astonished and scared. "Chuong — you very sick?" Dat's round eyes regarded him solemnly.

"Yeah. Better now." It was an effort for Chuong to speak.

Ann shooed everybody away. "You little kids watch t.v. or play *downstairs*. Go — right now! Chuong needs to rest."

He rested for many days. The illness had sapped his strength. Ann had thought his recovery might be faster, but she certainly didn't want to push him. She also had a private guess about why it was taking him so long. "I believe he has finally left Vietnam behind," she thought. The whole wrenching experience of being uprooted, torn from his family, had been like a great wound to the spirit. What hurt the spirit had to have hurt the body, too. Now Chuong seemed more at peace than she had ever seen him. He's getting over it, she thought — the infection of war as well as the infection in his throat.

Something else had happened during the long vigil beside Chuong's bed. Something Ann had longed for and feared might never happen. Dat had become her own baby the first moment she picked him up. With Hope, the feeling of real connection had taken longer, for the little girl was so withdrawn. However, as soon as she began to laugh and cry and respond to the life around her, it had been easy for Ann to feel like Hope's mother. But with Chuong, she had felt like a

Minh, 17

Megan, 11

Chuong, 11 (sixth grade)

Maria, 10

Jay, 9

Marcus, 5

Paddy, 4

Timmy, 4

Dat, 4

Faith, 3

Terry, 3

Hope, 2½

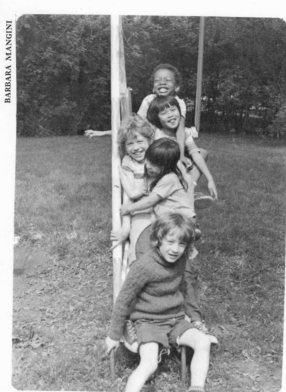

Terry, Dat, Marcus,
Hope, and Timmy
on the slide

The Rat Pack.
Hope, 5;
Dat, 7 (on top);
Terry, 5;
Marcus, 9;
Timmy, 7, riding
Big Wheels, on
bottom

rejected, if determined, outsider through all the months she'd been trying to help him. Yet at some point during the dark hours she'd spent at his bedside, Ann had finally become Chuong's mother, too, at last. It was a wonderful feeling. Even more wonderful was the fact that she knew he also felt the difference.

Chuong could not put into words what had changed, if anything. He felt totally drained, that was for sure. And somehow he felt it was okay to rest. He didn't have to fight back for once. Ordinarily he might have resisted being cared for like a little kid. The days drifted by, and when he awoke each morning he was always surprised when he looked at the place on the worn carpet by his bed. She had slept there! She did that for him. He never said, "Mom — thank you" in words. But his voice lost some of its harsh edge when he spoke to her. She looked at his eyes, which had so often blazed belligerently or turned away in defiance. They met hers now in a different way. She was glad.

It came as a surprise to Jay that he missed having Chuong to fool around with in the playroom or toss balls to out back. He had often ended up on the receiving end of Chuong's temper, but, gee, it was no fun hacking around with Marcus and the little kids. He tried lying on his stomach playing cars the way he used to with them. He got disgusted. They were babies! He went upstairs frequently. "Hey, Chuong — how you doin'?" Often he ended up sprawled in the hall watching whatever Chuong was watching. His mother, stepping over him as she went to and from the laundry room, thought, "They're beginning to be brothers. Thank God." "You know I'm so proud of Jay," she confided to John. "He took a lot from Chuong, and it wasn't fair and there wasn't much we could do about it at the time. But it's to Jay's eternal credit that he didn't carry a grudge from that time to this. He has a generous spirit. There's something — well, so *sound* about him."

"Yes," John agreed. "You mentioned that Dat might be our judge. Jay is probably too spirited for that job, but I'd certainly like to have him on my jury."

As for Megan, there was a certain relief in having a temporary cease-fire in the hostilities between her and Chuong. She had just turned eleven, and to have your *brother* in the same class with you, when you were trying to get started on the business of growing up and deciding which boys you liked a little bit — they were *all* impossible, of course, but maybe some weren't as bad as others — was like having an intruder watching your secret thoughts. She'd start to say something to somebody before class, and look up to see Chuong grinning at her or giving her a superior eye.

"Where's your brother? Where's Chuong?" a girl asked her one day when the boy had been sick for about a week.

"*He's* not your brother, is he?" said another girl who hadn't been in the class long. She looked incredulous, almost disapproving. "*Chuong?*"

"Of course he's my brother," Megan heard herself snap defensively. "Why shouldn't he be?"

"Well —" said the second girl lamely. "I mean, isn't he Vietnamese?"

"So?" said Megan. "I have two Vietnamese sisters, too. And a Vietnamese little brother." She was rather amazed at the strength of her feelings on this matter. Several weeks later, when Chuong came back to class, she made a point of being extra nice to him for a day or two. Before long, however, the situation returned to normal. Which is to say they went back to nipping at each other in the age-old way of brothers and sisters since time began.

TEN

❧ ❦

The Threat

SPRING CAME SLOWLY, on its hands and knees, as it always does in Connecticut. There'd be a few soft, bright days, then winter would blow in for an encore. But as the ground thawed, and the slippery mud finally gave way to good, hard dirt, the Sweeneys' backyard began to bloom with boys and all sorts of balls. Whatever game he played — soccer, baseball, basketball — Chuong was a natural. And playing with him, Jay began to learn some of the tricks of catching, kicking, and throwing that had eluded him. He was glad to have Chuong to bring him along. At the same time, it was hard to accept the age differences that naturally kept him from equaling Chuong's skills. Yet Jay at nine and Chuong at almost twelve showed all the signs of becoming staunch buddies. Family life was alive and well in the Sweeney backyard in 1977. Ann, watching from the kitchen window, was content.

Indoors, however, something seemed amiss. It took Ann a while to put the pieces together. During the late spring, as soon as driving became easier, there had been several visits by the Vietnamese who had originally been caring for the children. Ann and John had felt there was no way to prevent these meetings. Yet they certainly hoped such confrontations would be few. The pretense was a social visit, but the effect on Dat and Chuong was very upsetting. Hope simply went blank and paid little attention. Dat, however, climbed on Ann's lap the moment he saw the people he'd known before. Once he cried the whole time they were there. Another time Dat kept his hands over his face until they'd left.

"Dat's scared," Chuong told Ann later.

Chuong himself was not without fear of these encounters. On one occasion, when a woman clutched him by the arm, speaking to him in Vietnamese, Ann saw Chuong go pale. His mouth tightened, his eyes widened in the old terror. Two weeks later, when the group showed up again, Chuong ran away and hid till they were gone. Ann hoped then that they were gone for good. But while they didn't appear in person, there soon began to be phone calls for Chuong. At first the caller gave no name. Ann assumed the calls had something to do with school. But as Chuong began to grow nervous with each phone ring — and the household's two phones were always active — she began to have her suspicions. She tried to answer the phone herself as often as possible. Many times she heard a click following her own "Hello?" Yet if Chuong were to pick up the phone on the next call, he was obviously getting a message that was threatening. One day Ann decided she'd have to know what was going on. "Who was that? What did they say to you?" she said the moment he put down the phone. Chuong was so agitated he jumped. He hadn't known she was there.

"They tell me I have to go back!" he blurted out. "Dat and Hope, too. They say it's all settled —"

Fury rising in Ann's throat nearly made her choke. "Oh, Chuong — that's *not* true. You mustn't believe them. I won't let this happen —"

"They say you can do nothing. I don't know what to believe —" he said wildly. He grabbed his ball and baseball glove and ran outside.

"All our good work, all the trust we've built, down the drain? No way." Ann, trying to hold her rage within limits so she could function, dialed the New York State Department of Social Services. She explained the problem with as much force and tact as she could muster. Why, said the surprised person on the other end of the connection, this is the first we've heard of it. But of course we'll look into it and let you know.

"Soon," said Ann. "Please — it's really urgent. These children are being harassed."

"I understand."

The "looking into it" took two days. When the call was returned, Ann was in the front hall. John had just come back from picking up Jay at a friend's house. They saw her go limp after listening a minute. She said, "I see." Then she sat down and began to sob.

"What is it?" John went to her quickly.

"They're fighting custody. They've formally requested that Chuong, Dat, and Hope be returned. If we don't agree, they'll take us to court. My God, John — what'll we do?"

"We'll get a good lawyer," said John tersely.

No one noticed Chuong standing there, listening, in the kitchen doorway. No one saw him running upstairs a moment later.

Chuong and his new family had taken many a cautious but promising step in learning how to understand, love, and trust one another in the months since Christmas. But for every step that had been taken, they now took two steps backward. Old doubts reared their ugly heads. Ann and John tried never to discuss the custody worries in front of the children. Still, there was no way Chuong could have escaped the frightening message, with all these phone calls warning him that he'd soon have to go back to the overcrowded, dingy house he hated.

Was it really true? Whom should he believe? What could he do?

He did what upset youngsters usually do under heavy pressure. He was either stony and morose, or he lashed out at anyone who got in his way. Time after time in the days that followed, a crying child would come running to find Ann. "Mom — Chuong hit me!" Ann would pass out what comfort and scant justice she could, then she herself would go running to the bathroom. Eventually she ended up at the doctor's for a GI series and tests. She did not have that ulcer, not yet. But she did have a bad case of nervous diarrhea, she was losing weight, and worse than all this, she felt she was losing one of the most important battles of her life.

The Sweeneys had indeed found a good lawyer. A former foster child himself, he was immediately sympathetic to the problem at hand. They had also had no trouble finding friends, doctors, ministers, and even John Fisher of the Universal Learning Center, who were willing to testify on their behalf when the case came to court. But in the meantime the struggle was already being lost — or so it seemed to Ann — on the home front before a single legal shot had been fired. She was no longer trying to keep track of who was supposed to have done what to whom around the house. There were continual small wars going on in the sun room or at the supper table or out in the yard. Chuong, being the oldest, would ideally have been held more responsible for the welfare of others, would perhaps have been more patient, slower to swing. But under the circumstances, he was tinder-ready to explode every minute. Ann understood why very well, but this hardly helped the victims. Two days still stand out in her memory of that troubled time. Two days when she gave up, sank to the bottom, and let despair take over.

The first was a day when the victim turned out to be not just another kid wailing about an unfair punch or swat on the arm. The victim was Megan, Megan, who was nearly as old as Chuong and, at that moment, several inches taller, had taken a blow hard enough to give her a spectacular, bona fide black eye. Once again there had been a dispute during a game.

"Oh, Megan!" cried Ann when she surveyed the damage. This time it was the mother who cried harder than the child. The purplish wound seemed particularly insulting in the fine-featured face with its delicate ivory complexion.

"You want to know what makes me really mad?" said Megan in a tone of satisfied rage. "Tomorrow's the day we get our class picture taken!" Her pride as well as her eye had been jabbed. Ann shared this outrage in a very personal way. At eleven-and-a-half, Megan, with her long, slim bones and long blond locks, already showed signs of being everything Ann had always wanted to be. In addition, she was spirited and talented in her own right. Any blow that struck Megan struck Ann to the quick.

But it was on the following day, while she was still smarting sympathetically from the injury to Megan, that Ann received some bad news that gave her a fearful jolt. She had known all along that older refugee children from war-ravaged countries were likely to be poor risks when it came to adjusting to a new life. You could throw everything you had in the battle to save them — good food, good care, loving concern, psychiatric help, intelligent handling of many problems — and still lose. Ann didn't even like to think about it. But on that day, she learned through the grapevine of another local family who had taken on a Vietnamese boy just Chuong's age, given a year's good effort in trying to make him happy, and who had now just thrown in the sponge. The school and the psychiatrists had agreed that this child was much too disturbed ever to adjust or accept their help. He had also succeeded in disrupting the entire family. The worst of it was, they had simply called the state and asked that he be sent back! But back to *what?* Wasn't this the equivalent of throwing him off a cliff?

As upset as Chuong was, Ann was sure he could be saved if only the outside pressure would let up. The threat of having to go back kept him from moving on, making a new life, and kept Ann and John from doing their job. It also interfered with their enormous responsibility to all their other children, who now were suffering every single day from the chaos that kept overflowing all over the place. The August heat was now beating down, which didn't help, and the kids were at loose ends, with weeks to go before everybody went back to school. But even the structure of school wasn't going to be enough to save the situation this year. The Sweeneys had been told by their lawyer it might take months before the courts got around to resolving this custody dispute. How could she live through *months* of this uncertainty and emotional uproar? Ann hugged her aching stomach, rocking back and forth, worrying and pondering what to do?

She was a woman of forty-six who had given birth to seven children and chosen to add eight more to her family. It was a choice she and her husband had made together, freely and with love, and certainly with a great deal of knowledge of the joys and troubles they were likely to meet along the way. All this experience should count for something. Yet this problem was taking her to the bottom. There was something in her agony that felt familiar, like an old injury that had suddenly begun to ache again. Yes, now she was able to place the pain. It was very similar to the intolerable hurt she had felt following the loss of a wanted baby a few years after Jay was born. The threat of new loss brought it all rushing back. . . .

ELEVEN

Loss—and New Life

It was a day in December, 1969, when Ann Sweeney walked out of her obstetrician's office a very happy woman. He had just confirmed her own suspicion that she was pregnant with her sixth child. Five had never seemed a big enough family for the grown-up mother of all those dolls. Though she had never had smooth pregnancies or easy deliveries, Ann still insists, "I was never happier than when I was expecting a new baby. The bigger the bump, the better!"

But somewhere toward the end of the fourth month of that pregnancy, things began to go dreadfully wrong one day. John was in Texas on business. Ann, home alone with the five kids — it was early one Sunday evening — suddenly realized, to her terror, that she was going into labor. Months ahead of schedule! She dialed the doctor's number frantically, knowing she'd get the answering service. "Tell him it's an emergency — I need to hear from him right away," she told the operator.

"I'm sorry but your doctor is off call," said the operator. "Do you want me to contact his assistant?"

"Yes, *please*." In a few minutes the assistant called her back. Ann thought she could hear sounds of a gathering in the background. Voices, laughter, music. Was he at a party? "Ann, you wanted me to call?"

"Oh, yes! I'm afraid I'm going into labor — and I'm so scared —"

"Now, now, don't get all worked up. That baby's not due for months —"

"I *know* — but it's coming *now*! I need help —" cried Ann.

"You're a big girl, Ann," said the doctor. "You've been all through this many times before. Now you know what to do — just get into bed. Calm down. Relax —"

He wasn't coming. He said, call me in the morning. There wasn't any help on the way. The baby was born on the floor a few minutes later. Ann screamed for help. "Lynn, bring me the scissors!" Lynn, who was sixteen, ran to get them. Ann cut the cord herself. The baby — it *was a baby* — was lying on its side, she saw the feet, the tiny hands. She screamed again, this time for Randy. "Randy! Get us to the hospital — Randy! Oh, God — *quick*!" Randy, who was seventeen, ran to get the car. Ann wrapped the baby in a towel. Somehow they all got in — Ann kept on screaming — Randy drove as fast as he could to the emergency room.

It was too late. It had been too late from the moment of the first small but undeniable wave of pain signaling the start of labor. But it should not have happened the way it did. Miscarriages are always sad losses for women who want a baby, and they are unfortunately common. But this loss had been allowed to grow into a drama of abandonment and horror.

She kept falling down whenever she tried to get out of bed. They kept saying there was nothing wrong with her. There really was no reason for her to be in the hospital any longer. So she would get up again after a while. But then she would just fall down.

They said all she needed was rest, but every time she went to sleep she had nightmares and woke up screaming. She kept asking them what had been wrong with the baby. How big was it? Was it a girl? She couldn't be sure, it had all been so awful at the time, but she was almost positive the baby had been a girl. They said, "Now, now, you had a miscarriage." "No," she yelled, "I had a baby! What have you done with it?" It seemed very important to her to find out, for a baby was a *person* after all . . . and you can't just throw away a person like an appendix. They said, Please, Mrs. Sweeney, you mustn't get yourself excited. A year later she found out, finally, a few of the facts. The fetus had weighed less than a pound. There had never been any possibility of its surviving the spontaneous delivery. It had been disposed of in accordance with hospital policy, a policy which differed not at all from that found in hospitals anywhere in America. "What that meant," said Ann sadly, "was that it had ended up in the incinerator."

But at the time the event was new and painful, no one really wanted to talk to her about it at all. The result was that the more they didn't want her to talk, the angrier she got. She heard herself screaming things she'd never said out loud before. She heard ugly words bouncing off the walls, and saw startled looks on the people around her, so she supposed she must have said them, but she had gone away somewhere outside her body, so what did it matter? The baby was dead, she was dead, and she even screamed at John, too, because why hadn't he been there, why had he been off in Texas somewhere?

John was very tender with her, held her and comforted her. He had her moved to a private room so she could be alone, and finally he found a new doctor who was sure he could help her. In fact, the new doctor was quiet, gentle, and she thought maybe she could trust him. He ordered a change in her medication. Within thirty-six hours she was able to stand up and walk a little. Someone told her that an acquaintance of hers was two doors down the hall. It was the mother of one of her piano pupils. She had forgotten about that everyday world. On impulse she walked the few steps down to the woman's room. Unaccountably she found herself for the first time wanting to tell somebody, in her old normal voice, what had happened. "I lost my baby," she said.

The woman looked at her. "I know how you feel," she said. "I lost my first baby to leukemia. When she was just a year and a half old."

"Oh," said Ann. "I'm so sorry. Oh, I didn't know —" It was the first time she'd made a connection with somebody outside herself in many, many days. "That must have been terrible," she said softly.

"It was," said the woman. "But — I had to go on. And eventually, as you know, I had three lovely children."

When Ann got back to her own room she was feeling better. They had talked, two women sharing their losses, and for the first time it had dawned on Ann that other people had lived through much worse things, things she could barely imagine. She was, indeed, quite lucky. She had a husband who loved her, she had Randy and Lynn and Chris and Megan and Jay. A wonderful family! Within a few days she was able to go home and start trying to pick up the pieces. She still carried within her the ache of loss. But she knew life had to go on, and she hoped that some day things would feel right again.

The mourning that follows a miscarriage can often be every bit as painful and prolonged as the mourning of a real death. While Ann soon was back teaching, caring for her family as usual, she felt empty and depressed. She was doing her job, even doing it well, but underneath she still could not bear the knowledge that there was no baby on the way.

No one is quite sure who raised the question of adoption. It might well have been John, for over the years he'd become as excited by each new prospect of parenthood as Ann herself. He was also extremely anxious to find some way to raise his wife's spirits. Ann, of course, is sure that the idea was hers, that it had been in the back of her mind all along. The doctor treating Ann was so heartily in favor of the plan that he was later heard to claim some credit for urging an adoption. Obviously the parents of five healthy children would hardly be eligible candidates to adopt the usual Anglo-Saxon infant well matched to the family's coloring and background. Ann, however, found herself immediately thrilled at the thought of adding a totally different child to the Sweeney clan. As she said to John, "We need a baby. The important thing is to find a baby that needs us."

Ann's baby had been lost in mid-February. By July, when the baby would have been born, the adoption idea was gaining strength. "I really had to finish out that pregnancy first," says Ann, looking back. "And I had a lot of leftover anger. I was afraid I might run into the assistant somewhere in town and just begin to scream and fall apart again. The whole business peaked in a crisis of misery and loss over the July Fourth weekend, when the baby would have been born. I hurt so, physically, all that weekend with a strange, unfinished kind of pain I can still remember it. Then someone told me that the assistant had left to practice medicine in California, so I knew I'd never see him. But I really wasn't able to let go until I asked our minister if he and I could have a service for the baby I'd lost. He understood and so we did. Just the two of us. After that I did feel better. That anything so positive and delightful as Marcus should rise from the ashes of that situation of loss is a most unminor miracle.

"John wrote the initial letter to the adoption agency, and he always did in our subsequent adoptions, too. But it was November before we were put in touch with the caseworker, who invited us to come for an interview. She asked many searching questions, the most fundamental, of course, being, why did we want to adopt a baby? I found myself fumbling and blathering, never saying what I meant to. In retrospect I was always appalled at what I'd said, so I always wrote a letter the next day trying to clarify, emphasize, or unsay things I thought might damage my position.

"One of the important issues was, was I trying to replace my lost baby? I think I finally convinced the lady that, rightly or wrongly, nothing ever could. I knew this was really true. The sex, color, or background of any child they gave us didn't pose any problem for me. But I *did* want a young baby. About three months old seemed right. Well, the home study, as it's called, where they visit you, and interview you again and again, went on all through November, December, January, and February. Adoption proceedings have a gestation period all their own, like no other I've ever heard of. You never have any way of knowing whether you're making real progress — you don't get bigger — and there's no birthdate in sight for you to aim for. I crawled every wall in sight. During this time our emotional, financial, moral, legal, and other assorted attitudes were explored in depth. But it always came down to the same thing. I wanted a baby, *we* wanted a baby. And I did keep insisting it be three months old."

On January 22, Ann's fortieth birthday, John gave her a pair of yellow booties. She burst into tears at the sight of them. They were tears of longing for the new baby, but also tears of terror that she'd never be accepted as an adoptive mother. Somehow after that last loss, she couldn't believe her new dream might come true. Her defense was that it would never happen. "The yellow booties were too real for me to handle," Ann says now.

Then, on a perfectly ordinary Friday in February, Ann and John were called for "solo" interviews with the caseworker again. On the way home, afterwards, John mentioned casually that he'd been asked if he thought Ann would be willing to accept a baby a few months older than three months. John, with great perceptiveness, had answered that he thought once his wife knew a *real* baby might be theirs, he was sure she would.

The weekend was endless for Ann. All day Saturday, all day Sunday, the agency was closed. There was no way she could ask the questions that were pounding in her mind and heart. *What* baby? What age, what sex, what color? Ann is not a patient woman. By the time she was able to place a call to the caseworker at 9 A.M. on Monday morning, she was really fit to be tied. But she was given no real information over the phone, just a cool invitation to come into the office with John on Tuesday. "I was scared all day, waiting to go," Ann admits. "Cynthia McCall, the caseworker, always seems to be wearing mental white gloves at work, while I feel I'm wearing unmatched mittens. We had spent three days imagining herds of possible babies — male, female, black, white, tan, and everything in between, not to mention an age range from birth to twenty-one years old! So when Cynthia finally produced a picture of a six-month-old baby boy with a wisp of red hair, and inquired if we would be willing to consider such an old baby, I was ecstatic. I wanted very much to cry — my reaction to nearly everything that year — but was afraid that any show of emotion would disqualify me. We were also delighted with the baby's coloring, for John himself had been a redhead as a child. This augured well for the child's outward amalgamation into the family color scheme, despite the fact that his ancestry was definitely checkered — or plaid."

Marcus Taylor Sweeney, as he was to be called, was a black, American Indian, and possibly German or Scotch-Irish baby — who *looked* Irish — and who was very much himself from the first moment. He was the Sweeneys' first adopted child, and as such he played an important role in educating his parents.

Despite five previous babies, Ann felt she was totally unequipped to handle this new one. After all, he was adopted; he was interracial. She also found it impossible to believe that the little boy might arrive *dressed* — her other babies had all arrived naked. Her first move was to rush out and buy a com-

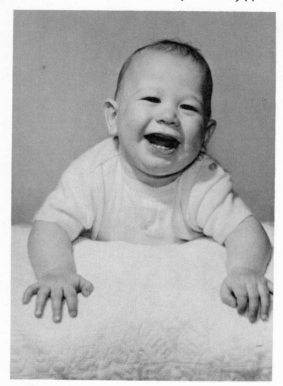

*Marcus, 6 months,
at adoption*

plete set of infant wear from the skin out. It never occurred
to her that he had to have been wearing *something* for all those
six months.

The day finally came when John and Ann drove to the
agency for the delivery of their baby boy, both of them in the
state of high excitement that usually precedes a "birth." The
agency was most un-hospital-like, however, with offices in a
small frame dwelling, and instead of the usual labor pains,
both parents listened to several pages of loving description of
the child written by the foster mother who'd cared for him
until that moment. The idea was to make the transition easier.
But Ann was beginning to shake. "It was all so unreal, unlike

Marcus, age 7

J. N. RASBACH PHOTO SERVICE, INC., SHELTON, CT

anything I'd ever been through before. Then suddenly there he was!"

Baby Marcus in a nice little yellow suit and white shoes. Almost bald except for a tuft of reddish hair. He had enormous ears. Bright brown eyes. Very pale skin. The social worker handed him to Ann, whereupon he began to howl. Ann looked down at him, amazed, apprehensive. "Then I saw one nostril was slightly dirty," she remembers, "and for some reason I was enormously relieved to be back on familiar ground again. I knew what to do. All I wanted was to leave immediately so I could clean him up — and of course so I could cry, too."

On the way home the family decided to drop in on big brother Randy, who was then in his freshman year at the University of Connecticut. "We all went out to lunch at a local restaurant and put Marcus, in his infant seat, right on the table like a centerpiece — which indeed he was." Ann recalls. "The waitress heated up his bottle, we had a good visit, and then we drove home very peacefully."

A woman does not necessarily become a mother, in the emotional sense, at the exact moment of birth or at the moment when she takes possession of an adopted child. Indeed there are some, like mothers of various species in the animal kingdom, who for some season or other fail to make the vital connection — ever. The cow who refuses to lick her calf after birth has many human counterparts walking around the streets of every city in our land. Every mother has moments before the child arrives when she fears that she, too, may become one of these repudiators. It is a terrible feeling, and it had struck Ann Sweeney on the night before they were scheduled to go pick up Marcus.

"Why am I doing this?" she thought in sudden panic. "How do I know I'll even be able to get along with this child, let alone love him?" She made a private vow that even if she could never love the baby, no one would ever know — especially Marcus, and she would always be a *good* mother to him. As she says now, "It's a marvelous indication of my naiveté at the time to remember that vow. As if you could be a good mother without loving! The other thing I didn't know was that loving is a whole lot easier than I thought that night. It just *is* — but the moment of truth, or love, doesn't necessarily come the first time you pick up the baby. And the older the child, the longer it seems to take."

Ann and John put little Marcus down for his first night in a crib right next to their own big round bed. It was the same crib they'd expected to use for the baby who'd never lived to be theirs. The new occupant was a small unknown quantity who'd come to them after months of suffering, soul-searching, and long delays. The officials presiding over his birth had been lawyers and caseworkers rather than doctors and nurses. But here he was. Ann was too exhausted that night to have any feelings beyond dull satisfaction as she drew the covers up to the soft little head. She tumbled into bed and fell asleep almost instantly.

Winter sun was weaving pale stripes of light across the walls when she woke up. Next to her, John was just beginning to stir and stretch. She glanced over at the crib and was instantly transfixed. "Hey!" she said softly to John. "*Look!*"

In the crib beside their bed, Marcus, on his tummy, was raising a wobbly head. He looked over at them — then he gave the most enormous, toothless grin. In that moment he became their baby.

Ann wrote to her parents in Mt. Clemens and John wrote to his in Grosse Pointe, telling them the happy news about Marcus. The two sets of parents were only about twenty miles apart in Michigan, but they were light-years apart in reaction.

Mary and Harry Taylor were delighted, as always, by anything their daughter decided to do. But unfortunately the adoption struck a vein of deep prejudice in John's father. He was a man of wealth and strong convictions. One of them was that family blood ties were one of the most important things in life. Yet while he was affectionate with his family, he tended to tie everyone up, using money as the string. That John should make such an important move that went against the elder man's feelings about family blood was intolerable. He reacted to the adoption of Marcus with rage. It was not Marcus himself he rejected. Any adopted child was an unwelcome outsider.

John's father had already had several serious operations, and it became apparent during the following year that he had not long to live. John flew out to his family home to try to say good-bye. He couldn't help hoping for some miraculous understanding. Perhaps his father would see how sad it would be if he left this world without an attempt at reconcilation of this painful clash of views. It was not to be.

There was a careful, almost formal, first day when relations between the two men seemed not too bad. But on the second morning the old man came downstairs in a terrible mood. "This is the most abominable thing you have ever done!" he raged. He demanded that John return every cent he had ever given him: a demand, of course, impossible to meet.

John went home deeply depressed. He knew that his gentle mother was in no way as prejudiced as his father, but she had had to live most of her life keeping her own quiet views to herself. When the father died, some months later, Ann was in bed with the flu, so John went to the funeral alone. After it was over he walked about in the old man's bedroom and picked up a few things — a pen, a letter opener, a glass paper-weight, other small things — thinking that perhaps in years to come his children might like to have some keepsakes from their grandfather. But that afternoon a lawyer came to read the will to the assembled family. John Sweeney's biological children were included. But any children that John and Ann adopted were specifically excluded now and forever. When he went upstairs to pack his bag, John looked helplessly at the small pile of mementos he'd gathered to bring home. They had lost all meaning. He left them there and took the plane back to his family.

The Sweeneys added rapidly to their patchwork clan in the years right after Marcus joined them. The joy that filled Ann and John to overflowing with the arrival of that engaging little fellow with the wide, crooked grin soon led them to start proceedings for taking still another baby. The miracle of adoption had touched them. They wanted it to go on and on.

As it turned out, life played one of its gorgeous tricks on

the Sweeneys. It was while they were waiting for adopted baby Number Two that Ann became pregnant with twins! Then baby Faith managed to arrive on their doorstep when the twins were but ten months old. She was a round, bouncing infant of six weeks. Her mother had been white, her father black. But Faith was like no other baby Ann had ever seen. A golden baby girl with honey skin, hair of tight, dark gold curls, great golden topaz eyes. The moment of true love came quickly with Faith, as Ann remembers. "She smiled up at me the first time I was changing her pants, and I just melted away. She had such a glow."

If Faith's adoption was remarkably smooth, the next was memorable for its difficulties. Terry, a beautiful black boy — "truly milk chocolate," as Ann says — was considered almost unadoptable, for he had a serious, perhaps incurable, lung condition at the time the Sweeneys found him. He was 16 months old, almost exactly the age of Faith, and both Ann and John were delighted at the thought of having a new set of twins. The state agency, however, did everything they could to discourage the Sweeneys. They preferred to place Terry with a black family. They thought the Sweeneys had too many children already. They felt that his closeness in age to Faith was another stumbling block. Only the fact that the Sweeneys had already had twins and understood how to cope with two the same age led the agency to reconsider. Also, they'd been unable to interest anyone else in a child that old with such a dubious health history. Terry had been in the charity wards of hospitals almost from infancy with a condition which was thought to be serious asthma. He had had pneumonia so many times he was still, at seventeen months, when the Sweeneys finally brought him home, almost unable to walk. He also had an active terror of people, especially men in white coats, and of cameras (which he thought were X-ray machines), so most of the Sweeney family pictures of the following few years show Terry wailing or with his face buried.

"We adopted him before I ever saw his real face," Ann recalls. "He'd start to scream when we arrived. Once we were allowed to take him out for a get-acquainted visit. We thought it would be fun to take him to a park. But the minute he saw all the people he screamed even harder. He was crying when they gave him to us, of course, and he cried half the way home. When he finally stopped, I looked down at this sad little boy in my arms and saw what a beautiful child he was. Oh, he had the sweetest smile. Terry is truly gentle, and I could tell that then. I guess that's the moment I really became his mother."

During those next years, as more children were added to the family, John's mother always managed to visit at least once every twelve months. At first she seemed a bit puzzled by what Ann and John were trying to do. Mrs. Sweeney was a gracious lady, used to a well-maintained home with servants to do the necessary. But here the constant bustle of kids running in and out, the laughter, the frequent tears, the crunch of toys underfoot, the thousand and one things that had to be done every single day, almost overwhelmed her. Yet as she began to understand how committed Ann and John were to raising this huge, fascinating family, she finally became the very model of an adoring grandmother. She knit beautiful sweaters in small sizes. She sent generous checks at Christmas because, as she said to Ann, "You will know what to get the children better than I" — and Ann made sure grandmother's name was on every present.

When first Minh, then Maria, then Chuong, Dat, and Hope joined the family only two years after Terry, the Sweeneys grew almost overnight from a comfortable brass band into a full-scale symphony orchestra. Ann often felt, in those days, that she'd have done better to study conducting rather than cello and piano. "In the conductor's score," as she says, "there's a line for each instrument, and a good conductor has to be able to read all the instruments at once. If you've got someone who's badly out of tune or off the beat over there, you've got to do something about it right away."

"Well, that summer in 1977, when we were afraid the Vietnamese kids were going to be taken away from us just as they'd all begun to thrive, it seemed to me our whole orchestra was falling apart. I felt, as a mother, I was trying to conduct a terribly difficult score that was just beyond me. There was so much discord, especially in Chuong's corner, I just didn't know from day to day how I was going to get through the piece we were trying to play."

TWELVE

❧ ❦

The Meaning of Marcus

IN SPITE OF EVERYTHING, the world kept right on turning. One summer day followed another until at last, on a hazy August Saturday, the family gathered to help Marcus Sweeney celebrate his seventh birthday. Maria and John Sweeney, whose birthdays were close by, also chose to celebrate their anniversaries along with Marcus. Randy and Vicki, Lynn and Gary, and Chris, too, came home for the big party out on the stone terrace. Marcus, being the youngest and therefore the least able to wait, was invited to dive into his presents first.

Ann watched the little boy with curly red hair tearing off the bright wrappings the way little boys always do, and suddenly felt a chord of peaceful resolution rising inside her. The chaotic music of recent days was, for this moment, stilled. Surrounded by family love and joy, she could not help but realize that in spite of many difficulties she was indeed a fortunate woman. She also couldn't help but remember the occasion years before when she'd burst into tears of disbelief at the gift of yellow booties on her own birthday. She hadn't allowed herself to hope that she would ever get the adopted baby she longed for — and yet here he was! Marcus, the realest, liveliest little boy who ever forgot a lunchbox or brought home a frog. She loved every freckle, every funny, appealing thing about him. "Marcus moves as if he'd been put together by a committee," she said once to John. "I don't think he can go through a room without bumping into something, but I wouldn't change a single thing about him."

Marcus had saved her life. He'd taught her to trust again. And now somehow she saw more clearly that this was what she had to do for Chuong. She'd been sorry for herself, wondering how long she could stand the uncertainty and tension of not knowing where they stood with regard to the custody cases. *How much worse it must be for Chuong!* She would simply have to hang in, be strong. If he saw that she and John were determined to keep them, that they were willing to take the bumps and the upsets in stride, perhaps he would become more calm in himself. Yes, she had to help him trust that there was a future out there for him and Dat and Hope — a good one, too. It wasn't going to be easy. . . .

Fate, as it sometimes does, took a helping hand in the Sweeney affairs that fall. One Saturday evening Ann and John decided to go out for dinner. The kids were finally back in school and the parents felt they had something special to celebrate. Paddy, Timmy, Dat, Faith, and Terry had all just crossed an important threshold. They'd graduated from John Fisher's Universal Learning Center and gone off on the school bus to kindergarten. "It's not the same as getting them into Yale, maybe," Ann said over her cocktail, "but we're gaining on the situation."

"I'm glad they took Terry," said John, who had written a letter to the principal explaining how important it was Terry not be left behind while four close brothers and a sister went off to the big school without him. Technically the little boy was eight days too young to start. Schools almost never bend the birthdate rule, but in this case they must have felt Terry's isolation would be cruel and unusual.

"Oh, listen, I forgot to tell you —" said Ann suddenly. "When I got home from the grocery this noon, there was this big chocolate cake on the front porch, with a note from the lady across the street. It said, 'Anybody with five children in kindergarten needs a cake.' And I've never even met her! Wasn't that sweet?"

"People in this town are so good," John agreed. "They really seem to understand what we're trying to do." They took their time over dinner; Ann even allowed herself to have her favorite chocolate mousse for dessert, then, after lingering over coffee, they looked at each other, smiled, and knew it was time to go home and pick up the reins again.

The baby-sitter met them at the door. "Dat hurt his leg," she told them. "He says it's broken but I don't see how it could be. All he did was jump from a low bed to the floor. Then he began to cry and say he couldn't get up. I'm afraid he's still upset, and he didn't want to go to bed until you came home —"

Ann ran upstairs. Dat was curled on the couch in the second-floor hall, and he immediately began to cry when he saw her. "Mom — my leg broken!"

"Oh, honey, I'm sorry you got hurt. Let me see —" There was nothing visibly wrong with the thin little leg. Perhaps he just needed some extra attention. She and John had gone out very seldom since these new three had arrived the year before.

"I'v got an idea — we'll put you in Mamma and Papa's bed for tonight. Then if you need comforting, I'll be right there." It was not unusual for Ann and John to end up with five or six little kids trying to outsnuggle each other in between them in their big bed. Dat readily agreed. She carried him herself. The tiny boy with the round gold face looked very small against the huge white pillows. Soon he was asleep.

But in the morning, when she tried to convince Dat his leg was probably all right, he cried some more. When she stood him up, he fell down immediately. They went to see Dr. Hecklau. Dat, as it turned out, had a hairline fracture. He must stay off that leg for four weeks!

Bad news sometimes has its uses. The simple, everyday

problem of coping with Dat's broken leg somehow lessened the tension that had developed between Chuong and the rest of the family. Everyone rallied around to amuse and comfort Dat. Ann tried all up and down the eastern seaboard to find crutches small enough for him. Finally she located a company in Delaware that would hand-make crutches the right size — in two weeks — for a large sum of money. Instead, she found a small wagon, and on nice days the kids took turns pulling Dat around the yard, up and down the driveway. The school protested on the first day when Ann took Dat, with his wagon, back to kindergarten. She had to sign a release absolving officialdom from any responsibility for further injury. Actually, Dat and his classmates were delighted by the whole situation. Every day the teacher assigned two children to be Dat's "helpers" and pull him around the classroom. The chosen two enjoyed the privilege; Dat enjoyed the ride.

The mystery of why a small jump should have resulted in a broken leg was never entirely solved. The condition of Dat's teeth certainly indicated severe malnutrition somewhere along the line. (The following year he broke his collarbone in gym. The teacher was having the children jump over a basketball. Dat, very small, didn't make it, and fell. It was a surprising break from an insignificant fall.) Ann made sure the lawyer fighting the custody case in behalf of the Sweeneys knew about Dat's unusual frailty. The lawyer wanted all the ammunition he could get in the approaching fight. He'd spent quite a bit of time researching the laws and interviewing the Vietnamese who were trying to get the three children back.

"They say it's because they want to do their duty by the children," he told the Sweeneys. "I think the second cousin may feel he could be criticized by the family. But I don't have any confidence that they would take better care of them if they *did* go back. They are having a hard time making ends meet, and there are many, many people in the house.

The situation remained frightening. Ann was glad Chuong, who had entered junior high that September, was still doing his usual good work in school. However he behaved at home, the boy knew how to shape up well in the outside world. Then one day Ann heard the crash of something heavy and harsh yells while she was teaching behind the closed library doors. More cries. She excused herself, ran out to the hall.

Chuong, coming in from the school bus, was giving way to rage while Jay and the little kids watched dumbfounded. He had slammed his notebook and schoolbooks down so hard they'd scattered all over the polished floor. "They can keep their school! I never go back!" he yelled hoarsely.

"Chuong! What happened? Tell me!"

But Chuong was too worked up to stop for conversation. He ran past Ann with blazing eyes and disappeared up the stairs.

She left him alone to work it out. Perhaps he would tell her what had happened when he cooled off. Following him and cornering him in his room would only fuel the fire. There were more pupils coming up until suppertime anyway. Ann went back to her piano.

Nothing was said that evening, and she thought maybe Chuong's small storm had passed. If he'd forgotten about it, so could she. But the next morning he didn't get up for breakfast. "Megan — go get Chuong, will you?" Ann was busy pouring milk in cereal bowls. "He's going to miss the bus —"

Megan sighed, got up, went off. She came back in a minute. "He says he's not going to school." She shrugged.

When she had all the kids started and lunchboxes packed, Ann ran up the stairs. "Chuong?" She knocked softly on his door. This was not the time to come on strong. "You're not sick?" She opened the door slowly.

"No." He wasn't huddled, he was dressed, sitting up rather defiant, on top of the covers. He stared straight ahead.

"Will you tell me what's wrong? What happened at school? Maybe I can help —"

"No — nobody can help."

"I could try —"

"*No!* It's a rule they have. A rule for everybody —"

"What rule?"

Chuong was silent for a long minute. "You don't take a shower, you don't play basketball. You don't get to use the gym. You *flunk*, that's what. Okay —" he shrugged — so *I* say no shower. No school."

So that was it. Ann tried to remember what she knew about the bathing habits of the Orient, and gave up. Whatever they might have been, they had to be a far cry from the American locker room. "What we have here is a simple collision of cultures," she thought, but simple or not, it was hardly going to be easy to get either the school or Chuong to back down from a position once taken. "The school has *got* to give," she said to herself. The pressures on Chuong were too big right now, and gym was too important to him to dismiss.

"Chuong," she said, "I'll make a deal with you. You go to school — and I'll try to fix it with the principal. I'll talk to her today. Don't worry. Just go on to gym. Forget the shower problem. Okay?"

He wanted to go; she could see that, and was encouraged. "What if they say no?"

"Then I'll take you home with me. I promise. But they won't." She'd gone out on a limb. But she had to get him moving. School gave his life structure. He needed that now, with chaos threatening to take over his world again. It was one place he'd never fallen apart —till now.

He thought it over. "Deal," he said shortly. "Okay, Mom."

Ann would bless the woman who was principal of Chuong's school for the rest of her days. A woman of understanding, who put children's needs ahead of the set procedures, she saw the point immediately. "— I'm sure he'll join the others soon enough," said Ann. "It's just that right now he's so upset about everything else, that he's not very cooperative when he doesn't want to do something. I *don't* want him dropping out of school."

"Neither do I," said the principal, standing up. "Don't worry, Mrs. Sweeney. I'll take care of it."

The junior high held an open house for parents shortly after that. When Ann and John had eaten the customary cookie and drunk the customary paper cup of punch, Ann decided to run a little interference for her son Chuong. "Be right back," she said to John, who was talking to a music instructor. Around the gym she went, a seasoned veteran of the old game parents and teachers must play together: Cooperation. She spoke to every one of Chuong's teachers, explained the situation briefly, assured the teacher that she, Ann, was very interested in having her child do well in the classroom, and then she said, "— But right now, I'd really appreciate it if you don't lean on him. He's having a hard time — we're having a hard time, but I know he'll be fine if we can just get this custody business settled." They saw it her way. They were so glad she'd talked to them. "If only more parents would take the time to tell us what's going on," said one. *Amen,* thought Ann exhausted but satisfied with her night's effort.

The legal battle was not going well. Because the Vietnamese trying to regain custody had a slight family tie — there *was* that second cousin — the Sweeneys' lawyer was afraid the opposition might have a strong case. "The courts always hesitate when there's a family tie," he explained.

"Dear God, it's not much of a tie!" Ann protested. "Those kids were at the tail end of the line when it came to passing out things in that house. They didn't even have beds! We can't let this happen —"

"We'll do everything possible," the lawyer sighed. "Our best hope is to see if we can't get them to drop the suit. I'm working on it."

While both parents continued to worry about losing Chuong, Dat, and Hope, unbeknownst to anyone, another member of the family was making plans to leave. So it was that Ann, glancing out the library window after giving a lesson one afternoon, saw a strange station wagon pulling into the driveway. Moments later Minh appeared, carrying two suitcases. Ann ran outside. "Minh! Where are you going? What's wrong?"

Minh said not a word, turned around, went back in the house and up the stairs. Ann followed, begging for an explanation. The girl had emptied her closet and dresser drawers. Now she gathered up her few remaining possessions and pushed past her mother. The two of them ran back down the stairs, Minh leading the way, Ann, in tears, still trying to find out why she was doing this. As soon as she reached the car, Minh jumped in quickly and slammed the door. The girl at the wheel, about Minh's age, swung the car around hard.

"But wait —" cried Ann.

"She's leaving!" the girl shouted. The car disappeared up the drive and took off fast down Old Mill Road.

There was nothing to be done. Minh was not a child runaway. She was eighteen, at an age when many young people decide to go off on their own. That she'd chosen to go without one word of discussion, without even saying good-bye, made Ann terribly sad. She could not say that she was entirely surprised, however. During the past year battles between parents and daughter had been on the increase. Most of them had to do with the way she treated the smaller children. Her "discipline" was harsh and often administered with little cause. Then if Ann questioned her methods, especially hitting the little kids, Minh would go her own way, sometimes not speaking for days. Actually she'd been trying to live in the midst of this busy, active family as if she were on her own. Now at last she would be.

That night Ann and John talked it all over. "The trouble

was," said Ann sadly, "that she just wasn't comfortable being a daughter. She'd never had a chance to know what it's like. She didn't even have a childhood, really. I feel I've failed with Minh. She was always in an unhappy situation, and I'm afraid she still is."

"Maybe." John nodded. He, too, felt a deep sadness that Minh had left. They had been able to enjoy small jokes together. He remembered telling her that one of the family cats spoke Vietnamese. Minh had always talked to that cat in her own language, enjoying its company after that. John realized how lonely she was but also how strong. Now he said, "I think she may be really happier once she's in charge of her own affairs. And so this move may not be as unfortunate as it seems to us right now —"

"What do you mean?"

"We were trying to give Minh things she didn't really want. I think she's going to find her own way and be all right."

"Oh, she's a survivor," said Ann. "Of that I'm sure."

"She might not have been if she stayed in Vietnam. She got herself here at the age of fifteen. She was just sitting there in Pennsylvania at the Indiantown Gap Reservation, waiting for a sponsor when we heard about her. We filled her need. We got her out of there. She couldn't spend the rest of her life in those army barracks —"

"But I wanted to do so much more —" Ann mourned.

"You always do," said John kindly.

"She never believed me, when I said, 'Same-same.' Remember? I'd put my arm around her and the other arm around Megan and say 'You are *both* my daughters — 'Same-same.'"

John shook his head. "She was almost a grown-up when she arrived. She could never be 'same-same,' really. I think we helped her. And you know, I'm sure she'll come back if she needs our help again."

Ann couldn't see that far ahead. In the midst of defeat her vision was apt to mist with tears for a while before she picked herself up off the floor to start swinging again.

Not too much time passed before Minh returned to get a few things she'd forgotten. The Sweeneys learned that she had decided to live with friends, she was working in a local restaurant at night, and still attending high school by day. Her attitude was not hostile, but it said clearly, "I am my own person now." Ann and John had no wish to interfere, and they were greatly relieved to find that indeed her life seemed to be taking sensible shape.

Indirectly there was to be a benefit from Minh's departure from the family. As long as she'd been around, she naturally tried to talk Vietnamese to Chuong every day. But Chuong himself chose to speak English in his daily life. He was looking ahead. She was nostalgic for the conversation and customs of her past. Sometimes she'd gone out of her way to try to please him with unusual Vietnamese dishes cooked just for him. Then there were other times when she could get angry with him, as if he were being unfaithful to his heritage by not preferring her company to the company of all these Americans. But if there was one thing Chuong didn't need at this time, it was to be pulled back and forth emotionally.

In his own heart there was confusion and fear. If he did, indeed, have to return to the house where he'd lived before, he didn't want to be accused of disloyalty to people of his own land. He dared not burn his bridges while the threat of being sent back hung over him. It could only mean that things would then be even worse for him and Dat and Hope. As ever, Chuong was a practical young man. And the truth was he was at last on the verge of feeling at home with his new American family and his new life. The past months had showed him clearly that Ann and John cared for him. He would not forget Ann's concern during his illness or the father's words, "We'll get a good lawyer," when the news came that there would be a custody fight. Then most recently there had been the surprise of Ann's willingness to help him have his own way in the argument with the gym teacher. Everything had been fine ever since. Chuong loved to win, whether in a dispute or a game. School was really fun now. He was very fast in math, too, and it made him feel strong to excel. He could see a good life ahead, he could see other kids he would like to be friends with, things he would like to do, if only. . . .

Unfortunately Thanksgiving came and went with the "if only" still clouding the holiday. The cloud lingered into December. On a Saturday before Christmas, while Chuong, Jay, and some of the other kids were waiting for John to give them rides, the phone rang suddenly. It was the lawyer for John. "I'm afraid I have bad news," he said. "I have to tell you I haven't been able to persuade these people to drop the case. The court date is set. They are going to bring you in —"

When John hung up the phone at last, Ann took one look at his face, and she knew. "They won't give up. We have to go to court." He nodded. She sank in a chair and buried her face. Watching her, Chuong felt his own heart sink back to an old wretchedness. It was a feeling he knew only too well. It said, "Don't hope, don't look forward, don't trust that life is ever going to get any better."

"I'm sorry," John said helplessly to everyone who stood there, the little children, sober-faced, not quite understanding why their mother was crying, the others upset because the family was losing — or might lose — some kind of important fight. "Well, now." John made an effort to pick up the pieces. "Paddy and Timmy and Terry and Dat all want to go to the museum, right? And Jay and Chuong were going to the football field?"

Jay put out a fist and punched Chuong lightly on the arm. "Let's go, man —"

Chuong brushed him aside. "*You* go — go wherever you want. I'm not going with anybody!" He opened the heavy front door and ran off down the driveway into the dark, gray winter afternoon.

It was family custom to eat dinner together once a week on Saturday night in the big, formal dining room. Chuong, as eldest son, always sat at the far end of the table opposite John at the head. That night they had finally begun their meal without him. But the normally noisy little kids, as well as the parents and older children, all seemed painfully conscious of the empty chair at Chuong's place. They were halfway through their pork chops and browned potatoes when there was the sound of the front door opening in the dark entrance hall. Chuong came in, slid into his place without a word, and began to eat. When he had finished, he looked questioningly at John presiding over the platter. "Have a second helping, Chuong?" said John.

The boy nodded and passed his plate. The threat of possibly having to go hungry again had made him ravenous. Now Chuong ate slowly, gratefully, again until his plate was empty. When he stood up to help take plates to the kitchen, he looked at Ann and said gruffly, "Good dinner, Mom."

John Sweeney pondered the impasse facing the family throughout the rest of that weekend. It was true their pediatrician and also the psychiatrist had agreed to testify if the case came to court. But the whole idea of a court battle, with the resultant wear and tear on Ann and the rest of the family, was repugnant. Even if they won, they were going to lose plenty of sleep and serenity during the next few months. In a family as big as theirs, with so many needs to be taken care of, the cost in emotional damage was going to be high. Not to mention legal costs! After a troubled Sunday, John woke up Monday morning with a sudden hunch. He talked it over with Ann at breakfast. But she was feeling too down to be very hopeful. "Go ahead," she shrugged, "if you think it might help."

John then decided he'd better consult the lawyer who would be presenting their case. The lawyer's reaction was, "Well, it can't hurt. Go ahead. Let me know what happens —"

Given the green light, John hung up and immediately placed

another call to the priest of the parish church in the city where Chuong, Dat, and Hope once lived. It was this man who had been instrumental in calling attention to the children's needs in the first place. Without his original concern, Chuong, Dat, and Hope might never have left that rundown, overcrowded house. Did he know what was going on right now? John asked him.

No, as a matter of fact, he did *not*, said the priest. He seemed very distressed to learn of the problem when John explained it.

Encouraged, John then said, "I'd like to come up and talk to you about this."

"I wish you would," said the good father. "Maybe there's something I can do —"

John told him the whole story. How they had been able to turn sad, lifeless Hope into a laughing, dancing, very talkative little girl. How they had repaired Dat's teeth and cared for his broken leg, how he loved his new family and new life in kindergarten. Above all, how much progress Chuong had made since the day he arrived, a disturbed and angry boy, suspicious of everything, still tormented by night terrors of war. "We are terribly afraid all these good things are going to be lost. Father, it would be a sin if these children have to go back," said John. "It's not only that we love them and want to keep them. We are truly worried about what may happen —"

"You are right to worry," said the priest slowly. He had listened closely to every word. Now he looked deeply concerned. "I can promise you nothing, of course. But I will do everything I can for these children."

No one will ever know exactly what took place when the priest called on the Vietnamese group that was to trying to regain custody of the children. They were members, or at least some of them were members, of his parish. He was one of the most influential men in their community. With his help they had furnished their house. More than once he had come to their aid in various emergencies. And it was his church that had made possible Christmas gifts for the many children of the household, as well as holiday treats for the meager table. There is little doubt that regarding the attempt to have Chuong, Dat, and Hope returned, the priest must have said in the strongest possible terms, "You must *not* do this thing."

On December 21 the lawyer called the Sweeney home. He told Ann the wonderful news that the case had been dropped. He told her that while he didn't know all the details, the priest must have been very persuasive in whatever arguments he used to effect this turnaround. He concluded by saying, "— and now have a Merry Christmas!"

"Oh, *thank* you! And Merry Christmas to you, too!" cried Ann.

The Sweeneys remember the Christmas of 1977 as one of the merriest ever. Their New Year was made a bit happier, too, when they received a bill for the lawyer's long months of work, a bill which should have been $3,000 but which had been cut in half because, as the lawyer said in his accompanying note, "I was a foster child myself, you know." This good man's action was one more proof for Ann and John of the importance of what they were doing, caring for the children who had come into their lives, and fighting for them when necessary. "You know," Ann said to John, "the words *foster child* sound a bit sad somehow. But they shouldn't —"

"Indeed they shouldn't," John agreed. "To foster is to nurture in the best sense of the word. I wonder if the dictionary puts it that way —" John was a man who cared about the words of five languages. Not infrequently in his work he had been called upon to translate the libretto of an opera. Always he had been aware that words could lose subtle meaning in translation. Now he reached for the big dictionary. " 'Foster,' " he read. " 'To feed, rear, cherish, sustain, promote.' The antonym is 'to deaden, kill, discourage.' "

With the custody fight finally settled, Chuong, for the first time, moved into his future. He joined the soccer team. He went beyond just tossing the ball around and went out seriously for baseball and basketball. He became very interested in piano lessons, and soon after that, he began to study on the drums. His schoolwork had always been good, but now he began to enjoy the social life that went with it. Where he had had casual acquaintances who changed from day to day, now he had friends. Of course there were days now and then when something would set him off-course. There would be a temporary return to the old days of flight and fury. His parents would have moments of despair, wondering if all was lost. But actually what they were all living through together was the gradual disappearance of severe trauma. No one could have experienced all the terrible upheaval of Chuong's young life, and suddenly become a whole, stable person overnight.

The good difference was that more and more the occasional storms resembled the normal storms of any boy on the brink of adolescence and his concerned mother and father. No longer did Chuong have to live looking over his shoulder for fear each day would bring some major unsettling change. His eyes lost their wary look. His sense of humor bloomed. He was even able to stand aside and lighten trouble when it erupted instead of jumping into the fray. A furious fight broke out one day among the smaller boys while Ann, who was hoping everyone would be on his best behavior, was being interviewed by a local news writer for a Mother's Day story. Chuong smiled right at the writer. "Just one great big lousy family, eh, Mrs. Baran?" The tension broke. Everyone laughed.

Ann enjoyed relating the story to John later. "I was so embarrassed — but he got me off the hook."

John listened with deep satisfaction. "Chuong is really on his way," he said.

THREE

1980

THIRTEEN

New Little Boys—March 1, 1980

SIX-YEAR-OLD MICHAEL SWEENEY threw first his pill, then a glass of orange juice, across the kitchen, missing his mother, Ann, by a matter of inches. The pill, an antibiotic prescribed by his pediatrician for an ear infection, disappeared forever. The orange juice splashed against the refrigerator door, dripped down, mingling with crumbs from the children's breakfast to make a lumpy puddle under the kitchen table.

Twenty minutes later the front door slammed as the last Sweeney child went running up the driveway hill to catch the school bus. Hearing the welcome thud of the heavy door, Ann poured herself a second cup of coffee and sank back on a plastic kitchen chair to survey the wreckage. At least the orange juice glass, which was plastic like everything else in the cupboard, had not shattered. But she had been too busy passing out school lunches and retrieving mittens or hats from their usual hiding places to mete out appropriate justice to Michael. What the hell *was* "appropriate justice" for throwing orange juice? she wondered. Well, whatever, the mess was now hers to clean up. And mess it was in more ways than one.

This year could have been a snap, Ann reflected. No more

nursery school car-pooling. This fall for the first time every Sweeney child had climbed on one of the big yellow school buses making the run up Old Mill Road. Tiny Hope was a kindergartener. Megan and Chuong had moved on to junior high. The remaining kids, including Maria, were all in the same elementary school. She could have enjoyed blissful hours of peace and relative quiet in which to count her many blessings. Instead, once again she and John had been smitten with the lure of adoption. Their last chance — John was fifty-two, she was almost forty-nine. What compounded the attraction was the fact that it was also, very likely, the last chance of rescue for two small black brothers, Carey and Michael. They'd been seven and five at the time. Their father was unknown. Their mother had given them up soon after Michael's birth.

It is a sad axiom in the world of adoption that black male children, once past the toddler stage, become increasingly hard to place with every passing year. For most, the alternative is foster care. Carey and Michael had already been fostered. Whether they had been well cared for was another matter. Ann would later hear tales from both boys about being beaten with a hot belt buckle. "The mother, she held it over the stove," Carey told her. There was a burn scar on small Michael's back. But at the time they first heard about the children, all the Sweeneys knew was that the jungle of New York had spawned them. That same jungle could almost surely be counted upon to let them grow up into city savages if something wasn't done — and done fast.

Ann and John had never seen Carey and Michael except from a distance when they started adoption proceedings. The New York agency's policy was to forbid any meeting in the early stages. The Sweeneys had been taken to a crowded city playground for a look. They'd stared through iron bars at two small boys indistinguishable from others in the pack. "Do you want them?" the official had asked.

The question, put that way, infuriated Ann. They might have been staring at animals in a zoo or convicts in a small jail. "We want two children," she said firmly.

"And we'll take these two —" said John. The idea, as so often in the past, had originated with him. Ann had been swept along by his enthusiasm. Both parents had been full of happy energy in the fall of 1979. Their three Vietnamese children were turning out to be wonderfully solid citizens. The rest of the crew, with the possible exception of Maria, was coming along in fine style.

Maria's problem was that maturity had hit her like a tidal wave at age ten. She had arrived in the family a tiny, appealing child of nine. Within one short year, she'd become a full-bosomed young woman. It would have been an enormous jump for any girl, but for a blind child in a new land, who had not yet completed her adjustment to a seeing world, it was an almost impossible leap. Maria was affectionate and outgoing, and loved the social life of her big family. But almost immediately she'd become locked into adolescent combat with her mother.

It was John's thoughtful opinion that the key to Maria had not been found. It was Ann's that she had, in fact, given Maria a whole handful of keys but she had yet to pick them up. Her Braille teacher and school teachers did not know what to make of the child. She was so competent in some things, so uninterested in others. Was her rebellion now simply the difficult but normal one of a thirteen-year-old? Ann was genuinely puzzled as to how to help Maria get on with the important business of growing up. The girl was far from dumb. Friends who visited the family over the years were always astonished at her memory. "Do you still have your little dog, Diego?" Maria would inquire solicitously after a visiting pet she'd met three years earlier. She could repeat whole conversations almost word for word from dinner-party talk of an occasion long forgotten by everyone else. Another thing: Maria was remarkably brave when it came to taking physical risks. For her last August birthday she had begged for roller skates. "Mom — all the kids are getting them. Please?"

Ann would never forget the terrifying, glorious sight of Maria flying down the driveway on her new skates. She made it the first time all the way down without falling until she knew she was safely in the backyard. Then she let herself tumble over on the grass, laughing with delight at what she'd done. There had to be lots of good stuff in a child who could do that. True, it was the same well-worn path she'd often traveled on her Big Wheel. But it was also the path where she'd struck her head on the steel fire escape sticking out of the truck. "I've got to help Maria use her courage," Ann thought. "She's also a very physical child. She may not like Braille and books, but she likes people and she adores animals." Suddenly it hit her. "Camp! I'll send her to a camp for blind children next summer. Maybe she can learn how to paddle a canoe, do all sorts of things." There had to be a good camp. "I'll find out about it, then I'll start saving my piano money so she can go. Besides, it's time she met other blind kids."

Once the decision had been made to send Maria to camp, Ann found that her daily worry about the child was not so intense. This freed her to move on and embrace the idea of adopting two more little boys.

There had been joy and excitement in preparing for them. Marcus, who'd always hated having to sleep alone while the four smaller boys bunked together, was thrilled when a new dresser and new bunk beds were installed for Carey and Michael up in his third-floor room. "Mom! Pop! When are they coming? Tomorrow?" As always, Marcus was impatient.

The process of adoption turned out to be the most tedious in all the Sweeneys' experience. There had been a hundred and one delays, legal complications, and several complete breakdowns in negotiations. But at last came the day in November when the family was able to drive into New York

The Sweeney family — September, 1979

Carey

Michael

to pick up its newest members. Ann would not soon forget how they looked. The boys were brought into the agency's meeting room wearing enormous navy blue hooded jackets, which, as she later remarked to John, "were clearly intended to see them through high school." Michael was just a dim yellowish spot way back in his hood, while Carey's blue-black face disappeared entirely except for an occasional slash of white teeth whenever he said something. That child should *never* be dressed in navy blue, she decided, her mother instinct going to work immediately to help her new child put his best foot — or face — forward. But while past experience had prepared her to do many important things for Carey and Michael, Ann had still, after four long months, not yet experienced what she called the moment of motherhood. These kids were now hers and John's. But she still had no idea who they were.

There were times when she felt overwhelmed, discouraged. This morning, staring at the puddle of orange juice on her kitchen floor, was certainly one of them. Then there was the night recently when Michael hurled a cat over the stair railing three floors down into the front hall, narrowly missing Maria, who was on her way from the kitchen to the library. The cat, a nine-year-old named Papa's Cat, or "Scat" for short, emitted an enormous yowl but otherwise seemed none the worse for his flying trip. Both Carey and Michael seemed to have almost no inhibitions when it came to throwing, hitting, or scratching. Perhaps the most frightening moment in the months since they'd joined the family occurred the day Carey snatched a Coke bottle during an argument, smashed the bottom off, and went after one of the twins brandishing the jagged neck. Ann grabbed him just in time.

"Do you know, I think whoever was supposed to have been caring for Carey and Michael just let them run absolutely wild," Ann had said then to John. "They haven't the faintest idea of right or wrong, good or bad. 'Bad' is just what happens to you when some grownup catches you and you get smacked —"

"The sad thing is," said John, "that while people were always hitting them for being bad, nobody ever took the trouble to teach them how to do better."

"What really grinds me," said Ann, "is the way the agency took its sweet time deciding *we* were desirable as parents." Among other things, the Sweeneys had learned that one of the hitches had been the fact that they were not black. They had no idea whether Carey and Michael's early foster parents had been black or white, but they had hardly done a great job.

"There were all these social workers worrying about whether Carey and Michael might lose their black identity," Ann went on. "Meanwhile those kids were losing their ability to live in *any* world — black or white." She gave a huge groan. When Ann's feelings sank, they sank all the way.

"Well," said John, tugging her gently back to the present problem, "let's not forget that they've got a chance now. The returns aren't in on these two. Remember how depressed you used to get about Chuong?"

She'd nodded forlornly, not really hearing him.

But now the message was getting to her in the messy kitchen two days later. Chuong! How strong and competent he was these days. And how proud she was to see him making his way successfully in the world of young teenagers. Yet there had been long months when she thought she'd never win his trust. Indeed, it had taken almost a year and a half before he gave up hitting other kids, withdrawing, or lashing out violently whenever he didn't get his way immediately. There were terrible similarities in the traumas suffered by children exposed to war in Vietnam and war in an American city's ghetto. But at least Chuong had known good family life and had some years of being well loved. While these two! They might just as well have grown up between cracks of broken

pavement in the South Bronx. She would have to be more patient, have to accept the fact that their turnaround was going
to take a long, long time. Lots of tough, hard work. She could
do it. She had always gotten up off the floor when the battle
demanded it. "Dear God," she prayed, "just help me to believe that one day Carey and Michael may have some of
Chuong's control and self-confidence and charm." Having
enlisted the Deity's support, Ann rose from her chair, reached
for a mop and prepared to attack her kitchen floor.

The phone rang.

Sighing, Ann leaned mop against the sink and went into
the sun porch to answer it.

"Sam Browning!" she cried, hearing a familiar voice.
"Where are you? Is Kate with you?"

"She's here. We're in New York for conferences, a little
fun. We'll be here at the Waldorf till Saturday. Then we're
driving to Boston for more of same. We'd like to take you and
John to dinner Saturday night on our way —"

"Oh, Sam — let me look." Ann ran to the calendar, which
told her what she expected. Saturday had a big red circle
around it. Dat's birthday, and a family party that night. "Oh
dear, wouldn't you know — it's Dat's birthday," she explained
to Sam. "We always celebrate on Saturdays so the bigger
kids can come when they get off work. But listen, it'll be
a hundred years before you get up here again. Come have a
drink with us — and join the party. It won't be fancy. But I
know John'll be dying to see you —"

"Oh, now, Ann — we don't want to add to your problems —"

"Listen, you couldn't, Sam. We've got two new little boys
who could keep a whole police force busy. But come ahead,
if you're game. You and Kate are family. I mean it. Please
come; it'll be so good to see you."

"Well — we feel the same way. All right, Ann. Wonderful!
We'll be there —"

Jesus, what have I done? thought Ann when she hung up.

The Brownings were two of their oldest, dearest friends from Michigan days. Kate was a head buyer for a big Detroit department store, who'd never wanted any kids. Elegant Kate, Ann could just see her coming in in a flawless suede suit and some Sweeney child rushing up to touch her skirt with sticky fingers. Oh damn, why did it have to be *this* weekend? Sam was one of their favorite people, though, and she and John really loved them. But at least I should have warned them to wear earplugs and shinguards. . . .

FOURTEEN

Stormy Weather

ANN WANTED DAT's birthday to be specially wonderful this year. Little Polka-Dot was a good man, and he'd been having rather a hard time lately. The addition of new figures into the family equation could be counted upon to provide excitement and high spirits, at first. It was later that worries about who might be the new underdog began to surface. She remembered a recent night when Carey had bitten Paddy on the arm. Paddy had the tooth marks to prove he had been wronged. But it was Dat all that evening who seemed to be the most insecure. And for Dat that was unusual.

Ann would have been teaching and missed the drift of it all if her last two pupils hadn't cancelled because it was snowing so hard. As it was, she relieved Alice, the babysitter of the day, from her post stirring the pot of spaghetti. "Here — I'll do that, Alice. I don't want you to get snowed in. Our driveway gets slippery and I know you have to get home." Alice had thanked her and disappeared, and Ann continued to stir. "Megan?" she called. "I'll want you to set the table in another few minutes."

"Okay, Mom." Megan was sitting on the stair landing helping Timmy with his reading. His teacher had thought he could use a little help. Megan was a good tutor and she could always use the money.

Things were peaceful enough at that moment. Little boys were sprawled all over the sun room floor, immobilized by t.v. Over their heads on the picnic table nearby, Chuong was making a kite from a bright-colored newspaper flyer of ads. Every so often he'd dash into the kitchen and grab a few strands of spaghetti for glue, just as he'd once stolen a bit of rice from the family pot in Vietnam long ago. But Chuong's thoughts were firmly anchored in the here-and-now as he talked away at Jay, who was half doing his homework, half listening. "Hey man, look at *this*," said Chuong. "They got soccer balls on sale for seven ninety-nine! This weekend only, it says —"

"Yeah? They can't be much good," countered Jay, who was trying to have character enough to save up for a good bicycle.

Chuong's needs were constant, however, and he went on reading as he cut and glued. "How 'bout this — pocket radios, only twelve ninety-nine! See me coming down the street?" He grabbed one of Jay's books and held it to his ear, practicing the teenage saunter.

Jay couldn't help laughing. "Hey, Chuong — cut it out."

"Boys! The show's over. Dinner's almost ready. *Megan?* The table —" Ann was ladling spaghetti onto plates, while sauce simmered in the huge dented pot.

"Okay, Mom."

In another moment thirteen places were set and Ann began to carry steaming plates into the sun room. As if by magic Hope and Faith appeared and quickly slipped into places at one end. This roused the little boys. Terry, who was closest, took the place at the other end. Dat had his eye on the spot opposite his brother and bunkmate, Terry, but Michael managed to slip in ahead of him. Immediately he began to eat. "Michael! That was my place!" yelled Dat.

"Here," said Ann putting a plate down next to Terry. "This is for you — sit here, Dat."

"I want to sit *there*. Michael's eating my dinner!" wailed Dat.

"Dat," said Ann firmly, "they're all the same."

"NO, THEY'RE NOT!" screamed Dat. For a tiny boy he could make the most enormous noise. Now his round face turned bright red and tears began leaping from his eyes.

"Eat your dinner, Dat — right here." She lifted him up, slipped him in next to Terry. But the minute she turned away to serve the others, Dat climbed down, threw himself on the floor, and began to sob. Dat hadn't had had one of his famous "lie-ins" to protest the injustice of society in quite a while, thought Ann. There was nothing to be done but to let it spin itself out. "He's feeling crowded so I won't crowd him at the same time." Half an hour later, when all the other kids had finished, Dat was still lying there moaning. She picked him up then, sat down, and began to rock him. His spaghetti was cold, but never mind. "Would you like to go swimming before bedtime, Polka Dot?" she said affectionately, kissing him above the ear. "Then you can have some cereal after you put your pajamas on?"

Before-bedtime cereal and milk had become a ritual a few years back when Ann was trying to get extra meat on the twins' small bones. It was also a comforting solution for little kids whose temper tantrums occasionally drove them from the dinner table. Ann didn't like her children to go hungry. There had to be other ways of handling uproar. A proud man, Dat was able to nod yes, now that his small Oriental face had been saved. "Well, then — go get ready. I'll call the others."

Dat wriggled out of Ann's arms and dashed upstairs to put on his bathing suit. "Thank God for the swimming pool," thought Ann. All year long it cooled off little hotheads, soothed injured spirits, and gave restless limbs a place to flail and splash without lashing out in blows. She poured herself a glass of wine to take down with her. Soon the flock was trooping down the back stairs and through the basement. At the first sight of green water there were screams of joy. Everyone jumped in quickly — everyone but Carey. He stood against the wall. It had become a pattern. Ann wondered what had happened to make him afraid. She tied a life bubble on him quietly. "This will keep you up if you want to get in, Carey" was all she said.

His younger brother, Michael, was giving a good imitation of swimming at the shallow end of the pool. "Hey, Carey!" yelled Marcus. "C'mon in." "Yeah, Carey — c'mon." Paddy dived under, came up blowing a few feet from where Carey stood. "Want to see me dive to the bottom?" It was the last thing Carey wanted to see. His blue-black face was impassive." I'm cool, I'm bored, what's a swim in an old pool to me?" said his look.

"I might have known Carey would be simmering, just waiting for a chance to boil over and get in a fight," Ann thought later. All the kids flew up the stairs fast after their swim so they could get into pajamas. The house rule was pajamas first, then you could have your cereal and milk. It was during the pajama period, while Ann, John, and Ann's mother, Mary, were finally having a late dinner, that a piercing, this-is-for-real scream was heard from the upper floors. Ann leaped to her feet. She got to the hall just in time to catch Paddy, who was howling his head off, flying down the stairs two at a time. "YAAAAAHHH!" cried Paddy. "Carey bit me!"

"Of course," thought Ann. It was in the cards. "Honey — I'm sorry. Let me see —" There were tooth marks but fortunately no broken skin. Bad business. But did this mean that Carey was a bad child? A budding criminal?

"Can I help?" John had appeared in the hall, napkin in hand.

"You can comfort Paddy. Here, you sit on Papa's lap for a minute. I think I know what's bothering Carey. I want to handle it —"

Carey was sitting on the bunk bed in his room, trying to

SIDNEY LUND

Grandmother Mary Taylor comforts Hope.

ACTION ART ST

Terry clings to his mother (1976).

Terry, 1981: "the bestest boy"

look blank-faced. His eyes were huge, scared. "I only wanted my marble," he mumbled. "Paddy — he took it. It was *mine* —"

"Carey, I want you to come with me. Downstairs." Ann wanted all the others to see that this was not going unnoticed. All of the children had crept into the dining room, drawn by the noisy drama. Paddy, still wailing on John's lap, was trying to explain through tears about the marble he'd found behind the drainpipe. Hope was clinging to her Grandmother "Dra," while Dat had sought refuge on Megan's knees. Everyone suddenly needed lots of loving. Faith, who had no place to sit at the moment, had draped herself around her papa's neck and was trying to play with his beard.

"Children, I want you to hear what I'm saying to Carey. I want you all to understand," said Ann in her most serious voice. "We don't allow biting in this house. It doesn't matter what happens to make you mad, you are *not to bite*. You must come find Papa or Mama and tell us what's wrong — but no biting. Do you understand? Carey? Look at me — do *you* understand?"

He nodded, drooping. The perfect picture of the outcast, the one who caused all the trouble. Ann couldn't leave it at that. She gathered him in her arms and sat down. "You're a good boy, Carey. I'm sure you're a very good boy, but there are some things you have to learn. It's Mama's job and Papa's job to help you learn them. We want you to be happy here —"

Dat, watching this love feast from Megan's knee, suddenly hopped off and came to stand beside Ann. "Is Terry still our bestest boy? And am I second bestest?"

"Oh, yes, yes, yes — everybody is just as good as can be." Ann sighed. "You are *all* wonderful children. Now will all of you go get your cereal and milk so Mama and Papa can eat what's left of their dinner? Megan — help them, will you?"

Megan jumped up. "C'mon, kids."

Carey got down quickly, eager for the subject to be changed

so he could slip back into the anonymity of the crowd. But before Ann's lap could cool off, Dat had climbed on for one last hug. Something was really bothering him. Finally he managed to get the question out. "Each time — each time you get a new little boy, do you have to give an old little boy away? Even if he's good?"

So *that* was it. Funny little Dat. So sweet, so serious, and still so worried about his place on this planet. "Never!" said Ann. "I couldn't do without my Polka-Dot. You are our little boy forever and ever, and whether you're good, whether you're bad sometimes, we always love you."

The dining room was empty. The sounds of children chattering and squabbling softly, sleepily, over their cereal and milk, drifted in from the sun porch. No need to oversee things at this point. John was right there loading the dishwasher. Besides, even the most wickedly determined kid wound down eventually and lost the capacity to think up a new script for trouble. But, Lord, she *was* tired. Ann rested her head briefly in her hands.

"Mom? Can I talk to you please?" Chuong stood in the doorway, his voice urgent, his black eyes ablaze with the need to right some wrong or other.

"Of course. What's the matter?"

"Everything. It's no good, Mom, what you're doing with the new kids. All this hitting and biting is real bad. You got to be tougher with Carey and Michael. You got be *real tough,* Mom —" His voice rose stridently as it always did when he had a point to make.

Ann allowed herself a minute to enjoy the beautiful irony of Chuong, the peacemaker, explaining to her, after all these years, that violence was not the way to go. It was rich. But oh, it was indeed wonderful that she had lived to see this moment. And besides, she was grateful for help from any quarter. "What do you suggest?"

"Well —" he hesitated. "You talk, but they don't listen. You got to make them listen to you, Mom —"

"Yes. I agree. And how do I do that?"

Chuong reached back to his past for the solution. "When they hit somebody, you hit them harder," he said in a loud, fierce voice. "Make them *see!* Make them see they can't get away with that."

Ann sighed. If Chuong had failed to solve the problem, he was in good company. The United Nations was no doubt, at that very moment, in late session arguing over how to make some country somewhere stop hitting another country. She said, "It's just not that simple, Chuong. Would it have helped you to stop hitting the other kids, if I'd hit you all the time?"

Chuong looked surprised. Even mildly embarrassed. "Maybe. I don't know —" he said, confused.

"You've probably forgotten how it was. But you were plenty rough on them lots of times. Especially Jay —" She waited.

He shook his head. It was hard for him to believe he'd ever given Jay a hard time. Jay was his best friend in the whole family right now. Sure, there was a difference in their ages, but somehow it was never a big deal. Jay was a neat guy. He respected Jay. *That* was it! People had to respect each other. He said to his mother now, "I'm sorry — if I was like that. But what I say now is we got to get Carey and Michael to have respect. I mean this is a family. In a family we have to respect each other, right? But they hit all the time, they don't understand —"

"Exactly. Now those two little boys have been hit a lot themselves. By grownups who should have been showing them how to behave instead of slugging them. So now *I'm* trying to show them. And if I give them love and respect, I hope they'll finally get the idea. You did. But it wasn't easy, Chuong. And it didn't happen overnight."

He grinned. For a minute he had just a glimpse of that long road he'd traveled. "I guess," he said finally, "I was really okay or I'd still be doing crazy things and — you know, making trouble. So maybe Carey and Michael are okay, too, underneath. It sure doesn't show much yet — but maybe they're good kids."

"That's my profound hope," said Ann wearily.

"Well, look, Mom — I'll help you. I mean if I can —"

"Thanks, Chuong." Ann was touched. His feeling for the family was all the more precious because it had been so long in building.

"I got homework," he said.

"Goodnight, then."

"Goodnight, Mom." He ran quickly out in the hall and up the stairs. "Now there goes a really good kid," she thought, watching him fondly. "Did I ever think he was really *bad?*" she wondered. Upset, yes. Disturbed by everything that had happened to him. But good and bad were such oversimple labels to paste on people. Right now, for instance, there was much too much competitiveness and worry among the little boys over who was "goodest." She thought about how it had all got started.

There had once been a time when Terry, who all the children now agreed was "the bestest boy," was the world's worst crybaby. To make matters worse, his lung condition had required Ann to hit him — yes, hit him! — two hundred times every night different places on his rib cage to knock the mucus off the surface of his lungs.

The Sweeneys hadn't been satisfied with a diagnosis of asthma for Terry. After adoption, they'd taken him back for more study. "This time we went in the *front* door," Ann explains. "Everybody paid attention and at first they said he had cystic fibrosis. I didn't know what it was. Then I learned it kills you! We really sweated out those tests on Terry. But they finally decided he had chronic interstitial pneumonitits, which explained why he was so pneumonia-prone. It really made me mad the way he'd been left to languish all those eighteen months. But as soon as he came in as a private patient, the same hospital shaped up and found out what was wrong with him.

"Anyway, this hitting business is called 'cupping' because you don't use the flat of your hand, you cup it. The doctors did it to me to show me how. It doesn't hurt, but it jars you. And it certainly isn't the greatest way to make friends with a scared new kid. We had to hit him every night till he was three years old. I felt awful. But I told him over and over, 'You're the best boy in the whole world, Terry,' so he'd understand this wasn't a spanking. That's how the legend of Terry as 'bestest boy' got started."

The little boy was in reasonably good health now and the doctors told Ann Terry could live a good life, "as long as he doesn't go out for track," said the specialist. "His lung function will always be impaired, so he won't make a champion runner." Even more remarkable than his physical recovery, was the fact that all that apparent "abuse" — for call it what you will, "cupping" had to be a punishing experience for a tiny boy — had not injured Terry's spirit. He was loving, gentle, rarely wanting to hit anyone back. Watching Terry had given Ann great faith in the innate goodness of a child. She realized that no one had done anything to bring out the best in Carey or Michael. Yet now and then she caught glimpses of wonderful possibilities hidden inside both boys. There was the day she found Michael picking up the newest kitten, Catalina. She'd rushed up quickly, remembering the incident with Scat being thrown downstairs. But Michael was stroking the little ball of gray fluff gently. "Soft," he whispered, looking up and giving Ann a wide smile of pure sunshine. And there was the day Carey brought home a valentine he'd made in school. "For Mom," it said in ragged crayon letters. He proffered it with great shyness. She hugged him close, telling him, "It's beautiful!" Then he was so pleased with himself, for that moment Carey Sweeney was beautiful, too. "If only the gentle Michael, the beautiful Carey could be with us this coming Saturday," she thought, as she wrote "Brownings" on the calendar under "Dat's birthday."

But the chances certainly didn't look good as the week wore on.

Wednesday evening, while Ann and John were out at a meeting, Carey gave his Grandmother "Dra" a hard crack on the wrist when she suggested he'd better go up with the other kids and get his pajamas on. Mary gave a yelp of pain, and one of the veins immediately puffed up in a big, hard knot. Chuong, who'd been left partly in charge with his grandmother, quickly swooped down on Carey, picked him up like a bad puppy, ran all the way up the stairs to Carey's third-floor room and threw him roughly on the bed. "Stay there!" he commanded. "No cereal, no milk. You go to bed *now!*" Carey had gone.

Thursday it was Michael's turn. The little boys had been playing hard outdoors in spring's first mud. They came in gloriously, totally dirty. All had gone happily up to their baths — all except Michael. "I *won't* take a bath!" he screamed at his mother when she urged him to get going. Before Ann could gather her wits together to deal with him, Chuong rushed in from the next room, grabbed Michael by the scruff of the neck and quickly hauled him upstairs, whereupon he dumped him in a full tub, clothes and all. "You *will* take a bath!" said Chuong, scowling at the little boy. "You do what your mother say — and what I say."

Ann was amused, if not quite sure how how effective this rough justice was going to be. But she couldn't help being very pleased to have a strong, young ally in the battle to civilize Carey and Michael. She noticed, too, that for the moment at least, Chuong seemed to have given up the idea of fighting blows with more blows. "Not bad," she thought. "Let's see how it goes. . . ."

As the week drew to a close, Ann found herself growing nervous. She could run a kid's birthday party in her sleep after all these years, but she'd never before combined it with trying to entertain sophisticated, childless friends. It was the "childless" part that made her feel vulnerable. Once she and Kate had been equally young, attractive, untouched by the battles ahead. Kate had opted for a career which could have only added to her original glamour. "While I opted for mud and mountains of laundry, Motherhood with a capital M," thought Ann. "If only Kate doesn't go home saying to everyone, 'Poor Ann!' If only she can see what I've been trying to do, how wonderful all of it is, even if the good times do seem to be few and far between sometimes. Especially right now when Carey and Michael are still going through the turmoil of being new in the family. Ah, well —"

Ann checked her supplies of birthday party stuff. Candles, holders, paper tablecloth? Yes. But she'd have to buy more paper plates and cups. And oh God, if only she could buy a magic potion to be administered to children ten minutes before a scheduled social event that would guarantee civilized behavior for at least three hours! Then she almost burst out laughing. It had already been tried in the adult world. It was called "cocktails." And it was far from foolproof.

FIFTEEN

❧ ❧

Dat's Birthday

THAT SATURDAY AT 5:15, the doors of the Sweeneys' elegant parlor were pushed wide. Kate Browning, cool and serene in a rose-beige Ultrasuede skirt and matching silk blouse, finished her first drink and was about to put it down. But John rose hastily and said, "Here, let me fix you another. I see Jay coming with the garbage can — that means the party is about to get underway."

Kate, startled, held out her glass. Indeed Jay *was* coming with a handsome new garbage can full to the brim with presents. As if by magic, children who'd been flashing up and down the stairs and whirling through the great front hall like flying objects all surged immediately into the living room. They crowded around Dat, the lucky birthday boy, shouting and squealing. "Happy birthday, Dat!" cried Ann above the din, and handed him the first package to open.

"How old is Dat?" asked Sam Browning.

"Eight years old today," said John.

The little boy was still very small, looking more six than eight. As if to dramatize this point, Dat had finally managed to lose his first baby tooth — or at least the short brown stump that was a remnant of a baby tooth — just the week

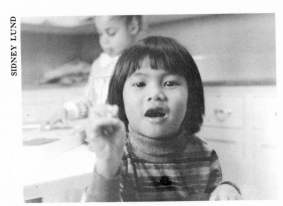

Dat on his seventh birthday

Faith and Hope try to get attention.

before. His parents now hoped his grown-up teeth would soon start coming in healthy and strong. But one thing was certain, with or without all his teeth, Dat gave the impression of being extremely thoughtful. Unlike the wilder kids, he opened his gifts gravely, giving each one his attention and appreciation. "Oh, I bemember when I asked you for *that* —" he said, holding up a small flashlight and smiling at his mother.

Dat's slow pace of enjoying was most pleasing for his parents to see. However, it was driving some of his brothers crazy. "*C'mon*, Dat — open this!" cried Marcus, grabbing a brightly wrapped package and thrusting it under his nose.

"Marcus! Will you *sit down?*" said Ann. "This is Dat's birthday. And he gets to do things his own way —"

In another week Paddy, Timmy, and Carey would all be celebrating *their* eighth birthdays. Much had been made of the fact that sooner or later, *everyone* in the family was sure to enjoy this peak experience and find himself surrounded by as much merchandise as one heart could possibly desire. But it was hard to keep the lid on anticipation. Now the natives were definitely restless and Ann decided to take charge and also involve them in the giving before they started a riot. "Here, Michael," she said, passing him a present. "You may give that to Dat. Quiet, everybody — each one of you will get a turn —"

Carey half-rose then, expecting to be called upon next. But Timmy, who was closer to his mother, whispered, "May I give this one, Mom?" His politeness got him the nod. Ann was about to tap Carey for the next present-giver. Too late. Carey stood up, and like some small, furious delegate from a Third World country, stalked from the Sweeney living room with his lower lip sticking out a mile. Ann sighed, watching the angry little boy disappear up the stairs. Kate was taking it all in with a slightly strained smile, trying not to look too aloof. Sam, however, looked completely relaxed, amused.

At that moment Chuong appeared in the doorway, a very welcome diversion. Ann couldn't help being secretly pleased at his dramatic late entrance. He was glowing from his afternoon of riding, and suddenly he looked so slim, so grown-up. But what she said was, "Chuong — why are you late? It's Dat's birthday —"

"I'm late because Mrs. Bennett doesn't drive as fast as you do when she car-pools," said Chuong smoothly. He smiled and said, "I'm sorry — Happy Birthday, everybody!"

"Chuong — how nice to see you. I wouldn't have recognized you." Kate Browning held out her hand. "She's impressed," thought Ann, gloating. "Well, she ought to be; it didn't happen overnight."

"You remember the Brownings?" John said. Chuong did, shook hands, excused himself to take a shower.

"Please hurry, Chuong," said Ann. "And when you come down, bring Carey with you —"

"Do all the children ride?" Kate asked.

"Just Chuong and Megan at the moment," Ann said. "Riding is Chuong's first love right now —"

"I imagine he's a beautiful rider. Such a graceful boy," said Kate admiringly.

"Yes," said Ann, smiling. Kate's remark reminded her of an interesting test of Chuong's "gracefulness" at a recent horse show. He had won the first event easily on Brandy, the horse both he and Megan preferred to ride during their weekly lessons. Then Megan had taken a third on Candyman, a horse she'd never ridden before, and she couldn't help being downcast. Chuong had tried hard to raise her spirits. "I didn't think I won, really," he said. "I thought you were better, and I was maybe third —"

In the next event Megan did well, while Chuong was disqualified and didn't even place because his horse refused the jump. But he was strong enough not to make excuses; he complimented his sister, too. "I wish I had time to tell Kate all this," thought Ann. "She sees Chuong the elegant, graceful athlete. She ought to see him in old jeans going off to take care of his lawn jobs up and down the street. And she ought to see

him coming in beat from long hours at his library job, too."
(For a year now he'd worked six days a week and hadn't had
to ask for a penny of spending money.) "What Kate doesn't
see is all the growing that had to take place before Chuong
could be graceful in a situation like that horse show. He didn't
boast when he won; he was generous. He was even a game
loser in the sport he loves best. *That's* the real triumph." No
time to talk now, though; Dat's birthday party was sagging.

The present-opening had lost some of its momentum. The
remaining participants, wavering between boredom and envy,
were anxious to move on to ice cream and cake. Faith, whose
case of jealousy was perhaps the most seriously advanced, ran
over to perch on Sam Browning's right knee. She had noticed
that Hope was already established happily on his left, and at
least she could strive for equal time in monopolizing the guest.
Now she began to play with Sam's handkerchief, pulling it
half out of his pocket, then stuffing it back in, giggling. Ann
spotted her out of the corner of her eye. "Faith! Leave Mr.
Browning's handkerchief alone —"

"She's fine," said Sam easily. "You take care of the boys,
Ann — I'll watch the girls." Faith's suffering had not escaped
him. He was amused. Now, to distract her, he said, "I remember meeting you when you were just a little baby. Can
you remember way back then?"

Faith, sulking because she had been reprimanded, shook her
head.

"I can!" Hope, bouncing on Sam's other knee, told him, "I
remember being born!"

Sam pretended amazement. "No!"

"Yes, yes," said Hope. "I had tiny little eyes — like this."
She squeezed her eyes tight shut. "But now, they're BIG —
like this!" She opened her eyes wide. "Some people think I'm
Chinese," she told Sam. "But Chinese people have eyes like
this — see?" Hope pulled her almond-shaped eyes up in an
exaggerated slant. "I'm *not* Chinese," she proclaimed vigor-

ously. She let go of her eyes, then laughed. "Maybe I am a little bit —"

Sam laughed heartily, throwing his head back. Hope peered up at him from her perch on his knee. "*You've* got a big nose!" she grimaced. "With hair in it. Why?"

"I don't know," Sam apologized.

"I've got a flat nose," said Hope, satisfied. "And look at Faith — she has a round nose."

Faith woke up from her sulk at this, felt her nose, and prepared to be aggrieved.

"Say," said Sam hastily, "did you ever think how lucky we are that our noses weren't put on upside down? Because if they were, and we went outdoors in the rain, our noses would get all filled up with water!"

Now both little girls had to turn upside down, leaning back on Sam's knees, to see how this would be. "Oh! Oh! My nose is all full of water — help, help!" shouted Hope.

Faith began to giggle. "Mine is, too." Now they're momentarily united in imagined misery. "Help *me!*"

But Hope, upside down, had got a good look at Sam's chin. "What's the matter with your chin?" she asked Sam. "It's got all that skin hanging under it —"

Sam sighed cheerfully. "That's because I'm an old man."

Kate Browning began to laugh. She was enjoying the party in spite of herself.

"I love my chin — see *my* chin?" said Hope.

"Beautiful," Sam agreed.

But now Faith saw her chance at last. "*You'll* get old some day," she told Hope. "You'll get a chin with wrinkles that hang down to — down to your waist!" She made an awful face at her sister.

Hope could not be vanquished. "No, I won't, I won't, I won't," she chanted. "I'm never gonna get old." Then she looked across the room where the boys were still handing presents to her brother Dat. "But I wish it was *my* birthday," she sighed.

The adults exchanged glances, shook their heads, and smiled. The room was full of children all certain of their immortality, all hungrily eyeing Dat's pile of presents, all wishing their own birthdays would hurry up and come. They saw no connection. But the adults had not missed it.

Enter Chuong in dark blue pajamas and tightly sashed printed kimono. He had a reluctant Carey in tow. "You know what this dude says?" Chuong was cheerfully scornful. "He can't live till next week when it's *his* birthday. Man, you're too much!" Chuong shook his head.

Ann saw she would have to rescue Carey, whose self-esteem could not yet survive public teasing. "Maybe you've forgotten, Chuong, that you arrived here the day *after* your eleventh birthday. And you had to wait three hundred and sixty-four days for it to come around again! You didn't find it all that easy. Remember?"

Chuong, trapped but ever agile, conceded with a grin. "That's right. Carey, I was worse than you. I thought it would *never* come —"

This concession wrung a small smile from Carey. Then he looked at the pile of loot accumulating around Dat — an oil truck, a car that ran on batteries, a puzzle, another car — it was too much. How could he trust he would do as well? Carey buried his head in Ann's lap. She stroked the black curls of his new Afro haircut rhythmically for a whole. Then, as he grew more relaxed, she said, "Now would you like to give Dat a present, Carey?"

He nodded and struggled to his feet. "A big one?" he said. At least he could be glorious by association. Ann agreed, handing him the biggest present left, a silver-wrapped box with a huge red bow. The present was grand enough to worry Faith. She had to wriggle off Sam Browning's knee and see for herself what was inside. Everyone groaned as Dat took his time getting the bow off, opening the silver paper so it wouldn't tear. At last he pulled out a big yellow shirt, a football shirt with huge black letters "88" on the front.

"Some shirt!" said Jay.

"That's really nice, Dat," said Chuong.

Carey, the present-bearer, began to expand. He was the man who had delievered this breathtaking garment.

But Faith, peering closer, said loudly, "It's a dumb shirt! Boys are *dumb*, too!"

Carey whirled in a rage. His hand flashed out. The pink nails ripped a formidable scratch across Faith's eyelid. She let forth an operatic scream.

"*Carey!*" Ann's scream was nearly as loud as Faith's. She grabbed the sobbing child, held her down quickly for a look. Thank God, he had missed the eyeball. The injury to Faith's golden face was nasty, but not serious. "Carey — you go to your room and stay there." Fear made her voice rough. Carey fled.

The prima donna was treated, soothed, comforted. John volunteered to go upstairs and deal with Carey. He was gone for several minutes. On occasion John resorted to prayer with serious offenders. "Well, we could use a little Divine Intervention," thought Ann. "Ah, here he comes!"

"I think Carey got the message, but I can't be sure," John told Ann. "We've got lots of work ahead of us to make it really stick."

"Well, let's get him down here now. These kids can't live another minute without ice cream and cake. And I can't live another minute if I hear one more word out of anybody —"

"I'll get him, Mom." Megan ran up the stairs. In a moment she was back. "He won't come. He's crying."

"Dear God — I *have* to serve the ice cream. And we can't have the party without Carey."

"Let me go. I'll carry him down." Chuong started up the stairs two at a time. Soon he deposited a weeping Carey at Ann's feet. "He says he's afraid you'll send him back," he told Ann.

"Back? To his room?"

"No — back where he came from. To New York."

This was too serious to be laughed off or dealt with super-ficially. She handed the big spoon to Megan. "Honey — dish the ice cream. John, would you bring in the cake?" Ann knelt down and put her arms around Carey. Then she picked him up and sat down in a big chair with the frightened boy on her lap. For a minute she just rocked him. Then she said, "Carey, did you really think we'd send you back where you came from?"

He nodded, whimpering.

"Then listen carefully. You will never be sent back, no matter what you do. You are *our* little boy now."

Carey opened his eyes. The tears still glistened on his blue-black cheeks. "You don't never send anybody back? Ever?"

"That's right." Ann had a sudden inspiration. "Go ask Marcus," she said. "He's the grand old man of adoption around here. He was the first one — and he's been in lots of trouble lots of times since he came. He'll tell you —"

The table was set on the sun porch. The children were climbing onto benches getting ready for the cake cutting. Ice cream was sitting in little dishes at everyone's places. Marcus, not yet sitting still, was hopping up and down as usual when Carey came up to him. "Is it true?" he asked Marcus sullenly. "They don't send you back ever? You get to stay here no matter what you do?"

Marcus, all freckles and red curls, gave Carey a big smile. "Yeah, that's right. When you're adopted, you're gonna stay. It's like in the supermarket. If you take a bite out of a tomato, you *can't* put it back."